A MANUSCRIPT *of* ASHES

Antonio Muñoz Molina

A MANUSCRIPT
of ASHES

Translated from the Spanish
by Edith Grossman

Harcourt, Inc.

Orlando   Austin   New York   San Diego   London

www.HarcourtBooks.com

This is a translation of *Beatus Ille*

This work has been published with a subsidy from the Directorate-General
of Books, Archives, and Libraries of the Spanish Ministry of Culture.

Library of Congress Cataloging-in-Publication Data
Muñoz Molina, Antonio.
[Beatus Ille. English]
A manuscript of ashes / Antonio Muñoz Molina; translated from the Spanish by Edith Grossman.
p.   cm.
I. Grossman, Edith, 1936– II. Title.
PQ6663.U4795B4313 2007
863'.64—dc22   2007036557
ISBN 978-0-15-101410-1

Text set in Adobe Garamond
Designed by Jennifer Kelly

Printed in the United States of America
First edition
A C E G   I   K J H F D B

For Marilena

A MANUSCRIPT *of* ASHES

PART ONE

Mixing memory and desire.
—T. S. ELIOT

I

SHE CLOSED THE DOOR very slowly and went out with the stealth of someone leaving a sick person who has just fallen asleep at midnight. I listened to her slow steps along the hallway, fearing or wishing she would return at the last minute to leave her suitcase at the foot of the bed and sit down on the edge with a gesture of surrender or fatigue, as if she had already returned from the journey she had never been able to take until tonight. When the door closed the room was left in darkness, and now my only illumination is the thread of light that enters from the hall and slides in a tapering line to the legs of the bed, but at the window there is dark blue night and through the open shutters comes the breeze of a night that is almost summer, crossed in the far distance by the whistles of express trains that travel under the moon along the livid valley of the Guadalquivir and climb the slopes of Mágina on their way to the station where he, Minaya, is waiting for her now without even daring to hope that Inés, slim and alone, with her short pink skirt and her hair pulled back into a ponytail, will appear at a corner of the platform. He is alone, sitting on a bench, smoking perhaps as he looks at the red lights and the tracks and the cars stopped at the end of the station and of the night. Now, when she closed the door, I can, if I want, imagine him for myself alone, that is, for no one, I can bury my face beneath the turned-down bedclothes that Inés smoothed with so much secret tenderness before she left, and then, waiting in the darkness and in the heat of my body under the sheets, I can imagine or recount what happened and even direct their steps, those of Inés and his, on the way to their encounter and mutual acknowledgment on the empty platform, as if at this moment I had invented and depicted their presence, their desire, and their guilt.

She closed the door and didn't turn around to look at me because I had forbidden it, I saw for the last time only her slender white neck and the beginning of her hair, and then I heard her steps fading as they moved away to the end of the hallway, where they stopped. Perhaps she put the suitcase on the floor and turned back to the door she had just closed, and then I was afraid and probably wished she wouldn't continue, but in an instant the footsteps could be heard again, farther away, very hollow now, on the stairs, and I know that when she reached the courtyard she stopped again and raised her eyes to the window, but I didn't look out because it was no longer necessary. My consciousness is enough, and the solitude, and the words I say quietly to guide her to the street and the station where he doesn't know how not to go on waiting for her. It is no longer necessary to write in order to guess things or invent them. He, Minaya, doesn't know that, and I suppose that some day he will succumb, inevitably, to the superstition of writing because he doesn't recognize the value of silence or blank pages. Now as he waits for the train that, when this night ends and he arrives in Madrid, will have taken him away forever from Mágina, he looks at the deserted tracks and the shadows of the olive trees beyond the adobe walls, but between his eyes and the world, Inés and the house where he met her persist, along with the wedding portrait of Mariana, the mirror where Jacinto Solana looked at himself as he wrote a poem laconically entitled "Invitation." Like the first day, when he came to the house with the ill-fated melancholy of a guest who has recently gotten off the worst trains of the night, Minaya, in the station, still contemplates the white facade from the other side of the fountain, the tall house half-hidden by the mist of water that rises and falls back into the over-flowing stone basin and sometimes goes higher than the rounded tops of the acacias. He looks at the house and senses behind him other glances that will converge there to expand its image by adding the distance of all the years that have passed since it was built, and he no longer knows if he remembers it himself or if rising in front of his eyes is the sedimented memory of all the men who have looked at it and lived in it since long before he was born. Undeniable perception, he thinks, amnesia, are gifts possessed completely only by mirrors, but if there were a mirror capable of remembering, it would be set up before the facade of the house, and only it would have perceived the succession of what was immobile, the fable concealed beneath the stillness of closed balconies, its persistence in time.

At nightfall yellow lights are lit at the corners, which don't illuminate the plaza but only sculpt in the dark the entrance to a lane, brighten a patch of whitewash or the shape of a grating, suggest the doorway of a church in whose highest vaulted niche there is a vague Saint Peter decapitated by the rage of another time. The church, closed since 1936, and the headless apostle who still lifts an amputated hand in blessing, give the plaza its name, but the width of the plaza, never opened and very rarely disturbed by cars, is defined by the palace. The palace is older than the acacias and the hedges, but the fountain was already there when it was built, brought from Italy four centuries earlier by a duke who was devoted to Michelangelo, as was the church and its gargoyles, black with lichens, who when it rains expel water onto the street as if it were vomit. From the plaza, behind the trees, like a casual traveler, Minaya looks at the architecture of the house, still hesitating at the bronze door knockers, two gilded hands that strike the dark wood and produce a somber, delayed resonance in the courtyard, under the glass dome. Marble flagstones, white columns supporting the glass-enclosed gallery, rooms with wooden floors where footsteps sounded as they would in a ship's cabin, that day, the only one, when he was six years old and

they brought him to the house and he walked on the mysterious parquet floor as if he were finally stepping on the material and dimensions of a space worthy of his imagination. Before that afternoon,
when they walked through the plaza on their way to the Church of
Santa María, his mother would squeeze his hand and walk faster to
keep him from stopping on the sidewalk, trapped by the desire to
stay there forever looking at the house, imagining what was behind
the door that was so high and the balconies and the round windows
at the top floor that lit up at night like the portholes of a submarine.
At that time Minaya perceived things with a clarity very similar to
astonishment and was always inventing mysterious connections
among them that didn't explain the world to him but made it inhabited by fables or threats. Because he observed his mother's hostility
toward the house, he never asked her who lived there, but once,
when the boy went with him to visit someone, his father stopped
next to the fountain and with the sad irony that was, as Minaya
learned many years later, his only weapon against the tenacity of his
failure, he said:

"Do you see that big house? Well, my cousin Manuel, your
uncle, lives there."

From then on, the house and its mythological resident acquired
for him the heroic stature of a movie adventure. Knowing a man
lived in it who was inaccessible and yet his uncle produced in Minaya a pride similar to what he felt at times when he imagined that
his real father was not the sad man who fell asleep every night at the
table after making endless calculations in the margins of the newspaper, but the Coyote or Captain Thunder or the Masked Avenger, a
comic book character dressed in dark clothing and almost always
wearing a mask, who one day, very soon Minaya hoped, would come
for him after a very long journey and return him to his true life and
the dignity of his name. His father, the other one, who almost always
was a shadow or a melancholy impostor, sat on one of the red easy
chairs in his bedroom. The light had red tonalities when he closed

the curtains, and on a pink background, as if in a camera obscura, small inverted silhouettes were outlined on the ceiling in the warm semidarkness: a boy with a blue apron, a man on horseback, a slow cyclist, as detailed as a drawing in a book, who glided, head down, toward an angle of the wall and disappeared there behind the blue boy and the tenuous rider who preceded him.

Minaya knew something was going to happen that very afternoon. A truck had stopped at the door, and a gang of unknown, frightening men who smelled of sweat had walked calmly through the rooms, picking up the furniture in their bare arms, dragging the trunk that held his mother's dresses out to the street, throwing everything into confusion, shouting to one another words that he didn't know and that made him afraid. They hung a grapple and pulley from the eaves, ran a rope along it, stood on the balcony, attached the furniture he loved best, and Minaya, hidden behind a curtain, watched how an armoire that seemed to have been damaged by those men, a table with curved legs where a plaster dog had always stood, and his disassembled bed swung over the street as if they were about to fall and break into pieces to the guffaws of the invaders. So that no torture would be denied him that afternoon, his mother had dressed him in the sailor suit she took out of the closet only when they were going to visit some gloomy relative. That's why he was hiding, aside from the fear the men caused in him, because if the boys on the street saw him dressed like that, with a blue bow on his chest and the absurd tippet that reminded him of an altar boy's habit, they would laugh at him with the uniform cruelty of their group, because they were like the men devastating his house: dirty, big, inexplicable, and wicked.

My God, his mother said afterward in the now empty dining room, looking at the bare walls, the lighter spots where the pictures had been, biting her painted lips, and her voice didn't sound the same in the stripped house. They had closed the door and were holding him by the hand as they walked in silence, and they didn't answer when he asked where they were going, but he, his intelligence sharpened by the sudden irruption of disorder, knew before they turned the corner of the Plaza of San Pedro and stopped at the door with the bronze door knockers that were a woman's hands. His father adjusted the knot of his tie and stood straighter in his Sunday suit as if to recover all his stature, prodigious at the time. "Go on, you knock," he said to his mother, but she refused, sourly, to listen. "Woman, you wouldn't want us to leave Mágina without saying good-bye to my cousin."

White columns; a high dome of red, yellow, blue glass; a grayhaired man who didn't resemble any movie heroes and who took him by the hand and led him to a large room with a parquet floor, where the last light of the afternoon shone like a cold moon while a large shadow that may not belong to reality but to the modifications of memory inundated the walls supernaturally covered with all the books in the world. First he was motionless, sitting on the edge of a chair so high his feet didn't touch the floor, awed by the size of everything: the bookshelves, the large windows that faced the plaza, the vast space over his head. A slow-moving woman dressed in mourning came to serve them small steaming cups of coffee, and she offered him something, a candy or a biscuit, using formal address, something that disconcerted him as much as finding out that the case that was so tall and dark and covered with glass was a clock. They, Minaya's parents and the man whom they had taken to calling his uncle, spoke in quiet voices, in a distant, neutral tone that made him drowsy, acting like a sedative for his excitement and allowing him to retreat into the secret delight of looking at everything as if he were alone in the library.

"We're going to Madrid, Manuel," his father said. "And there we'll have a clean slate. In Mágina there's no stimulus for an enterprising man, there's no dynamism, no market."

Then his mother, very rigid and sitting next to him, covered her face with her hands, and it took Minaya a little while to realize that the strange, dry noise she was making was weeping, because until that afternoon he had never seen her cry. For the first time it was the weeping without tears that he learned to recognize and spy on for many years, and as he learned when his parents were already dead and safe from all misfortune or ruin, it revealed in his mother the obstinate, useless rancor toward life and the man who was always on the verge of becoming rich, of finding the partner or the opportunity that he too deserved, of breaking the siege of bad luck, of going to prison once because of a run-of-the-mill swindle.

"Your grandmother Cristina, Son, she was the one who began our misfortune, because if she hadn't been stupid enough to fall in love with my father and renounce her family in order to marry him, we'd be the ones living now in my cousin's palace and I'd have the capital to be a success in business. But your grandmother liked poetry and romanticism, and when my poor devil of a father, may he rest in peace and may God forgive me, dedicated some poems to her and told her a few vulgar clichés about love and twilight, she didn't care if he was a clerk at the registry office or that Don Apolonio, her father, your great-grandfather, threatened to disinherit her. And he certainly did disinherit her, as if it were a serialized novel, and he didn't see her again or ask about her for the rest of his life, which turned out to be short because of that unpleasantness, and he ruined her and me, and also you and your children if you have any, because how can I raise my head and give you a future if bad luck has pursued me since before I was born?"

"But it's absurd for you to complain. If my grandmother Cristina hadn't married your father, you wouldn't have been born."

"And you think that's a small privilege?"

A few days after the funeral of his parents, who when they died left him some family portraits and a rare instinct for sensing the proximity of failure, Minaya received a condolence letter from his Uncle Manuel, written in the same very slanted and pointed hand he would recognize four years later in the brief invitation to spend a few weeks in February in Mágina, offering him his house and his library and all the help he could offer in his research on the life and work of Jacinto Solana, the almost unpublished poet of the generation of the Republic about whom Minaya was writing his doctoral dissertation.

"My cousin would like to be English," said his father. "He takes tea in the middle of the afternoon, smokes his pipe in a leather arm-chair, and to top it off, he's a leftist, as if he were a bricklayer."

Not daring yet to use the knocker, Minaya searches in his over-coat for his uncle's letter as if it were a safe-conduct that would be demanded of him when the door was opened, when he crosses once more the entrance where there was a tile frieze and tries to reach the courtyard where he wandered that afternoon as if he were lost, ex-pecting his parents to come out of the library, because the maid who had used *usted* with him led him away when his mother's weeping began, and he was possessed by the enduring fascination of the solemn faces that looked down at him from the paintings on the walls and by the light and the design of large flowers or birds formed by the panes of glass in the dome. At first he limited himself to walk-ing in a straight line from one column to the next, because he liked the sound of his own methodical footsteps, and it was like inventing one of those games that only he knew, but then he dared to climb very silently the first steps toward the gallery, and his own image in the mirror on the landing obliged him to stop, a guardian or sym-metrical enemy that forbade him to advance toward the upper rooms or enter the imaginary hallway that extended to the other side of the glass and where perhaps oblivion keeps several faces of Mariana that are not exactly the same, the print of Manuel when he went up after her in his lieutenant's uniform, the expression that Jacinto Solana's eyes had only one time in the small hours of May 21, 1937, unaware it was the eve of the crime, after being carried away by her caresses and tears on the grass in the garden and telling each other that guilt and the war didn't matter on that night when giving in to sleep would have been a betrayal of happiness.

In that mirror where Inés will not see herself again, Minaya knows he will look for impossible traces of a boy dressed in a sailor suit who stopped in front of it twenty years earlier when a voice, his father's, ordered him to come down. In the courtyard his father was taller than his cousin, and seeing his impeccable jacket and spotless boots and the opulent gesture with which he consulted the watch whose gold chain crossed his vest, one would have said he was the owner of the house. "If I'd had just half the opportunities my cousin has had from the time he was born," he would say, trapped between rancor and envy and an unconfessed family pride, because when all was said and done, he too was the grandson of the man who built the house. He spoke of Manuel's errant ways and the lethargy into which his life seemed to have fallen since the day a stray bullet killed the woman he had just married, but his irony was never more poisonous than when he recalled his cousin's political ideas and the influence this Jacinto Solana had on them, a man who earned his living working for leftist papers in Madrid and who once spoke at a meeting of the Popular Front in the Mágina bull ring, who was sentenced to death after the war and then pardoned and who left prison to die in the way he deserved in a skirmish with the Civil Guard. And in this manner, ever since he had the use of his reason and the memory to recall sitting at the table after meals when his father made conjectures regarding senseless business deals and did long arithmetical operations in the margins of the newspaper, cursing the ingratitude of fortune and the insulting indolence and prosperity of his cousin, Minaya had formed a very blurred and at the same time very precise image of Manuel that was always inseparable from that one afternoon in his childhood and a certain idea of ancient heroism and peaceful seclusion. Now, when Manuel is dead and in Minaya's imagination his real story has supplanted the mystery of the gray-haired man who occupied it for twenty years, I want to invoke not his flight this evening but his return, the moment when he holds the letter he received in Madrid and prepares to knock at the door and is afraid it will be opened, but he doesn't know that returning and fleeing are the same, because tonight too, when he was leaving, he looked at the white facade and the circular windows on the top floor where a light that illuminates no one is shining, as if the submarine he wanted to inhabit in his childhood had been abandoned and was sailing without a pilot through an ocean of darkness. I'll never come back, he thinks, enraged in his grief, in his flight, in the memory of Inés, because he loves literature and the good-byes forever that occur only in books, and he walks along the lanes with his head lowered, as if charging the air, and he comes out on the Plaza of General Orduña, where there's a taxi that will take him to the station, perhaps the same one he took three months earlier when he came to Mágina to find in Manuel's house a refuge from his fear. *It will be my pleasure to help you any way I can in your research on Jacinto Solana who, as you know, lived for a time in this house, in 1947,* when he left prison, he had written, *but I'm afraid you won't find a single trace of his work here, because everything he wrote before his death was destroyed in circumstances you no doubt can imagine.*

2

A PRETEXT, AT FIRST, a secondary lie learned perhaps from those con-
trived by his father so he could go on wearing a suit and tie and polished shoes, a casual alibi so that the act of fleeing and not
continuing to resist the harsh inclemency of misfortune would resemble a positive act of will. Minaya was alone and in a kind of daze
in a corner of the cafeteria at the university, far from everything,
brushing the rim of an empty cup with the tip of his cigarette and
silently putting off the moment of going out to the wintry avenue
where hard, gray horsemen stood guard, and he hadn't yet thought
of Jacinto Solana or the possibility of using his name to save himself
from persecution; he thought, having recently emerged from a de-
tention cell on the Puerta del Sol, only about interrogations and the
sirens of police wagons and the body that had lain as if at the bottom of a well on the concrete or paving stones of a courtyard at State
Security headquarters. Around him he saw unfamiliar faces that clustered at the counter and at the nearby tables with briefcases of notes
and overcoats that seemed to protect them with identical efficiency
from winter and the suspicion of fear, secure in the warm air and cigarette smoke and voices, firm in their names, their chosen futures, as
irrevocably unaware of the silent presence among them of the emissaries of tyranny as they, children of forgetting, were unaware that

the pine groves and redbrick buildings they walked past had been a battlefield thirty years earlier. He was alone forever and definitively dead, he later told Inés, ever since the day the guards trapped him and with punches and kicks from their black boots forced him into a van with metal gratings, ever since he left prison with his belt in a pocket and his shoelaces in his hand, because they had been confiscated when they took him to the cell, perhaps to keep him from dismally hanging himself, and were returned only a few minutes before he was released, but they said the other one had committed suicide, that he took advantage of a moment's carelessness on the part of the guards who were interrogating him to throw himself down into the courtyard and die in handcuffs. He, Minaya, had survived the blows and the ghastly wait to be called for another interrogation, but even after he was out, the slightest sound grew until it became the deafening noise of bolts and heavy metal doors in his dreams, and every night the sheets on his bed were as rough as the blankets they gave him when he entered the cell, and his body retained the stink it had acquired in the basements, behind the last grating, when they took away his watch, his belt, his matches, his shoelaces, and handed him those two gray blankets that smelled of horse sweat.

But deeper than his fear of footsteps in the corridor and the methodical fury of hard slaps in the face, those five days left Minaya with an unpleasant sensation of impotence and helpless solitude that refuted all certainty and forever denied the right to salvation, rebelliousness, or pride. How to redeem himself from the cold at daybreak that penetrated beneath the blankets where he hid his head in order not to see the perpetual yellow light hung between the corridor and the cell's peephole or to invent in the name of what or whom a justification for the smell of confined bodies and cigarette butts, where to find a handhold to keep him steady when he didn't know if it was day or night and he leaned the back of his neck against the wall waiting for a guard to come in and say his name. It was on the second night that he thought of returning to Mágina. The cold woke him, and he remembered that he had dreamed about his father putting on his boots in the red bedroom and looking at him with the pale smile of a dead man. He told Inés that in his dream there was a pink, icy light and a feeling of distance or ungraspable tenderness that was also the light of May coming in and waking him from a balcony of his childhood where swallows built their nests or lingering in midafternoon over a plaza with acacias. In vain he closed his eyes and tried to resume the dream or recover it whole without forfeiting its pleasure or the exact tone of its color, but even after he lost the dream, the name of Mágina remained as if it were an illumination of his memory, as if saying it were enough to tear down walls of forgetting and to have before him the intact city, available and remote on its blue hill, more and more precise in its invitation and its inviolable distance, while for Minaya all the streets and faces and rooms in Madrid were transformed into snares of a persecution that did not end when they released him, that continued to crouch behind him, all around him, when he drank a cup of coffee in the cafeteria at the university; and on the other side of the windows, among the dark green, rainwashed pines, he saw the gray horsemen, dismounted now, serene, the visors of their helmets raised, like weary knights who without disarming allow their steeds to graze on the grass wet with dew, near the waiting jeeps.

Then someone came and talked to him about Jacinto Solana: dead, unpublished, renowned, heroic, disappeared, probably shot at the end of the war. Minaya had finished his coffee and was getting ready to leave when the other man, armed with a briefcase and a glass of cognac, spread before him his combative enthusiasm, his friendship, which Minaya never asked for, the evidence of a discovery that in the future would probably provide him with a summa cum laude. "His name was, his name is, José Manuel Luque," he told Inés, "and I can't imagine him without running the risk of anachronisms, impassioned, I suppose, addicted to clandestine conversations, ignoring discouragement and doubt, carrying forbidden papers in his briefcase, determined to have destiny fulfill what they affirm, and with a beard and rough workman's boots."

"Jacinto Solana. Make a note of the name, Minaya," the other man said, "because I'll be sure you hear it in the future and read these poems. They were published in *Hora de España,* in the July 1937 issue. Though I warn you this is only an appetizer for what you'll see later."

"Invitation," read Minaya, fifteen lines without rhyme, without any apparent rhythm, as if the person who wrote them had with absolute premeditation renounced indicating any emphasis, so that the words would sound as if spoken in a quiet voice, with sustained coldness, with the serene purpose of achieving perfection and silence, as if perfection, and not even the act of writing, mattered. A man alone was writing in front of a mirror and closing his lips before saying the only name that dwelled in him in order to look at himself in a tranquil invitation to suicide. At the end, "Mágina, May 1937." Each line, each word sustained on the negation of itself, was an ancient call that seemed to have been written only so Minaya might know it, not in a vast future but on that precise afternoon, in just that place, thirty-one years and eight months later, as if in the mirror where that man was looking at himself as he wrote he had seen Minaya's eyes, his predestined loyalty.

"Valuable, Minaya, it's true, I don't deny any of the value you attribute to it, but you haven't seen the best things yet. Read these ballads. You can see they're photocopies from *El Mono Azul.* They were published between September '36 and May '37."

With gestures of clandestinity, of mystery, he pawed through his briefcase among smeared, duplicated pages and notebooks of notes, looking all around the cafeteria before showing Minaya a pile of photocopies that appeared in his hand like a magician's pigeon, just arrived from Mexico, he said, fragile, as sacred as relics, like the manuscripts of a persecuted, hidden faith, heavy with heroic memory and conspiracy. *El Mono Azul,* Weekly Pamphlet of the Alliance of Anti-fascist Intellectuals for the Defense of Culture, Madrid, Thursday, October 1, 1936, the black rectangle of an undecipherable photograph: *Rafael Alberti, José Bergamín, and Jacinto Solana in the headquarters of the Fifth Regiment.* Then the other man spread out before Minaya the ballads "The Iron Militia," "The Ballad of Lina Odena," "The Twentieth of July," "International Brigades." The name at the bottom of each one, Jacinto Solana, almost erased among the large letters of the titles, like his face in the photograph, lost in forgetting, in a time that never seemed to have existed, but the voice wasn't the same one Minaya had heard when he read the first poem. Now it was confused with the others, exalted by the same fervor, by the monotony of rage, as if the man who had written the ballads was not the one who looked at himself, enclosed and alone, in the mirror of a shadowy room. He read the name of the city and the date again, "Mágina, May 1937," like a countersign that the other man, José Manuel Luque, could not see, like an invitation deeper than the one offered by the poems, without calculating yet the possible alibi, only astonished that for the second time in a matter of days the inert territory of his consciousness where the city lay, his own wasted, distant life, had opened again like a wound. "I know he didn't die," he was going to say, recalling his father's sad monologues in which the name of Jacinto Solana sometimes appeared, "I know he didn't disappear from the world when the war ended, that he got out of prison and went back to Mágina to go on fighting as if the fury that had moved him when he wrote the ballads still lived in him and perhaps came to an end only when they killed him." But he didn't say anything; he nodded in silence at the other man's enthusiasm, then listening to the usual predictions about the irremediable decay and fall of the tyranny, about the united general strike that would bring it down if everyone, including him, Minaya, devoted themselves to the struggle, shoulder to shoulder. For it seems that after thirty years they are still using the same words that had not been exhausted by the evidence of defeat, the same blind inherited certainty that they could not have learned back then because they hadn't been born yet, the secret, single word said in a quiet voice in rooms full of smoke and conspiracy, the initials written in red brushstrokes on the walls of midnight, in the vacant fields of fear. Blind, bold, fearless, between the legs of the Cyclops that takes a step and squashes them without even noticing, who lifts them up in his hand to throw them down into a courtyard sealed off by gray walls, in handcuffs, already dead, still undamaged in their condition of the heroic dead.

"And nobody knows about it, Minaya, absolutely nobody, and it will remain unpublished until I bring it to light, I mean, if you keep my secret. I've even thought of the title for my doctoral dissertation: 'Literature and Political Engagement in the Spanish Civil War. The Case of Jacinto Solana.' You can't deny it sounds good."

Minaya cleaned a section of clouded glass and saw the motionless horsemen at the corners again. Gray overcoats in the January dusk, hard faces restrained under helmets, black rubber truncheons hanging from the saddlebows, raised like swords when they galloped in pursuit among the cars. He drained his glass, vaguely noted the date and password for a clandestine appointment he wouldn't keep, promised silence and gratitude, left the cafeteria and the university, crossing in front of the horsemen and the barred windows of the jeeps, hoping fear wouldn't be noticed in his calm step, his lowered head. Abruptly, that night, he imagined the lie and wrote the letter, and later he told Inés that it took ten interminable days to receive Manuel's reply, and on the night train that brought him to Mágina he didn't hear anybody speak, and there were indolent guards in civilian clothes smoking as they leaned against the dark windows in the corridors, looking at him at times as if they recognized him.

3

INÉS SAID SHE SAW HIM standing among the acacias, not yet decided, examining the house, the balconies, the white plaster moldings, as if giving time to his memory to recognize them, still and solitary behind the fountain's rim, not protecting himself from the fine spray that dampened his hair and overcoat, indifferent to it. She was changing the sheets on the bed in the room that Manuel had told her that same morning to prepare for the guest, and she said that from the first time she looked out from the balcony and saw him there in the plaza, staring so intently at the house, she knew who he was, and that very soon, when he tossed away the cigarette and picked up the suitcase in a gesture of brusque resolve, the bell would ring in the silence of the courtyard and then Teresa's footsteps would sound on the marble flagstones. She went out to the gallery and hid behind the curtains to see him from the front when the door opened, framed in the light of the threshold, tall, his hair tousled and damp, with a gray-checked overcoat and sloping shoulders that emphasized his air of fatigue and a small suitcase he didn't want to give to Teresa when she asked him into the parlor room where the fire was already lit.

"Inés," Teresa called, going to the stairwell, "tell Don Manuel that his nephew's here, the one from Madrid."

INÉS REMAINED QUIET on the other side of the curtains, her face very close to the glass, because she liked to stand that way for hours, behind the windows, looking at the street or the courtyard with white columns or the animal pen with a poplar tree and a dry well that she has to cross for the last time tonight on her way to the Mágina station. She liked to look at everything from a distance, immobile things, the passage of light across the glass in the dome, and without anyone noticing her presence—she was so stealthy and slim that only a very attentive ear, one alerted ahead of time, could detect her—she pressed her nose and forehead to the glass and traced lines or words left by her breath, returned to an extremely slow time, the time of her childhood, lost in it, immune to the voices calling her. Before going back to the kitchen with her swaying walk, Teresa looked up from the middle of the courtyard, searching for Inés' shadow behind the gallery curtains, because she suspected she hadn't obeyed her and was still there, watching her, perhaps choosing a favorable angle that would allow her to still see the new arrival, and ordered her again to hurry and let Don Manuel know. The clocks struck six, first the clock in the parlor, very close to Inés, and a few seconds later, when the girl was already climbing the stairs to the pigeon loft, the bells of the clock in the library, sounding deep and distant to her, startled Minaya, who hadn't dared to sit down and remained standing, very firm and attentive, at the closed door, his coat over his arm and the suitcase close by, as if he still weren't sure he would be accepted in the house. Reality, I calculate, imposed unpleasant corrections on his memory. The ceiling wasn't as high as he remembered, and the books no longer prodigiously covered every wall, but the parquet floor shone exactly as before and creaked slightly under his feet, and a fire was burning in the marble fireplace to receive him. There were two large windows divided into rectangles by white woodwork, almost like grillwork, and through the panes the plaza he had left a few minutes earlier seemed imaginary or distant, as if the city and the winter did not maintain a precise connection to the interior of the house, or only in the sense that an intimate landscape was added on to look at from the balconies and a sensation of hostile twilight that made its enclosed space more inviting. Then, as he waited and was afraid, he saw the first two images of Mariana, which later, day after day, would be repeated and extended in others when her face, not always recognized, would appear to him in the rooms of the house, the writings of Jacinto Solana, a plaza, and some churches in the city. First he saw Orlando's framed drawing between two shelves in the library, the face foreshortened, almost in profile, of a young woman with short hair hanging over her cheeks, a fine-drawn nose, a short chin, and wide-open eyes fixed on something that wasn't outside her but absorbed into her consciousness, her slight smile. "Orlando," he read, "May 1937." On the mantel over the fireplace, in a photograph that despite the glass protecting it was taking on a sepia tone, the same young woman walked between two men along a street that undoubtedly was in Madrid. She wore a coat with a fur collar opened over a white dress and high-heeled shoes, but all that could be seen clearly of her face was the large smile that mocked the photographer, because she had the brim of her hat pulled low on her forehead and a veil hid her eyes. The man who walked to her left held a cigarette and looked at the spectator with an air of irony or misgiving, as if he did not completely approve of Minaya's presence or had discovered a spy in him. Minaya thought he recognized his uncle in the one on the right, the tallest of the three and clearly the best dressed. Manuel was surprised by the photographer's shot while he was turning toward Mariana, who unexpectedly had taken his arm and pressed it against her without noticing the gift she was granting him, attentive only to the eye of the camera, like a mirror in which she liked to look at herself as she walked.

"That man, the one on the left, is Jacinto Solana," said Manuel, at his back.

Minaya recalled a tall figure with gray hair, a large, pale hand on his shoulders, but the face that bent down toward him that afternoon to kiss him lightly on the cheeks had been erased forever from his memory by the almost terrifying exactitude of the large clock whose golden pendulum slowly moved back and forth behind the glass of a box that resembled a coffin. Now, when the clock and the bookshelves and the entire house took on dimensions without mystery, the earlier figure with gray hair disappeared before Minaya, supplanted by the features of a stranger. He was not nearly as tall as in memory and not as heavy as in the photograph, and he had white hair and a posture ruined not by old age but by long neglect and the habit of illness, the cardiac ailment left over from his war wounds, made worse by the passage of the years and nourished by his own negligence because he continued to smoke and never took the pills Medina prescribed for him. Any shock provoked violent palpitations and a dark, tenacious pain that did not allow him to sleep and was like a shadowy hand that penetrated his chest and squeezed his heart to the point of asphyxia at the precise moment sleep conquered him. He would sit up, shaken by the certainty that he had been about to die, turn on the light, and remain motionless in the bed, his hand at his heart, attentive to its beat, and he could not get back to sleep until dawn, for as soon as he closed his eyes the vertigo of fear would break free and the invading hand would slip again inside his body, groping between his lungs and his ribs, coming up from his belly like a reptile silently coiling around his heart. Fear of the definitive attack and the obsessive attention with which he listened to his own heart probably made his ailment worse, but eventually they also allowed him to acquire a serene familiarity with death, for he knew how it would come, and when he could recognize it from a distance, he gradually had stopped fearing it. It would be, as it had been so often, that pain in his left arm, the stabbing pain in his chest piercing without warning, like a bullet or a knife thrust, perhaps when he was eating breakfast alone in front of the large windows to the garden, or in the afternoon in the library, or striking him dead on the plank floor of the pigeon loft. It would be that same stabbing pain turned into a sudden shot or blade and the tide of terror rising from his stomach and taking on in his chest the form of that familiar, lethal hand that would not stop this time but penetrate until it tore out his breath and his heart so that he would never return again from that anguish and could remain sweetly dead and abandoned on the bed, or even better, in the pigeon loft, on the same planks where Mariana had died, her forehead punctured by a single bullet. The habit of solitude and the longing for death were for him residual or secret ways of remembering his wife and Jacinto Solana, and having survived them for so many years seemed to him a disloyalty unmitigated even by the devotion of his memory. In the bedroom he shared with Mariana for only one night, he kept her wedding dress and the white shoes and the bouquet of artificial flowers she carried on their wedding day. He had catalogued not only all his memories but the photographs of Mariana and of Jacinto Solana as well, and distributed them around the house according to a private and very strict order, which allowed him to transform his passage through the rooms into a reiterated commemoration. He was not satisfied with the few images a man can or has the right to remember: he demanded of himself dates, precise locations, exact tones of light and nuances of tenderness, enumerations of meetings, of words, and with so much thinking about Mariana and the man who had been his best friend, his recollections became worn, so that he was no longer sure they had really existed outside the photographs and his memory. This is why he was so surprised that in his nephew's letter the name of Jacinto Solana appeared: someone not himself and not connected to his house had heard that name far from Mágina and even had knowledge of his life and some poems which for Manuel had not existed until then except as attributes of his most secret autobiography. Reading that name, Jacinto Solana, written by another hand, in Madrid, at the end of January 1969, was proof that the man it designated had in fact lived and left in the world traces of his presence that could not be erased by time or the voracious executioners in blue uniforms who one day made the flagstones in the courtyard and the parquet in the rooms tremble with the tramping of their boots and who burned in the garden all of Jacinto Solana's books and kicked his typewriter to pieces.

In the midst of the pigeons' muffled cooing he heard the footsteps of Inés, who was coming up to tell him something—perhaps he thought then, but that too was part of an old habit, that this was how Mariana's footsteps must have sounded on a certain dawn in 1937—and before the girl came into the dovecote he already knew that Minaya was waiting for him in the library, a witness to the photographs and Orlando's drawing, but also, remotely, to the existence of Jacinto Solana and the time that in response to the incantation of his name was returning after a silence of twenty-two years. "In some newspapers from the war I found not long ago a few admirable poems by Jacinto Solana, who, I know through my father, was a good friend of yours, and to whom I would like to dedicate my doctoral dissertation," Minaya had written, trying with difficulty to reconcile dignity and lies. How it would have amused him to know that someone, after so many years, was attempting to write a solemn doctoral dissertation about his work.

"*Oeuvre*, Manuel, everybody is looking for and has an *Oeuvre*, with a capital O, just like Juan Ramón. They go down the street with the O of their *Oeuvre* around their necks, as if it were the frame of the portrait in which they are already posing for posterity. And I've been writing since long before I had the use of my reason, and at the age of thirty-two I don't have a bad book I can call my *Oeuvre*, and I'm not even sure I'm a writer."

That was all he talked about in the spring of 1936, about the need to leave the bad life of newspapers and banquets with their toasts and literary magazines and return to Mágina and lock himself inside his father's house and not leave or talk to anybody until he had finished a book that wasn't called *Beatus Ille* yet and was going to be not only the justification for his life but also the weapon of an uncertain vengeance because, he said, with the smile that expressed no pleasantness or bitterness but rather a very calculated complicity with himself, sometimes the success of the best was personal revenge. He thought about him and his wise, cold smile as he slowly descended the steps of the pigeon loft on his way to the courtyard where night had definitively fallen and the library where Minaya was waiting for him. In the mirror on the last landing he looked at himself to find out how his nephew would see him: he seemed old and disheveled, and there were tiny white or gray feathers on his stained trousers and his tweed jacket with the torn pockets. He smoothed back his white hair, and not without a certain uneasiness, because he was still very timid, he opened the door to the library. Minaya, his back to the door, was looking at the photograph on the fireplace, which in Manuel's catalogue had an invisible number one written on it, because it was the first one taken with Mariana and also the oldest image he had of her. After the initial silence and the stupefaction of not recognizing each other—for a moment what seemed to divide them was not immobility or the great empty space of the library but a chasm in time—Manuel came toward Minaya and embraced him, and then, resting both hands on his shoulders, stepped back to look at him with blue eyes circled in weariness beneath his lids. At close range he was a stranger, and Minaya could barely find in him any characteristic that reminded him of the tall figure glimpsed in his childhood: perhaps the hands, his hair, the set of his shoulders.

"The last time I saw you, you came just to my waist," said Manuel, and he invited him to sit down on one of the armchairs arranged in front of the fire, as if that too had been anticipated because of the delicate talent he always had for hospitality. "Did you remember the house?"

"I remembered the courtyard and the tiles, and the clock that frightened me back then. But I thought it was all much larger."

Slowly the fire, the attentive voice, Manuel's gestures, stripped away the feeling of flight, the dejection of the trains, and for the first time Madrid and the memory of prison were as distant as the winter night thickening in the plaza against the windowpanes and the white shutters, closed to protect him. Leaning back in the chair, Minaya gave in to fatigue and the warm influence of the cognac and the English cigarettes that Manuel had offered him, hearing himself talk, as if he were someone else, about his life in Madrid and the death of his parents, which occurred when a doubtful stroke of good luck in business allowed them to buy a car and treat themselves to a vacation in San Sebastián, because his father, who had hereditary nostalgia, always wanted to spend the summer like the aristocrats in the illustrated magazines he had read in his youth. He lied without will, without excessive guilt, as if each of the lies he devised had the virtue of not hiding his life but correcting it. He didn't say that in recent years he had lived in a pensión, or that the incidental pieces he occasionally published in literary magazines slipped inevitably from indifference to oblivion, he didn't speak of his fear of prison or the gray horsemen, but of the poem "Invitation," which someone had shown him in the cafeteria at the university. He had copied it, he said, and read it so many times that by now he knew it by heart, and he recited it slowly, not looking at Manuel, grasping at the only fragment of indubitable truth that sustained his imposture. Manuel nodded gravely, as if he too remembered the lines, and when Minaya finished saying them neither of them spoke, so that in the end the urgent will to die in those words remained suspended and present in the library like the final striking of a clock, like the smile and gaze of the man who had written them. Later, when they went upstairs so that Minaya could see his bedroom, Manuel opened the door to a room that contained only an iron bed and a desk placed in front of a mirror.

"Here it is," he said, "the window and the mirror in that poem. This is where he wrote it."

As they went up, the piano music that had been playing since Minaya entered the house sounded more clearly and closer. It invaded the silence and suddenly broke off in the middle of a phrase, though nothing had announced the proximity of its ending, and then all that could be heard was the beating of pigeons' wings against the glass dome. "That's my mother," said Manuel, smiling, as if excusing her for her eccentric way of playing a habanera that never advanced, that stopped abruptly and returned to the first phrase, like the exercises of a student who does not achieve the certainty of perfection. Minaya climbed the stairs, sliding his hand along the varnished, curved wood of the railing as if guided by a silk ribbon that dissolved in the music and traced lingering art nouveau curves in the angles of the labyrinth. Always, ever since he was a boy, he had liked to climb shadowy staircases in houses and movie theaters this way, and he half-closed his eyes so he had only the polished touch of the wood to guide him.

"This house is too big," said Manuel in the gallery, gesturing toward the large windows of the courtyard and the line of doors to the rooms. "It's all Inés and Teresa can do to keep it clean, and in winter it's very cold, but it has the advantage of allowing you to lose yourself in any room as if it were a desert island."

Lost forever, Minaya swore, safe, enclosed behind the white shutters to the balconies, in the heat of the fire burning in the marble fireplaces, and the clean sheets, and the water in which he dissolved with closed eyes, abandoned and alone, undamaged, naked, not fearing anything or anyone, as if fear and the obscene possibility of failure had not been able to pursue him to Mágina. Manuel had left him alone in the bedroom, and before unpacking and taking a long bath that made him lose his awareness of the time and place where he found himself, he examined with gratitude and discretion the large, high bed that yielded so sweetly under the weight of his body, the deep closet, the paintings, the modern lamp on the night table, the desk facing the balcony that made him imagine tranquil afternoons of literature and indolence when he would look out at the tops of the acacias and the dark rooftiles of the houses in Mágina. I'll be thrown out of here, he thought as he dried himself before a mirror, as he shaved and dressed and used the comb and razor as the tools of an actor who isn't sure he has learned his part and doesn't have time to rehearse before he's called on stage: "I'll be thrown out or I'll have to leave when I can't pretend anymore that I'm writing a book about Jacinto Solana and I don't even have enough money to take a taxi to the station." Lost forever, for two weeks, he calculated, using each hour as if it were his last coin, a respite for an impostor or a condemned man. When he left the room, bathed and relatively decent in his only suit and tie, he found himself in the parlor that opened onto the nuptial bedroom. Before they married, Manuel had assigned the front rooms on the second floor to his conjugal life with Mariana so they could have their own area separate from the rest of the house, but of that original plan all that remained was the bedroom no one had used since May 21, 1937, and the wedding photograph hanging on the wall of the parlor over the sofa with yellow flowers. Tall and erect in his lieutenant's uniform, with a small blond mustache and his hair fixed with pomade, in the photograph Manuel had the unwilling appearance of a hero frozen by the shock of the flash, his eyes staring and lost. Mariana, on the other hand, and this was not a coincidence, I suppose, but an indication of their different characters, looked at the spectator from whichever angle you contemplated the photograph. You entered the parlor and there were her large, almond eyes looking at you without expression or doubt, her white veil and ambiguous smile, her long, extended fingers resting on Manuel's arm, very close to his two lieutenant's stars. The straps, the pistol at his waist, his military bearing, were no longer anything but a simulation or testimony to what had ended, for when the photograph was taken it had been two months since Manuel had definitively been discharged from the army because of the bullet that had grazed his heart on the Guadalajara front and kept him on the verge of death for several weeks. But the clarity of his blue eyes was the same that Minaya had encountered when he met with him in the library, as well as that air of useless solidity and excessive generosity, limited only by modesty. Dressed now in a dark suit that he wore very few times during the year and prepared, because he was a gentleman and knew the norms of hospitality, to receive his nephew properly, he again resembled the tall, solemn man in the wedding photograph.

That was when Inés heard them talking about Jacinto Solana. She had gone in to serve them sherry, and when she heard that name she paid more attention to what they were saying, and she remained still, very attentive, without their noticing her, in a dark corner, choosing to be invisible, the same attitude of absent submissiveness she had adopted as a child at the orphanage; but when she had poured the glasses and placed a tray of appetizers on the table—the other one, the stranger, watched her moving around them and spoke in a peculiar tone about a book he was going to write—Manuel told her she could leave, since Amalia and Teresa undoubtedly had prepared supper for Doña Elvira, and he began to recall his friendship with Solana only when he supposed that Inés was no longer listening.

"It would be inexact to say he was my best friend, as your father told you. He wasn't the best friend but the only friend I've had in my life, and also my teacher and my older brother, the one who guided me through Madrid and found the books for me that I had to read and took me to see the best films, because he was very fond of movies and had been in Paris with Buñuel for the opening of *L'Age d'Or*. Before the war, one of his jobs was writing screenplays for that film studio of Buñuel's, Filmófono it was called, he did screenplays and publicity too, but he kept writing for the newspapers, short things, film reviews in *El Sol*, poetry in *Octubre*, a story or two that Don José Ortega published in the *Revista de Occidente*. You can read it all if you like, because I have those things in the library, though he always told me he didn't care anything about them and they deserved to be forgotten. When we were boys, at secondary school, we imagined we'd become war correspondents and rich, famous writers, like Blasco Ibáñez, and our success would make the girls like us, the ones we fell in love with so futilely. We planned to go to Madrid together, not to study for a career but to live a bohemian life and achieve glory. But my father died when I was in my second year of law, and I had to come back to Mágina to help my mother, and I didn't finish my studies and I lacked the will to leave here, as Solana had done. He came from time to time and talked about Madrid and the world, the cafés where it was possible to sit beside the writers who were like gods to me, and he brought or sent me newspaper clippings with his byline, always saying it was nothing compared with what he was about to write. At the end of Primo de Rivera's dictatorship, he published a good number of articles and some poems, especially in the *Gaceta Literaria,* because he had become a surrealist, but I believe his only friends in Madrid were Buñuel and Orlando, the painter who illustrated his stories, and then, just before the war, Miguel Hernández, who was younger than us and saw in him something like a mirror of his own life. Solana really disliked the way Hernández boasted about his origins. "I've tended goats too," he would say, "but I don't think that's something to be proud of." He didn't stop writing when the war broke out, but I suspect he wouldn't have liked knowing that those ballads from the *Mono Azul* that you've read have survived him for so many years. In May '37, when he came to Mágina for my wedding, he was one of the editors of that paper and belonged to the Alliance of Antifascists, and they had just named him cultural commissar in an assault brigade, but suddenly nobody heard anything about him, and he didn't attend the writers' congress they were holding that summer in Valencia. Not even his wife knew where he was. He had enlisted as an ordinary soldier in the popular army under another name, and he didn't publish a single word. He was wounded on the Ebro, and at the end of the war he was arrested in the port of Alicante. But all of this I found out ten years after he disappeared, when he left prison and came to Mágina and to this house. He still wanted to write a book, one memorable book, he said, and then die afterward, because that was the only thing that had mattered to him in his life, to write something that would go on living when he was dead. That's exactly what he told me."

I can imagine him now, in his leather armchair, in the precise spot in the library where Inés said he had sat across from Minaya, his hands joined, his cigarette forgotten in the ashtray, all the lost years written on his face and on his hair that had been blond and that gave him, along with his blue eyes and his manners from another country and another time, a foreign air exaggerated by his shyness and his loyalty. Like a prolongation in his memory of the words he had said after an infinite respite of silence, Manuel looked at the pencil drawing of Mariana and repeated to himself the date and name written in the margin, but when he stood it was not to take down the drawing and show his nephew the words Solana had written on the back, but to pick up from the mantel over the fireplace the photograph taken on the same day they learned about the victory of the Popular Front in the February elections and hand it to Minaya. Look at us, he could have said, smiling at the proximity of war and death, contemplating with open eyes the dirty future reserved for us, the shame, the useless enthusiasm, the miracle of a hand that for the first time rested on my arm.

"What your father told you was true. It was Solana who introduced me to my wife. Ten or fifteen minutes before this picture of us was taken, on February 17, 1936."

4

HE HAD A NOTEBOOK where he wrote down dates, Inés said, places, names, a notebook that he kept in the top drawer of his desk and in which at first he didn't write anything, as if it were only a part of his meticulous simulation, except, on the cover, the date he arrived in the city, January 30, Wednesday, and on the first page, in the middle of the empty space, just the name Jacinto Solana, 1904–1947, like a funeral inscription, like the title of a book that was still blank, destined perhaps never to be written, to be nothing but a volume of ordered pages without a single word or any other marks except those of its blue squares. Then he began to write down dates and names, at night, when he went to bed, as if he were outlining the rough draft of a future biography that his indolence would always postpone, the names of all the inhabitants of the house and the titles of the magazines he had consulted that afternoon in the library, when he was alone and turned red if Inés came in to ask him something, to offer him something, because Manuel had told her to, a cup of tea or a drink. He always listened, very silent, solicitous, and stayed very late conversing with Utrera, with Manuel, with Medina, the doctor, and with brief questions, with silences that contained the questions he didn't always dare to ask, he tried to have the conversation gravitate to Jacinto Solana, to his profiled shadow, elusive and laconic like his gaze in the photographs, like the dedications to Mariana or Manuel in some of the books in the library, on some postcards sent from Paris in 1930, from Moscow in 1935, in December.

He writes in his bedroom, Inés said as she undressed, first pulling off her blue tights, dazzling the semidarkness of the room with her white thighs, her white feet, the pink heels numb with cold, and after taking off her skirt she got into bed and sat on it, covering herself to the waist, her icy feet in the deepest part of the sheets, and then, when she removed the red wool sweater, her head disappeared for an instant and emerged again, beautiful and disheveled, to submerge completely, up to her chin, lying still and shivering, unveiling one hand to toss her bra and shirt to the floor, naked now, clinging, pushing her knees forward, her thighs, with her eyes closed, as if feeling her way, her skin cool and then warm, her small breasts, the brush of nipples hardened by the cold and then soft again and pink and docile to the caress or slow bite that she confirmed, still without the assistance of sight, so that when her eyes opened she, Inés, would be recovered and close, intact, breaking free of the embrace, bending her long body that lay in the dark corner of the sheets that had to be moved away to see her whole, the brief, smooth pubis between closed thighs, the angular, raised hips, and when the hand moved down until the fingertips felt the straight, wet cleft, that touch, like a countersign, advised of the transition to the celebration of odors, deep salty vagina and delicate breath and mouth that sometimes closed pink and wet and a smile of thin lips pressed tight that was the candid, wise smile of happiness and rest.

"But he stops talking when I come in, and he looks at me a lot, almost never in the eye, he looks at me when I turn my back, but I see him watching me in mirrors," she said, laughing only with her lips, certain of her body, grateful to it in a way that excluded adolescence and chance. For Minaya she had prepared the room located to the left of the parlor, symmetrical with the empty bedroom of Manuel and Mariana, and on the first night, when he went down to the library after bathing, Inés examined his suitcase and his books and the papers he had put in the desk, and when she opened the closet she confirmed her suspicion that the recent arrival had no suit other than the one he was wearing. Then she went to the courtyard, hovering near the half-opened library door, pretending to clean the paintings or the tiles, but then Utrera appeared, back from the café, and he began to ask her things about Minaya in his slow, drunkard's voice, what he was like, what time he had arrived, where he was now, brushing against her body in a siege either casual or cowardly, so close she could smell his breath rotten with tobacco and cognac. Utrera, who didn't go into the library because he couldn't walk a straight line and his hands were trembling, looked at her for the last time, not at her face but at her hips and belly, and then he disappeared into the depths of the house, no doubt to shut himself inside the carriage house where he had his studio, or what he called his studio, because in all the years Inés had been in Manuel's service, the old man hadn't done anything but carve a Saint Anthony for a village church and repeat to the point of satiety a series of Romanesque-looking figures that he sold regularly to a furniture store.

"You can stay here as long as you like, even when you've finished your book," she heard Manuel say, and she moved away from the library door because the voice had sounded very close by. She saw him walk out, head bowed and more distracted than usual, and she was surprised he didn't ask for his hat and coat, as he did every night, to take the long walk past the watchtowers on the wall that Medina had prescribed for him. "Inés," he said, turning to her from the stairs, "see if our guest needs anything," but she couldn't do as he asked because Teresa came out of the kitchen then and asked her to help prepare supper for Doña Elvira—Amalia, the other maid, lethargic and almost lost in blindness, gave them vague orders as she sat next to the stove. Broth, a plate of boiled vegetables, and a glass of water that she, Inés, usually took up to the señora's rooms, attending to the most unpleasant part of her work, because Doña Elvira frightened her, like some of the nuns at the orphanage where she had spent her childhood, and she looked at her in the same way. Doña Elvira spent her days examining accounting books or fashion magazines from the time of her youth with a magnifying glass, and she always had the television set on, even when she played the piano, and never looked at it. I estimate that she must have been almost ninety, but Inés says there is not a single sign of decrepitude in her eyes. She wears a black dress with lace collar and cuffs, and her hair is short and waved in the style of 1930. This afternoon, for the first time in twenty-two years, she has left her rooms and her house to go up to the cemetery and witness without tears, with a rigid expression of grief very similar to that of certain funerary statues, the burial of her son.

"Your supper, Señora," Inés said.

"Is my nephew's son, Minaya, here yet?"

"He arrived at six, Señora. He's in the library now."

"What's he like?"

"Tall, Señora, and he seems pretty quiet."

"Is he good-looking?"

"I didn't notice."

"That's a lie. He's good-looking. I can tell by looking at you. And of course you noticed. Will he stay very long?"

"It seems about two weeks."

"We'll see. He'll deceive my son, like that Utrera, who still says he's a sculptor, and he'll stay until he gets tired of living at our expense. He's bound to be a sponger, like his father."

When she came down again with the untouched tray, she saw that the light in the parlor was on, and following her custom of spying on everything—it wasn't curiosity but an instinct of her large, always open eyes and her body trained in stealth, like the eyes and body of a nocturnal animal—she could see Manuel without his detecting her, trapped in Mariana's dead gaze and then locking himself in the marriage bedroom with a key that he alone possessed, and she knew then that this return to an abandoned custom was the first consequence of the stranger's arrival and the conversation in the library. She distrusted Minaya as an affable invader, and with the same attention she had used to search his suitcase and books and smell the traces of his body in the bathroom and on the damp towels, she studied him later, in the library, enjoying his uneasiness when she looked directly into his eyes, when she brushed against him as she leaned over to fill his glass during supper in the dining room, or caught in the mirror his look of interrogation, of proclaimed desire. Silent and hostile, alert to the danger, she entered the library to see Minaya up close now that he was alone. They would remember afterward that it was the first time they spoke to each other, and that Minaya stood when he saw her and didn't know what to say when Inés asked if he wanted anything as she waited in the doorway, undecipherable and submissive, her chestnut hair pulled back in a ponytail and her beautiful girl's hands abused by the murky water in washtubs. She had just turned eighteen, and with her mere presence she knew how to establish an invisible distance between herself and the things that brushed against her without ever touching her, between her body and the looks that desired it, and the obscure, exhausting work she did in the house. She scrubbed the floors and made the beds and spent hours on end kneeling beside a bucket of dirty water to clean the flagstones in the courtyard, and five times a day she carried food or tea to Doña Elvira, holding the silver tray with the same absorbed elegance as those figures of saints in old paintings who hold before them the emblems of their martyrdom, but she and her body kept themselves safe, and every night at about eleven, from the balcony of his bedroom, Minaya saw her go out to the plaza in her coat that was too short and her flat shoes, haughty and suddenly free and moving away to another place and another life that neither he nor anyone else knew about, just as no one, not even he, could determine her thoughts or find out about her past before the day she came to the house recommended by the nuns of the orphanage where she had lived until she was twelve or thirteen years old. She walked to another life every night, to a rented room off the plaza where Utrera's Monument to the Fallen stood. But at first, that afternoon in the library, before desire and the will to know, Minaya was moved only by gratitude and fear of her beauty and his customary predilection for very slim girls.

"Still a little skinny, but wait until you see her in a couple of years," said Utrera, examining her shamelessly from across the table with his little damp eyes, as lively as points of light in the midst of the wrinkles on his eyelids. When the clock struck nine, Minaya had entered the empty dining room that was too large, thinking that the setting placed across from his was his uncle's, but after a few minutes of solitude and waiting it was not Manuel who came in but a tiny, talkative old man who smelled vaguely of alcohol and wore a white carnation in his lapel. Everything about him, except his hands, was small and carefully arranged, and his impeccable baldness seemed like an attribute of his orderliness, like the gleam of his dentures and the bow tie that topped his shirt.

"Since it's very possible that Manuel won't have supper with us," he said, tense and extravagant, "I'm afraid I'll have to introduce myself on my own. Eugenio Utrera, sculptor and unworthy guest in this house, though I must inform you that very much against my will I find myself a step away from retirement. You're young Minaya, am I right? We had a real desire to meet you. Your father was a good friend of mine. Didn't he ever tell you? On one occasion the two of us were about to organize an antiques business. But sit down, please, and together let us do honor to these delectables brought to us by the beautiful Inés. I understand that you are planning to write a book about Jacinto Solana. A difficult undertaking, I would imagine, but an interesting one."

He spoke very quickly, leaning his body forward to be closer to Minaya, with a smile greedy for responses that he didn't wait for, and as he sipped his soup the air whistled through his false teeth, which at times, when he adjusted them, emitted a sound like bones knocking together. He had large, blunt hands that seemed to belong to another man, and on his left ring finger he wore a green stone, as extravagant as his smile, a testimony, just like his smile, of the time when he reached and lost his brief glory. He smiled and spoke as if sustained by the same spring, about to break, that kept his figure of an anachronistic gallant standing, and only his eyes and his hands did not participate in the will-o'-the-wisp of his gesticulations, for he could not hide the fever in his eyes sharpened every morning and every night in the mirror of old age and failure or the ruin of his useless hand that in another time had sculpted the marble and granite of official statues and modeled clay and now lay still and slowly became dull in an immobility driven by arthritis. Behind his words and the smoke of his cigarettes, his eyes, not veiled by vanity or lies, scrutinized Minaya or pursued Inés with the devotion of a dirty old man, and when she leaned over to serve him something or remove the tablecloth, Utrera remained silent and looked at her neckline out of the corner of his eye, sitting a little more erect, very serious, the fork in his hand, his napkin carefully placed in the collar of his shirt.

"She lives with an uncle who is ill, I think he's an invalid, there's something wrong with his legs or his spine. From time to time he must suffer some kind of relapse, because Inés stops coming or leaves in the middle of the afternoon, with no explanation, you must have noticed by now that she doesn't talk very much."

He ate slowly, as if he were officiating, cutting the meat into very small pieces and sipping the wine like a bird, hospitable, always careful that Minaya's glass was never empty, recalling or inventing an old friendship with his father, in those days, he said, so reviled now and so prosperous for him, when he was somebody in the city, in Spain, a well-known sculptor, as his father had perhaps told Minaya, as he undoubtedly would confirm if he visited his studio one morning and looked at the albums of press clippings where his photo and his name were reproduced and it was stated that he, Eugenio Utrera, was

destined to be, as they said in *Blanco y Negro,* a second Mariano Ben-
lliure, a present-day Martínez Montañés, and not only in Mágina,
where he had recarved for the Holy Week brotherhoods all the pro-
cession statues burned by the Reds during the war, but in the entire
province, in Andalucía, in the distant plazas of cities he had never
visited, where the Monuments to the Fallen bore his signature written in learned Latin capitals, EVGENIO VTRERA, sculptor. Now
he drank without pretense the rest of the bottle that Inés, responding to a discreet signal from him, had not taken away when she
cleared the table, and he looked at his hands remembering with
threadbare melancholy the unrepeatable years when his workshop
was visited by presidents of brotherhoods and local heads of the
Movement to commission Baroque Virgins and statues of fallen heroes, somber busts of Franco, granite angels with swords. The empty
spaces of plundered altarpieces had to be filled and Holy Week
thrones had to be remade that perished in the bonfires lit in every
plaza in Mágina during that summer of madness, their flames leaving behind high trails of soot that can still be seen, he said, on the
facades of certain churches abandoned since then, closed to worship,
like the one opposite, the church of San Pedro, some of them converted into warehouses or garages. During the years following the
war, Utrera's workshop teemed, like an animated forest, with Virgins
pierced by daggers, Christs carrying the cross, crucified, expiring,
whipped by executioners on whom Utrera without the slightest
scruple depicted his enemies, Christs resurrected and ascending, motionless, on clouds of metallic blue paint. In 1954, he recalled, on the
first of April, the minister of the interior came to Mágina to inaugu-
rate the Monument to the Fallen. In the midst of the hedges, among
the recently planted cypresses, a monolith, a stone cross and altar, a
great block of imprecise edges covered by a huge national flag. He
wasn't a politician, he was an artist, he explained, but he could not
remember without pride the moment when the minister pulled on the
cord, making the red and yellow cloth fall to one side and revealing

to applause and hymns an angel with lifted wings and a hard, wind-blown mane of hair who sheltered the body of the Fallen and grasped his sword, raising it with muscled arms like Caravaggio's dead Christ, which perhaps Minaya knew.

"Now I go into my workshop, and it seems a lie that any of it happened. They gave me a medal and a certificate, and the *ABC* published my picture in the photogravure section. I should have left Mágina then, when there was still time, just like your father did. We're isolated from everything here. We turn into statues."

He, who had been in Paris, who had seen the marbles of Michelangelo and Bernini in Rome, who had been somebody and succumbed to the conspiracy of envy, of dubious enemies established in Madrid, he said, a victim now, a melancholy artist conquered by the world's ingratitude. The Monument to the Fallen in Mágina was his last official commission, and since 1959 he had not carved another Holy Week image. "And it isn't that tastes have changed," he would say to whomever wanted to listen, sitting on the divan in a shadowy café where he spent the afternoons with a snifter of brandy and a glass of water, "they've simply become depraved, those plastic-looking Christs, those elongated Virgins with girls' faces that look like something Protestant, or Cubist." At first light he would go down to the immense workshop, which had first been a stable, when the house was built, and then a carriage-house where Manuel's father kept the trophies of his mad passion for cars, and there he would spend the morning, not doing anything, perhaps sketching models of statues that were impossible now, carving Romanesque saints, cheap falsifications that had no future, looking at the vast empty space.

"I came to Mágina on July 5, 1936. I had spent a month in France and Italy, and before returning to Granada, it occurred to me to visit Manuel. We had met when he was studying law, and we continued corresponding after he returned to Mágina, when his father died. I was here a little more than a week, and when I was leaving, when I was saying good-bye to Manuel and his mother, Amalia came out of the kitchen and told us she had heard on the radio that the garrison in Granada had sided with the rebels. How can you go now, Manuel said, wait a while and see if the situation clarifies. And so I came to spend a few days and stayed for thirty-three years."

He was also ready to leave in 1939, but he no longer had anywhere to go, because his mother had died during the war, or at least that's what he told Manuel to justify remaining in the city and in his house. He packed his suitcase then, too, and consulted the schedules of the trains that stopped in Mágina, but this time he, who for three years had wanted the victory of those who won, knew he was probably contaminated not by the defeat of the Republic or by Manuel, who would very soon be dragged from his invalid's bed to prolong his dying for six months in the Mágina prison, but by a future, his, the one he had imagined in Rome and in Paris and in the Granada discussions of his youth, definitively upended or broken in the bitter spring of 1939, wiped out, like his right to dignity and to the skill of his hands, by three years of waiting and silence, both less brutal than guilt. With his hands in his trouser pockets and his hat tilted over his face in an expression of petulance that he would improve on years later and that back then only he was capable of admiring, he would wander through the cafés looking for someone who could treat him to a drink or a cigarette, or he would spend the slow afternoons strolling through the Plaza of General Orduña, as if waiting for something, among the gray men in groups who were waiting just like him, with their hands in their pockets and their eyes fixed on the clock in the tower or on the profile of the general whose statue had been rescued from the garbage dump where it had been thrown in the summer of '36 and raised again in the middle of the plaza on a pedestal of martial allegories. He visited offices, unsuccessfully laying claim to old loyalties from long before the war, using up the hours of tedium and despair until nightfall, when the light in the clock on the tower was lit, and then, when it was too late to return to the house and pick up his suitcase and go to the station before the train arrived that would take him back to a city where no one was waiting for him, he walked slowly down the narrow lanes and swore to himself that tonight he'd have the courage to ask Manuel for the exact amount he needed to buy the ticket. He never managed to do it. Six months after the victorious troops entered Mágina, a general competition was announced to replace the image of Nuestro Padre Jesús Nazareno, an apocryphal work by Gregorio Fernández, which had been publicly profaned and burned in July '36.

"Never, never, even if I lived a hundred years, could I repay the debt I owe your Uncle Manuel, my boy. Although he knew I admired the Movement, he allowed me to live in this house throughout the war and then, when I won that competition and received a commission for my first piece of sculpture, he offered me the carriage house to set up my workshop, because I didn't have enough to even rent a room. It's true I interceded for him when things became difficult, but that doesn't repay him. I owe everything I am to his generosity back then."

Because his greatest pride wasn't official glory or the medal or the yellowed clippings he kept as relics in a box in his workroom, but his undeniable loyalty to a friend, to the custom of gratitude, to this house. He spoke to Minaya about Manuel's family as if it were his own, and he knew by heart the names and ranks of the gentlemen depicted in the indistinct portraits in the gallery and in the photo albums that only he bothered to exhume from the library shelves, showing Minaya solemn ancestors he had never heard of, because the oldest face he could recognize belonged to his grandmother Cristina.

"You should have known Doña Elvira when I met her. She was a lady, my friend, as tall as Manuel, and so elegant, a true aristocrat. The death of her husband was a terrible blow, but she would have overcome that if it hadn't been for the things that happened later. I can still see her on the day Manuel came home from the hospital, recovering from that serious wound and ready to marry Mariana. Because, as she said, it was one thing for her son to be for the Republic, and even a little bit of a Socialist, and quite another to see him married to that woman after dropping his lifelong sweetheart. I remember Doña Elvira standing at the door of the library, dressed in mourning, and when Mariana offered her hand she turned and withdrew to her rooms without saying a single word."

Her eyes wide open, Minaya thought, her lips resolute and her eyes flashing and fixed on the offense as they would remain afterward, unmoving, in the time without hours of the wedding photograph, in the blind persistence of the things she looked at and held in her hands and brushed with her body and the air where her perfume resided. It was the wine, he suspected when he stood and shook Utrera's hand again, which remained flaccid and dead in his as the old man reiterated his pleasure at having met him and begged his pardon and invited him to visit his studio any time, it was the wine and his fatigue from the train and his lethargy after the bath and everything muffled or blurred by the strangeness of the house, but as he climbed the stairs and turned the shadowy corners of the gallery, he suddenly felt the physical certainty that Jacinto Solana, the name written at the bottom of the poems he had in his room, had actually existed and breathed the same air and walked on the same tiles he was walking on now knowing as if in a dream that after a few steps he would come to the parlor where Mariana's eyes had been waiting since long before he was born to look at him exactly as they had looked at Solana and the world in 1937. He smoked as he lay on the bed, looking up at a ceiling with painted wreaths that no longer resembled any memory, and then, in the empty exaltation of alcohol and insomnia, he opened the shutters to the balcony and continued smoking with his elbows resting on the marble balustrade, facing the tops of the acacias and the tile roofs and the towers of Mágina submerged in the damp darkness, in the inviting, frightening night that always receives travelers in strange cities. He heard the street door closing with a heavy resonance, and after a moment, when it struck eleven in the Plaza of General Orduña, in the library, in the parlor, he saw Inés passing under the acacias and disappearing into the shadows of a lane, her hair loose and her walk more energetic than the one she used in the house, her head bowed and her hands in the pockets of a coat too short for the raw January night.

5

PERHAPS NOW, IN THE STATION, when he remembers and denies and wants to rein in his will and desire so that they offer him only the necessary future of desertion, departure and the train and eyes vengefully closed, he will want to comprehend the length of time he has spent in Mágina and the order in which things happened, and he will discover he doesn't know or can't know that the precise time of calendars doesn't concur with that of his memory, that two months and thirty years and several lifetimes have gone by without his being able to assign them connections of succession or cause. Now he remembers and is astonished by the speed with which the house took hold of his actions of a new arrival and turned them into habits, and he doesn't know precisely the day he desired Inés for the first time or when he was irremediably trapped by the biography of Jacinto Solana, even before finding his hidden manuscripts and visiting the Island of Cuba and the landscape where they killed him and the plaza where he was born and lived until he was twenty. He doesn't remember dates, only sensations as extensively modulated as musical passages, habits of tranquility sustained in the restlessness of waiting for Inés or stealing after midnight into rooms where he searched for clues and manuscripts fearing he would be caught.

Apart from the house and the present into which he had settled like someone who locks a room from the inside to sit quietly by the fire and doesn't feel the cold or hear the rain or the clock striking the hours, and absorbed in reading a book, the city almost didn't exist, and Madrid even less, or the mediocre past. When he arrived he had crossed the city without recognizing it through the taxi windows, first the empty lots around the station, and the avenue of linden trees with bare branches raised against a vast gray sky that clung like mist to the edge of the plain where church towers were outlined. But that wasn't the city he remembered, and it wasn't the winter light that belonged to it but the exalted light on whitewashed walls and thresholds of sand-colored stone, the one that flowed out of the tunnel of darkness at entrances and gathered in pools like shaded lagoons at the rear, in the vine-arbored courtyards of Mágina, when in the first morning hour, a woman, his mother, opened the door and all the windows and swept the pavement then sprinkled it with water until it gave off the odor of damp cobblestones and wet earth after a storm. Which was why he couldn't recognize the city when he arrived and took so long to walk its streets like a stranger, because Mágina, on winter afternoons, becomes a Castilian city of closed shutters and gloomy shops with polished wood counters and faded mannequins in the display windows, a city of cheerless doorways and plazas that are too large and empty where the statues endure winter alone and the churches seem like tall ships run aground. His light was of a different sort, golden, cold, blue, stretching from the ramparts of the city wall in an undulating descent of orchards and curved irrigation ditches and small white houses among the pomegranate trees, extending in the south to the endless olive groves and blue or violet fertile lowlands of the Guadalquivir, and that landscape was the one he would recognize later in the manuscripts of Jacinto Solana, flat as the world in ancient maps and limited by the outline of the sierra beyond which it was impossible that anything else existed. And he, Solana, had also looked as a child at that place of unlimited light and returned there to die, the open streets of

Mágina that looked as if they would end at the sea and ramparts like steep balconies or high crow's nests from which he looked out on all the clarity of a world unviolated except by the avidity of his eyes and the fables in his imagination.

"His father had a farm," Manuel said. "It's abandoned now, but from the watchtower of the town wall you can see the house and cistern. Every afternoon when we left school, I went down with him and helped him load the produce onto their white mare, to carry it to market. Then we would ride across the city on the mare, but I got down a few streets before we reached here, because if my mother found out I had been with Solana, she would punish me and not let me go out on Sunday. My son, she would say, unloading fruit in the market, like a farmhand. But my father had a certain fondness for him, always somewhat distant, similar to how he would have viewed the child of one of his foremen who showed an aptitude for studying, and when Solana went to Madrid, he carried a letter of recommendation, written by my father, for the editor of *El Debate,* who had known him back when he was a member of parliament. 'I like that boy,' he would say when my mother wasn't around, 'he has ambition, and you can see in his eyes that he knows what he wants and is prepared to do anything to get it.' I've always suspected those words weren't so much praise for Solana as a reproach for me."

He doesn't know when that custom began either, because now it seems to him it lasted for many months or all his life, and that it's impossible Manuel is dead and won't converse with him again every afternoon in the library, when Inés would come in with the tray of coffee and they would smoke English cigarettes with their backs to the window where the light was dying until their only illumination came from the fireplace, interrupted at times by the arrival of Medina, who came to examine Manuel with his medical bag and useless prescriptions and to censure coffee and tobacco and the absurd habit of always talking about the dead, about Jacinto Solana, regarding whom he once told Minaya that he had been nothing but a timid adulterer, and then laughed with his chuckle of a libertine physician addicted to hygiene and what he called the physiology of love.

"I don't know if you realize it, young man, but your presence in this house is having an effect on your uncle as beneficial as a swim in the sea. In my capacity as physician allow me to entreat you not to leave yet. I look at Manuel and don't recognize him. On any afternoon he spends with you he talks more than he has talked to me in the past twenty years, which isn't all that meritorious, because you're young and educated and know how to listen, and I can almost never keep quiet. How's that book of yours on Solana coming along?"

Inés said it was as if Manuel had returned to his own house, as if when he saw it again he observed with astonishment and guilt the signs of the decay into which his neglect had plunged it. He reimposed a fixed schedule for meals, took care of discussing the day's purchases with Amalia and Teresa, and even renewed the supplies of wine in the cellar, finding in these occupations that he had forgotten for so many years a pleasure that surprised even him. Punctually each morning, before withdrawing to the pigeon loft, he went down to have breakfast with his nephew, and from time to time their afternoon conversations were prolonged in slow walks along the watchtowers of the wall, where Manuel would point with his walking stick to the white road that led to Solana's father's farm, the house with its collapsed roof, the cistern blocked by weeds. One day, as if he had guessed that his hospitality was turning into a debt for Minaya, he asked him not to leave yet, to help him organize the books in the library, left for thirty years to an abundant disorder, offering him a justification for remaining in the house that was in no way humiliating. He wouldn't need to abandon his dissertation on Solana, he said, he could work on it a few hours a day and then devote himself, perhaps in the afternoon, to creating a catalogue for the books and perhaps also for the furniture and valuable paintings that were now scattered in no order throughout the rooms and attics. "You'll be my librarian," he said, smiling, as if requesting a favor he wasn't sure would be granted, not daring yet to offer a salary, always afraid to offend. This work, whose proportions very soon revealed themselves as disheartening, had the virtue of calming Minaya in singular fashion because it offered him a new time limit so far off it no longer made him afraid to imagine his departure. At about ten in the morning he would go to the library and begin working with a silent, constant passion, nourished in equal measure by the solitude and stillness of the books and by the tight golden light that came in from the plaza, where there was always the sound of water ascending higher than the acacias and then spilling over the rim of the fountain. When his eyes grew tired of so much writing on file cards in a very small and voluntarily meticulous hand that had allowed him to discover the serene pleasures of calligraphy, Minaya put down the pen and lit a cigarette and sat looking at the white shutters on the windows, the squared, reduced landscape of the acacias and hedges where a feminine figure passed by who sometimes was Inés, back from her other life, ready to enter the library and roil with her perfume the peaceful smell of the books that Minaya tended to as a refuge so he could pretend he wasn't watching her.

From higher up, from the circular windows on the top floor, Jacinto Solana had contemplated the plaza in the winter of 1947, the night still as a well, the only light the insomniac lamp in the shelter Manuel had prepared for him and that wasn't enough for him to finish his book or escape the persecution of his executioners. Minaya saw the metal bed with the bare mattress, the desk by the window where the typewriter had been, the empty drawers that once held his pen and the sheets of paper, blank or written on in the same parsimonious, almost indecipherable hand that traced on the back of Mariana's picture the veiled, precise words, like an augury of his "Invitation." Beyond the circular windows and the shuttered balconies was the same city his eyes had seen and that had remained in his memory like a vengeful paradise during the last two years of the war and the eight years he spent in prison waiting first for death and then for a freedom so remote he could no longer imagine it. Mágina, suspended high on the prow of a hill too far from the Guadalquivir, as beautiful as any of its marble statues, as the sand-colored caryatids with bare bosoms that on the facades of palaces hold up the coats-of-arms of those who left them to the city as a useless inheritance, undeserved and pagan. Dissolved in the city, contained within it like a narrow stream that flowed invisibly and almost never touched his consciousness completely, was Minaya's early life, but there was a fog-bound area beyond the final reaches of his memory that without a break was becoming confused with Jacinto Solana's. He sensed him in the house, just as he came to sense the proximity of Inés before his ears or eyes announced her, he surmised his attentive presence on the other side of things, witnessing everything with the same renegade or ironic indolence that was in his gaze on the morning the photograph in the library was taken. Because he lingered in the city and in the house and in the landscapes of roofs or blue hills that surrounded them, but above all in the library, in the dedications in the books he sent to Manuel from Madrid and that at times rose up before Minaya like a warning that he, Solana, was still there, not only in the memory or imagination of the living but also in the space and matter that had survived him, as enduring and faint as the fossilized trace of an animal or the leaf of a tree that no longer exist in the world.

"If you could have seen," Manuel said, "the expression in his eyes when he entered the library for the first time. My mother had gone to spend a few days at the Island of Cuba, and my father was in Madrid, at the Congress of Deputies, and for a week the entire house was ours. We were eleven or twelve years old, and Solana, when he walked into the courtyard, stood very still and silent, as if he were afraid to move forward. 'This is like a church,' he said, but in reality it wasn't the house that interested him but the place where the books came from that I would lend him behind my mother's back, and which he read with a speed that always bewildered me because he did it at night by the light of a candle when his parents had gone to bed. In his house there was only one book. I remember it was called *Rosa María or the Flower of Love,* a serialized story in three volumes that Solana had read when he was ten and toward which he always felt a kind of gratitude. 'What else could I ever want than to write something like those two thousand pages of misfortunes?' he would say. He entered the library as if he were going into a cave filled with treasure, and he didn't dare touch the books, he only looked at them, or gently ran his hand over them as if he were stroking an animal."

Solana's tightened lips, his dark rage, his lucid, precocious hatred of the life that denied him that house and that library, his desire to rebel against everything and flee Mágina and his father and the two hectares of land and the future in which his father wanted to confine him. It wasn't his love of books that made him clench his fists and wait in silence in the middle of the reception room that smelled of leather and polished wood, but his consciousness of the miserable poverty into which he had been born and the brute fatigue of the work to which he knew he was condemned. The books, like the opaque gleam of the furniture and the golden lamps and the white cap and starched apron of the woman who served them chocolate at teatime in large porcelain cups decorated with blue landscapes, were merely the measure or sign of his desire to flee in order to calculate at a distance his future revenge, longed for and planned out when he read in books about the return of the Count of Monte Cristo. Manuel, alarmed by his silence, suggested they go to the rooms upstairs, but at that moment Jacinto Solana had become a stranger. He ran up the stairs to induce him to follow, but from the gallery balustrade he saw that Jacinto Solana was looking at himself in the mirror on the first landing, distant from him and his voice and everything he so eagerly wanted to offer him in order not to lose the friendship he felt was in danger for the first time since they had met. Solana looked in the mirror at his shaved head and his hemp espadrilles and the gray jacket that had belonged to his father, signs of the degradation against which he could defend himself by imagining with obstinate fervor a future in which he would be a rich, mysterious traveler, implacable with his enemies, or a correspondent and a hero in a war from which he would return and humiliate at his feet all those who now conspired against his talent and his pride. Manuel did not see his tears before the mirror or hear his silence, but a half century later he still recalled the hostile resolve with which Jacinto Solana had said that some day the books he was going to write would be in the library too.

Beatus ille, thought Minaya: what an elevated life and work he desired until his death and never had. His books weren't there, but his words and eyes were, like scratches in the shadow, obsessively contemplating from the mantel over the fireplace the area of serene semidarkness and volumes in a row that he never reached. Crossed-out words or scratches of his poor handwriting suddenly appearing in the margins of a novel that Minaya leafed through for the sheer pleasure of touching the pages and looking at the romantic prints that interrupted them from time to time. He was cataloguing the beautiful volumes of the first French edition of *Les voyages extraordinaires*—Manuel's father, a devotee of Verne's, must have bought them in Paris early in the century—when he noticed that *L'île mystérieux* was missing. He searched all the shelves in vain for the book and asked Manuel about it, who didn't remember having seen it. One morning, when he went into the library, Inés was there dusting the bookcases and the furniture and replacing the bottles in the liquor cabinet. *L'île mystérieux* was on Minaya's desk.

"I brought it back," Inés said. "I finished reading it last night."

"But it's in French," said Minaya, and immediately regretted saying it because she set aside the duster and stood looking at him with an expression of impassive mockery in her chestnut-colored eyes.

"I know that."

To escape his embarrassment, Minaya feigned a sudden interest in his work and didn't stop writing on the file cards until Inés left the library. This was how she would always leave him, so often lost in stupefaction, halted at the brink of a revelation he never could attain and besieged by the desire not only for her body but above all for everything her body and her gaze concealed, because in her, caresses and hungry kisses and fatigued, final stillness were the mask and the lure that hid her from Minaya, so that each boundary of desire he crossed with her was not its assuaging consummation but an impulse to go even deeper and tear away the veils of silence or words that inexhaustibly imposed themselves on Inés' consciousness. But the sensation of advancing was completely illusory, for it wasn't a question of successive veils that would eventually end in the true, unknown face of Inés, but of a single, reiterated, immobile one: the eyes and mouth and thin lips she tensed to apologize or to smile, the voice and face that Minaya never could fix for any length of time in his memory. Slowly he turned the large yellow pages of *L'île mystérieux* and stopped at the last print: when those who had been shipwrecked have abandoned the *Nautilus,* fleeing the eruption that will destroy the island, Captain Nemo dies alone in the splendor of his submerged library. There was a handwritten note at the bottom of the print, and it was difficult for Minaya to decipher it because the blue ink had almost faded. "3-11-47. If only I had the courage of Captain Nemo. My name is nobody, says Ulysses, and that saves him from the Cyclops. JS."

But between himself and the words written by Jacinto Solana, which always had the quality of a voice, there now was Inés, mocking his clumsiness, and the book she had brought back was proof of her irony and her absence, for Minaya still found himself in that trance in which desire, not yet revealed in its deceitful plenitude, advances like a nocturnal enemy and makes accomplices of all the things that are transformed into emissaries or signs of the creature who has touched them or to whom they belong. The large house on the Plaza of the Fallen, one of Inés' shirts on the clothesline in the garden, her coat, her pink kerchief on the coatrack, the bed and the glass of water on the night table in the room where she slept when she stayed at the house, the leather sofa where he kissed her for the first time at the beginning of March, Orlando's drawing that fell to the floor, interrupting the shared excitement of their embrace with a crash of broken glass when she pushed him with her hips against the wall and kissed him on the mouth with her eyes closed. As if the sound of the glass had awakened him from a dream, Minaya opened his eyes and saw before him the half-closed lids and eager wings of Inés' nose, who had not stopped kissing him. For a moment he was afraid that someone had come into the library, and he moved away from the girl, who still moaned in tender protest and then opened her eyes, smiling at him with lips wet and inflamed by his kiss.

"Don't worry. I'll tell Don Manuel the drawing fell when I was cleaning it."

When he picked it up, Minaya saw that something was written on the back. "Invitation," he read, and again it was the tiny, familiar, furious hand he had found a few weeks earlier in the novel by Jules Verne and that very soon he would secretly pursue through the most obscure drawers in the house, a slender thread of ink, a flowing stream not heard by anyone that led only to him, not to the key to the labyrinth he had already begun to imagine, but to the trap he himself was setting with his search. He saw the desk, the mirror, the hands on the paper, the pen that was tracing without hesitation or rest the final verses Jacinto Solana wrote not realizing until the end that the sheet he had used was the one where Orlando had drawn his portrait of Mariana. That night, when Minaya entered the library after supper, the drawing was back in its place with new glass. Sitting across from him, meditative and calm, Medina examined it with the attentive air of someone who suspects a falsification.

"I'll tell you something if you promise to keep it a secret. I never thought that poor Mariana was as attractive as they said. As Manuel and Solana said, of course, though Solana was very careful about saying it aloud. And do you know what they both suffered from? An excess of seminal fluids and literature—forgive my vulgarity. I suppose they've already told you that Solana was in love with her too. Desperately in love, and long before Manuel, but with the disadvantage that he was already married when he met her. Piously married in a civil ceremony, like the good Communist he was, feeling Christianly remorseful for the temptation of deceiving his wife and his best friend at the same time. Your father really never talked to you about it?"

6

TIME IN MÁGINA revolves around a clock and a statue. The clock on the tower of the wall built by the Arabs and the bronze statue of General Orduña, whose shoulders are yellow with rust and traces of pigeons and whose head and chest have nine bullet holes. When Minaya can't fall asleep and tosses and turns in the arduous duration of his insomnia, he is rescued by the great clock on the tower striking three in the empty Plaza of General Orduña, where the cab drivers stretch out and fall asleep on the backseats of their cars and an officer sitting in boredom at the entrance to the police station guards the door with his elbows on his knees and his flat-peaked cap down over his face, and perhaps he gives a start and sits up when above his head he hears the striking of the hour, which then, like a more distant, metallic resonance, is repeated in the tower of El Salvador, its bulbous, lead-colored dome visible over the roofs on the Plaza of the Fallen, where Inés lives. Then there is almost a half minute of silence and suspended time that ends when it strikes three inside the house, but still very remote, on the clock in the library, and immediately, as if the hour were approaching Minaya, climbing the deserted stairs with inaudible steps and slipping along the checkered corridor of the gallery, the three bells strike very close to his bedroom, on the clock in the parlor, and so the whole city and the entire house and the consciousness of whoever cannot sleep eventually merge in a unique submerged and bidimensional correlation, time and space or past and future linked by a present that is empty and yet measurable: it precisely occupies the seconds that pass between the first bell in the tower of General Orduña and the last one that sounds in the parlor.

Wide towers crowned with brambles, made huge by solitude and darkness, like the Cyclops whose single eye is the clock that never sleeps, a lookout that informs all those condemned to ceaseless lucidity and unites them in a dark fraternity. The sick undermined by pain, those in love who do not sleep in order not to abandon a shared memory, killers who dream about or remember a crime, lovers who have left the bed where another body sleeps and smoke naked beside the curtains trembling in the night breeze. But this may be the final insomnia of all, the one that flows into death, and enduring it is like walking at night along the last street in a city without lights and suddenly discovering that you've reached the flat wasteland beyond the houses.

The bottles are lined up on the night table, within reach, as are the glass of water, the cigarettes, the capsules that are pink and white, blue and white, blue and yellow: delicate pastel tones for administering the minimal methodical death each of them contains. Diluted blues, yellows, pinks, like the ones in Orlando's last sketches, his watercolors of Mágina seen from the south, from the esplanade of the Island of Cuba, in which the sensation of distance—a long profile of roofs and towers and white houses spread out across the top of the hill toward which the gray lines of olive trees and the pale green of wheat fields ascend—was also an indication of its distance in time, for they weren't painted on the eve of the wedding but during the last winter of the war in a house in Madrid, half destroyed by bombs, in whose hallways and rooms with their boarded-up windows no light like the one Orlando had seen in Mágina in the spring of 1937 ever penetrated.

At that time the Plaza of General Orduña had lost not only the bronze statue but also the name written on the stone tablets at the corners. For three years, and until the day the general returned from the garbage dump swaying like an intrepid drunken charioteer on the back of a truck and watched over by a double row of Civil Guard and Moorish soldiers on horseback, it was called the Plaza of the Republic, but no one ever used that name to refer to it, and even less the name of General Orduña. It was, for the inhabitants of Mágina, the old plaza or simply the Plaza, and the statue of the general belonged to it because it had entered the natural order of things, like the clock tower and the gray pigeons and the arcades where men gathered on rainy winter mornings or at dusk on Sundays with their hands in the pockets of their wide dark suits, their curly hair damp with pomade, cigarettes dangling from their mouths. The large taxis as black as funeral carriages are lined up beneath the trees on one side of the central gazebo, facing the clock tower and the police station. The cab drivers talk or smoke, leaning against the rounded hoods, as if taking refuge in tedium under the protection of the statue of the general who ignores them, standing quiet and alert in the center of the plaza. "One of the most distinguished sons of Mágina, from our family, I think," Minaya remembers his father saying, leading him by the hand on any forgotten Sunday, after eleven o'clock Mass at El Salvador and a visit to the confectioners, where with a magnanimous gesture he gave him a coin so he could take a candy out of the great glass ball that gleamed in the semidarkness, spotted with light from the street. A flock of pigeons takes flight abruptly at Minaya's feet and settles on the head and shoulders of the general, and one of them pecks at the hole that a vengeful, precise bullet opened in his left eye. "To the most excellent Señor Don Juan Manuel Orduña y León de Salazar, hero of the Ixdain Beach, Mágina, in gratitude, MCMXXV," his father would read aloud, and Minaya recalls that it frightened him to contemplate the height of the statue and the holes made by bullets that had penetrated his head and chest and gave him the appearance of the living dead in horror movies. Rigid, like them, invulnerable to gun shots, and looking out with a single eye no more obstinate and fearsome than the other empty socket, the general seemed to sway back and forth on his marble base and his entire golem's bulk weighed on Minaya. In his right hand he holds a pair of bronze binoculars, and in his left, adhering to the high leg of the boots with spurs, a whip or saber that he is about to raise. Indifferent to pigeons and oblivion, the general has his one eye fixed on the south, on the straight street that descends from the plaza, hugging the ruins of the wall, to the embankments of the spillways and the farms and the distant blue of Sierra Mágina, as if there, on the elevated horizon that on rainy days displays the purple mist of Velázquez' Guadarrama, he caught a glimpse of a military objective that was unreachable now, a column of white smoke that he will decipher with the binoculars before raising the whip or saber and shouting a bold, heroic order.

"Those are bullet holes, Son," said his father, solemn and pedagogical. "Since they couldn't shoot General Orduña, because he was already dead, those imbeciles shot the statue."

They arrived in a ragged formation of blue coveralls and espadrilles, unbuttoned tunics over white shirts, military trousers held up by a rope around the waist and militia caps and helmets tilted or fallen over the back of their necks. They carried old muskets from the Cuban war and Mausers stolen during an attack on the barracks of the Civil Guard, and some, especially the women, brandished no weapons other than their raised fists and their voices repeating an Anarchist anthem. Someone shouted for silence and the best-armed men lined up in front of the statue, aiming their muskets at his face. A silence like that of an execution had fallen over the entire plaza and over the crowd waiting in the arcade. The first shot hit General Orduña in the forehead, and the explosion frightened away the pigeons, which flew in terror up to the eaves and went astray in the air each time a volley was discharged that was greeted by the crowd with a vast, single shout. When the guns were silent, a man carrying a long hemp rope made his way through the mass of people and threw an accurate noose over the statue's head that had been punctured nine times, calling for the help of the others who placed their guns across their backs and joined in his effort to bring down the general's likeness. With the rope tense and the harsh knot closed around the hollow torso that resonated like a great wounded bell when it was penetrated by the bullets, General Orduña rocked very slowly, still vertical and not entirely humiliated, and then it moved back and forth and finally fell with a bronze clamor, pulling down in its slow fall the marble pedestal that splintered on the flagstones of the plaza. They adjusted the slipknot around the neck of the statue and dragged it bouncing on the paving stones of the city until they threw it into the chasm of the garbage dump. Three years later, a municipal crew spent an entire week looking for it in the trash and debris, and before they raised General Orduña onto a new base, men in white coats who had come from Madrid—in Mágina they were immediately called statue doctors—repaired the dents and cleaned the bronze, but no one thought of covering the holes scattered like scars over the forehead, eyes, firm mouth, haughty neck, and the chest armor-plated in a general's medals. On the same day his statue was erected again on the base that had been empty for three years, the bells of the clock on the tower sounded again, because the men who pulled down the general had also shot at the white sphere, whose motionless hands marked the exact moment the statue fell and Mágina entered the exalted and voracious time of the war.

"THAT WAS THE FIRST THING he must have noticed when he returned to the city after ten years," Minaya thinks in the plaza and writes later that night in the notebook that Inés punctually opens and examines every morning when she comes in to clean his bedroom, "and what gave him the measure of their defeat and of his sentence, which had not ended when he left prison: not only the red and yellow flag that hung now from the balcony of the police station but also the restored statue and the clock that began to tell time again only when the city had been conquered by the fascists." Like Solana, imagining what he did or feared, he avoids the more traveled streets and goes down toward the southern wall along cobblestoned lanes and white walls that lead to intimate plazas with abandoned sixteenth-century palaces and tall poplars quivering with birds, to the hidden Plaza of San Lorenzo, where the house is located in which Jacinto Solana was born and lived and before whose door he stopped one dawn in January 1947. From the half-closed doors, from the open windows through which the music of a radio soap opera reaches the plaza, attentive women watch Minaya and question one another, pointing at the stranger, who stands beneath the poplars and looks at all the entrances one by one, as if he were searching for someone or had lost his way in the city. That's how they looked at Solana when he arrived there, and perhaps they didn't recognize him because he was ill and had aged and ten years had passed since the last time they had seen him in Mágina. And so, with a slow step and bowed head, he came to his father's house and saw the balconies and closed door that nobody opened when he struck the door with the knocker. Number three, said Manuel, the corner house, the one that has a coat of arms over the doorway with the cross of Santiago and a half moon. The house with deep animal pens and barns where he would hide behind sacks of wheat to read the books Manuel gave him and that had, like the library, the profound fragrance of serene time and money that isolated him from his own life and from the shouts of his father calling him from the door to come down and clean the stable or give the animals their feed. In his house the golden miracle of electric light did not exist, and when his parents went up to bed, they took with them the kerosene lamp whose yellow, greasy light swung between their sleepy voices and lengthened their shadows in the hollow of the staircase, and he remained alone in the kitchen, his light the embers of the fire and the candle he lit in order to continue reading the adventures of Captain Grant or Henry Morton Stanley or the journeys of Burton and Speke to the source of the Nile until his eyes began to close. He groped his way up to his room, and from his bed he listened to the coughs and snores of his father, who fell asleep with the same brutal resolve he brought to his work, and as soon as he had fallen asleep, sinking into the mattress of corn husks as if it were a bed of sand, his father was knocking at the door and calling him because it was almost dawn and he had to get up and saddle the white mare and take her to the farm along the road that began at the Gothic door in the wall. He tied his book bag to his back, and it was already morning when he returned to the city, running along the paths on the ramparts to get to school on time, and there Manuel, blond and clean and just recently awake, was waiting for him to copy the composition and arithmetic homework from his notebook.

What a strange logic of memory and pain conspires silently to transform the prison of another time into paradise: he trembled with gratitude and tenderness when he turned the corner of the plaza and saw the poplars and the familiar doorways, loyal to his recollection, and the illuminated air that became blue over the high, ivy-covered belfry of San Lorenzo. For a moment, as he walked toward the house recognizing even the irregularities in the ground, he thought his whole life had been one long mistake, that he never should have left the place with serene light that received him now as if he were a stranger. It was the time of the olive harvest, and a man he didn't recognize immediately was loading empty sacks and long poles of heather wood for shaking down the olives onto a mule tied to the grillwork over the window.

"How could I not remember him if we grew up together," the man says to Minaya, and he chokes and coughs without taking the cigarette wet with saliva from his mouth, sitting in the sun on a wicker chair that creaks beneath his large, defeated body. "But he went to Madrid during Primo de Rivera's dictatorship and found a job on a newspaper and got involved in politics, because he had a lot of ideas and never liked the countryside, so he left his father alone with all the work they had on the farm, and they didn't speak for years."

"Be quiet, Manuel," murmurs a woman beside the old man who has her white hair pulled back and a black shawl over her shoulders, who had been sweeping the sidewalk and saw Minaya stop in front of the house next door, as if he didn't know that no one had lived in it for many years. The man—"Manuel Biralbo, pleased to meet you"—had stopped braiding the rope he was holding in his large hands when Minaya arrived and offered him another chair facing his, in the corner of the plaza where there's a smell of damp earth, in the light that sifts through the thick foliage of the poplar. "Be quiet, Manuel," the woman repeats in a low voice, looking out of the corner of her eye at the stranger who asks questions about forgotten things, but her husband, as if he were not aware of the risk she observes and fears, goes on talking and not only invites Minaya to sit down but also offers him his tobacco pouch and cigarette papers and becomes entangled in senseless explanations that no one has asked him for.

"Justo Solana, the father, they shot him when the war was over, and nobody knows why. He must have done something, people say, like so many others who had fingers pointed at them back then, but I don't know what he could have done since he wasn't a man who got mixed up in politics, and for the whole war he stayed at the farm. But he came back a little while before the troops marched in, and in three or four days they came for him in a car and took him to jail, in handcuffs like a criminal. Then I found out they killed him. But his son, Jacinto, didn't know until he came here from prison. I can see him as clearly as I see you, with his black coat and hat and the suitcase tied up with a rope in his hand. At first I didn't know him. I was in my doorway when he knocked at the door of his house, and I saw his face when they told him his father didn't live there anymore. Jacinto, I said, don't you remember me? And when I shook his hand, I saw that he was crying. He said, 'Manuel, what did they do to my father?' and I didn't know what to tell him because I had a thing here, in my throat, and I couldn't even talk. 'They killed him,' I said, and he looked at me and lowered his head and left the plaza without saying another word. And I never saw him again. That summer I heard they had killed him too."

His footsteps returning, the inert sound of his footsteps on the paving stones of the street that takes him away from the Plaza of San Lorenzo, where Manuel Biralbo sat watching him leave, never to return, sitting on his wicker chair, braiding a rope to occupy his hands, explaining to his wife that there's no danger, that this boy who's so polite is writing a book about Jacinto Solana, you remember, Justo's son, the one who went to Madrid and then they killed him. Like the ticking of a clock, like the beating of the suicide's heart and the ringing of bells in Mágina, his footsteps drummed on the empty street, not subject to his will and his consciousness, indicating the only possible road left to him in his banishment. He thought he would never reach the white palace on the Plaza of San Pedro as he walked along the Calle de la Luna y el Sol, remembering other dawns when the mare's hooves sounded in the silence to invite him to gallop and imagine an adventure, but the now unfamiliar city continued to be a firm habit of his footsteps. Clinging to the walls, Minaya thinks, his face hidden beneath the brim of his hat, between the lapels of his overcoat, the face without eyes or nose or mouth, only a straw hamper of shadow to waylay the besieged presence of the Invisible Man. But he still doesn't know the street plan in Mágina—long medieval streets, curved like a bow, that never let you see their ending, you simply have to guess gradually at the shape of nearby houses and discover a plaza only when you've reached it—and wanting to repeat Solana's exact footsteps on that cloudy early morning in January, he soon found himself lost in narrow lanes that have the names of ancient guilds and saints, and when he finally thought he had found his way to Manuel's house, it isn't the Plaza of San Pedro he comes to but another larger square he had never seen before and in whose center there is a scraggly garden with cypresses standing like guards around the monument erected by Mágina in 1954 to honor its fallen. The house, Minaya recalls in a sudden rush of tenderness, the house on the corner where Inés lives with her sick or paralyzed uncle at the back of a courtyard in an apartment house, where the motionless man waits every night at the highest window for her to return.

Because he doesn't know how to renounce the custom of waiting for her, Minaya lingers in the Plaza of the Fallen, looking from time to time, like a zealous spy, at the closed door and balconies where it's possible she may appear. Utrera's monument shines in the midafternoon like a great block of marble against the dark backdrop of the cypresses. "An entire year of work, my boy, my hands, these hands, bloody every night from struggling with the granite. It was like Jacob wrestling with the angel, but tell me if art, great art, doesn't always consist of that." As if exhausted under his mineral wings, the angel bends over the fallen and tries to lift him up from the stone altar where his sword lies, but the naked white body overflows his arms, and his face is turned toward the wall, toward the high stone slab where the cross is sculpted with the names of the fallen of Mágina, so that it is very difficult to see his features. "Because Utrera wanted no one or almost no one to see them," Minaya wrote in his notebook, "because he wanted only a very small number of viewers, or perhaps none at all, to discover his most perfect work, and in this way publicly keep it secret, the treasure of a strange avarice."

One night when he had taken up his post in the Plaza of the Fallen to look for Inés, because she hadn't come to the house for a week, Minaya heard at his back the sound of a body moving through the hedges, and he saw the glow of a small flashlight wielded by someone who seemed to be hiding on the other side of the statues. He's following me, he thought, suddenly recovering the fear of his final days in Madrid, but Utrera was too drunk to recognize him in the dark and hadn't even seen him. He was looking for something between the pedestal and the cypresses, cursing in a quiet voice, and when he heard Minaya and turned the light on him, he didn't know what to say and stood there in front of him, the flashlight in his hand and his mouth open and an alcoholic somnolence clouding his eyes.

"I dropped my watch. I tripped over a tree, and I dropped my watch in that garden. A family memento. Thank God I found it. Would you be so kind as to walk home with me?"

Minaya felt the intolerable certainty that he wouldn't see Inés that night, and perhaps not tomorrow either, and to go on waiting for her was not a way to prod destiny into making her appear.

"My friend, my young friend and guide," said Utrera, who accepted his own drunken clumsiness and Minaya's firm arm like an aristocrat who had resigned himself to ruin without, for that reason, losing pride in his lineage. "There is no way to deceive you. Have you looked carefully at my monument? The signature is there, wait until I shine the flashlight on it: E. Utrera, 1954. Have you already seen all my works in the churches of Mágina? Well please don't go to see them. Maybe there'll be another war and they'll burn them all and then they'll begin to give me commissions again. Do you believe those students who are organizing demonstrations in Madrid will burn any churches?"

But Minaya might never have found out what Utrera was looking for that night with the flashlight if Inés hadn't told him. It was Sunday afternoon and he was waiting for her in the plaza, paying attention to the clock and the slow-moving minutes left before she would arrive with her perfumed hair hanging loose and her blue shoes and the white or yellow dress she put on only on Sundays to go out with him, which for Minaya was, like the afternoon light and the scent of the acacias, an attribute of happiness. Like an adolescent on his first date, he looked in the windows of the parked cars to make sure the part in his hair was still straight, and he smoked without stopping as he watched the door of the house where she would appear like an undeserved gift, walking toward him through the cypresses with a slight smile in her eyes and on her lips. But that afternoon he didn't see Inés arrive, and when he heard her voice she was already at his side, brushing his hand with a gesture as casual and precise as a countersign, the same one she used some nights in the dining room to tell him secretly that when everyone was in bed she would be waiting for him, naked and distinct in the darkness of her bedroom and attentive to the sound of his cautious footsteps in the silence. "Do you like it?" Inés asked, pointing at Utrera's monument. Minaya shrugged and tried to kiss her, but she eluded his lips, and taking him by the hand made him turn toward the pedestal of the statue.

"I want to show you something," she said, smiling, as if she were inviting him to play a mysterious game, and she asked him to look carefully at the face of the fallen, hidden between the legs of the angel. "I realized it once when I hid here playing hide-and-seek."

The fallen hero has a body of barely chiseled hard angles, but his face, which cannot be seen head on and is revealed only from one, very difficult vantage point situated behind the pedestal, shows the incontrovertible features of a woman and seems sculpted by another hand. The straight nose, the delicate cheeks with the smoothness of marble, the half-opened lips, the almond-shaped eyes about to close, and the sleepy charm of hair falling across one side of the face.

"It's as if she had just fallen asleep," said Minaya, following with his index finger the line of the lips that suggested a smile not completely unknown to his memory, "as if she had turned in her sleep to face the wall."

That was when Inés showed him the darker, slightly sunken circle in the middle of the young woman's forehead.

"She isn't asleep. She's been shot in the head, and she's dead."

7

FASCINATION OF HALF-CLOSED or closed doors, like the eyes of the statue that has a man's body and the secret face of a woman, like Inés' body, always, before first kisses, when she becomes someone else and is unreachable by words or the caresses that touch her as if they were touching the inert smoothness of a statue, immune to silent pleading and to silent despair. In the house there are hospitable half-closed doors that invite one to go into the successive rooms of memory, but there are also, and Minaya knows it, in a cowardly or greedy way he guesses it, closed doors that he is not permitted to violate and whose existence is hidden from him or denied, like a man crossing the empty salons of a Baroque palace who discovers that the door he wanted to pass through is painted on the wall or reflected in a mirror. The house is so large that its inhabitants, including Minaya, are lost or erased in it, and if each one is secluded in a precise space that they almost never leave, it is not because they desire or have chosen solitude but because they have surrendered to its powerful, empty presence that is taking over, one by one, all the rooms, the length of all the hallways. Every night Minaya makes notes, enumerates on his pad: Utrera carving improbable Romanesque saints in his workshop at the back of the house, behind the garden; Amalia and Teresa in the kitchen or the laundry, in the dark rooms of what in another time was called the service area; Manuel shut in the pigeon loft all morning, smoking silently beside the fire in the library, when Minaya isn't there; Doña Elvira with her magnifying glass bending over the glossy pages of a magazine devoted to celebrities as if it were a case of insects, or playing the piano in front of the television set she never looks at. Shipwrecked people, Minaya writes, in a city that is now, and has been for three centuries, a motionless shipwreck, like a galleon with high Baroque rigging thrown onto the top of its hill by some ancient maritime catastrophe. Medina, an unbelieving local scholar, says that Mágina was first the name of a peaceful city of merchants and shady Roman villas extending along the plain of the Guadalquivir, and occasionally a plow or an archaeologist's pick unearths a millstone or the headless statue of a Carthaginian or Iberian divinity on the banks of that muddy stream, but the other Mágina, walled and high, was built not for happiness or life fertilized by the waters of the river and the goddess with no chapel or face but to defend a military frontier, first against Christian armies and then against the Arabs, who came up from the south to reconquer it and were defeated along the wall they themselves had raised, and on one of whose highest towers is the clock that now measures out the days of Mágina and the duration of its decadence and its pride. For it was pride, not prosperity, that constructed the churches with bas-reliefs of pagan gods and battles with centaurs and palaces with courtyards of white columns brought from Italy, like their architects, in the by-now mythological times when a man from Mágina was secretary to the Emperor Carlos V. Orlando's judgment in the Plaza of Santa María, before the palace of the Vázquez de Molina who administered the finances of Felipe II: "What I like most about this city is that her beauty is absolutely inexplicable and useless, like the beauty of a body you encounter when you turn a corner." Now those palaces are abandoned or converted into apartment houses, and all that is left of some is, like a painted curtain, the high facade and empty windows that reveal a site strewn with rubble and columns fallen among the hedge mustard flowers, but the white house on the Plaza of San

Pedro doesn't resemble any of those, because it was built more that two hundred years after the ancient pride of Mágina had been extinguished forever. The marble balustrade that crowns its facade and the garden walls and the garlands sculpted in white stucco over the arches of the balconies give it an air between French and colonial, like a serene extravagance. In 1884, Manuel's grandfather, Don Apolonio Santos who, they say, had been a gilder of altarpieces in his youth and left the city without saying good-bye to anyone after winning two hundred silver duros in the casino, came back from Cuba weighed down with a fortune as barbarous as the means he used for twenty years to obtain it, and he had the house built and a neo-Gothic mausoleum erected in the Mágina cemetery. Ten years after his return, Don Apolonio owned the best palace in the city and had bought eight or ten thousand olive trees within its boundaries, but he barely had enough life to enjoy his fortune, because some poorly treated fevers—and, they said, his displeasure at seeing his youngest daughter married to a clerk with no future—brought him to his neo-Gothic tomb during the first winter of the century.

"Which means you should pay no attention to Utrera," said Manuel, with the sad irony he always used when he talked to Minaya about his family, "when he recounts the merits of our ancestors. All those paintings in the courtyard and the gallery were bought by my grandfather, your great-grandfather, from the same penniless aristocrats who sold him their country estates."

As if ashamed of having been born where he was born and bearing the name he bore, but not daring to reveal his shame completely or to cultivate his disdain openly, for he was not unaware that only the house and the name connected to it had saved him from being shot and from the obligation for courage, demanding from him instead a passive loyalty that, as he grew older, stopped being the never-demolished boundary line and the exact measure of his resignation and failure to become one of his habits. Who then was the man with the haughty, almost heroic bearing in the wedding photograph, the one who was promoted to lieutenant for bravery in action after he jumped undefended into an enemy trench with no help other than a pistol torn from a corpse and a group of frightened militiamen and who shot to death those who were firing an Italian machine gun at them, where did he look for and find the valor needed to marry Mariana, abandoning without the slightest misgiving the girl in whose languid company he had spent a six-year engagement with the always alert indulgence of Doña Elvira, who took this sudden fit of her son's as a personal insult and never forgave him for it?

"And not only that," Medina recalled, "he was also capable of finding a position in the Spanish embassy in Paris, I suppose through the mediation of Solana, and he had everything prepared for going there the day after his wedding, imagine, the same man who had come home from Madrid without finishing his studies in order not to oppose his mother. Which means that if Mariana had not died the way she died, your uncle would now be a member of the republican government-in-exile, or something like it."

Many times in the course of the two years granted him to survive the slow surrender of his will, Manuel looked at his wedding photograph and felt he wasn't the man who appeared in it, not because he didn't believe he had once possessed the spirit or the madness needed to confront his mother and overcome the fear that made him vomit before an attack at the front but because he had never thought he deserved Mariana's blind tenderness and proffered body, and he looked at her photographs and Orlando's drawing with the same unlimited, incredulous devotion and the same astonishment with which he looked at her and he saw himself in the bedroom mirrors when he finally had her white and naked in his arms. It was Solana, declared Mágina or that part of Mágina where unconquered pride survived, he was the one who made him a Red and encouraged him to become involved with that slut, said aggrieved voices in the salon where the embroidered table linen and silver table service were still displayed, what was going to be the dowry of the bride so abruptly abandoned, relics now of her melancholy destiny. And without saying anything to her, even though she was preparing the wedding dress and my cousin knew it, Minaya's father recounted many years later, because Mariana was dead and the war that had brought her to Mágina was over, but her pride and imperious capacity for contempt were still intact, perhaps even ennobled, like the statue of General Orduña, by indications of heroism and ignominy.

"And don't think that girl was a scarecrow because she belonged to one of the best families in Mágina, almost as respectable as ours. Ask your mother, who knew her very well. Of course in the end she was lucky and recovered from my cousin's betrayal. She married, and it was a very good match, a captain in the Regular Army."

Inexhaustible, intact, and useless, like Mágina's light and its statues with Greek profiles, rancor is the only thing they save or that saves them from oblivion and strengthens the persistence of pride over the void. Each morning, attended by Teresa and Amalia, who climbs the stairs very slowly and holds the railing and the walls and breathlessly reaches the top floor of the house, Doña Elvira dresses ceremoniously before a mirror and combs her white hair waved according to the by-now blurred style of 1930, at times permitting herself a drop of perfume at her wrists and on her neck and a light shadow of pink powder on her cheeks. How is my son, she asks without looking at anyone or expecting anyone to answer, directing her gaze over the heads of the two women moving around her, because she was taught that this was how a lady ought to address her servants, remind Inés that today is Thursday and she has to bring me the magazines. Has the administrator called? Have someone let him know. I want to settle the olive accounts with him before I forget about it and he cheats me. Dressed and perfumed as if she were going out, though she does that only early in the morning on Good Friday, Doña Elvira contemplates her own firm body in the mirror and smooths with her index finger the deleted line of her eyebrows.

"Teresa, when you've made the bed, water the geraniums. Don't you see they're withering?"

Still in front of the mirror, without turning around or raising her voice, Doña Elvira sees Teresa pulling the sheets and quilt from the large double bed where she still sleeps forty years after becoming a widow, and she suddenly notices, with secret satisfaction, how much the maid who was only a girl when she entered her service has aged. The cold yellow sun of February enters obliquely through the large window to the terrace, leaving on the tiles a damp stain of light, sifted down like pollen, which surrounds things without ever touching them and slides over to the doorway where Amalia, who almost doesn't see it, is standing and waiting.

"Does the señora want anything else?"

"Nothing, Amalia. Tell Inés she can bring me the paper and my breakfast now."

Before he was allowed to meet her, Doña Elvira imposed herself on Minaya's consciousness like a great absent shadow, depicted, with severe precision, in the fear with which Jacinto Solana imagined her many years earlier, in certain customs and words that ambiguously alluded to her, almost never naming her, not explaining her seclusion or her life, only suggesting that she was there, in the topmost rooms, appearing at the balcony of the greenhouse or looking at the garden from the window where her figure sometimes was outlined. A tray with the silver teapot and a single cup set out at midafternoon on the kitchen sideboard, the *ABC* folded and unopened, the illustrated magazines that Inés bought every Thursday at the kiosk on the Plaza of General Orduña, the account books next to the coat and hat of the administrator, who talks to Amalia in the courtyard, waiting until Doña Elvira wishes to receive him, the sound of the television set and the piano canceling each other out and confused in the distance with the fluttering wings of pigeons against the glass in the dome. He had learned to catalogue and discover the signs of Doña Elvira's presence and always to fear her when he walked alone down the hall-ways, and one day, without anything foretelling it, Inés told him that the señora had invited him to tea that afternoon in her rooms. The way up began with a door at the back of the gallery and crossed a dark region of rooms, perhaps never occupied, that had religious paintings on the walls and porcelain saints enclosed in crystal urns. Solitary figures on credenzas looking into empty space with lost, glassy eyes, looking at Minaya like motionless guardians of no-man's-land as he crossed the deserted semidarkness behind Inés' footsteps and the muffled clink of teaspoons and cups on the silver tray that she held solemnly, as if they were objects of worship.

"Come in," he heard the hard voice on the other side of the door first, and then, when he went in, Inés' faint scent was lost in an un-familiar, dense perfume that occupied everything, as if it too formed part of the invisible presence, the enclosed solitude and the clothing and furniture of another time that surrounded Doña Elvira. It isn't the aroma of a woman, he thought, but of a century: this was how things, the air, smelled fifty years ago. Without looking up, Inés made a vague curtsy and left the tray on a table near the window. "Leave now," said Doña Elvira and didn't look at her, because she had been observing Minaya since he came in, and even when he helped her to sit next to the tea table, she continued watching him in the closet mirror, clumsy, solicitous, bending over her, conscious of the silence he didn't know how to break and of the cold, wise eyes that had already judged him.

"You look like your mother," she said, contemplating him at her leisure behind the steam and the cup of tea. "The same eyes and mouth, but the way you smile comes from your father. The way my husband and all the men in his family smiled, and even your grand-mother Cristina, who was as good-looking as you. Haven't you seen her portrait that my son has in his bedroom? All of you smile to ex-cuse your lies, not even to hide them, because all of you have always lacked the moral sense needed to distinguish between what is just and what isn't, or why that should matter to you. That is why my poor husband excused himself before committing an error or telling a lie, never afterward. For him there was nothing he did that could not be pardoned. His smile was never more candid or more charming than when he informed me he had sold a farm with a thousand olive trees to buy one of those Italian cars, Bugattis, they were called. He took it and a slut to Monte Carlo and returned in a month without the car or the slut, and, of course, without a cent, but he did come back with a very elegant dinner jacket and a bouquet of gladiolus and smiled as if he had traveled to the Côte d'Azur only to buy me flowers. My son, on the other hand, has never even known how to smile like his father, or like yours, who also was an extremely dangerous liar. He's been wrong as often as either of them, but with all the solemnity in the world, as if he were taking Communion. He went voluntarily into that army of the hungry who had taken half our land to divide it among themselves, and he almost lost his life fighting against those who were really his people, and as if that were not enough he married that woman who was already used goods, you understand me, and even wanted to go to France with her. But I'm sure you're not entirely like them, like my husband and my son and that madman your father, or like your great-grandfather, Don Apolonio, who infected them all with his deceptions and madness but not with his ability to make money. All of them liars, all of them reckless or useless, or both things at the same time, like my husband—may God have mercy on his soul—but if he had taken a few more years to die, he would have left us in poverty, with that mania he developed for collecting first thoroughbred horses and then women and cars. That's why, when he was a deputy, he became such good friends with Alfonso XIII. They had the same enthusiasms, and neither one bothered to hide them. Your father probably told you that when the king came to Mágina in '24, he took tea with us one afternoon, in this house. The people with titles were green with envy when they saw the friendliness the king displayed toward my husband, who after all was the son of a man who made his money in the Indies and whose only coat of arms was invented for him by your grandfather José Emilio Minaya, the poet, who I think was the only man who could deceive him, he seemed so guileless, because he got five hundred pesetas from him to publish that book of poetry and made off with his daughter, though not with her inheritance. On the last night of his visit to Mágina, Alfonso XIII disappeared, something he apparently did habitually, and no one, not the queen, or Don Miguel Primo de Rivera, who had come here with him, or his military escort knew where to find him. At two in the morning, the telephone woke me. It was Primo, so nervous he didn't seem drunk. 'Elvira, is His Majesty in your house?' 'But Don Miguel,' I said, 'does Your Excellency think that if the king were here, I would have gone to bed?' And do you know where he was? At the Island of Cuba, which by then was the only estate we had left, drinking champagne with two deluxe sluts my husband had found for him, because I believe playing go-between for his friends gave him more pleasure than being a fighting cock. He returned at dawn, undressed as casually as if he had come from the opera, and told me before he fell asleep, 'Really, darling, His Majesty is a sportsman.'"

Doña Elvira's laugh, he later told Inés, was a short, cold outburst that shattered like glass and gleamed for an instant in eyes unfamiliar with indulgence and tenderness, eyes open and inflexible and rigorously sharpened by the lucidity of her contempt and the proximity of her death: the taut translucent skin at her temples, the white needlework at cuffs and neckline to hide from herself and the mirror the worst ravages of old age. All that could be seen of her hands were the short, slender fingers that drummed on the table or grasped the cup to hide their tremor.

"No, you're not like them. You're better-looking and more intelligent, and you owe both things to your mother, because your father, that stupid man, never could console himself for having been born disinherited, and he did nothing to give her the life she deserved. What was he doing when he killed himself?"

"Something in real estate. He said he was going to earn a good deal of money. He bought a car."

"Was it an honest business?"

"It seemed to be. But after his death they impounded even the furniture. I had to find a job and move to a pensión."

"From time to time, before the three of you went to Madrid, he would come to me and lament his bad luck and ask for money for his business without your mother knowing. I never gave him a cent, of course, among other reasons because even if I had trusted him—and I never made that mistake—I had nothing to give him. My husband left everything to Manuel; that was another of his jokes, the final one. There's still a copy of his will around here somewhere. 'I declare my son Manuel sole inheritor of all my goods,' it said, in order not to break some tradition or other, which naturally was false, and he left me a painting, nothing but a painting. 'To my dearly beloved and faithful wife, María Elvira, I leave the portrait of Reverend Father Antonio María Claret, to whom I know she is very devoted.' He didn't do it for revenge but to go on laughing at me after death. But I'm the one who saved this house, and if we still have a little land and some capital in the bank, it hasn't been thanks to my son, who never took care of anything and was as much a bungler as he is now, but to me, who spent forty-four years struggling to preserve what my husband didn't have the time or desire to sell at a loss in order to pay for his whims. Look at those books. I spend entire nights over them, revising the accounts of the administrator, who is a scoundrel and cheats me if I'm careless. Since he knows my eyes are failing, he makes the numbers smaller and smaller, but I've bought a magnifying glass, and with it I can see even what isn't written down. There never was a man who could deceive me, and I won't permit it now, in my old age. Neither can you, but you know that. Tell me why you've come."

That was the question and the hidden challenge and the conclusion that all her words had led to, not a confession but a raw challenge in which she, after displaying her weapons, put simulation and words to one side like a gambler who clears the table to leave a single card and then turns it over with marked slowness. That was the only question and the only reason she had received him, and Minaya had been waiting for it since he entered the room, long before that, since Inés announced the señora's order and the moment designated for his audience. This afternoon, at five, Doña Elvira had said, and he spent the entire morning calculating the tone and precise words and manner in which he should present himself, docile, Manuel warned him, because she would look at him searching for confirmation of an ancient threat that was once, but not always, called Mariana or Jacinto Solana, well dressed and combed as she imagined a young man of evident dignity, though limited funds, ought to dress and comb his hair, but not so impeccable or servile that Doña Elvira might suspect the premeditated use of a mask.

"Before you can see her," said Manuel as they ate lunch, "she will have looked you over from head to toe, especially your collar, cuffs, and hands, because she has always said that in the collar and cuffs of his shirt one can discover if a man is or is not a gentleman. Since you arrived she's been asking about you, questioning Inés and Amalia, and even Medina when he goes up to examine her, but especially Teresa, who's afraid of her and feels hypnotized when my mother speaks to her. She already knows everything about you, and of course why you have come, but she wants to hear it from your own lips to decide if you're a danger."

And now he was sitting in front of her, in front of her only question, pouring himself a little more cold tea in order to break or prolong a truce and looking before responding, for ten extremely long seconds, at the garden conquered by darkness and the roofs and the sky where it was still day. I want to write a book, he said at last, about Jacinto Solana, anticipating a grimace or wounded rejection but not the laughter that sounded again like the rattle of bones and immediately died out.

"Solana. That Solana. No one has said his name before me for the past twenty years. I thought that thank God he had been erased forever from the world, and now you come to tell me you're going to write a book about him, as if one could write about nothing, about a fraud. But he was such a liar that after he died he continues telling lies just as he told lies from the time he was a boy until the day they killed him. And so he's deceived you too, just as he deceived my son and his own wife, who waited for him for ten years without his sending her a single letter or telling her he was leaving when he abandoned her. But many years earlier he had deceived my husband. Perhaps you don't know that it was he, my husband, who was responsible for Solana getting out of the dung heap and receiving an education that those of his class have never needed. There was a kind of charitable committee or something like that, and every year it tested the children in the schools for the poor and selected the most outstanding and paid for them to study with the Piarists. My husband, who was deputy for Mágina at the time, presided over the committee, and it was his vote that decided Solana's fate and my son's misfortune. A great writer, they said, but I never saw a book signed by him, not even the one he seemed to be writing when he came back from prison to live at our expense, first in this house and then at the Island of Cuba. What happened in the war was being forgotten, and Manuel, who escaped dying in prison because of the name he bears, seemed to have recovered his senses, or at least one could no longer detect the madness that drove him to become a Communist or a republican or whatever it was—because I believe he didn't know himself—and to enter into that absurd marriage. We all thought Solana was dead or had escaped to another country. But he came back. He came back saying what he had always said, that he was going to write a book, though he didn't deceive me. 'Don't call attention to yourself, Manuel,' I told my son, 'that man is an ex-convict, and he'll be your ruin again.' I knew something bad was going to happen, and I waited for the disaster until some Civil Guards came to tell me, very courteously, I must say, because the lieutenant colonel was related to me, that they had to search the house and question Manuel, because that friend of his, Solana, had killed two of their men at the Island of Cuba. That was the book he was writing, and of course no one could find it afterward. He used the farm to meet with his accomplices, a gang of those Red bandits who were wandering the sierra then. And again they dragged Manuel out of his bed in the middle of the night to take him to their barracks in handcuffs. Once again I had to cover my face with a veil and humiliate myself by knocking at the doors of those who had been my friends to save him from death or a sentence that would have killed him a little more slowly. And do you know the first thing he did when he was free? Look for his friend in the morgue and pay for his funeral and a marble gravestone. It's still there, I suppose, in the cemetery, in case you want to visit it. Manuel never comes up to see me, but every year he takes flowers to the graves of his soul mate and of the woman who turned his life upside down. And took his honor, if truth be told."

She didn't say good-bye or order him to leave, she simply stopped seeing him or forgot she wasn't alone, and her words faded into a very slow silence, just as her features faded in the same semi-darkness that was erasing the shapes of the furniture and the corners of the room, coming up from the garden, from the empty hallways and rooms where Minaya had to feel his way back like a traveler surprised by darkness in a thick wood where there were no roads, only closed doors. Solitary doors, suspended in air, hermetic like the book Minaya was looking for and that perhaps never was written. Half-open doors that invite one in and then close, as if in a sudden gust of wind, behind the person who dares to cross them. He stood noiselessly and murmured an excuse or a farewell, but the small woman in mourning continued to look at the garden with her hands folded in her lap and her back ridgidly erect, as if posing for a photograph.

"You're not like them," she said, and seen from above she was smaller and almost vulnerable, with her bones sharp beneath her skin and the white needlework on the velvet of her mourning. "Come back to see me whenever you like."

As he was leaving he saw her in profile, the dark silhouette, her white hair dazzling against the pale light from the window and the purple and opaque blue of nightfall on the roofs. He closed the door slowly and when he turned he found the light, staring eyes of Inés, who seemed to have been waiting for him to leave and was carrying on the silver tray the supper that Doña Elvira wouldn't taste that night either.

8

HE, TOO, DEFEATED AND OBSCURE beneath the blankets where a sick body lies, I imagine, he, too, looking at the ceiling or the semidarkness or the faint light that comes through the curtains that someone partially closed before leaving him alone. There are medicine bottles on the night table and the odor of the alcohol Medina used to disinfect the needle is still in the air. He closed his bag at the foot of the bed, slowly moving his head, the hands that so delicately lifted the back of Mariana's neck from the droppings, as if he didn't want to wake her. He looked at his watch and placed it back in his vest pocket, studying Manuel, who seems to be asleep but who is watching him, high and distant, from a fog not of physical pain but of melancholy, prepared to close his eyes in order not to sleep and surrender to the last light of day fading in the plaza and on the white curtains at the balcony with the same sweet slowness with which he wishes to be extinguished, let it be tonight, he thinks, with no fear or urgency, with his eyes closed, with the picture of Mariana and the one of his Aunt Cristina attending with their solemn presence as silent witnesses. For a moment he sees Medina or dreams him as he was in 1937, slim and with a black mustache, in his captain's uniform, leaning not over him but over the body of Mariana, who wears a sheer nightdress and has a red, round stain on her forehead. Medina, slow and heavy again, presses his hand for an instant and then leaves the room, and his cautious voice can be heard speaking to someone, Teresa or Amalia, in the hallway. Now Manuel curls up on his side and raises the fold of the sheet until it covers his mouth, his back to the balcony, and stares at the moldings on the closet, dissolving in the night. The only vestige is a vague muscular pain in his chest, the quiet hand, the tranquil reptile that isn't even asleep beneath closed eyelids. It only waits for the next, the definitive day, the hour when it will move up his left side brushing against the warm pink tissue of his lungs and then encircling his heart before squeezing it, closing the ring of asphyxia around its frightened beating, like a blind animal that had been incubated in Manuel's chest thirty-two years earlier to pay, day after day, the extremely long installment plan of anguish and longed-for death. He had spent the afternoon in the library, not doing anything, lacking even the will to climb the stairs to the pigeon loft, waiting for Minaya to come back from his visit to Doña Elvira, and perhaps the disquiet of waiting and cigarettes had caused the reawakening of the old wound near his heart, like a road that precisely indicates its white line in the growing light of dawn. What will she say about me, he thought, about all of us, fearing his mother's hatred less than the manner in which she might show it to Minaya, the indiscretion, the very probable slander. Since the proximity of the pain in his chest was more certain with each passing minute—now the reptile or hand was lodged in his stomach and groping its way upward, animated by brandy and tobacco—Manuel put on his coat and hat and took the bamboo stick that had belonged to his father to walk out to the watchtowers on the wall. But there was no respite because fear and pain were already moving up his veins like a single knife thrust, already hastening his breath and opening before his feet a pit that separated him from the world and left him alone with the bite of terror. He walked, slow and anachronistic, down Calle Real, very close to the building walls, ceding the sidewalk to the ladies, whom he greeted when he thought he knew them, touching the brim of his hat with a distracted and completely involuntary gesture, but the air on the street was not enough to ease the incessant pounding that cracked a whip in his heart and temples, and in an instant of vertigo the dark hand oppressing his chest sometimes even stopped the flow of his blood. Leaning against the walls, he was able to reach the Plaza of Santa María, and when he felt in his heart the last peck and the shadow's slap that knocked him to the paving stones, he recalled an April morning when that same plaza and its backdrop of palaces and distant bell towers seemed more boundless than ever to him, because Mariana, in a white blouse and summer sandals, came toward him, smiling, from the facade of El Salvador. It was that same image, intact, that he found before him when he woke from his brief death not knowing who he was or in what part of the world the room and the bed he was lying in were to be found. He heard voices, pigeons, the notes of a strange habanera that never ended, he heard, as he was overcome by the dense lethargy of sedatives, little girls' voices in the plaza singing the funeral ballad of Alfonso XII and Doña Mercedes, and in the not-yet-unfathomable waters of sleep the melody of the habanera became entwined with the voices of the children's song, the nocturnal footsteps in the hallway, the murmur like that of a hospital, the wakefulness that reached him from the other side of the door.

"He's fallen asleep," said Teresa, closing the door again with extreme care. Minaya and Medina were smoking beside the darkened glass doors of the gallery, talking in that muffled tone of voice used in churches and in the vicinity of the sick.

"The worst thing afflicting your uncle, my boy, isn't that he drinks and smokes and exerts himself too much given the fragility of his heart, but that he doesn't want to live. Understand what I'm saying: when you reach the age that Manuel and I are, living becomes an act of will."

Inés passed them with Doña Elvira's untouched tray and looked for a second at Minaya with an expression so rapid it seemed unreal.

He saw her walk away with the clink of porcelain and silver, like a perfume or a melody that followed and announced her.

"You speak about will, but my uncle has had a cardiac lesion since a bullet grazed his heart."

"My friend . . . " Medina, smiling, picked up his bag from the floor, ready to leave. "Manuel has told me you're a kind of writer, so perhaps you'll understand what I am going to tell you. In my work, one becomes very skeptical with the years and discovers that in certain cases the heart and its ailments are a metaphor. Manuel had his first serious attack on the day following Mariana's death. That was when his real illness began, and it wasn't caused by the bullet you mentioned but by the one that killed her."

They went downstairs in silence, trying to keep their footsteps from resounding on the marble, less to respect Manuel's sleep than to avoid committing an uncertain profanation. In the courtyard, Medina ceremoniously shook the hands of Teresa and Amalia and accepted the hat and coat that Minaya handed him with the quiet gravity of a priest who dons his liturgical cape at the door of the sacristy. They were alone, in the doorway, and only then did Minaya dare to ask the question that had been troubling him since they came down from the gallery. Who killed her, he said, regretting it instantly, but there was no censure in Medina's glance, only a serene wonder, as if he were surprised to discover that after so many years there was still someone asking that question.

"There was shooting on the roofs, on the other side of the house, above the lanes that the pigeon loft looks out on. A militia patrol was pursuing a rebel, whom I'm sure they never captured. Mariana, who was in the pigeon loft, went to the window when she heard the shots. One of them hit her in the forehead. We never found out anything else."

He thought about Medina as he groped his way up the last steps to the pigeon loft, not daring yet to turn on the flashlight, about

Medina, about his slow eyes that had seen Mariana barely covered by the nightgown under whose silk folds one could make out the faint shadow of her pubis, about the way he cleaned his eyeglasses so unhurriedly or looked in his vest for the watch he used to measure with equal composure the time of his visits and the passage of his life toward an old age as irreparable and mediocre as the tyranny he once had fought and now tolerated—without accepting submission but also without the vain certainty that he would witness its downfall—as one tolerates an incurable disease. Some nights, after the game of cards in the parlor, when the others had withdrawn, Medina delayed drinking his last glass of anisette and remained seated in silence across from Manuel, who gathered up the deck counting the cards on the table with that distracted air of his, as if he were counting coins. At first, from his bedroom, Minaya listened to the silence, perhaps Medina's cough or a few words in a quiet voice that almost never became a conversation, asking himself why the two men were still there doing nothing, facing each other, smoking in the light of the lamp that enclosed them in a conical bell of silence and smoke. When it was after midnight, Medina would ask Manuel something, who agreed, and then a sound could be heard like whistles and tearing paper, voices that interrupted one another or were inundated by a remote babel of words in foreign languages. "It's no use," said Manuel, "there's too much interference tonight, and I can't find it." And then, when he was about to fall asleep, the music of the 'Anthem of Riego' woke Minaya, and he knew what he should have guessed long before: Manuel and Medina stayed in the parlor that late to listen to Radio of the Pyrenees. "Don't have any illusions, Manuel," he heard Medina say one night, "you and I will never see the Third Republic. We're condemned to Franco in the same way we're condemned to grow old and die." "Then why do you come every night to listen to Radio of the Pyrenees?" Medina burst into laughter: he had the sonorous laugh of a bishop. "Because I like the

'Anthem of Riego.' It rejuvenates me. That anthem of Franco's is for third-rate funerals."

After kneeling beside Mariana and confirming that she had no pulse, Medina stood up, brushing off the knees of his military trousers. Death had been instantaneous, he said, but no one paid attention to his words. Near the door, Minaya imagined as he slid the circle of the flashlight around the walls, there would be the others: Doña Elvira, in mourning, Manuel, Amalia, perhaps Teresa, if she was already working in the house then. Utrera, Jacinto Solana, biting their lips, wanting blindly to die. When it reached the window without glass or shutters, the illumination from the flashlight dispersed in a well of night, and then the very weak circle shed light on the roof on the other side of the lane. Leaning on the sill, Medina saw two Assault Guards crawling with difficulty along the neighboring roof, rifles over their shoulders, examining the broken tiles. "There's a trail of blood here, Captain," one of them said. "The militiamen say the Fascist hid behind the chimney and fired from here." In the darkness, Minaya, who had turned off the flashlight because its light made the pigeons restless, thought he heard footsteps, imagined that the staircase was creaking, that someone was going to discover his useless investigation, but the footsteps and his fear were simply the way his conscience felt guilt, the invincible and secret shame of being an impostor that had pursued him his entire life and now, in the house, in the places of the time he dared to enter clandestinely, it hounded him more than ever. They're asleep now, he thought, while I climb like a thief up to this place that doesn't belong to me and shine the flashlight on an empty space, they're asleep or probably they never sleep and their eyes are open in the dark as they listen to my footsteps over their heads. For a moment, the murmur of the sleeping pigeons and the sound of the blood beating in his temples seemed like the combined breathing of all those who slept or didn't sleep in the rooms of the house. Above the roofs, in the center of the window, was a half-moon as precise and fragile as the illustration in a children's book. Minaya closed the door of the pigeon loft and felt his way down the steep staircase. Only one of the lamps in the gallery was lit, and its light projected his own very long shadow in front of Minaya. The afternoon's conversation with Doña Elvira, Manuel's relapse, the time spent in darkness in the pigeon loft, had plunged him into a state of singular fatigue and nervous excitement that denied in advance the possibility of sleep. His sudden image was that of a sleepwalker in the tall mirrors along the stairs. But when he reached the courtyard, he knew he wouldn't be alone in the library. A line of light slipped under the door, and in an easy chair next to the fire, her lips painted, her hair loose over her shoulders, holding a cigarette and a book in her hands, was Inés, who looked at him without surprise, smiling, as if she had been waiting for him, knowing he would come.

9

ORLANDO SHOULD HAVE SURVIVED to sketch Inés just as he had sketched Mariana. He, who never desired women but was never indifferent to the beauty of a body, would have known how to sketch in exact equilibrium the cold lines of her profile and figure and the passion they incited: the pencil tracing with distant tenderness Inés' nose and chin, her lips, on the white paper, the modeling of her hands and ankles, the invisible smile that sometimes lit up her eyes and that the most attentive camera would never have captured in a photograph, because it was an inner smile, like the one provoked so slightly by the splash of a fish's tail on the surface of a lake. But that night, when Minaya found her in the library, or the days and dawns that preceded it, the line of the pencil on untouched white would not have been enough to draw Inés, desired by two men who situated her body on the balance of an obscure symmetry. A single red stroke for her smile, a red or pink spot for her lips, the same as the one left by her lipstick on the towels in her maid's room, when she locked her door to put on makeup at a mirror hanging on the wall, as if it were a secret rehearsal or a brief performance meant only for herself, for in the end, when she had succeeded in combing her hair and painting her lips in a way that satisfied her, she would pull back her hair again and wipe off the lipstick with a wet towel and return silently to her earlier, hermetic simulation.

Very soon the game acquired new characteristics: she liked to put on makeup and look at herself naked in closet mirrors and go down to the library when she was sure no one would surprise her to repeat a scene she had relished in certain fashion magazines. Sitting next to the fire, with a glass she never finished and a cigarette pilfered from Manuel's case, she read in the oblique light of a low lamp, absorbed in the adventures presented in the book but conscious at the same time of each one of her gestures, as if she could see herself in a mirror. When she heard the door she closed the book, marking the page where she had stopped with a peculiar sliding of her fingers that Minaya could not help but notice because it had the quality of a caress, and she contemplated with irony and tenderness the surprise of the newcomer. It had to happen there, in the library, and nowhere else, at that time and with that light, which invited and seemed to accentuate Inés' features and the unfamiliar perfume that Minaya distinguished among the usual odors of wood and books. It was easy, that night, to imagine what was going on, to calculate the particulars of the scene and the words Inés would use to recount it afterward, interrupting the kisses to add a minor detail: the way Minaya sat down across from her, not looking at her yet, searching for his cigarettes, his momentary evasion, asking about the book she was reading, overwhelmed by the terror and vertigo of knowing that Inés had painted her lips and combed her chestnut hair in that new, dazzling way to wait only for him at two o'clock in the morning. Sitting on the chair, her legs extended so that her heels rested on the precise spot where he had to sit, with that inexplicable cigarette between her lips, for she didn't know how to smoke and every time she exhaled the smoke it gave rise to the cough of a fourteen-year-old with clandestine cigarettes.

"You've been in the pigeon loft."

"You saw me?"

"I saw the feathers sticking to your sweater."

"Do you see everything?"

Never until then had he seen that smile in Inés' eyes and on her lips, or perhaps he had, he would remember later: that same morning, when they were talking about *The Charterhouse of Parma* and she, in their shared enthusiasm for the adventures and courage of Fabrizio del Dongo, smiled at him for an instant, as if he were her accomplice in a secret passion. She talked about Fabrizio the way she talked about Errol Flynn, because her literary imagination had been educated visually by Technicolor movies on Sunday afternoons, and when she read a book she moved her profile forward as attentively and greedily as if she were contemplating the illuminated screen. Ever since he saw her come into the library at ten in the morning, as she did every day, with the feather duster and the white apron around her waist, her gestures had acquired for Minaya the quality of signs about to be revealed. Useless to seek refuge in the severe protection of the books, the pasteboard filing cards that he wrote and put in order with a purpose whose conclusion was so distant it was becoming impossible. Inés sat across from him, forgetting the duster on the table, her face lazily resting on her hands, which held and framed her angular pink cheekbones, while he gave himself over to his enduring task of calligraphy and pasteboard.

"Last night I was up until three o'clock reading *The Charterhouse*. I've never read a book I liked as much as that one. What about you?"

"Only *The Mysterious Island*. Where did you learn French?"

"At the orphanage. There was a French nun."

It was the same smile, the same way of looking at him as if she finally were seeing him, and of using literature, the sonorous name of Fabrizio del Dongo and the illusory recollection of the landscapes of northern Italy, to speak about herself, about Minaya, whose face she instinctively attributed to Fabrizio, for since then their conversations about books on tepid mornings in the library were the veil for other words neither of them dared to say. On the mantel over the fireplace, in the semidarkness across the room, Jacinto Solana smiled at them from an afternoon in 1936 with his obscene loyalty to every unconfessed desire. Inés, Minaya said then, interrupting a phantom conversation in which books and Mariana's picture intervened, calm now and a little drunk, firm in his twenty-six years as a man alone and in the certainty that he desired her that night with the clarity of an axiom. "You never say my name. Did you realize that? As if it embarrassed you." But he didn't explain that it was modesty that kept him from pronouncing her name in front of her, because naming her would be saying everything, his sleeplessness, his solitary love under the sheets, memory retrieving her body to desire her more, closing his eyes until all of him melted in a hot, despicable spasm, mornings without her in the library, the inconsolable emotion when he saw her coat hanging on the rack in the courtyard or passed by her room and saw her stockings and white apron on the bed. Saying Inés aloud was like doing what he perhaps would never do, like taking her hand and slowly removing the glass or caressing her breasts. Inés, the two beloved syllables, the hand that offered him a cigarette stopping at the boundary beyond which a caress would begin, the music she had put on Manuel's phonograph as if at random and that was incredibly, premeditatedly the trumpet and voice of Louis Armstrong on a record from 1930, at last her lips, the girl barefoot and kissing him in the darkness like no one, not even she, would kiss him again, gratitude broken into delicate bites of silence, into caresses of the blind who search each other for characteristics driven not by desire but by an urgent wish for acknowledgment. Inés' cheekbones, chin, wet lips, the tears that moistened Minaya's fingertips in the darkness, the perfume, the music sounding in a closed room in 1930 just as it sounded seven years later, that same song, on Manuel's piano, and he translated the title for Mariana before he began to play "If We Never Meet Again."

The end of the music and of their caresses came at the same time, and then, when Minaya and Inés drew back listening to their double and single breathing, they could see each other as strangers in an uncertain light that came from the plaza, because they had turned off the lamp when they began to kiss, and they heard, as if they had just returned to the world, that the record was silently turning with the needle still on it and the pendulum of the clock had not stopped moving back and forth in a corner of the library. Now their voices were different, slower and warmer, as if made denser by the darkness, and they extended their hands to stroke the other's hands or simply to touch the clothes or skin or perfumed air that surrounded them, run aground not in peaceful fatigue but in the stupefaction of having survived happiness. Inés said afterward that when she wanted to get up to turn on the light, Minaya kept her at his side. He wanted to stop time, not take a step beyond the instant in which the darkness still enfolded them like a silken wing, not return to the usual light that leveled everything and would return them to their modesty, strangers once again, their hands hurrying to straighten their clothes and erase from the library the signs that could expose them the next morning. A glass of wine overturned in the grass, an empty bottle, a rectangle of light advancing without mercy on the shadows of the garden like a river whose flooding the lovers would move away from without undoing their embrace. Mariana, sitting up, leaned her beautiful disheveled head against the trunk of the date palm, immune to the fear that had made them move back when the light went on and they saw in its squared patch the shadow of someone who perhaps had been spying on them. "Solana," she said, the cigarette between her lips, taking in her hands the dark face in front of her, then caressing his neck and drawing him to her, as if guiding him, until she sheltered him between her white breasts under the moon, "Jacinto Solana," like a challenge and an invitation that would never be accepted because they were already consuming the ashes of the time they had been granted.

SUDDENLY MINAYA WAS ALONE, and it was as if nothing could attest to the fact that he had been kissing Inés on a sofa in the illuminated, unmoving library. The sensation of the caresses and the darkness remained in his consciousness, with no reason to connect it to the present, even less so to the blurred scene that had preceded it, just as an apparition leaves no trace when it fades away. In front of the fire was the glass table where she placed the book she was reading while she waited for him and that held the bottle and glasses and ashtray with cigarette ends stained crimson, but Inés, before she left, had put the book back on the shelf where it belonged and removed the glasses and the bottle as urgently as she had straightened her skirt and buttoned her blouse, then disappeared as if she were never going to return. "Now she's in her room, probably naked under the sheets, because she may still be waiting for me, and this flight has been a trick to get me to follow her." But he didn't do anything except insist on the alcohol, on his cowardice and good fortune, except to look at Orlando's drawing and the photograph in which Jacinto Solana was smiling at him, Minaya, guessing, understanding everything, with the air of someone who confirms with disdain that what he always imagined has happened and that the gift of prophecy is a melancholy privilege. Then he went up without even daring to pass Inés' bedroom, going along the hallways in the house as if they were the last streets of a city not entirely recognized or inhospitable, obedient to sleep and the mature night where, as if in a kind of future memory, there were to be found Inés' embraces and the placidity of the sheets waiting to remind him of the commandment of abandonment and forgetting, because out in the world it was February 1969, tyranny and fear, but inside those walls what endured was a delicate anachronism, a plot he was also a part of though he didn't know it: Inés, who didn't belong to this time or any other because her presence was enough to cancel it, Mariana in the drawing and in photographs, Manuel in his lieutenant's uniform, and Jacinto Solana not motionless in his figure and in the date of his death, but always writing, even now, narrating, Minaya imagined, like the impostor and guest who enters the parlor at three in the morning and discovers that there is a key in the lock of the forbidden room, that it will be infinitely easy to push the door and contemplate what no one but Manuel has seen in the last thirty-two years. A large, unexpectedly vulgar room, with dark furniture and white curtains across the shutters to the balcony that overlooks the Plaza of the Acacias. He moved forward uncertainly, closing the door behind him, he lit a match and saw himself in the double mirror on the closet, his pale face emerging from the darkness as if in a chiaroscurist portrait. But it wasn't entirely a funereal place, because the top sheet was clean and looked recently ironed and the air didn't smell of enclosure but of a cold February night, as if someone had just closed the balcony door. He locks himself in here, he thought, to caress the embroidery or the edge of the sheets as if he were caressing the body of the woman who lay on them for a single night, to look at the plaza from the balcony that only he can open, or to look at the mirror searching for a memory of Mariana, disheveled and naked, and perhaps he no longer feels anything, because no one is capable of incessant memory. He opened the closet, as empty as one in a hotel room, he searched through the dresser drawers and saw Mariana's lingerie and stockings and a mirrored compact that contained a pink substance as delicate as pollen, and in the bottom drawer, under her wedding dress, which became entwined in his hands like silken foam, he found the packet of old handwritten pages tied with a red ribbon. There was no need to hold it up to the candle to read the name written on the first sheet: he could recognize Jacinto Solana not only in his insomniac handwriting but above all in the talent for secrecy that seemed to have endured in him even after his death. They killed him, they thought they could demolish his memory by stomping on the typewriter that he was heard pounding constantly for three months in the highest room in the house, they ripped the papers he had written and burned them in a fire they set in the garden, but like a virus that lodges in the body and returns when the patient thinks it has been exterminated, the furtive words, the incessant writing of Jacinto Solana appeared again twenty-two years later, and in a place, Minaya supposed, that would have pleased him: the most untouched room in the house, the drawer where the wedding dress was kept and the intimate silk things of the woman he loved, so that the odor of the paper blended with the scent of her clothes, a distant heir of other scents that were in Mariana's skin.

Only later, when Minaya had read the manuscript, could he understand why Manuel had lied and told him that not even a page remained of the book Solana had been writing when they killed him. It read "Beatus Ille" at the top of the first sheet, though it wasn't or didn't seem to be a novel but a kind of diary written between February and April of 1947 and crisscrossed with long evocations of things that had happened ten years earlier. At times Solana wrote in the first person and at other times he used the third, as if he wanted to hide the voice that was telling and guessing everything and in this way give the narration the tone of an impassive history. Kneeling next to the open drawer, next to the wedding dress that spread around him, Minaya untied the knots in the red ribbons with clumsy, eager slowness, and when he touched the manuscript pages one by one with the incredulous fervor of a man who has witnessed a miracle, he heard the door of the bedroom closing quietly, and before he turned around, he recalled in a moment of lucidity and terror that he hadn't taken the key out of the lock. But it wasn't Manuel, it was Inés at his side, Inés who turned the key so that no one could take them by surprise and who, tall and ironic, looked at him as if he were a thief who, when he was discovered, forgot the fruit of his greed between his hands. Still on his knees, he let the manuscript fall, unable to say anything or think of a possible excuse. "I saw Utrera walking around the gallery," Inés said, "he almost caught you," and her voice wasn't the voice of an accuser but of an accomplice when she kneeled beside him to put away the dress. "Look what I've found. Manuscripts by Jacinto Solana." But Inés didn't seem to hear him; she had seen, among the bride's clothes, a rose of yellow cloth that Mariana must have removed from her hair before the wedding photograph was taken, and she put it on one side of her forehead, with transitory elegance, and looked in the mirror for an instant, smiling at herself, at Minaya's stupefaction and passion. With a caress he removed the rose from her hair as he kissed her with his eyes closed.

10

IN THE MIDDLE OF THE GARDEN, next to the palm tree that's so tall its top can be seen from the plaza, Manuel, convalescing, sat in the sun and talked to Minaya, sitting on a wicker chair, wearing no tie and a light-colored suit that seemed to have been chosen to match his white hair and the tone of the paint on the small round table with a glass of water sparkling in the light and an opaque bottle of medicine. Dominating his figure, beyond the fatigue of his convalescence visible only in the flat pallor of his skin and a certain tremor in his left hand, was a serene inaugural air, as if he had dressed so carefully to attend a fiesta or receive a group of guests in the garden. Disobeying Medina's orders without excessive pleasure, though with absolute premeditation, Manuel smoked his first cigarette since the afternoon when his heart knocked him down in the Plaza of Santa María. Still intact was the delight of taking it out of the cigarette case and fitting the filter in the holder with a light pressure of thumb and index finger, but the tobacco had a taste somewhere between unfamiliar and neutral, and Manuel, after the disappointment of the first few inhalations, continued smoking only because of loyalty to himself, just as he had allowed himself the useless elegance of going out to the garden, wearing his linen suit and an Italian scarf instead of a tie.

"Utrera told me you were going to visit his studio. He's a little nervous, and I think a little ashamed. You know, he considers the works they commission now humiliating. So you shouldn't praise his Medieval Virgins too much. He has a high opinion of you. He says you've inherited the artistic temperament of your grandfather Minaya and your grandmother Cristina."

Minaya couldn't imagine his grandmother as an old woman. In fact, he had never thought about her until he saw her oil portrait in Manuel's bedroom: a blonde girl with singularly delicate features looking into empty space and holding on her lap a half-open book on whose cover one can read with some difficulty the title written in Gothic letters: *Arpeggios,* by J. E. Minaya.

"My father rarely spoke of her, and then only to reproach her until after she had died for what he called her bad marriage. 'Dear God, what have I done that You gave me a poet for a father, a disinherited mother, and a son who's a Communist.' He said that once when he found a clandestine journal among my papers."

THERE WAS NOTHING STRANGER FOR MINAYA than remembering his father in the garden of the house that his bad luck had denied him. Death, he thought, isn't that boundary, that unmoving trench one imagines when it has just happened, but a slow distancing that ends in forgetting and disloyalty. In Madrid, in the sad streets and doorways of the district where they had taken him when they left Mágina, in a cell at Security Headquarters, the shadow of his father had moved very slowly away from Minaya, but it survived, transfigured and abstract, in the sensation of failure and fear, in the disagreeable need to take the metro every day and work and know he was alone. Now he was smoking in the garden and listening to the extremely hospitable voice of Manuel, who was telling him something about the visits he and Jacinto Solana made in their adolescence to the blonde girl in the painting, and the figures of his parents faded irremediably, like his own life and his future, abolished in time, in the pink fragrance of the wisteria that sifted the early light and brought him the memory of Inés, as if the day he would leave the house would never come, as if there were no days beyond the one indicated by the calendars that morning, no cities on the other side of the blue sierra. Even the next few minutes seemed remote to him: "If the smoke stopped in the air, if the light at the end of the cigarette stopped burning, if the splotches of shadow did not advance along the gravel in the garden." He walked toward the rear, toward the door of the carriage house where Utrera was waiting for him. "Triumphant," he had read in a passage of the manuscript, "solicitous, offering smiles and black-market cigarettes, appealing, as he says, to forgetting past rancors, to friendship, which is stronger than political differences. Wearing one of those dustcoats that mechanics used thirty years ago, he rules over the three workers who help him in the studio and over the statues like dismantled mannequins to which he barely applies a touch of paint or varnish when they are presented to him, for he claims that his art, like Leonardo's, *è cosa mentale.* Beneath the dustcoat he always wears a suit with spectacular shoulder pads for his slight figure, and a white carnation in his lapel. In the late afternoon, a worker acting as his *valet de chambre*—the mockery is Manuel's—helps him remove the dustcoat, and then Utrera emerges ready to prolong his reign in conversation at the café and at the tables with heaters under them in the brothels. He returns in the middle of the night with a drunkard's wariness and usually enters his studio through the back gate in the lane. He uses too much cologne and too much pomade, but I suppose that's another sign of success. He never looks me in the eye."

The same dustcoat, Minaya thinks, the same smile roughened by the gleam of his false teeth, almost the same cafés, darker now or more deserted, as excessive and empty as the workshop where Eugenio Utrera, leaning over a low table that looks something like a cobbler's bench, scratches with his sharpened gouge at a piece of wood to obtain something that resembles a saint or a Romanesque Virgin. His hands, the long yellow index fingers and blue veins, a cigarette that has gone out in a mouth wet with saliva, a man who isn't exactly

Utrera murmuring at the back of the carriage house, diminished, erased by the empty space and high ceiling that has a large glass skylight toward the center. He finishes a carving, leaves it on the table covered with old newspapers and shavings that allow him to smell at least the sweet, almost faded aroma of fresh wood, shakes off the lapels of his dustcoat and looks at his work and hates it with a devotion he only uses secretly to curse himself. Tacked to the wall, next to the shelf where the varnished figures are lined up, are newspaper clippings no longer legible, because years ago the dampness faded the photographs and headlines announcing the inauguration of a new monument sculpted by Utrera. "Orthopedic Virgins," wrote Solana, "wire nudes and amputated hands: the head, the wax lips that smile as if at the top of a pike, the hands extended at the end of a body of wires and wicker rods. Then, over nothing, over so light an armature, tunics and embroidered mantles are added so that no one can see the obscenity of these Virgins. Utrera isn't copying Martínez Montañés, as he supposes, but Marcel Duchamp."

In a corner of the workshop was the last car Manuel's father bought before he died, gloomy behind its windows closed like certain glass urns. "Look," said Utrera, pointing at it with pride, "look at how it still shines. Doesn't it look like a viceregal carriage? Nowadays they don't make automobiles like this one." He cleans off a chair, tossing the stained newspapers that covered it to the floor, offers it to Minaya, puts into a chest the piece of wood where there was the beginning of a suggestion of crude oval eyes.

"Romanesque Virgins," he murmurs, as if apologizing, "now everybody wants to have a Romanesque Virgin in the dining room or a bearded saint as a bookend. Of course there are more serious clients: for them I make special counterfeits, though you shouldn't think the store pays me much more for them. Shall I tell you a secret? Last week I finished a fourteenth-century crucifix."

His incessant talk, Minaya notices, is muffled in the workshop, as if here he weren't permitted the petulance he exhibits in the dining room, the library, the card games in the parlor, the Mágina cafés where he has occasionally seen Utrera lethargic in front of a glass of water and a snifter of cognac, pale in the damp semidarkness that smells of wood soaked in alcohol and urinal drains. He has seen him, without Utrera noticing him, at the back of cafés where the light of day never reaches, he has followed him at night along the lanes of his cowardly return, when he comes down to the house from the Plaza of General Orduña staggering and murmuring those things solitary drunks say to thin air, the alcoholic sidelong glances still not exempt from shame. Since Minaya's arrival in Mágina, his own consciousness had been pared down and reduced to a gaze that ascertains and desires, like a spy in a foreign country who has forgotten his true, distant identity in order not to be more than an eye and a hidden camera. He has visited the Gothic cloisters of the Church of Santa María and in its chapels, lit by candles, he has seen Eugenio Utrera's statues elevated on thrones that women in mourning adorn with large bouquets of flowers. The eyes blank, lacking the half-moon of glass eyes, the hard features of the Virgins gleaming in the semidarkness with a waxen smoothness. But in all those faces there is a unique, ambiguous air that isn't due simply to negligence and the monotony of a studio overwhelmed by commissions. Looking at Utrera's Virgins and Veronicas and penitent Magdalenes in the chapels of Santa María sounded an alarm for Minaya, a warning that he was about to discover something so hidden and fragile that only an abrupt revelation could give it definitive form. He recalled the photographs, Orlando's drawing, he recalled a Sunday afternoon when he waited for Inés next to the Monument to the Fallen and a night when he surprised Utrera looking for something in the gardens surrounding the statue, on his knees, drunk, holding a flashlight that barely illuminated his face. The Fallen Hero has the hair and features of a woman and a small circular mark on the forehead. Now he dares to say it, in Utrera's studio, as the old man catalogues humiliations and scorn, the persistence of ingratitude and forgetting. His hands are the same bloodless color of the old newspapers that cover the table and lie on the floor and the chairs and the shelf with the rows of wooden saints and cans of varnish. When he hears the name, Mariana, spoken by Minaya, Utrera moves his eyes away from his own hands and slowly raises his line of sight until he is looking at the other man and he smiles at him with the same questioning, suspicious air he used the first time they met in the dining room.

"It was because of the eyes, wasn't it? The eyes and cheekbones. Her mouth was admirable and her nose, as you must have noticed, was just a little longer and sharper than the accepted norms of sculpture. But her beauty lay above all in her almond-shaped eyes and those extremely high cheekbones. They weren't perfect, but when one looked at them, one's hands almost felt the sensation of modeling them."

It wasn't in the church but afterward, when he left there to look at the face in the Plaza of the Fallen, that could only be seen between the angel's legs and from an angle as unusual as it was difficult, when Minaya realized that all of Utrera's female faces were partial portraits of Mariana. A minor variation in the mouth or in the rendering of the face was enough to transform her into an unknown woman, but the long, pensive eyes were always the same in the dark air of the chapels, the same cheekbones that Orlando had summarized forever with a single stroke of his pencil. Now Utrera has forgotten all suspicion as he gives himself over to pride: standing and facing Minaya, with his dirty dustcoat and the tense or involuntary smile of his false teeth, he smokes and agrees to remember, to grant him the status of accomplice.

"You're right. The face of the Fallen Hero is a portrait of Mariana, a funerary portrait, to be more exact. I had made her death mask, but I lost it before the war was over. I found it again many years later, in '53, I think, when I was already working on the Monument to the Fallen. It was in the drawer of an old armoire, in the basement, so forgotten that finding it seemed like a miracle. At first

I thought the angel ought to have Mariana's face, but exposing it to light after all the years it had been hidden in the basement would have been a profanation. Have you seen photographs of those Egyptian statues that appear in the tombs of the pharaohs? They were made for the darkness, so that no one but the deceased could contemplate their beauty. In fifteen years no one, absolutely no one, discovered my secret. Now I have to share that portrait of Mariana with you. Promise me you won't say anything to anybody."

I promise, Minaya says, lying, imagining in advance how he'll tell these things to Inés and the words Solana would have used in the manuscripts to describe the conversation and the scene. All things, he thought then, have already been written and matter only to the extent I can recount them to Inés to provoke in her eyes a flash of longed-for mystery. Like her on certain clandestine nights, when she is naked and embraces his body, which never stops desiring her, to tell him about a book or a film or the brief dream she had while he was smoking in the dark and didn't know she was asleep, Minaya wants to tell her what he knows now, Utrera's pride and hidden rage, the pride and rage of looking at the empty car and his useless hands but always knowing he has added to the world a single memorable face, the unique shape of the eyes and cheekbones concealed, as if by a veil, with features that didn't belong to them, the precise lines of the face of a sleeping girl who smiles inside a dream disintegrated in death. He returns to the house from which he vindicated his glory with no witnesses other than a glass of cognac or a clouded mirror, and sometimes, when he is ready to open the door to the lane, he stands proudly erect on the aberration of alcohol and decides to prolong his steps to the shadowy plaza where the portrait of Mariana and the certainty of his pride await him with a constant loyalty possessed only by statues and paintings. At night, so that no one will follow him, like a miser who goes down to the basement where he counts and contemplates his coins every night and lets them slide through avid fingers, he stumbles, flips on his lighter, cannot manage to hold up the flame and shelter it from the wind, gropes at the granite he so delicately polished, recognizes every undulation, and stops his index finger at the small sunken circle in the middle of the forehead. He hears footsteps very close by, but it's too late when he gets to his feet because someone, a tall, familiar figure, has seen him kneeling next to the statue. When he stands so abruptly the blood pounds in his temples and a cognac nausea comes up from his stomach, but he cares more about his certain embarrassment, his obligation to pretend. It's that young man, Minaya, Manuel's nephew; it's midnight and very cold and what is he doing here except spying on me.

"Now you're thinking I fell in love with Mariana too. I hope you'll believe me when I tell you that didn't happen. She was the kind of woman every artist wants as a model, but nothing else, at least for me, especially if you keep in mind that she was going to marry the man to whose hospitality I owed my life. I don't betray my friends."

"And Solana?"

Utrera remains silent: premeditatedly grave, almost wounded, when he speaks again he avoids Minaya's eyes, as if forced against his will to take a step beyond discretion. "One shouldn't speak ill of the dead." When he leaves the studio, the noon light dazzles Minaya in the garden. With his back turned to him, Manuel in his wicker armchair remains in a repose belied only by the blue cigarette smoke that rises until it disappears in the clusters of wisteria.

II

THE NARROW GAUGE TRAIN slowly descends the Mágina slope to the Guadalquivir. In the distance, among blue olive trees and dunes of wheat or drab fields lying fallow, the river glitters like a thin plate of metal, of silver, of the same livid, glassy blue in the air at the edge of the sierra. As it goes down to the Guadalquivir, the train advances more rapidly between the olive groves, whose long rows open like fans into successive vanishing points. In profile next to the window, Inés looks at the olive groves and the white houses that appear for an instant like islands in the geometry of their thick growth, holding on her knees a wicker basket covered with a blue-checkered cloth. The olive trees and the dense line of poplars that announces the river, the distant sierra with clusters of white houses hanging from the slopes, are for Minaya like those landscapes of blue mountains and curving rivers visible in the background of certain quattrocento portraits in which a girl smiles in profile. With a casual air he caresses the hand resting on the basket, Inés' hands and knees, her ankles close together, the glance that recognizes and waits for a sign among the oleanders and the olive trees. "When we reach the river, the house where I was born is after the next curve." The rolling plain vibrates with the hedge mustard's greens and silvers and yellows, and before the river can be seen through the windows, an odor of mud and shaded water announces its vast, almost motionless, proximity.

"Look," Inés sits up, lowers the glass, and points at a house on the other side of a little grove of pomegranate trees and cypresses, "that was my grandfather's mill, that's where I was born." But the house is immediately left behind, barely glimpsed, like the new gleam in Inés' eyes when they looked at it. He would have liked to stop there, get off with her, go along the path that leads to the house among the pomegranate branches, acknowledge the grapevine in whose shade her uncle told her tales of travels, and the bedroom where she waited for sleep every night, hearing the passage of the water through the vault of the mill and the distant wind that shook the trees and carried to Mágina the deep whistles of trains or improbable ships. "At night, so I'd forget my fear of the dark, my uncle would come into my bedroom and sit beside me, leaving his crutches on the bed. He made me listen to the water and the whistles of the trains, and when you could hear one coming from very far away, he'd tell me it wasn't a train but a ship passing through the Straits of Gibraltar."

He would have liked to know, one by one, all the places and moments in the life of Inés, the childhood days at the mill, the seven years at the boarding school for orphan girls, the house where she lived now that she never allowed him to visit, transforming all of it into a part of his consciousness with the same urgent thirst of eyes and lips with which he sometimes undressed her and caressed her and opened her. But just as Inés' body always emerged somehow untouched and alone from their mutual sieges, her thoughts and memories were not revealed to Minaya except in flashes of chaotic images that tended to have, because they almost always alluded to the girl's early childhood, the ecstatic air and unsettled disorder of illustrations in color. Motionless for a moment to his gaze, despite the landscape passing the train window, the first illustration has been fixed now in Minaya's eyes: around 1956, a little girl cradles a cardboard doll at the feet of the crippled man who looks at her and smokes as he sits under a grapevine, scratching at the ground with his crutches. "We're almost there," says Inés. On the other side of the tracks is an abandoned shed that once must have been a station, and beyond the river, the shore of red mud and the banks covered with oleanders and reedbeds. "Give my respects to Don Manuel," says the conductor from the step as the train starts up again. They cross the stone bridge over the slow waters, and when they reach the other side Inés, turning around, shows Minaya the hilltop where Mágina is spread out, gray and remote, high with pointed towers, Mágina alone on the hill of spillways and ramparts, open to the blue, as in Orlando's last watercolors.

It had been Manuel who suggested to Minaya that he visit the Island of Cuba, offering Inés as a guide on his way down, but now, when he looked at the city and the valley again from the esplanade of the country estate, when he shook the large hand of Frasco, the caretaker, witness to Solana's final days and death, he felt he hadn't been brought there by Manuel's suggestion or by his own desire for knowledge, but by the clandestine order of the manuscript he had discovered in the marriage bedroom, its last page dated March 30, 1947, one day before Jacinto Solana went down to the Island of Cuba in his penultimate flight, knowing perhaps that he never would return to Mágina. As if he were moving on a blank page where the total absence of words concealed invisible writing, Minaya followed Inés up the path through the olive trees until they reached the esplanade where Jacinto Solana's dead body had been lain, at the entrance to the house. "Ask Frasco," Manuel had said, "he was the last of us to see Solana alive."

ON THE FIRST DAY of April 1947, at dawn, Jacinto Solana was tempted to go up to the cemetery to look for the pauper's grave where his father was buried. Without mentioning his intention to anyone, he left very early so they wouldn't see him when he crossed the Plaza of General Orduña, but he was not aware of his error and didn't realize that the commemoration was in progress until a shout made him raise his head as he passed the Church of La Trinidad. In front of the facade, at the top of the Baroque stairs, were three poles and three flags and a kind of burning censer next to which five men stood guard, looking down at him with folded arms in their blue uniforms and dazzling boots. One of them called to Solana, taking pleasure in repeating his first and last names and insulting him with predictable coldness, indicating the flags with a not entirely enraged gesture as he took his pistol out of the holster. "Raise your arm, and sing nice and loud so we can hear you." His eyes fixed on the ground, his hand raised and cowardly and shaken by a trembling that wasn't fear but an unfathomable future shame, Jacinto Solana heard from the depths of his consciousness his own voice singing the anthem of those aiming weapons at him with the same piercing clarity with which he heard the laughter and the usual insults. "That morning I went up to his room and saw that he kept his things in the same suitcase he had brought from prison," said Manuel. "He wanted to leave Mágina without telling me where he was going, and without his knowing either, because there was no place he could go. Then I told him to go to the Island of Cuba for a while, at least until he finished his book. Sometimes, when we were boys, we'd ride the white mare there from his father's farm to swim in the river. He left that same afternoon, I took him to the train station myself. I never saw him again." Beatus ille, thinks Minaya, with a melancholy not entirely his, sudden and general, as indifferent as the landscape of olive trees that extends to the spurs and the faded blue of the sierra. Inés has gone into the house, calling Frasco's name, and when her voice can no longer be heard, Minaya is temporarily lost in the solitude, which he always imagines as definitive, of unfamiliar, empty places. Across from the house is a small hill planted with almond trees, and from it comes a breeze with the scent of damp earth, risen perhaps from the river. Then Frasco appeared among the almond trees, a clay-encrusted hoe on his shoulder and a wide straw hat covering his face. You could hear his trouser legs brushing harshly against the hedge mustard, and from the energy of his step and the muscular tension that could be guessed at in the way he held the hoe, Minaya would have said it wasn't an old man but a forty-year-old who was approaching him. They walked together to the house, chatting at random about the recent rain, Manuel's illness, the distant time when the estate, which had been the best in the entire district of Mágina, had ten thousand olive trees. But that was long before the war, explained Frasco, who still remembered the visit of Alfonso XIII in his sportsman's outfit and high hunter's gaiters and the dust raised on the road by the cars of his entourage. Sitting in the entryway, at the bare wooden table, they watched Inés in silence as she served them their meal. In the entryway, on the entire ground floor of the house, a damp semidarkness like the breath of a well prevailed and made the paving stones, as worn as pebbles, glisten.

"I was told you saw them kill Solana."

"I didn't see it. Only they saw it, the ones who killed him. I heard the burst of the three-and-a-half-inch caliber weapon the Civil Guard carried and shots from Don Jacinto's pistol; he jumped into the river gorge from the shed. I spent a whole year on the Córdoba front, and I could identify every kind of weapon. They had me handcuffed right here, two of them, pointing their rifles at me, as if I could escape, and I heard the gunfire and the shouts, and from time to time Don Jacinto's pistol, he always carried it, even when he was writing. He kept it on the table, next to his papers, and when he went down to the river to swim, he left it with his clothes, because he knew they were going to come for him. I remember it took them several hours to find the body, because he was dead when he fell into the river and the current dragged him, so it was already daylight when they brought him here and threw him in the middle of the esplanade, full of mud, his whole face covered with blood. They didn't let me near him, but I could see from a distance the broken lenses of his glasses glinting on his face."

Inés listened to Frasco's story with the same fascinated attention she had felt when she was a little girl in the dark listening to tales of islands and tall empty ships that sail up the valley of the Guadalquivir on moonless nights. She was standing behind Minaya, and from time to time she touched his shoulder or brushed his neck with a very light touch, because nothing pleased her as much as enveloping any sign of tenderness in secrecy. With a shiver of gratitude he squeezed the hand she held out to him in the shadows as they followed Frasco up the stairs to the room Solana had occupied during the last three months of his life, a large hay loft with a sloping roof and long beams with halters tied to them, and in the back a single window covered with a piece of burlap that tinted the light the yellow of pollen. Under the bed was the trunk no one had opened for the past twenty-two years, because Frasco hadn't wanted to touch anything after the Civil Guard left carrying the dripping wet body of Jacinto Solana.

"I swept up the ashes. The floor was full of burned papers everywhere, even under the bed, I don't know how the roof didn't catch fire—you can see it's made of wood and reeds—and burn the whole house down. They didn't burn all the papers at the same time, in a bonfire; it seems they burned them one by one."

"Did they burn the books too?" asked Minaya as he examined the blue ink stains on the table. Stains of a finger sometimes, like fingerprints, long stains like the shadow of Jacinto Solana's hands.

"There weren't any books. Don Jacinto didn't bring any when he came here. Nothing but the suitcase tied with rope and the pistol in his jacket pocket. He wrote with a pen Don Manuel had given him. The Guards must have taken it with them because I didn't see it again."

Moving aside the piece of burlap that covered the window, Inés leaned her elbows on the sill to look at the river and the walled blue line of the city, as if she weren't listening to Frasco's words. The water formed dark clotted eddies around the pillars of the bridge and the reedbeds on the shore. Beneath the window was the sloping roof of the small shed from which Jacinto Solana had jumped to the embankment, rolling blind through the slippery leaves of oleander, between the darkness and the mud, then getting up and pushing his elbows into the red earth to fire at the Guards pursuing him. Inés, said Minaya, and from the tone of his voice she knew they were alone now in the loft and all she had to do was remain motionless and he would embrace her from the rear and caress her breasts, saying her name again in a darker voice as if it were hidden in her hair, which he explored with his lips. But this time Minaya didn't embrace her: Frasco had gone, he said, and would be right back, and while they were alone he wanted to open the trunk under the bed. When he raised the lid Minaya had the sensation that he was opening a coffin. "There's nothing," said Inés, kneeling beside him, "just old clothes." They searched down to the bottom of the trunk, where there was a pair of cracked shoes, a fountain pen, a cigarette lighter, a red ribbon like the ones tied around the manuscripts in the marriage bedroom. Like the metal bed with the bare mattress, and the ink stains on the table, each of the things they exhumed added obscurely to the others to lay out before them the empty mass of Jacinto Solana's presence. "Memory doesn't last," Minaya thought as he opened the pen that perhaps Solana touched a few minutes before he died, as he attempted to work the lighter that for so many nights had occupied a precise place between the habits of writing and insomnia, "the only things that last have always belonged to forgetting, the pen, the lighter, a pair of shoes, an ink stain like a fingerprint on the wood." It was Inés who found the notebook and the small cartridge wrapped in a piece of newspaper. She was folding a gray jacket to put it back in the trunk when she noticed a hard, smooth surface in the lining, and then, as she continued searching, a bundle so small that at first her fingers didn't distinguish it from the fold where it was resting. There was a tear in the inside pocket, and the cartridge and notebook had undoubtedly slipped through it. "Look, it's the same handwriting as on the manuscript." It was a notebook whose pages were graph paper, it had a blue cover and a schoolboy air, and it was irregularly filled by writing that seemed disciplined by desperation. That afternoon as they returned to the city on the train, Minaya examined the pages where the lines of ink were now as faint as the grid marks, and when he deciphered the words, which at times he read aloud to Inés, the images of the river, the esplanade in front of the house, the room with the table and the single window through which you could see the silhouette of Mágina, specified the details of a nocturnal setting surrounding the figure who in the light of a candle writes incessantly even after he hears the uproar of rifle butts banging on the door of the country house, when the Guards' boots thundered like galloping horses on the stairs, but he knows he's going to die and doesn't want his final words to end up in the fire. "He hid the notebook in the jacket lining himself," Minaya told Inés excitedly, as if he were talking to himself, to his yearning to find out and know, "because this diary was his will, and he knew that when he began to write it." He kept the notebook when they reached Mágina station, not having read yet the long account that filled the last pages and consequently not understanding the reason why there was also a cartridge in the lining wrapped in a piece of the Republican *ABC* of May 22, 1937. Only that night, last night, when Manuel was already dead on the rug in the marriage bedroom, did Minaya lock the door of his room and discover that Solana had recounted the death of Mariana in the last pages of the notebook, and that the bullet that killed her hadn't come from the roofs where militia men were pursuing a fugitive, but from a pistol that someone held and fired from the doorway of the pigeon loft.

12

He had telephoned Medina himself and gone downstairs to unbolt the outside door so the doctor would find it open when he arrived, bringing to these actions a useless urgency, a somnambulistic haste similar to that shown by Teresa and Inés in preparing coffee, bottles of hot water, clean sheets for making the bed where Minaya and Utrera had lain Manuel, as if death were not something definitive, as if it could be stopped or mitigated by pretending they were ministering not to a corpse but a sick person, and their hurry to arrange everything in the marriage bedroom in silence, not speaking to each other or to anyone else, avoiding looking at each other just as they tried not to look at the man lying on the bed, was motivated by the sense of propriety that the imminent arrival of the doctor provokes in houses where someone is ill. Wandering in a waking state as dark as the film over her eyes, Amalia drifted between the gallery hallway and the parlor and marriage bedroom, setting herself vague tasks she didn't complete, bringing a glass of water to Doña Elvira or clumsily smoothing the quilt around Manuel's feet, and she murmured things that to Minaya's ear were confused with Doña Elvira's murmurs or prayers and the profusion of footsteps that exaggerated the silence. Like fish in an aquarium they all passed one another in the area of the bedroom and the parlor, their bodies sometimes making contact but not their eyes, and if Minaya, overcoming for a moment the stupefaction of a guilt that resembled our guilt for the crimes we commit in dreams, searched out Inés' eyes when he found himself alone with her in the hallway, he encountered an attitude of flight or a fixed stare that did not seem to notice him. He wasn't afraid then that they would be discovered: with a fear that wiped out all culpability or sense of danger, he was afraid only that Inés had stopped loving him.

Now death was Manuel, with his silk scarf around his neck and his touseled white hair that Doña Elvira smoothed as if in a dream with a dry caress, it was open eyes at the threshold to the room and the hand he had raised as if to curse them or expel them, then curving as if wanting to clutch at his heart and the hoarse sound of air escaping his lungs and of his body slowly collapsing then falling all at once onto the disorder of Minaya's and Inés' clothes and the bridal veil she had worn to initiate the game of pretending to be or being Mariana on her wedding night. But everything was very distant and as if it hadn't happened, because death demolished the possibility of remembering and fleeing, and the moment when Manuel died was now as imaginary or remote as Medina's voice, torpid with sleep, when he promised Minaya he'd be at the house in twenty minutes. Minaya went out to the hallway, with the useless intention of confirming that the courtyard light was on for Medina's arrival, he refused a cup of coffee that Teresa offered him, looked for Inés and when he saw her coming didn't dare look at her, brusquely opened the door to his room and locked himself in and saw on the desk Jacinto Solana's manuscripts, the blue notebook, the cartridge that in a few minutes, when he had read the final pages in the notebook, would be established as the conclusion of the story he had pursued for three months. But now there was only a culpable lucidity in his mind. He understood that in looking for a book, he had discovered a crime, and that after Manuel's death there was no possibility left to him for innocence.

They had returned from the station that afternoon, pursuing

each other down the lanes and embracing with an obstinacy of desire that for the first time excluded all modesty or tenderness, delaying the moment they would arrive at the house and daring rough caresses at the empty streetcorners and sweet, dirty words they had never said before. But the game and the fever didn't end when they knocked at the door of the house. As they listened to Teresa crossing the courtyard and repeating "Coming," they arranged their clothes, their hair, they solemnly stood erect at either side of the door, feigning indifference or fatigue, and now simulation excited them more than the chase.

"Don Manuel is worse," said Teresa. "He had to lie down after lunch."

"Did the doctor come?"

"Of course, and he scolded him for smoking and not taking his medicine. How can he get better if he pays no attention to what they tell him to do?"

When she heard Minaya, Amalia felt her way down the stairs, clutching at the banister. She was coming from Manuel's bedroom and brought with her the weary smell of the sickroom. "Your uncle wants to see you." There was a dirty gleam of tears beneath her painted lids. When Minaya knocked gently at the bedroom door Manuel's voice inviting him in sounded unfamiliar, as if it had been infected prematurely by the strangeness of death. But he thought about those things afterward, when he was alone in his room waiting for Medina, because one always remembers the eve of a misfortune imagining vague presentiments that could not be verified while there was still time and that perhaps did not exist. The same voice coming out of the semidarkness asked him to open the curtains. "Open them more, all the way. I don't know why they have to leave you in the dark when you're sick." Because light is an affront, Minaya thought when he turned to his uncle, looking at his sunken cheeks against the white pillow, the slender, motionless hands on the quilt, the wrists with long blue veins emerging from the sleeves of his pajamas. In the plaza, above the tops of the acacias, the sand-colored church tower, crowned by gargoyles under the eaves, shone brilliantly in the afternoon against a violent blue crisscrossed by swallows.

"Bring over that chair. Sit here, closer. I can't speak very loudly. Medina prohibited my talking. He's spent thirty years prohibiting my doing things and ordering absurdities."

Manuel closed his eyes and very slowly brought his hand to his left side, holding in the air and then expelling it with a very long whistling sound. Once again it was the stabbing pain, the knife, the dark hand splitting open his chest until it squeezed his heart and then released it as slowly as it had seized it, as if offering a respite, as if advancing only as far as the precise boundary where asphyxia would begin.

"This morning, when you went to the estate, I entered the library and saw you had forgotten to put away some written pages. I was going to do it myself because I thought they were notes for the book that I don't know if you still want to write, and I was afraid Teresa would disturb them when she cleaned, but when I put them together I saw without meaning to that you had written and underlined my name and Mariana's several times. Don't look at me that way: I'm the one who ought to apologize, not you. Because I was tempted to open the drawer again and read what you had written about us. Since you came here I've answered all your questions, but this morning it frightened me to imagine what you must think of us, of Mariana and me, and of Solana, who did what you're doing, who looked at everything the same way you do, as if he were verifying the history of each thing and what one was thinking and hiding behind the words. With that novel of his that he never finished, the same thing would have happened to me as with your papers. I wouldn't have had the courage to read it.

If he knew I wasn't a witness but a spy, that I've gone into his marriage bedroom and discovered the manuscripts he didn't want to show me, perhaps because they recount what could be seen only by a shadow posted above the garden that night in May when Solana and Mariana wandered around in the dark kissing each other with the desperation of two lovers on the eve of the end of the world." Manuel had spoken in a voice that grew increasingly faint, and finally, in silence, he pressed Minaya's hand for a long time, not looking at him, as if he wanted to be certain he was still there. Then the hand, yellow and motionless, the palm turned up and the fingers curved like the claw of a dead bird, the hand that moved sluggishly through the air not to curse or expel Inés and Minaya but to make them disappear like smoke in a closed room, their two naked bodies shadows or premature apparitions that announced to Manuel the dream of death when he, pursued by her, got up from his bed and left the bedroom and crossed the dark hallway to look for the last time at Mariana's face in the photograph in the parlor and open the door of the room where he had embraced and possessed her. He awoke, caught off guard by the sudden awareness that he was going to die, but not even when he was standing and dared to walk barefoot on the cold chessboard of the tiles could he elude the sensation of inhabiting a dream in which, for the first time, the stabbing pain in his heart and the suffocating lightness of the air, like the vertigo in his temples and the cold on the soles of his feet, were things alien to his own body. Which is why it shouldn't have surprised him that there was a line of light under the door of the marriage bedroom or that above the noise of his respiration he could hear the obscene panting of entwined bodies, the bitter breath of a man murmuring and biting as he closed his eyes to empty the impossible instant of desperation or joy and the long shout or the tears or laughter of a woman whose fierce pleasure exploded like the brash noise of breaking glass in the silence of the house. He understood then, on the verge of passing out, the unreality of so many years, his status as a shadow, his interminable and never mitigated memory of a single night and a single body, and perhaps when he opened the door and stood on the threshold, sensing in the air the same candescent odor of that night, he didn't recognize the bodies captured on the bed, gleaming in the semidarkness, and died, obliterated by the certainty and the miracle of having returned to the night of May 21, 1937, to witness behind the glass of death how his own body and hands and lips laid siege to a naked Mariana.

"No," Inés had said, leaning against the closed bedroom door when Minaya, who had returned the manuscripts to the drawer where he had found them, prepared to go out. "It has to be here. I like that bed and the mirror on the closet." She said it in a voice that wasn't so much inviting as determined in advance to fulfill that specific desire even if Minaya didn't agree to stay, as if he weren't an accomplice but a witness to the pleasure she imagined and in which she would somehow be alone. She said "It has to be here," smiling with serene audacity, and he knew immediately that he would stay even if he couldn't share her courage or forget his fear of being discovered, which hadn't stopped since Inés had come to his room and said, with the same smile, that she had found the key to the marriage bedroom in one of Manuel's jackets. It was Minaya who had asked her to look for it: some day, some night when he couldn't sleep, it was possible that Manuel would look in the bedroom for the manuscripts he himself must have hidden after Solana's death. For a time Minaya was confident that at some point the accident that allowed him to find them would be repeated, but Manuel didn't forget again to lock the bedroom, which, Minaya suspected, might have been proof that his uncle already distrusted him. He heard footsteps approaching, and he still hadn't dared to hope they were Inés' footsteps when he heard the three quiet knocks of their signal and she slipped into the room dressed and made up for the usual secret game of their nocturnal rendezvous, pushing aside, in her yellow skirt and her Sunday afternoon blouse and stockings and the shadow of cosmetics on her cheeks, the semidarkness of midnight, the solemn presence on the desk of the blue notebook and the manuscripts, the pages where Minaya was outlining the biography of Jacinto Solana. But now, when he had Inés in front of him, all that mattered was her beauty and the devastating certainty that he would be in love with her for the rest of his life. He didn't turn around immediately to embrace her: he first saw her reflected in the windows to the balcony, standing behind him, while he was still writing, and that image acquired for Minaya the immobile quality of a symbol or a future memory, because in it was summarized the only inhabitable future he conceived of for himself.

Hiding and alone, at three or three-thirty in the morning—he didn't have a watch and hadn't heard the clock in the parlor and was incapable of estimating the time that had passed since he had spoken to Medina—he sat down again at the desk and saw in the glass the same light that had illuminated it three hours earlier, but now he saw only himself, knowing that never again would the serene figure of Inés, uselessly searched for now in the empty glass, in the disloyalty of mirrors, be reflected next to his. The present had shattered and condemned him irremediably to the usury of memory, which was already urging him to commemorate with obsessive details the first embrace at midnight and the smile in Inés' eyes when she showed him the key like an ambiguous invitation that was revealed completely only in the marriage bedroom, after Minaya had placed the manuscripts under the wedding dress.

"Nobody will hear us. Don Manuel's asleep with the pills Medina gave him, and the others sleep very far from here."

It would have been enough to say no a second time, oblige her to move away from the door, go out alone perhaps and accept insomnia and rage, but he did nothing, only looked at her, sick with desire and fear: she sat down on the bed, dropped her shoes, raised her skirt to undo her stockings. Minaya saw her long white thighs, her raised knees, her feet finally bare and willful under his kisses, pink and white and moving like fish in the semidarkness of the mirrors. When he opened her thighs to descend to the damp rose of her belly he thought he heard the sound of a distant door, but he didn't care anymore about fear, or even decency, or his life, or his awareness that he was disintegrating like the shape of the room and the identity and limits of his body. He heard Inés' voice confused with his own, and he bit her lips as he looked into her eyes to discover a gaze that never had belonged to him until that night. Holding on to each other like two shadows, they rolled to the floor, dragging the sheets from the bed with them, and on the rug, on the stained sheets, they sought each other and overthrew and bit each other in a persecution multiplied by the mirrors in the dark, purple air. As if they had survived a shipwreck at sea and the temptation to succumb to a sweet death underwater, they found themselves once again motionless on the bed and couldn't recall how or when they had returned to it. "Now I don't care if I die," said Minaya. "If you offered me a cup of poison right now, I'd drink it down." Sitting on the bed, Inés caressed his hair and mouth and slowly made him turn toward her, between her thighs, until Minaya's lips found the pink cleft that she herself opened with the thumb and index finger of both hands to receive him. But there was no urgency now, no desperation, and the serene cupidity of his palate was prolonged and ascended in the inquiry of his gaze. Urged on by the dark breath that had revived more deeply when he was drinking from her womb, he moved up to her breasts, her chin, her mouth, the damp hair that covered her cheekbones, and then he felt that he was disappearing, quivering motionless, lucid, suspended at the edge of a sweetness from which there was no return. "Don't move," said Inés, "don't do anything," and she began to move back and forth, gyrating under his hips, clutching at him, wounding him, draining the air and expelling it very slowly as she rose and curved and sank her elbows and heels into the sheets, and smiled with her eyes fixed on Minaya, murmuring "slow," saying in a quiet voice words he had never dared say to her. Like a wounded animal he rose up, lifting his head, and that was when time ripped as if a vengeful stone had broken the mirrors reflecting them, because they heard behind them the sound of the door and saw the terrifying slowness with which the knob moved and the long stain of light entered the bedroom and stopped at the foot of the bed when Manuel appeared on the threshold, barefoot, in his pajamas of an incurably sick man and his Italian scarf around his neck, looking at them with a stupefaction from which anger would have been absent if it hadn't been for the unmoving hand that ascended when he took a step toward the bed, as if in a frozen gesture of malediction. He opened his mouth in a shout that never was heard, and even took one more step before his eyes became empty and staring, not at Inés or Minaya but at the hand that had descended until it lay open beside his heart, curving as it clutched at the cloth of his pajamas at the same time that Manuel fell to his knees and raised his blue eyes again to look at them. Inés didn't see that last look: she said she had buried her face in Minaya's chest and dug her nails into him when she heard something rebound heavily on the wooden floor. Trembling with cold she opened her eyes and saw in the dresser mirror that she was alone and very pale on the bed. Minaya, still naked, was leaning over Manuel's body, feeling his chest under the pajamas. He's dead, he said, and locked the bedroom door. Manuel's open mouth was against the floor and his eyes fixed on the light on the night table. Inés, in order not to see them, got off the bed like a sleepwalker and extended a cowardly hand until she touched his eyelids, but Minaya stopped her and obliged her to stand up, shaking her as if she were a child who doesn't want to waken. For the first time in his life he was not paralyzed by fear: now fear was an impulse to intelligence or the dirty courage to simulate and flee.

"Listen. Now we're going to get dressed and straighten up the bed and the room. We'll leave the window open to get rid of the smell in the air. That won't make them suspect anything: Manuel could have opened it before he died. You'll go to your room, and I'll go to mine, and in an hour I'll go and wake Utrera. I'll say I couldn't sleep and heard a shout and something falling near the parlor. Nobody will find out about us, Inés."

Later he told the story with the desperate fervor used to tell certain necessary lies, he told it to the incredulous gaze of Utrera, who was already dressed when he went to call him, he repeated it a few more times, adding details that made him feel despicable, but not less persecuted, and when he heard Amalia telling it to Doña Elvira, it seemed to him that the story, when it took place in a different voice, entered reality completely, and he was temporarily relieved of its weight. But Utrera, when they picked up Manuel's body to lay it on the bed, had examined the open window, the quilt, the half-burned candle still smelling of wax in the candlestick on the night table. I'll leave here tomorrow, Minaya said aloud, when he was alone and in the room, facing the window to the balcony that overlooks the Plaza of the Acacias, suddenly possessed by the premonition of exile. He heard a distant bell and then footsteps and voices on the stairs, the slow footsteps, the unmistakable voice of Medina, but still he didn't leave the room. He could hear them and recognize each of their voices, because they were all in the parlor, on the other side of the door, but also in the blue notebook, on the last pages that he was beginning to read now, asking himself which of them, which of the living or the dead had been a murderer thirty-two years earlier.

PART TWO

*After all the years I have spent asleep in the
silence of obscurity.*
—Cervantes, *Don Quixote*, I, Prologue

I

I still could hear the concave sound of the galleries, metal gates
closing behind someone's footsteps, the pounding of the guards'
heels, a thicket of voices that resounded in the high vaults like the
ocean in a shell and seemed like voices and footsteps that were infinitely distant, the dark ocean heard in dreams. I had left behind the
gate of the final gallery, high and painted black, like the wrought-
iron grillwork in a cathedral, and now I was walking down ordinary
corridors with floors of tiles and not damp cement, with gray doors
and peaceful offices on the other side of the doors, where I waited
interminably and acquiesced, signed typewritten forms, docile, cowardly, always fearing I hadn't completely understood what they were
saying to me, repeating my name without avoiding the suspicion
that when he heard it, the man bent over the typewriter would lift
his head and order the guard who accompanied me to handcuff me
again. There were countless offices, all the same, and in all of them
there was someone who shook his head when he heard my name and
didn't look at me, only read something on a list and asked something
and, with an engrossed air, opened a large record book and then
closed it without having found what he was looking for or asked me
to sign somewhere, handing me a pen across the counter that I no
longer knew how to hold between my thumb and index finger, too
thin and too fragile for my fingers made clumsy by the cold, by ten

years of not touching or using a pen. Now the guard was walking in front of me, rhythmically hitting the bunch of keys against the side of his trouser leg, and I no longer expected freedom and the street to be on the other side of any door. Now the doors were made of wood and not metal and were painted green like the shutters at the windows, but they still resounded in the same deep, definitive way when they were shut and there were no prisoners sweeping the corridors. I said my name again and signed a receipt; they gave me an open suitcase, and I put my papers and clothes in it while two guards with unbuttoned tunics watched me and smoked in a room without windows that had numbered metal lockers and a low-hanging lamp that swayed above the table, thickening the cigarette smoke in its cone of light. The other guard, the one who had led me there, ponderously left the bunch of keys on the table and ordered me to follow him, but this time the last door we passed through didn't have a lock and opened onto a small courtyard with very high walls of ocher brick and sentry towers rising at the corners of the roof, where two Civil Guards in gleaming oilskin capes were profiled like symmetrical statues against a low, pale gray sky. They didn't look at the courtyard, they didn't do anything when I crossed it trembling with fear and unknown joy and with twitching fingers grasped the handle of the suitcase as I approached the entrance, as closed and undifferentiated as a wall, where someone, another Civil Guard, opened a gate and stepped to one side to let me pass, saying something I didn't stop to hear, because the gate had closed behind me with a long clanking of locks and I was alone before the facade of the prison, under the yellow and red flag that snapped in the wind like the wings of a large bird.

THE PRISON WAS A HIGH ocher island in the barren ground and fog. Facing it, on the other side of the highway, was a building with long whitewashed walls and broken windows that looked like an industrial ship or an abandoned warehouse. I walked toward it, stepping on mud crisscrossed by tracks of horses and cars, but I still didn't see the black car parked at a corner: perhaps I saw it without noticing it, and I remembered only when I heard the engine starting that I had seen it and that the blades of the windshield wipers were moving even though it wasn't raining. To shield myself from the wind, I walked very close to the wall, the brim of my hat down over my eyes and the lapels of my overcoat raised, and I didn't turn around when I heard the engine and then the tires skidding in the mud. I heard it moving slowly behind me, as if it didn't want to get ahead of me, and I walked faster and moved closer to the wall that never ended, on my way to the single tree and the shack made of debris that sometimes, from a high window in the prison, I had seen beside the highway, the only indication that a city existed beyond the wasteland my eyes could glimpse briefly. The men who left the city at dawn on slow bicycles would stop there to drink a glass of aguardiente and then leave rubbing together their hands numb with cold, exhaling the hot breath of the alcohol as they grasped the handlebars again and pedaled down the highway with their heads sunk down between the lapels of their dark jackets, as if they were leaving for a wintry, distant exile. From the tin roof rose a column of smoke that the wind dispersed among the branches of the tree. Without turning around to look at the black car, I pushed the door of poorly assembled planks and entered a narrow, warm place filled with smoke and cases of bottles. The counter was a board that smelled strongly of wood soaked in alcohol, lying across two barrels. Behind it, lit by an oil lamp, a very fat woman nursed a child red-faced with crying. Nailed to the wall were yellowed posters announcing remote bullfights and a 1945 calendar on which a black woman with a red shawl tied around her waist smiled as she displayed a tin of cocoa. The woman behind the counter, motionless on an empty case, slowly and methodically examined my face, my suitcase, the mud on my shoes. I asked for a glass of cognac, and she didn't detach the child from her large white breast or stop looking at me as she stood to find the bottle. She didn't look at my eyes but at the indications of what she had known since she had seen me come in: the awkwardness, the still undiminished distrust, the way my hand held the glass and raised it, with a slight tremor. I drank the cognac in one swallow and nodded in silence when the woman asked if I wanted another one. The glass in the small window that faced the highway was dirty and opaque with vapor, but through it I could see the black silhouette of the car, which had stopped. The alcohol burned in my throat with violent sweetness and intensified the colors of things. With the second glass still intact, I went to sit beside the window, wrapped in my overcoat, in the warm blur of the alcohol, raising the faint mask of abandonment and smoke that was between my eyes and the door that perhaps was going to open. I smoked with half-closed eyes, waiting, not indolent, lost, feeling the alcohol rising in my veins like successive undulations in the water of a lake, I half-closed my eyes as if waiting for sleep so I wouldn't see anything but the blue smoke rising and the dirty semidarkness of the barrels and the row of bottles, the red spot on the calendar whose pages numbered the days of a time when I hadn't existed. I took a drink and closed my eyes completely, and on the other side of the window, the door of the black car slammed shut. When I opened them again she, Beatriz, was looking at me through the smoke that the icy outside air had shaken, taller than I remembered, as if immune to time, as if she had just turned thirty, her age the last time I saw her, tall and solemn with her blonde mane and gray overcoat and the beret she held in her hands as if she weren't sure how she ought to behave. The fat woman had lain the child down, and now she was cleaning a row of bottles on the counter. From the corner of my eye I saw her looking at us as Beatriz embraced me, touching me with her blonde hair from which there rose an unfamiliar perfume and taking my hard face in her hands to recognize and touch what her eyes saw, undimmed by tears. She watched us without interest or modesty, with inert fixity, wiping the dust from the bottles with a dirty rag that she sometimes passed slowly over the counter, and when I approached to ask her for another glass, she studied Beatriz' coat and stockings and high-heeled shoes and then looked at me, with a different expression, as if comparing us, asking herself perhaps why a woman dressed like that had come into her tavern to find me.

We didn't speak at first, or between long silences we said only the necessary, useless words, looking for a respite with cigarettes and drinks, leaning on our elbows in the gray light that came from the other side of the window, from the field where the black car waited, occupied now only by a man who smoked as he rested his elbows on the steering wheel. "We thought you were dead," said Beatriz, caressing her lighter of smooth, gold-colored metal, very close to my hand on the stained wood, moving her fingers close, her unpainted nails trailing across the veins in the table, then stopping when they seemed about to touch me, then brushing against the acknowledged metal boundary, the pack of American cigarettes that now formed part of her perfume and her distance. "Nobody knew where you were. Nobody could tell me if you had died or were in prison or had managed to escape over the French border at the last minute. A woman told me she had heard that you were seen sick or wounded in the camp at Argelés, but they also said you had escaped to the sea and were arrested in the port of Alicante. After a year I began to write and receive letters. I wrote to friends in exile asking about you, but you weren't in France, or Mexico, or Argentina. You weren't dead or alive anywhere, but I waited every day to receive a letter from you. Last month a comrade just out of prison came to the house. He was the one who told us you'd be getting out very soon."

So THE AMBIGUOUS, the sacred plural was still true in spite of the gold-colored lighter and the silk stockings, and they were still called comrades and not shades or survivors and as a plural they had waited for me and thought I was dead and now they had come to receive me and welcome me not in the warm interior of the car or in a probably clandestine house but in the ancient, failed, intact plural behind which were hidden, in succession, impotence and fear, the fervor of old names, of lost banners, the unconfessed tenderness of Beatriz, who searched for my hand on the table and didn't dare touch it, always brushing against the boundary in the space that divided us like the blade of a knife, the one, desperate question she never would ask me now. From a great distance, behind the smoke, I watched her talk to me and estimated the words beneath each eruption of silence, indifferent, like a doctor who does not need to examine the body lying next to him to know the exact place where the pain is lodged. It was as if time or the chance that governs such transfigurations had used the past ten years to complete a work—the face, the hands, the figure of Beatriz—which earlier, when I knew her, had only been foreshadowed and that reached their plenitude in the prelude to their decadence. There was something dry or cruel in her slender hands, perhaps the shadow of an obstinate, useless determination, a hardness not rooted in any purpose, faint wrinkles, like the slashes of knives, next to her lips, around her covetous, firm eyes. I looked at her, still not asking, I heard her talk to me about her life during those years, perceiving the same chasm in time already proclaimed by the dates on the bullfight posters nailed to the dirty walls of the tavern and that month of July 1945 that remained inert on the calendar like a rip in my memory. She had waited for me, she said, wanting to involve me in the invocation of her waiting and her remembering, wanting to vindicate as attributes of a shared suffering the letters that never arrived anywhere, the empty letterbox in the hollow of the stairs, the horror and hunger and loneliness of the winter of 1941, and when she remembered, she claimed me for herself and demanded the part of my sorrow I had denied her. "And while you were in prison, condemned to death, and I didn't know anything," she said, as if she were demanding not only sorrow but also blame for not having found me, but then she raised her damp eyes to me and suddenly understood that she was becoming vulnerable because she was alone in her remembering, and to defend herself she was forced to turn to pride and pretended serenity. She sat up straight before her glass, before me, lighting a cigarette with excessive resolve, her fingers firm on the gold-colored lighter, as if in that gesture she were using all the determination she had needed to survive from the May night in 1937 when I had gone to Mágina without saying a word to her. "I can see you're surprised at my appearance. At first I was too, when I looked at myself in the mirror. I didn't tell you that since '42 I've been working in a dress store on the Gran Vía, selling expensive clothes to the richest women in Madrid. Sometimes I even design a model. Do you find it strange? It was like a story or a miracle, I was making things for a dressmaking shop where I didn't earn enough to pay my rent, and one day that man, Ernesto, the owner of the dress store appeared, and asked if I wanted to work exclusively for him, imagine, I was so hungry I almost didn't sleep so I could sew all night. I think he's in love with me, like an old-fashioned gentleman, you know, he invites me to the theater and takes my arm almost without touching me when we go into a restaurant, he always gives me things, the lighter, this coat, this perfume, which is very expensive. That's his car, he brought me here."

The man alone, behind the car window, perfumed and cowardly, I imagined, drumming his nervous fingers on the steering wheel, turning from time to time toward the prison building to make certain there were no Civil Guards at the door who suspected and were watching him, dying of jealousy, no doubt, of dignity and rage, the cuckolded gentleman. "Of course I've told him who you are and why you were in prison. He also knows I belong to the Party, and he doesn't care. He says he's glad I work with him because that means I'm in less danger. Imagine, who can suspect me, if I try dresses on the wife of the General Director of Security." But there were very few, she said, returning unexpectedly to the plural of persecution and secrecy in which without counting on me she included me, we were, myself also included, very few and inactive and dispersed, slowly we were recognizing one another and grouping again following the disaster in which the illusion had been undone of the underground, basements, secret cells that met to count the dead and discuss repeated, exhausted slogans, they or we had to resist without letting silence resemble surrender, and somewhere in Madrid the same house I had left ten years earlier was waiting for me. "No one has gone in, not even Ernesto, since you left." I drank without saying anything, turning toward the gleaming, quiet automobile in the bare field, in a cowardly way I supposed that Beatriz was going to accuse me now. The woman behind the counter had plugged in the radio and a bolero played from a filthy distance. But the obscene voice of the radio and Beatriz' words passed through me as if I didn't exist, as if I had died in some other empty field in the world, lost my way and died, for example, on any of the rectangular identical days in the month of July 1945. "I remember as if it were yesterday, the day you went away. It'll be ten years on May 15. Do you remember?" Now Beatriz was speaking to another man who wasn't me, and she knew it but no longer cared, in the same way she had stopped caring that someone else was waiting for her in the black automobile. Imperiously she spoke to a shade, to someone who may have been me thirteen or fourteen years earlier, when Mariana did not exist yet or the shame of desiring what had been denied to me, the kind of injustice or error that no one corrects and no one accepts. But neither Beatriz nor I were to blame for Mariana appearing before me in Orlando's studio, sitting naked and facing a recently begun canvas, with her legs crossed and the smile of a patient model, as if she were in a café, innocent and shameless, dazzling forever the deepest, blindest essence of my desire. "You don't remember anything, Jacinto. I came home and you weren't there, and at first I felt an awful terror because I was afraid you'd been caught in that afternoon's bombing. It was midnight and you still hadn't come back, and I went out to look for you. I ran into Orlando in a bar on the Puerta del Sol, but he didn't hear what I was asking him because he was so drunk he had to walk leaning on one of those adolescents who were always with him. Finally he looked at me as if he didn't know who I was and didn't understand what I was saying, and he started to laugh that disagreeable laugh he had when he was drunk and said you had taken the train to Mágina. He was still laughing when I left."

I'd had too much cognac and the frontiers of time and the limits and profiles of faces had begun to disintegrate. Mariana or Beatriz, 1937 or 1945 or 1933, years and bodies and blame not recovered from its own ashes, a fervor for nothing, the loyalty of the dead, hard eyes looking without tenderness to demand and accuse, immune to the present, to the exact January morning on which the impossible acknowledgment had not taken place. All I wanted was to be alone, hidden in my overcoat, drinking until my consciousness was very slowly obliterated, my legs together under the table, coat collar raised, everything as far from me as the city whose first house I had seen from the highway. "And where are you going to go, then?" said Beatriz, and I didn't say anything at first, I put the glass on the table and looked at the empty field, the air free of fog, like an engraving of ice. "To Mágina. I'm going to my father's house." Unhurriedly she got to her feet, putting the lighter and the pack of cigarettes in her leather handbag, and when she leaned over her hair suddenly fell to one side of her face. Through the window I saw her walking with long strides over the mud. I got up to order another drink, and when I returned to the table the black car was no longer in the empty field.

2

MANUEL REMEMBERS HE WAS sitting at the kitchen table, looking through the panes in the white doors at the dark morning beginning in the garden and raising a late mist, sourly bristling with rain. Amalia had served him a large cup of lukewarm café con leche that was the dirty color of mud and a slice of unusually white bread that he crumbled slowly over the cup and stirred into the coffee with a spoon. "Eat it all up, Don Manuel, that's real bread," Amalia said, "I bought it on the black market for twelve pesetas." The delight of the white bread, the porcelain cup with blue designs, the silver spoon and the linen napkin on his knees. In those years, he recalls aloud to his nephew Minaya, one gave oneself over to minor tactile pleasures as if they were the unique, hidden happiness that no one could detect or snatch away. He touched the loyal things to which he had always belonged, searching them for the possibility of a narrow escape accessible only to his fingertips, and the presence of the linen, the curved porcelain, the silver flatware, secretly saved him from the unpleasant taste of the coffee at dawn and the smoke from the stove, filled with damp wood, that turned the air in the kitchen gray like an extension of the bad weather and cold fog from which the garden and the city, his own lethargic life, were emerging so slowly. The doorbell rang in the courtyard, and it was still so early that Amalia and Teresa and even Manuel remained motionless, not deciding to open the door and not even acknowledging they had heard it, because at that hour, as it did at night, the sound of the bell always seemed to announce a threat. Amalia stopped moving dishes in the sink, and Manuel, with involuntary caution, went out to the courtyard, making a silent gesture to Teresa so that she wouldn't open the door yet. On the translucent glass of the entrance door, a tall masculine figure was outlined. "Open it," said Manuel, and he went back to the kitchen. A man alone didn't frighten him. He carefully fit the first cigarette of the morning into the holder and prepared to wait and listen, his back to the courtyard and to the voice it took him a little while to recognize. "Don Manuel," said Teresa, "Don Jacinto Solana has come."

He saw him standing in the courtyard as if in the middle of time, returned not exactly from prison but from memory and death and the ten years that had passed since the night in 1937 when he took a train to Madrid. The time of his absence and the mystery of his fate during those years surrounded him in the emptiness like the paving stones and columns of the courtyard and gave his return the sudden quality of an apparition, because he seemed to have come from nowhere, wearier and older but untouched in his pride, his solitude, his ironic way of saying "Manuel," smiling before he embraced him, as if the irony and the smile could maintain the old virtue of eluding the hideous edges of things and he hadn't come from a prison where they had amputated eight years of his life. His hair was gray, cut very close, white at the temples and the badly shaved tips of his whiskers. His voice was more serious, but perhaps it was always that way and Manuel didn't remember it. "But he's the same," he thought, seeing how he took off his hat and placed the cardboard suitcase tied with a rope on the ground to look with his sharp gray eyes at the columns in the courtyard, the gallery, the stained glass of the dome. "The library door to the left," he said, as if reciting a lesson, "to the right the marble staircase with the mirror on the first landing. I liked imagining it all. I set myself the discipline of remembering each thing with absolute exactitude. To the rear the kitchen, and the piano room, and the window shutters painted white that open to the garden." It wasn't his more serious voice, it was the tone, the slowness with which he said the words, as if he didn't care about them or didn't see to whom he was saying them: it was his eyes, Manuel realized later, remote from the smile and the voice and endowed with an expression as dark as his consciousness, as the true nature of his despair. In the kitchen Teresa and Amalia approached reverentially to greet him. "But your hands are frozen, Don Jacinto, come over to the stove, I'll give you breakfast right now." The dirty nails, the sides of his eyeglasses secured with black string, the eyes avidly fixed on the coffee and the piece of bread that Teresa set before him. He wore a heavy overcoat that was big on him, with a belt and buckle and very wide coattails, like the ones worn a few years before the war. He had put his hat on the table but didn't take off his coat or lower the lapels to eat breakfast: he rubbed his large, unfamiliar hands together as he hunched inside his vast overcoat next to the stove, so close to it that the smoke choked him, he drank the coffee holding the cup with both hands and didn't use the napkin to wipe his mouth when he had finished. With the spoon he scooped up the crumbs of bread remaining at the bottom of the cup and only then raised his eyes to Manuel, who smoked and looked at him from the other side of the table, melancholically confirming the indecency of hunger and the ravages of time that had brought them down and reunited them now as brutally as it had divided them: to offer them not the relief of recognition but the certainty of its impossibility. "White bread," Solana said, "I had even forgotten its taste. Do you know the last time I ate it? In March of '39, the day before the Fascists entered Madrid. They threw us white bread from their planes, Manuel." Never, says Manuel, never since he returned to Mágina had he heard him take pleasure in sorrow or recall hatred or lost battles. In his voice, the war, when it did come up, was as distant as everything else, and he never stopped to tell him why at the beginning of June 1937 he left his job at the Ministry of Propaganda to enlist voluntarily in the army or what the circumstances of his arrest had been when the war was over. He knew only that when he was wounded at the Ebro, he was an artillery sergeant, that between January and March 1939 he was in Madrid and saw Orlando, that in 1940 he shared a cell for prisoners condemned to death with Miguel Hernández. When he finished breakfast, he stood and plunged his hands into the pockets of his overcoat, and for an instant Manuel recognized him: it was his old gesture of determination, the secret, sudden way he always had of leaving even though he didn't move. The sun had come out in the garden, and an icy wind beat at the glass and shook the swing under the palm tree. They looked at it at the same time when they heard the creak of the chains that held it down, and perhaps they both saw the same phantom suspended over the white swing, but they didn't talk about Mariana yet. "I've begun to write a book," said Solana, pointing vaguely at his suitcase, where he might be keeping the first drafts. "In prison, like Cervantes," he half-opened his lips to smile and Manuel noticed he was missing several teeth. "It will be called *Beatus Ille.* Do you like the title? It's about Mágina, and all of us, Mariana and you, Orlando, this house. That's why I needed to see it again. In January of '39, when I returned to Madrid, I happened to find out where Orlando lived, and I went to see him. It was a very dark, very large apartment, in Argüelles, an old building with all the windows boarded up, still standing by some miracle, because it was very close to the Ciudad Universitaria front, it was like an island surrounded by rubble. It was hit by a bomb a week later, and I suppose Orlando died buried in the ruins. He wasn't living anymore with that boy who came with him to your wedding and scandalized Utrera and your mother. He had gotten married, and don't ask me why because I don't know. He looked very sick, constantly spitting into a handkerchief stained with blood, shivering with cold on a mattress that looked as if it had been rescued from a garbage dump, because in that apartment there was no bed, no furniture, only bare tiles and frozen radiators. His wife was a nurse, an unsociable type who didn't say a single word while I was there. She stood and watched us from the door to the room, and from time to time she took his temperature and brought him cups of broth that he drank down immediately, as if he were afraid. At first he didn't seem to recognize me. He laughed a great deal, with a laugh as strange as his cough, he made fun of my sergeant's stripes and called me a Communist hero and didn't know or remember anything about the war, as if he didn't care that we were about to lose it. 'I fooled them, Solana,' he said with that miserable laugh of a dying man, 'they wanted to send me to the front and had to declare me unfit. Look there, in those papers on the floor, look for one where it says I'm unfit for military service.' I asked about that picture he had decided to paint when he was in Mágina, you remember, the one he imagined in the country house the day before your wedding. He had decided to call it *Une partie de plaisir* and told all of us it was going to be his masterpiece. He didn't remember it, of course. 'I've retired from painting, Solana. Art and happiness are incompatible.' But on the floor I saw the last things he had painted. They were all watercolors, and the same landscape was repeated in all of them. Mágina's hill above the olive groves, the outline of the city just as we saw it that day from the country house. The watercolors had a beauty that wasn't of this world, it wasn't perfection but something beyond that, something that didn't even belong to art, and even less to the man who had painted them. Then I thought that just one of those landscapes was enough to justify Orlando, and all of us, because we were participants in his brilliance. I remembered with shame all the things I had written, the articles in *El Sol* and in *Octubre,* the ballads in *Mono Azul* and in the war murals, and I realized I had to break with it all and forget it all to write something that would resemble Orlando's watercolors." Abruptly Solana fell silent, still walking up and down past the glass doors to the garden, his head bowed and his hands fiercely thrust into the pockets of his overcoat. He's left again, Manuel thought. As he spoke he slowly had been recovering his gestures, the way he looked and moved his hands, the cold fervor of another time, but now silence returned him to his present form, unfamiliar and a little frightening: the hard, unshaven jaws, the scraped, long nape like a sign of obstinacy or failure, the myopic eyes reddened by sleep that rested on him like two spies when Jacinto Solana took off his glasses to clean the fogged lenses and said what Manuel had foreseen and feared since he saw him in the courtyard: "Tell me how they killed my father."

3

I CALLED TO HIM from the top of the path, but the din of the water overflowing into the irrigation ditch from the cistern kept him from hearing me, and then, instead of going over to him or calling him again, I stayed next to the dead poplar where we had tied the mare when I was a teenager and watched him for a long time before he noticed my arrival, watched him alone and absorbed in his work, as he always had wanted to live. He was squatting, leaning over the edge of the cistern, in the shade of the pomegranate tree, with his straw hat that hid his face from me and the black smock he had always worn buttoned to the neck. I saw his large reddened hands vigorously shaking a bunch of onions in the water to clean the mud from the roots, and when he stood to place the onions in a wicker basket, I finally saw his face with the cigarette end glued to one side of his mouth. From the top of the path the farm descended a slope of meticulously cultivated terraces, with angles as precise as those on a sheet of paper, bounded by irrigation ditches and the fig and pomegranate trees on whose trunks I so often had carved my name with a knife. I walked along the path and stopped halfway down to call him again. He stood slowly, wiped his damp, red hands on the tails of the smock, and carefully put out the cigarette before kissing me twice, as he had always done, but now he was not nearly as tall as me and he had to stand straight to reach my face. "You didn't even write me a damned letter, you bastard." With him I always was paralyzed by an old shyness that wasn't completely separate from the fear I had of him once, when he was a frightening man as big as a tree who told me I'd turn into an idiot from reading so many books. "It's the war, father," I apologized, without his paying attention, "it doesn't leave me time to write to you." "The war?" he said looking around, as if when he didn't see its traces on the peaceful cultivated earth and in the irrigation ditches he might think I was lying to him. "What do you have to do with the war?" I wanted to stand firm, even indict him, say something with the necessary fervor, but when I spoke to him in my own voice, I recognized the same vacuous tone of exaggeration or lies that official communiqués had then. "Here you don't know, or don't want to know, but we're teaching the Fascists a lesson," I concluded. I remember that he sat down, shrugging his shoulders, on the stone bench under the pomegranate tree, and then he looked through the smock, searching for the cigarette he had put out, looking at me as if confirming that after twenty years his suspicion had come true that reading books would turn me into an idiot. "That's what they told us when they sent us to Cuba. That we were going to teach the insurgents a lesson. And now you see, a little more and you wouldn't have been born."

He lived alone on the farm he had plowed himself, in the house he had built with his own hands before I was born: a shed with mangers, a small stall for the pigs, a single room with the fire, the bed, the sacks of seeds, the tools, the earthenware dishes in which he prepared his food with exactly the same pleasure he found in all the chores of solitude, because now, when he's dead, I know he was a man dominated by a fierce will to be alone, and if he left Mágina on July 19, 1936, it wasn't because he was afraid of the war but because the war offered him the excuse he always had wanted to leave the city and escape his tedious dealings with other men. On the afternoon of that July 19, he went out and saw a man running across the Plaza of San Lorenzo, and he stationed himself at one of the corners. The man, a stranger, wore a shirt stained with perspiration and looked at my father with his mouth open, saying something he couldn't understand because immediately afterward a shot was fired in the empty plaza, and the stranger, pushed to the wall as if by a gust of wind, rebounded against it, holding his stomach, and fell to the paving stones dead.

The next morning, without talking to anyone, my father loaded the mare with a mattress, a disassembled metal bed, and the second book of *Rosa María or the Flower of Love,* a serialized novel in three volumes of infinite pages and lugubrious lithographs he had inherited from his father and that very probably he never finished reading. As a boy I had entered those volumes with the exaltation and horror of someone crossing an uninhabited forest at night, and many years later, when I returned to Mágina to attend my mother's funeral, I discovered that in the middle of the second book of *Rosa María or the Flower of Love* my father kept, carefully cut and folded, some of the articles I had begun to publish then in Madrid newspapers. I never told him I had seen them; he never acquiesced and revealed to me, even indirectly, that he read and kept them with a pride stronger than his desire to renounce me, for I had fled Mágina and the future that he himself assigned to me even before I was born, when he dug a well in the living rock and leveled a hillside of barren earth and built the house I didn't want to share or inherit and where he finally spent the last three years of his life inflexibly alone, far from a city and a war he didn't care about, just as he never cared about Alfonso XIII or Primo de Rivera or that vague Republic that had changed the flags on the public buildings and the names of some streets in Mágina. Because I talked about it and defended it, he must have thought the Republic belonged, like Madrid and literature, to the same kind of illusions that had poisoned my imagination ever since I went to school and was irremediably turned into a stranger in his eyes and he could do nothing to get me back.

———

OLD AND SLIGHT in the black smock, but still endowed with a physical strength that had remained intact because it was an attribute of his moral courage, he loaded the basket of onions on his shoulder and carried it up to the house without letting me help him. Piled in the shed were baskets and sacks of damp vegetables that he showed to me with pride. "Look how much I care about that war. When I saw how they killed that man almost at our door, I said to myself, 'Justo, they've finally gone crazy, and this is none of your business.' And so I loaded a few things on the mule, double-locked the house, and came to the farm. I haven't set foot in Mágina since that day. People come here and buy my vegetables, or I trade them for what I need, which is almost nothing because I even make my bread. And you, how do you make a living?" "I have a job at the Ministry of Propaganda." He looked at me in silence, shaking his head with an air of disillusionment I already knew: he, who never asked anyone for anything or obeyed anyone, who never wanted to work except for himself or have anything he hadn't earned with his own hands. "Eating off the government . . . It ought to make you ashamed, Jacinto." But I couldn't explain anything or even defend myself, and not because I knew he wouldn't understand me, but because in that place and at that moment, I myself could not conceive of a reason that would justify me. The usual words, the still sacred words, the pure sensation of joy and rage that still moved us in the spring of 1937 were things as improbable and distant that afternoon as the war in the consciousness of my father: an unknown man killed in the white-hot light of a July siesta, a sound of sirens at midnight confused at times with the whistle of the trains that crossed the valley, a squadron of planes that flew higher than any bird and glittered in the sun before being lost on the other side of the sierra. I had felt it since I passed through the gate in the wall and recognized just beside it the post where when I was a boy I would take the white mare and then start to gallop along the farm road. I had come from Manuel's house and had Mariana's eyes fixed in my memory, but as soon as I left the wall behind and walked on the fine dust of the paths, it was as if I had shed my present form to become, as I walked down to the meeting with my father, the shade of what I had been when those roads and the valley and the blue sierra were the only landscape in my life. I thought that time wasn't successive but immobile, that the regions and boundaries of its geography can be drawn with the precision that the world has in school maps. Like Orlando's watercolors, my father's farm was a region immune to time, and I couldn't go back to it, just as one can't cross a mirror or join the figures in a painting: I could only, if my will didn't intervene, accept the forgetting, the transfiguration, the fear, the impossible tenderness I had felt for so many years before my father, the share of guilt that was mine because of his disillusionment or his old age.

THEN, AS NOW, when I write so uselessly to bring him back to life, gratitude was impossible. In the mild May afternoon, the shadow of the ramparts and Mágina's south wall extended over us, and the air had the damp odor of pomegranate leaves, the cold transparency of water in the irrigation ditches. Before me the terraces of the farm descended to the valley like the stanzas of a successive garden. He was sweeping the packed-down earth of the shed, and he stopped when he reached my side, looking where I was looking, as if he had guessed the temptation that possessed me so suddenly, not like a desire or a purpose, but with the imperious certainty of a pain that wounds us again when we had already forgotten it: "The world ends here; there's nothing on the other side of the sierra, only that sea of shipwrecks and dark cliffs I imagined then, because I had seen it in a print in *Rosa María*." But perhaps I'm trying to correct the past. Now, ten years later, it is shut in this room with circular windows like a fugitive, when I feel the blind, the useless temptation of tearing out my consciousness like Oedipus tore out his eyes so that nothing's left in me but the memory of that orchard and my father: tall, buttoned up, choked by the hard collar and the half boots that creaked in a strange way when he walked down the corridor of the school, because he put them on only to attend funerals, tall and suddenly a coward when he knocked at the door and asked permission without daring to go in before the headmaster stood to receive him. I had just turned eleven, and one night, after giving the animals their last feed and barring the street door, he sat in front of me and moved aside the book I was reading to look into my eyes. "Tomorrow I'm taking you out of school. What you know now is enough." Behind me, next to the fire, my mother was sewing something or simply looking at him, not impassive but defeated beforehand, and even though I would have liked to say something to her or ask her for help, it would have been impossible because weeping choked my voice and everything was very far away behind the mist of tears. "Don't cry, you're not a little boy anymore. Men don't cry." He picked up the oil lamp from the mantle over the fireplace and signaled to my mother. They left me alone, illuminated by the red embers of the fire, my eyes staring at the book and the words that dissolved as if they were written on water. The next day, before dawn, I saddled the white mare and took her to drink at the post at the wall. Dawn was breaking as I rode slowly along the road to the farm. I intended not to stop: I'd continue to the end of the white road, beyond the farms, the olive groves, the river, the distant blue hills that undulated before the first spurs of the sierra. But when I reached the dead poplar, I got down from the mare and left her tied by the bridle, and I sat down in the manger to wait for the full light of day, because I had brought my book bag with my notebooks for school and I wanted to finish an arithmetic exercise, as if that mattered, as if I had before me a placid future of schoolyards and desks and examinations in which, not for love of studying but out of a kind of vengeful obstinacy, I always received the highest grade. That morning, sitting at the desk I shared with Manuel, I let him copy the exercises from my notebook without saying a single word to him, and I didn't play with him or anyone else when we went out to recess.

With their blue aprons and white collars, the others ran shouting after a ball or climbed the bars in the schoolyard, but I wasn't like them. I looked at the large clock on the facade of the school, forever stopped at a quarter past ten, and that stopped hour was more fearsome because it hid the true passage of time, the other invisible hands that brought the moment close when my father, after selling the last produce and closing his stall at the market, would put on his hard collar and suit and boots for funerals to inform the headmaster that I, his son, Jacinto Solana, would not return to school because now I was a man and he needed me to work on his land until the end of my life. But when at last he arrived and we went into the headmaster's office together, I saw him infinitely docile, lost, vulnerable, murmuring "With your permission?" in a voice I had never heard from him. He nodded, murmured things, and held his hat in his two large hands that I suddenly imagined as useless, keeping himself erect with difficulty on the edge of the chair where he had dared to sit only when the headmaster indicated it to him, and then I felt the need to defend him or to squeeze his hand and walk with him the way I had when I was little and I went with him to sell milk to the houses in Mágina. "But you don't know the foolish mistake you're about to make, my friend": defend him from the headmaster and his bland smile and his words that acquired the same hostile quality from the oak desk where he rested his hands and from the portrait of Alfonso XIII he had hung above his head. "I must tell you that your son is the best student we have in the school. I predict a magnificent future for him, whether he leans toward the sciences or the arts, both of them paths for which nature has endowed him with exceptional qualities. No, it isn't necessary for you to tell me so: agriculture is a very worthy profession, and a great source of wealth for the nation, but young heads like that of your son are called to a destiny, if not worthier then of a higher and greater responsibility." He paused to catch his breath and rose decisively to his feet, resting his soft, small hands on my shoulders with a gesture in which, after so many years, I suspect a vague allegorical intention. "Your son, my friend, should continue under the care of his teachers. Who can say that we do not have before us a future engineer, an eminent physician, or, if I am pressed, a statesman of impassioned oratory? Very great men have come from humble homes. For example, Don Santiago Ramón y Cajal." After an hour, when we left the headmaster's office, we walked in silence down a very long corridor to the door of my classroom. Above the vague sound coming from the rooms that lined the hall I listened to my father's footsteps and the uncomfortable creak of his boots, and I recalled his voice finally saying the words I hadn't even dared to wish for—"Well, if you say so, I'll leave him here, even though I need him, and we'll see if he gets to be a useful man some day"—but I found in them not the temporary salvation they seemed to promise but a dark guilt more certain than gratitude: the consciousness of a debt that perhaps I didn't deserve, that I never would repay. Before he left, my father bent down to give me a kiss, smiling at me in a way that wounded me because it was the smile of a man I no longer knew. "Go on, go back to your class, and don't play around when you get out, you have to bring my lunch to the farm." He turned to wave good-bye in the last light in the hall, and when I went into the classroom and Manuel moved to one side to give me room at the desk, I covered my face with my hands so he wouldn't know I had been crying.

As if brought in by the immense shadow of the wall, at the top of which they were turning on the distant lights of the watchtower, night had fallen over the farm and the valley—very slow, perfumed and blue and deep, like the gleam of motionless water in the irrigation ditches. He took the oil lamp from the house and hung it on one of the beams in the shed. On nights like this he cooked supper on a fire outdoors. Outside the circle of that light, which shone before the house like the flames of stubble burned on summer nights, there was the darkness of a waveless ocean, of black hills and trees like ghosts or statues. But he didn't fear the darkness or the uninhabitable silence. He cleaned the fireplace of ashes, trimmed the light, stood with an agility that disconcerted me to show me where the pan and oil were. In a tower in the city the bells had struck ten. "I have to go now, Father." He stood still, next to the fire, shook his head with an air of melancholy or exhausted disillusionment. "All the time it's been that you don't come to see me and you don't even stay for supper. Where are you staying in Mágina?" "In my friend Manuel's house. He's getting married the day after tomorrow. He asked me to invite you." "Well you tell him thank you and say your father's sick. I'm not going up to Mágina until all of you end that war." When we said good-bye he kissed me without looking at me and turned immediately to stir the fire that was going out. From the road to Mágina I saw him absorbed, sitting back, alone in the light of the fire as if he were on an island, angrily alone against the darkness and surrender. I imagined him putting out the fire when he finished supper, going into the house with the lamp in his hand, acknowledging the semi-darkness and the order he had chosen. He would hang the lamp at the head of the bed, and lying on it he would open the second volume of *Rosa María or the Flower of Love,* which was a book longer than his patience and his own life, finding perhaps the old clippings that were now as yellow as the pages of the novel. But he never told anyone he knew how to read and write: it was important to him not to leave traces of his presence in the world, and in writing, as in photographs, he suspected a trap he always tried to avoid, the invisible snare laid by fingerprints.

The road to Mágina gleamed like moondust in the dark. I reached the gate in the wall and walked alone down the paved lanes toward Manuel's house, but the impulse that led me wasn't my will: it was desire pushing me, the warm, recovered despair of knowing that Mariana's eyes would receive me.

4

TENSE AND SERENE, in the center of the photographs and in Orlando's drawing and in the essence of a plural memory that became one when interwoven in her, like men's glances at a girl walking alone between the tables in a café: firm in her unknown desire, in the certainty of the fascination she exercised, and in the slight tilt of her hat with a veil that concealed her eyes and reached just to the middle of her nose and cheeks. Solana on one side, and on the other Manuel, both welcomed by her, who had taken the arm of each in order not to lose them in the crowd that filled the Puerta del Sol and held herself up between their twofold and denied tenderness with a grace as indifferent as the profile of a tightrope walker who does not look at the slender cord or the pit or the dizzying emptiness over which his feet move forward. "But when that photo was taken Manuel wasn't in love with her yet," Medina explained. "Or he didn't know it and had only a few hours to find out." With the years she had stopped being a single face and a single woman to become what had perhaps always been her destiny, not interrupted but consummated by her death: a catalogue of glances and recollections fixed at times by a photograph or a drawing, profiles on coins incessantly lost and recovered and spent by the covetousness of hatred or remembrance, coins of ash. Voices: hers, unimaginable to Minaya, a little dark, according to Solana's words, the other voices that continued naming her when she was already dead, in solitude, before mirrors, saying her name into the pillows of insomnia, repeating for her sake the three syllables into which defamation continued to be condensed with no less fervor than remorse or desire.

"Born of the water," said a jovial Medina, laughing, as he usually did, with his mouth closed, "she appeared walking in her white high heels on the pavements of Madrid, next to Solana, risen from the water or from that crowd, the largest and most inspiring Manuel had seen in all the days of his life, celebrating the triumph of the Popular Front and shouting, demanding amnesty and a new government in the same plaza where they had heard the Republic proclaimed. You've read books, I suppose, you've seen photographs, but you can't know what happened then. On Sunday, election day, I had been with Manuel, here, in Mágina, and when we realized we were going to win, he said to me in a fit of daring, 'I'm going to Madrid tonight.' That was February 16, and a month later Manuel was going to marry his lifelong sweetheart, Señorita de López Cabaña, whom I called de López Carabaña, because she was as exciting as a bottle of Carabaña mineral water. The trousseau was already on display in the house of the bride-to-be, which was the custom back then, and almost every night Manuel had a visit from the tailor who was making his cutaway coat. That's why I mentioned daring to you: instead of going to the house of Señorita López Carabaña, who that afternoon, I imagine, after virtuously voting for Gil Robles, would be saying a rosary for the victory of the right wing with her mother and her infinite Carabaña sisters, Manuel held me by the arm so I wouldn't leave him alone and took me into the presence of Doña Elvira, to whom he communicated with all the solemnity the wine allowed, because we had been drinking in the worst taverns in Mágina, that it was urgent he go to Madrid to settle some piece of family business. His mother didn't say anything but kept looking at me as if I were the one responsible for this reckless escapade of Manuel's. I suppose she feared something, but neither she, nor I, nor anyone, could imagine what would happen five days later, when Manuel returned from Madrid with a certain photograph in his pocket and went to Señorita López Carabaña's house to tell the poor martyr and her mother and sisters, more Carabañas than ever, that he considered his engagement canceled, provoking a bereavement of Carabaña tears that lasted until 1941, when the young lady in question again became engaged to a former captain in the Regular Army who now manages the family oil factory."

First came the photograph, recounts Medina, the vague snapshot taken on the Carrera de San Jerónimo by a street photographer who caught Mariana's laughter and the passage of her white high heels, but also, as a witness, the distracted gesture of Jacinto Solana, the way in which Manuel turned his head very slightly to look at her without her noticing, her two hands resting on their arms with the kind of impartiality that cannot always be distinguished from indifference. Manuel opened his leather wallet and showed Medina the photograph as if it were a valuable secret document. "Her name is Mariana. She models at the School of Fine Arts. Jacinto met her three years ago, in Orlando's studio." Medina examined the photograph and then looked attentively at Manuel, as if he wanted to confirm a doubtful resemblance. "But he was a different man," he recalls, with theatrical exaggeration, passing his hand over his own face, "and I wouldn't have been able to say how he had changed, but he had the same expression Saint Paul must have had the day after he fell off his horse. Love, I imagine, that thing that should have dazzled him when he was sixteen and left him immune, but not at the age of thirty-two, because then there was no way to defend against it or to avoid his walking around with that photograph in his pocket like the lock of hair of a medieval damsel." Manuel delicately put the photograph back in his wallet and questioned Medina. "Insufficient, Manuel. I'm referring to the photo. But the proofs of miracles always are, aren't they?" Manuel took Medina's irony as an insult, but that didn't stop him from talking about Mariana: her large almond eyes, her laugh, her wavy chestnut hair, which she combed, he stated precisely, with the part on the left, her way of looking at him and talking to him as if they had always known each other: her name, which he repeated even when there was no need to for the sheer pleasure of pronouncing the three syllables that referred to her. "I can't understand how there can be other women in the world named Mariana," he said once to Medina, for he understood that Mariana wasn't a name given to someone arbitrarily at birth but a word as definitively and exactly connected to her as the moon was to the word *moon*. They came, then, like secret emissaries, the photograph and the name, and only a year later Mariana herself, like a silent, attentive nurse to Manuel, who was convalescing from the wound that had left him close to death on the Guadalajara front, but long before Mágina and Mágina's pride finally met that woman who from so far away and without even setting foot in the city had insulted them, in their closed houses, in the salons where they so cautiously tuned in at night to the stations of the other faction to hear the voice of Queipo de Llano and the anthems that would not be played publicly for another three years along the conquered streets of Mágina, persistent voices repeating her name and Manuel's and enumerating the details of their insolence, their undoubted madness, with the same rancor they used to tell one another the bad news of another church burned or another execution at the cemetery walls. Very soon they ignored her name to call her only "the militia woman" or "the Red": they said she had danced nude in a cabaret in Madrid, and then, when the war began, a relative of the Señoritas López Cabaña stated with certainty that he had seen her marching with a musket, cartridge belt, blue coverall, and militiaman's beret worn at a slant down the Calle de Alcalá, along with Manuel and Jacinto Solana. But the part of the story they preferred to tell, perhaps because it was the first part they had known, or because they found in it a certain dramatic quality, was the moment when Manuel appeared at the house of Señorita López Cabaña, treacherously carrying a bouquet of violets, and, after asking her mother and sisters to leave him alone with his fiancée—this added bit of drama was, of course, false, but it had a symbolic value no one wished to disparage—he sat down beside her, offered her the violets with the impeccable smile of an impostor, said in a quiet voice, looking perhaps at his own hands holding his hat on his knees: "María Teresa, our relationship has to end, and it's going to end right now."

In his early adolescence, Minaya had heard that scene intact and with those exact words, their bland harshness born not of reality but of certain worldly plays by Benavente; now, as he listened to Medina's narrative, he understood perhaps that they weren't a slander, that the lie and added details were the ironic attributes of truth. "But Manuel didn't care about anything," Medina said. "At first it didn't even occur to him to think of the possibility that Mariana might love him. I think her mere existence was enough to make him happy. She was a goddess, you know, and goddesses don't fall in love with you. Perhaps they smile at you from their pedestal, permit you to look at their photograph as if it were a statue, touch your hand distractedly in the café, offer you a cigarette stained with lipstick. The old school, my friend. I don't know why I have the impression that you belong to it too. And so Manuel, when he left the inconsolable Señorita López Carabaña, which made me infinitely happy, didn't do it because he was ready to marry Mariana: you don't ask for Aphrodite's hand in marriage when you see her emerge from the water, preferably nude, as on the pornographic postcards of my youth. It's just that one day early in July, without his even knowing how he dared to do it, Manuel took her hand on a tree-lined walk in the Retiro when no one else was around and told her all at once everything that had not let him live or sleep over the past few months, and she, instead of laughing, stood looking at him as if she didn't completely understand what he was saying, and responded that yes, she too, ever since that day in February when Solana introduced them. And now their only problem wasn't how to tell Doña Elvira but Jacinto

Solana, whom they were going to see in an hour, because they both knew, and would rather have died than confess it to each other, that Solana had been in love with her for three years."

Medina saw him arrive, pale and still in uniform, recently discharged from the military hospital where Mariana had been with him for the past few months, during the nights of agony and fever when pain made worse by nightmares so frequently made him feel submerged in death, with no other hold on lucidity and life than the hand that held his and wiped his forehead and caressed his unshaven face in dreams. Mariana's face dissolved into sphinxlike animals, into faces of doctors who bent over him from an infinite height, into shadows without bodies to contain them, into a tranquil light similar to the light of dawn that gradually took on again the shape and features of Mariana. Once—he couldn't remember when because in the hospital the measurement of time disintegrated and lengthened like the faces in nightmares—he awoke and Mariana wasn't alone, but it wasn't a doctor who was with her. Rising blindly from the darkness and the mire of sheets soaked in cold sweat in order not to lose an extremely slender possibility of consciousness, he recognized a voice saying something to her, her forgotten name perhaps, a fine-drawn face and the flash of eyeglasses, and before he passed out again he knew who it was and said "Solana," immediately returning to a suffocating dream in which he continued to hear her voice, their voices, as if he were already dead and they were talking beside his coffin. But on the day he finally awoke, free of the slime of dreams, Mariana was alone at the head of his bed, wearing a white blouse and a blue ribbon in her chestnut hair, smiling at him, overcome by happiness. This is how Medina saw her, in Mágina, a week later, sitting beside Manuel at the round table in the garden, and he immediately thought she wasn't the kind of woman he had imagined from looking at the photograph, and even less the one Mágina had predicted and feared. "You're Medina, aren't you?" she said to him as she stood, shaking his hand with an absolutely masculine gesture, with the immediate fondness certain women feel for the friends of the man they love. "Manuel and Solana have talked a great deal about you." The fine skin, translucent at the temples, the green or gray eyes, the short chin, the nose like an attentive bird's that Orlando had drawn with so much delicacy. It was a very warm morning in April, and Mariana had her white blouse unbuttoned down to the top of her breasts.

"And so that was Mariana," said Medina, shaking his head as if he still felt the astonishment of that distant morning. "If you were to see her, you wouldn't recognize her, because she didn't resemble the Madrid photograph at all, or even the one they took on their wedding day. Only Orlando's drawing is more or less faithful to reality. But the dead immediately stop resembling their photographs. I estimate that Mariana must have been twenty-seven or twenty-eight at the time, but she didn't look it at all: her body was a little like that girl's, Inés, but she didn't have Inés' serious walk or that reserve you can see in Inés' eyes when you look at her. Mariana's glance was absolutely transparent, which always made me uneasy for some reason I never could fathom. It was as if her eyes were asking for something, as if they were empty, as if just by looking at her, you saw her naked. When I met her here that day, I thought she resembled Hedy Lamarr a little. Back then I liked women like Jean Harlow."

It was there in the garden, at the beginning of May, when they decided to write to Solana, and Medina knew they had torn up a good number of drafts at the round metal table painted white before they found the exact words, the circumspect and earnest and cowardly words of invitation, written in Manuel's English hand, that Solana read in his house in Madrid, swearing to himself there would be no truce, that he would never agree to smile and accept and be a witness to the culmination of his failure, and then tearing up the letter with meticulous rage not toward Manuel or Mariana but toward himself, promising the empty wall, the pieces of paper he still held in his hands, that on May 20, 1937, he would not be in Mágina.

5

I OPEN MY EYES but still cannot see or remember anything. On my stomach, face against the sheet, hands tensely grasping the bars at the head of the bed, I touch the cold metal and recognize its moldings as if I were recognizing and touching the limits of the body that slowly is becoming mine. In the first darkness that my eyes have encountered, areas of dim light are taking shape, the light patch of the curtains, the form of the door, the window, circular like an eye that had been spying on me as I slept, fixed on me and on the plaza that the sound of water falling over the rim of the fountain brings now to my memory, adding it to the world. It seems as if when I awoke, I had suddenly started the clock on the night table: pale green in the semidarkness, luminous face and hands indicating an hour vaguely suspended between four and five in the morning. I brush the wall with my fingers, behind the bars at the head of the bed, searching for the light switch, but it's useless because they cut off the light at eleven. On the night table, next to the alarm clock, I always keep the candlestick, cigarettes, a box of matches, paper, a pen. Sometimes I wake because of an intuition that seemed memorable in my dreams but crumbles into nothing when I try to write it down. I dream I'm writing a definitive and perfect page, that there isn't enough paper or I can't find enough to receive all the words that continue flowing and spilling out and getting lost and disappearing in the air while I look for a single blank page, a piece of paper, a smooth surface where I can write them down and save them from my dream. I write, and the ink disappears into large blue stains on suddenly liquid paper, I trace signs with a knife on the damp stone of a wall that is the one in any of the cells where I've awakened for the past eight years and the steel point breaks without penetrating that hard material. I want to write, but I've forgotten how, and I'm alone in front of the desk where I sat in school. I dream insomnia, fear, the blank page. I fumble and light the candle: a point of light that ascends, when it seemed extinguished, a pointed yellow tongue that illuminates the clock, the night table, my own hands rolling a cigarette because I know I won't get back to sleep. I carry the candlestick to the table, arrange around me the inkwell, the pen, cigarette papers, blank pages in a pile, the ashtray. I draw a long line on the unmarked paper and look at it as if it were the writing of a language I don't know.

"Why don't you write a real book," my father would say, "a novel like *Rosa María*, so I can read it." One book that would have the mysterious appearance that all the books of my childhood had: a dense, necessary object, a volume made weighty by the geometry of the words and the materiality of the paper, its hard angles and covers worn by longstanding dealings with the imagination and with hands. Perhaps now I'm not writing for myself or to save a forbidden memory; obscurely I'm being led by the desire to plan and create a book in the way a potter models a clay jar, so that his dead man's hands can touch it and his eyes blinded by the final fear and stupefaction of a fate that wasn't his can read it and revive it. They tell me, Manuel says, that nobody knows why they killed him, but that is a pious or cowardly way of not saying that they killed him because he was my father. They were probably afraid that I had managed to escape; they may have calculated that a single death was not enough to exhaust my punishment or my guilt. I know, they've told me, that on the second or third day of April 1939, they saw him come to the Plaza of San Lorenzo just as he had left it three years earlier. He tied the mare's bridle to the grillwork at the window, opened the door with the large metal key, unloaded the mattress and the disassembled bed and asked a neighbor who had won the war, shaking his head pensively when he was told. For several days he didn't leave the house. He listened to the radio until very late at night, watched the plaza through the shutters at a balcony, and when someone knocked at the door, he hurried to answer it, breaking an old habit.

On the fourth day a van painted black drove to the plaza and stopped under the poplars, directly in front of the house. With a clamor of violently slammed doors and military boots five men in blue shirts and red berets got out. Inside the van, next to the driver, sat a man in civilian clothes who made affirmative gestures to the others indicating the door that was still closed. When he opened to see who was knocking they pushed the barrel of a pistol into his chest, forcing him back inside, shouting at him to keep his hands at the back of his neck. "Are you Justo Solana?" said one, the man who had first pointed the gun at him. Hitting him with the butts of their pistols, they pushed him out to the street, until he was close to the window through which the man in civilian clothes was looking. He stood there for a time, motionless, surrounded by pistols, his hands clasped at the back of his neck, and finally the man in civilian clothes, who had lowered the window to look at him more carefully, said, "That's him. I recognized him right away," and the others, as if obeying an order, hit him with the butts of their pistols and forced him into the van and then jumped in after him still pointing their guns at the closed windows of the plaza, which opened again very quietly only when the sound of the engine had disappeared down the narrow lanes.

I've seen the place where they took him. A convent, abandoned now, that during the war was a storage depot and barracks for the Anarchist militias, on one of those treeless little plazas that one sometimes finds unexpectedly at the end of a street in Mágina. In 1939 they whitewashed the facade of the convent to cover the large red letters painted on it, but the years and the rain have delicately dissolved the whitewash and now the initials, the condemned words can be made out again. F.A.I., he must have read on the facade when they made him get out of the van. PRAISE DURRUTI, but undoubtedly he didn't know who Durruti was or the meaning of the Anarchist initials furiously scrawled in red brushstrokes. They were only a part of the war that had trapped him in the end, as indecipherable as the war itself and the faces of the men who pushed him and the reason they gave for arresting him. The cellars, the chapel, the cells of the friars were filled with prisoners, and they had stretched barbed wire between the columns in the courtyard to hold the ones who couldn't fit into the cells. From the street one could see a cloud of dark faces adhering to the gratings at the windows, eyes and hands clutching at the bars or emerging from the semidarkness like strange animals or tree branches stretching in vain to reach the light. There was also, I suppose, in the upper corridors, where one could hardly hear the noise of pounding heels and orders and the engines of trucks filled with prisoners that stopped on the plaza, the busy sound of papers and typewriters, fans, perhaps, lists of names endlessly repeated on carbon paper and confirmed by someone who ran a pencil down the margin and stopped from time to time to correct a name or make a brief mark beside it.

I know that every day at dusk, a string of donkeys loaded down with cauliflower leaves came to the convent. They emptied the panniers at the entrance, and a gang of prisoners watched over by Moroccan guards gathered the fodder in big armloads and threw it over the barbed wire to the others in the courtyard. The large leaves of a green between blue and gray spilled into the outstretched hands of the prisoners, who fought to get them and tore them apart and then bit greedily into the ribs, sucking at the sticky, bitter juice. He didn't eat. He didn't want to humiliate himself among the groups of men who fought over a leaf of cow fodder and crawled on all fours around the feet of the others searching for a trampled leftover that had gone unnoticed. After eating those leaves that crinkled like wrapping paper and left a dirty, wet, green stain around their mouths, some prisoners, perhaps the ones who had fought most savagely to get them, writhed on the tiles and vomited and clutched at their bellies and the next day were dead and swollen in the middle of the court-yard or in a corner of a cell. Silent and alone, he looked at the un-known faces and strange things happening around him and thought that this, after all, was war, the same cruelty and disorder he had known in his youth when they sent him to Cuba. Sometimes, at midnight, he heard a truck shaking to a stop at the door to the con-vent. Then silence was suddenly imposed on the murmur of bodies crowded together in the dark, and all eyes remained fixed on the air, never on the faces of others, because looking at another man meant seeing a prefiguration of being called, of death. The sound of the truck was followed by the noise of locks and the pounding of boots along the corridors. Between two columns in the courtyard, at the doorway to a cell, a group of uniformed figures came to a halt and one of them, shining a flashlight on the typed list he held in his other hand, read the names slowly, stumbling sometimes over the pronun-ciation of a difficult last name.

One night they called his. His bones were swollen with damp-ness, and he had a disagreeable taste of ashes in his mouth. Two guards picked him up from the floor and tied his hands behind him with a wire. He thought about me, about whom no one had heard anything for two years, about his closed house, about his land lying solitary in the night. They made him climb into the body of the truck and tied him to the back of a chair beside a man whose head hung low and who shuddered in his bonds with silent, continual weeping. They had nailed a double row of rush chairs to the boards of the truck, and the men tied to the backs remained lined up and rigid, as if they were attending their own wake, solemnly moving back and forth on the curves of the streets and bouncing up and down, shaken, when the truck left the last lit corners behind and drove onto a dirt road in the barren lands to the north of the city. He smelled the limitless odor of the air and the empty fields in the night that the headlights cut through looking for the road to the cemetery. The truck finally drove between dark cypresses, and when it reached the iron gate, it turned left and continued down a narrow path that ran the length of the low, whitewashed walls. Someone shouted to the driver to stop, and the truck drove in reverse until it stopped in front of a section of wall where the whitewash was pockmarked with bullet holes. Two soldiers were untying the ropes that secured them to the chairs and then pushing them until they jumped out of the truck. They lined them up in front of the wall, lit by the yellow headlights that lengthened their shadows on the turned over, stained ground. Long before the sound of the bolts on the rifles and the single detonation that he didn't hear, he had stopped being afraid because he knew he was on the other side of death: death was that yellow light blinding him, it was the shadow that began behind it and took on the shape of the nearby olive trees and the men hiding in them or confused with them who raised their rifles and remained motionless for an endless time, as if they were never going to move or shoot. Not the pain of the void or the vertigo of falling with tied hands to the ground or onto another body but a sudden sensation of lucidity and abandonment and the raw taste of blood in his mouth that was closed against the dark.

I light a cigarette in the candle that I put out slowly when I exhale the smoke. The smoke is blue and gray and hangs in the air like the gray light out of which emerge the room painted white, the unmade bed, the blue plaza beneath the roofs, the acacias. Smoking, motionless next to the glass, beyond the circular windows, as if in a cabin on a ship, I see the Mágina dawn, as if day were dawning in a city where I am dead too.

6

"AND NOW HE'S LYING DOWN in the room," Manuel thought, "with the shutters closed, his eyes closed, his hands folded over the buckle of that absurd coat that smells of the train and that he hasn't taken off because he's trembling with cold even though Teresa lit the fire that faces his bed, his hands folded, his fingers interlaced over the coat, his thumbs rhythmically tapping each other, as if he were marking shapeless, limitless time with no precise destination, just as one marks the beats of one's heart or the drip of water falling at night from a half-closed tap. He heard me when I went in and he pretended he was sleeping, or perhaps he really was sleeping and his sleep resembles an exhausted insomnia as he lies on the bed, dressed, his unopened suitcase in the middle of the room, his shoes with the laces untied dirtying the edge of the bedspread with mud, and that smell of rough blankets and cold dawn that I had forgotten." Even before his mother came into the dining room, examining everything in a single glance as she searched for some sign that would proclaim the arrival of her guest and enemy, Manuel knew that Solana's presence in the house would weigh on the predictable silence in which supper would take place, even if his name weren't spoken, for Doña Elvira had always known how to use silence as an accusation and an insult, and Solana was one of the names she never pronounced, obeying a fierce standard of pride inculcated in her in her youth.

When she finally appeared in the doorway of the dining room, flanked by Amalia as if she were an ancient lady-in-waiting, Manuel and Utrera stood at the same time, but it was Utrera who hurried to pull out the chair reserved for her at the head of the table, holding the back while Doña Elvira sat down, bowing too deeply, like a hotel waiter. In those years, Medina said then, Utrera seemed determined to maintain a certain air of a cinematic hotel receptionist, always solicitous, somewhat South American, slightly oily, with his pinstriped suits, hair stiffly waved with pomade, and the very thin black mustache that exaggerated his smile, the soft line of his mouth.

"Señora," he said, as Doña Elvira opened her napkin and placed it on her lap, looking without expression at the other side of the table but also, very much out of the corner of her eye, at Manuel, who was sitting to her left, "I have no words to thank you for accepting my invitation tonight. With your permission, I shall tell Amalia to begin serving supper." The municipal council of a nearby town had commissioned a very large allegory of Victory, and since, like the painters of the Renaissance, he was paid according to the number of figures, he had invited Manuel and his mother to a supper that he himself classified as special. After requesting permission from Manuel, who shrugged, Amalia had agreed to serve supper on the silver table service, and to place on the table the two bronze candelabra that normally were on the sideboard and were a partial testimony to the time when Manuel's father was still alive and gala suppers were held in the house, like the one attended by Alfonso XIII and General Primo de Rivera. In the light of the candelabra, the dining room and the three figures gathered around the table that was too large had the melancholy appearance of an unfortunate simulacrum. As he had done at the formal suppers of his adolescence, Manuel looked obsessively at his shirtcuffs and the hands that held his fork and knife, sometimes lifting his head to agree with what Utrera was saying, with his solicitude and his smile, distant, like the gestures of an actor who has been left alone on stage and attempts to move the audience in a half-empty hall. He noticed, suddenly, that Teresa had left the dining room and had not returned, and a sideways glance at his mother let him know that she too had noticed the girl's absence. "Teresa," said Doña Elvira, interrupting something Utrera was telling her. Amalia took a step and approached her but looked at Manuel as if asking for a sign. "Yes, Señora?" Doña Elvira slowly placed the knife and fork on the tablecloth and spoke, barely separating her lips. "I didn't call you. Isn't Teresa here?" Amalia was still looking at Manuel, nervously smoothing the edge of her white apron with her fingers. "She'll be right back, Señora." It was then that Manuel spoke, understanding, accepting the trap that had been laid, daring to look in his mother's eyes just as he had looked in them on the day he told her he was going to marry Mariana, imitating without realizing it their blue fixity, stripped of any desire to explain or defy. "Teresa has gone up to take Solana his supper."

She had heard the bell from her bedroom, sensing in its long ring a danger she couldn't specify, because she didn't recognize the voice of the person who had just arrived, but as soon as she heard the street door closing she rang the bell imperiously for Amalia to come up, and she asked and found out, while the maid helped her dress, that the old threat had never died but had only been incubating for ten years, ready to return at any time from a future she had always feared and that was being realized now as inevitably as the coming of autumn or old age. "So they didn't kill him in the war or after the war," she said, "they condemned him to death and pardoned him, and now he's left prison to come to my house." "I heard him say he'd be leaving soon," said Amalia, behind her, placing the embroidered peignoir over her shoulders. "It doesn't matter if he stays or leaves today. He came, and my son has seen him. The harm has already been done." But she asked every morning if he had left, not saying his name, alluding with a movement of her head to the part of the house where the outsider was staying, and every day during the first week she received the same reply, which didn't explain anything, because no one, not even Manuel, knew Solana's intention. They told her he probably was sick, because he coughed and his hands trembled and he almost never left the room or got out of bed, and when Teresa brought him a meal and left it on the night table he acted as if he hadn't seen her, but then, as soon as the girl left the room, he sat up and ate without taking off his coat or using the cutlery or the napkin, stopping abruptly if he heard a noise outside his door, as if he were ashamed to let anyone discover how hungry he was. "He still hasn't opened his suitcase," said Amalia on the morning of the fourth day, "and he hasn't even untied the rope he had around it, or moved it from the spot where he left it when he came." The untouched suitcase, the overcoat, the empty closet, even the attitude of Manuel, whom they rarely saw talking to Solana, were gradually being established as signs of an immediate departure, a respite, at least, because as the days passed the presence of the outsider seemed to dissolve without anything taking place. Doña Elvira never crossed paths with him in the dining room, as she had feared, and she didn't see him in the courtyard or the hallway in the gallery. But it was enough for her to know he was near her, in the house, in the same room he had occupied in 1937, to imagine him alone, waiting for something, poisoned by a purpose that she would discover only when it was too late to put an end to his evil spell. "Just like it was before," she said to Utrera, "when my simpleminded son would bring him here for a snack and do everything to keep me from knowing. But the smell of the rubber in his espadrilles was left in the library."

They ate alone, Doña Elvira and Utrera, because Manuel had stopped coming to the dining room and spent his time in the pigeon loft, in the upper rooms, occupied, as they learned from Teresa, in supervising the work of the masons he had hired to restore the roof. He chose the huge room with the circular windows, which for thirty years had been a storeroom for old furniture and religious paintings stowed against the walls, and chests like tombs where solemn ballroom dresses were kept and carnival costumes that hadn't been worn since the turn of the century. The masons moved everything to an attic, sealed the rat holes, and painted the ceiling and walls of the room white, as well as the shutters at the two windows. With the help of Teresa, to whom he had suggested that she say nothing, not even to her Aunt Amalia, Manuel had the wooden floor cleaned until its former chestnut color was restored and he arranged the new furniture in the room so thoughtfully that Teresa suspected he intended to move into it himself. A bed with a thick mattress and clean sheets and blankets that had never been used, facing the two circular windows that were oriented to the southeast so they would receive the first light of day, an oak desk between the two windows, its Isabelline moldings newly varnished, a shining Underwood, an English fountain pen and an inkwell and a packet of blank sheets carefully arranged in the top drawer, and on the wall, above the desk, a darkened, Arcadian eighteenth-century landscape depicting the ocher outskirts of a city and a long gondola crossing the waters of the lagoon of Venice. But if Manuel was going to banish himself to that room where the other voices in the house didn't reach, it would not be only to sleep, Teresa thought: it was as if he had decided to prepare everything and definitively cut himself off from the world, because he hung a curtain across one end and behind it he placed a small kerosene stove and a locker with dishes and cutlery for one person, sausages, canned goods, bottles of wine that the two of them brought up more or less secretly from the wine cellar, and even a pack of candles to illuminate the room when the electricity was cut off every night at eleven. By the light of one of the candles, on the night of the fifth day after Solana's arrival, Manuel and Teresa checked all the things one by one as if they were inspecting the staterooms and pantries of a ship that was about to sail, and Manuel, exhausted, because he hadn't stopped working since dawn, lit a cigarette and sat in front of the typewriter, brushing the keyboard with the tip of his index finger, not daring to strike the grouped, identical letters, only feeling their brief metal touch like a possibility of interminable words. Then he remembered something Jacinto Solana had told him in a very old letter: words, literature, are not in the consciousness of the person who writes but in his fingers and the paper and the typewriter, just like the statues of Michelangelo were in the block of marble where they were revealed.

The next morning, when Teresa came into Solana's bedroom with the breakfast tray, she found him standing in front of the mirror, fastening the belt of the coat that he may not have taken off the night either before when he slept. "He said he's leaving today," she hurried to tell Manuel when she went back to the kitchen, and a few minutes later Amalia was already repeating the news to Doña Elvira, who showed no sign of relief when she heard it. "I saw him in the hallway in the gallery," Amalia said, "with his hat on and his suitcase in his hand. I didn't hear him cough, and he's not as pale as he was when he came." He went down the hallway in the way he had walked since leaving prison, slowly and very close to the wall, as if he wanted to take shelter in it, fatigued, tenacious, one hand in the pocket of his overcoat and the other clutching the suitcase with contracted knuckles that jutted out of his dirty sleeve, and it wasn't the odor of prison and of trains or the weariness of his shoulders that pointed to his future of bad weather and stations with no destination, but that pallid gesture of his hand that held the suitcase as if it were an accepted and necessary attribute of his condition, like the brief tie, the dark shirt collar, the overcoat that belonged to another time and another man who perhaps was still in prison. He walked with his head bowed, looking through the glass in the gallery at the amber light descending to the courtyard, but he never went down the stairs because Manuel was waiting for him and didn't seem to hear him when he said he was leaving. "Come. I want to show you something." "I'm in a hurry, Manuel. They told me a train to Madrid comes through at eleven." Manuel took his suitcase from him and had him go up with him to a part of the house that Solana had never visited: dark staircases, empty salons with mirrors on the walls and pale painted wreaths in the corners of the ceilings, vaulted glass niches where the staring eyes gleamed of saints modeled in wax with ringlets of human hair. Finally they came to the first door in a hallway whose other end was lost in darkness, and when Manuel opened the door, it was as if the daylight were spilling violently over them. The desk between the two windows, the high typewriter that sparkled gold and black and metallic in the icy sun of the January morning, the white walls that still smelled faintly of paint, the air full of a fragrance of clean sheets and varnish that repeated in Solana's memory the distant invitation he took as an offense the first time Manuel had him go into the library, standing in the doorway, just as he did now, so that he would enter only in the glare of delight. He took a few steps, as he had then, not daring to go all the way in, he stood still before the typewriter, before the light from the circular windows, picking up the pen and then putting it down carefully, as if he were afraid to damage it with his hard, clumsy hands, and it may have been when he saw the pack of black tobacco and the cigarette papers that he definitely realized that the room and the typewriter and the bed with its white sheets had been prepared for him, because Manuel smoked only light tobacco. "You know I can't accept, Manuel. You know I'd never be able to repay you," he said, looking at all the untouched offerings, and he made a brusque movement as if to leave and renounce them while it was still possible not to surrender to temptation, but Manuel remained in front of the door, blocking his way. "Write your book here. In the top drawer of the desk you have all the paper you'll need. I'll make certain nobody bothers you." He put the key on the desk and went out, closing the door very slowly. He heard Solana's footsteps, silence, then the bedsprings, and again silence and footsteps on the parquet, the typewriter, sounding as if an index finger were hitting over and over again the same letter chosen at random and repeated with tireless fury on the paper, on the black, empty roller.

7

WHEN SHE HEARD the still distant whistle, Mariana stepped to the edge of the platform to look at the deserted track that vanished among the green fields and the first olive groves, and the south wind, the one that announces rain, blew her hair and skirt and the white cloth of her blouse as if she were standing on a pier by the ocean. "It's coming," she called to me, pointing at the almost motionless column of smoke bending over the tops of the olive trees, and then she turned toward me smoothing her hair and the skirt that had revealed her knees for a delicious moment, but the smile on her lips now was no longer mine, and her impatience for the arrival of the train carrying Orlando was an affront very similar to the uneasiness of jealousy. I hated the train and I hated Orlando, because they were coming to decapitate my being alone with her, they were emissaries of the time that would snatch her away from me and the future hours when her absence would destroy me. Stripped of will, of resignation, of pride, I consisted of nothing but two yearning eyes that looked at Mariana, and consciousness of the last respite that had venomously been granted to my imagination. She was already leaving, although she seemed immobile, I felt her becoming lost as slowly as the hands of a clock or a train that begins its departure in silence slipping away toward the red lights in the darkness, and when the second whistle sounded and I saw the column of smoke coming closer, the empty station, the indolent quiet of the May morning, were suddenly the landscape of a desert island where I had been abandoned and left alone, looking at the clock that pointed to noon, calculating the place and destination of my next flight, not going more than three days into the future because beyond that time limit nothing would remain. The respite that for me was disintegrating like a face of smoke lasted interminably for Mariana, and this mutual discord in our perception of time wounded me like a disloyalty more certain than her marriage to Manuel. "I count the days, Jacinto, I can't live in that house, with that woman who doesn't look at me and hates me without saying anything to me, with that man, the sculptor, who always looks at my neckline and has clammy hands. Even Manuel is like a stranger to me."

It was at the beginning, that morning, when we arrived at the station in the Ford that had belonged to Manuel's father, crossing the lit empty streets of the city, the avenue of linden trees that ended in the high esplanade with its flags where a boy in uniform saluted us with a raised fist. There were silent women in mourning and wounded soldiers on the benches along the platform and on every wall violent war posters that had an anachronistic, distant air, as if the war they exalted had nothing to do with the peaceful station and the morning in Mágina. We were alone, Mariana and I, we had been alone in the house when I came down to have breakfast and found her waiting for me in the dining room, recently bathed and light-hearted, with her damp hair and her white blouse unbuttoned almost to the tops of her loose, pale breasts that I glimpsed in their slight semidarkness every time she leaned toward me to tell me something, bringing me back with sudden clarity and sorrow to the afternoon in 1933 when I saw her, unknown and naked, in Orlando's studio. It had always been like this, I thought, always touching her with my eyes and hands and never crossing the chasm that divides bodies when they are so close that a single gesture or a single word would be enough to tear apart the cowardly spiderweb that joins desire to despair, exactly four years that resolved into ashes and nothingness with the cold visible serenity of what has already happened, like the sugar that I poured into the cup and that dissolved in the coffee as I sat across from Mariana and stirred it with a spoon, impassive, attentive, darkly absorbed in my breakfast and in her half-opened blouse. But we were alone and the silence in the house was like a final gift I never would have dared to ask for, and just as the war didn't seem to exist in Mágina because sirens didn't sound at night and there was no burned rubble in the middle of the streets, the absence of the others allowed me the clandestine privilege of imagining that nobody would come to argue with me over Mariana, cleanly offered to my eyes in the empty dining room. Manuel had left very early for the country estate, using the train and not the car so that Mariana and I could drive to the station to pick up Orlando. When I sat next to her on the leather seat and slammed the door shut at the same time that Mariana turned on the ignition, it was as if I too was stirred by its thrust, very violent at first, barely controlled by her when we turned into the first narrow lane on the way to the Plaza of General Orduña, then passing like a sound or a long gust of wind against the windows when we drove down the broad empty streets to the north, and Mariana, who had been tense and hunched over the wheel, leaned back and asked me to light a cigarette for her. She belonged to me boundlessly now, not to me, who was going to lose her, but to the tenderness of my eyes that in the warm interior of the car added new, unknown images to the figure of Mariana. Mariana in profile against the glass of the window, her hands sliding or firm on the wheel, her chestnut hair lifted and then falling again over her forehead and the rapid movement of her hand that brushed it aside and then immediately rested again on the brake lever, her forehead and her nose and her mouth and beyond them the fleeting, familiar streets of Mágina, the distant cemetery among the empty fields, the shadows of the linden trees that successively hid her face and returned it to the light, her laughter when she stopped the car in front of the station, as if we had completed an adventure.

They told us that Orlando's train would be two or three hours late. The delay irritated Mariana, as if the wait would lengthen hers to escape Mágina, but I secretly was grateful for the unexpected hours granted to me. It had been so long since I had been alone with her that I was incapable of calculating the exact duration of what I now had: each future minute was a coin from those excessive treasures we find in some dreams, a thin thread of dizzyingly spilled sand that I clutched at in order to retrieve it. I saw her approaching, returning from the precise moment when I knew I had known her only to lose her, the Mariana of 1933 who had just appeared, the possible Mariana, not yet desired, the girl with no name and the lock of hair hanging straight over her brows and her eyes made up like those of Louise Brooks, whom I had seen before I met her in some photographs that Orlando showed me. I saw her return as we walked on one side of the tracks, beyond the platform, past the long banks of young hedge mustard that extended it, our heads bowed, slightly apart, looking at the slow advance of our own steps or the distant gray of the olive groves. "I spend all my time with Manuel, imagine, today is the first day we've been apart since he got out of the hospital, but in that house it's as if I were always alone. Everything frightens me, even counting the days left until we leave. It frightens me to think about the trip to Paris, and I'm so adventurous that the first time I left Madrid was to come to Mágina. I can't tell you how grateful I am that you've come. After we mailed you the letter I was waiting for your answer and always afraid you'd stay in Madrid. Somebody would knock at the door and I'd run out to see if it was the mailman, and if the phone rang, I closed my eyes, hoping it was you. With you in the house, that woman, those people, no longer frighten me. Medina was sure you wouldn't come. I started to hate him for the way he said it, so much the doctor, as if he could know everything."

By now we were very far from the platform, and when we reached the first olive trees we slowly began our return. Mariana took my arm and rested her weight on me with a gesture that was usual in another time, in Madrid, before Manuel, in the uncertain streets of the small hours and the never satisfied temptation to embrace her. "Tomorrow," I said, rigid and cowardly when I felt her hand and the proximity of her hips, tomorrow and then never, the other house, the dark bedroom, the insomnia, the silence and the waiting and the darkness where Beatriz wasn't sleeping. "I almost can't remember what I did before I knew you," Mariana said. A step away from the platform, the lazy soldiers looked at her, the clock was about to strike eleven. But she still leaned on my arm, and when she raised her head to look into my eyes, I saw in the transparency of hers something that had nothing to do with her words, that wasn't mine, or Manuel's, or anybody's, that belongs now only to the memory of the man they fixed on for the last time, the certainty of an appointment and a shot in the pigeon loft, the will to die, I know it now, to never be vulnerable again to abandonment or fear. "A model," she repeated, laughing: "Who remembers that? You shouldn't remind me of it now. I was nobody, less than nobody, I was nothing when I met you. I went from one place to another, never stopping, because if I had paused at someone or something I would have disintegrated immediately, like a face in the water. When you appeared and looked at me, it was as if I finally had been embodied in myself. I can see you now, so quiet, so firm, looking at the painting and not at me because it embarrassed you to look at me naked. That day it was as if I were seeing myself in the mirror for the first time. You didn't need to speak or even move for people to know you were in the world. I never had read anything with as much attention as the poems of yours that Orlando gave me. 'Look, this is what Solana has written. Except for the two of us, it's a secret.' I didn't sleep at night, reading the books you gave me. I brought the first one with me, *The Voice Owed to You,* with the dedication you asked Salinas to write for me.

To Mariana Ríos, with affection, September 1933. When I read those poems I always had the feeling it was you who wrote them."

"There's another creature I'm looking for in the world," I quoted, but Mariana was no longer beside me, she was looking at things beyond my desire to immobilize them in her, torn by the hands of the clock that joined to indicate twelve o'clock and by the still distant whistle and the column of smoke that thickened into a soot-stained cloud when the train, stained by war and with ripped banners hanging from the sides of the locomotive, obscene like an old animal with wet skin, stopped in front of us. Through the smoke that dissipated to reveal dark anxious faces at the windows looking at the platform, I saw Orlando, who signaled to Mariana by waving his drawing portfolio over the heads grouped at the windows, taller than the others, and before he saw me, because I was still sitting on the bench on the platform, I heard over the din of the cars and the shouts of the soldiers his huge voice and laugh as he embraced Mariana, picking her up and swinging her around. "Solana, you old satyr, prince of your own darkness, you're even paler than you were last Sunday. Or was it Saturday when we got drunk the last time?" Big, tired, his clothes in the disarray of nighttime drunkenness, with thin damp hair at his temples, smelling of alcohol and medicine because he suffered attacks of asthma, laughing with an obstinacy in his intoxicated eyes that sometimes seemed close to madness, Orlando got down from the train bringing with him like an emissary all the excitement of the war and the blind urgency of Madrid. He brought portfolios of drawings that fell to the ground when he embraced Mariana and that I collected from between people's feet, and a suitcase that had been mislaid somewhere in the corridor or in his compartment. When we climbed into the train to look for it, urged on by Orlando's despair, who said he had packed the sketches for a masterpiece in it, a slim boy with long, very black hair whose face I vaguely recognized appeared with it. "God, here at last," Orlando said in a way that didn't reveal if he was referring to the suitcase or the boy. "I was afraid I had lost them both, and I swear to you that I would have preferred to lose the suitcase than him. Santiago, this is Mariana, who has been kind enough to invite us to her wedding with a local landowner. I think you already know Solana. He's the one who writes those fine articles in *Octubre* on art and the proletarian revolution. He aspires to a position in the political bureau."

He talked so much and so rapidly and with such a perverse edge that I estimated he had been drinking right up to the moment the train arrived in Mágina. The flask of liquor bulged in his jacket pocket, but when he introduced us to the boy he had brought with him, I understood that pride and not alcohol was the real reason for his elation. "Solana, you ought to get right back to Madrid. The front is going to collapse if you don't go in and recite some of your Communist ballads for our soldiers. Even the intellectuals are clamoring for you. The other day I ran into Bergamín, with that face that always looks as if he's just taken communion, and he said that as soon as you get back he was going to name you as his secretary for that congress you're all preparing in Valencia. Don't miss it, Marianita, the Congress of Anti-Fascist Intellectuals or something like that. Everything with capital letters." He put his hand on my shoulder not to be amiable so much as to keep his balance, and leaning on Mariana and me, he left the station. There he stopped beside the open car where Santiago and I had put the luggage, looking as if dazed at the vast blue sky and the double avenue of linden trees that cut across the plain toward Mágina, whose highest towers looked like pointed needles above the empty fields. Orlando took off the red and black handkerchief he always wore around his neck and wiped the sweat off his face, staring at the light, the handkerchief paused by his mouth, like a mask he hadn't decided to remove. "Solana," he said, his back to us, "Solana you infidel, you should have told me, you should have warned me about the light. Didn't you realize that this is the light I've been waiting for? Even Velázquez is darkness compared with this." He staggered with his head turned toward the blue, and when Santiago got out of the automobile that was already running to take him by the arm as if he were a blind man, he suddenly became disheartened and closed his eyes and seemed to fall asleep against the back of the rear seat, his mouth and nostrils wide open, as if he were dreaming about the beginning of an asthma attack.

We were already crossing the first streets of low villas and dusty gardens where Mágina ends in the north when I saw in the rearview mirror his open, reddened eyes staring into mine in an absent lucidity that his waking, or the silence that had overtaken the four of us since Mariana had started the car, stripped of any sign of mockery or pride. He let his head fall slowly onto Santiago's shoulder, and the boy remained solemn and firm beside him, looking at the long lines of houses, and when he lit a cigarette without moving his eyes away from the rearview mirror I thought I could detect in his expression an old countersign of desolation or renunciation, as if the illusions of alcohol had abruptly abandoned him. He moved his head a little and then I knew he was alluding to Mariana and was asking me about her without words. "You look beautiful when you're driving, Mariana," he said, his eyes half-closed to complete his indolence, "you remind me of that heroine in *Orlando Furioso* who rode on a winged horse wearing brilliant armor." He rested his hand on the back of Mariana's seat and caressed her hair with fleeting tenderness, like a dozing faun, as if he were touching the air or liquid silk that dissolved between his large, stained fingers. She looked away from the road for a moment to smile at him in the mirror with the tranquil gratitude of an accomplice, which was always present in the way she looked at Orlando. I was jealous when I caught their eyes meeting in the rearview mirror, because I desired the candid, offered part of Mariana that she revealed only in her behavior with Orlando as much as the other darker, more carnal part that belonged to Manuel, and I would have liked to join the two in a single indubitable woman not closed to my intelligence and desire, like the third Mariana, the only one I knew, shadow or reverse of the others or of herself, who always seemed to be to one side of things, who sometimes, that very morning, would take me by the arm and stop to tell me the exact words that burned inside me and that I would never say to her. "I'll always be with you. Whatever I do and no matter who I'm with, even if I don't see you again. I want you to know that and never forget it, not even when you don't care about me anymore."

SUDDENLY I NOTICED that we were proceeding more and more slowly now, because as we approached the Plaza of General Orduña, the sidewalks and streets were filling with a slow-moving crush of people. They came out of the narrow lanes, at first in silence, unarmed men in white shirts and corduroy trousers, tense women clustered at the corners who talked quietly and turned inquisitively to look at the car that by now was almost at a standstill and surrounded by a single-minded crowd who walked toward the plaza and seemed to inundate us and then drag us along to the rhythm of their movement forward. The voices still had the same vast, muffled sound as the footsteps, but very soon, when we finally entered the plaza—the small tree tops surrounding the amputated pedestal of General Orduña stood out above their heads—the great sound broke apart into a clamor of shouts and raised fists rhythmically beating the air as they leaned toward the closed balconies of the police station, toward the cubic tower where a red and yellow and purple flag hung over the broken sphere of the clock. Mariana sounded the horn several times, but by now it was useless, because we couldn't open a passage and there were hostile faces looking at us through the windows as if we were fish in an aquarium and furious fists pounding on the car body to the rhythm of their shouts, the single shout in which all the voices had already converged when Mariana stopped the car at one side of the plaza and we managed to get out by pushing the doors against the bodies that seemed to adhere with the tenacity of mollusks. "Give him to us," they shouted, "give us the traitor," convulsing in violent eddies toward the closed balconies of the police station, and no sooner did I get out of the car than I found myself lost and far from the others in a dense pulsation in which bodies and voices were confused, driven by instinct or a determined rage as indecipherable in its purpose as the energy of the ocean. Like swimming in sand, I moved forward until I reached the hand that Mariana held out to me, but I could no longer see Santiago or Orlando. We drifted together toward the center of the plaza, where the bodies had erased the benches and the line of the gardens and covered in their flood tide the pedestal of General Orduña. Now we saw the closed doors of the police station and the only space not yet engulfed by the crowd: nine Assault Guards formed a semicircle in front of the building, standing firm, their legs apart, with hard somber faces under shining visors and rifles held against their chests, as if they didn't see the surging crowd that besieged them or the closed fists that stopped so close to their rifles. Then a side balcony opened and I saw a man in uniform who looked at the plaza without stepping outside entirely, smoking, partially protected behind opaque glass, but that image, endowed with the serenity of an illusion, vanished when I felt people shoving me and separating me from Mariana, because a police van was making its way unhesitatingly through the crowd and approaching the semicircle defended by the Assault Guards. I saw Mariana moving away and calling to me with her hand, as if she were being dragged out by the sea, my blind fear was that I had lost her and I shouted her name over the agitated heads that again occupied the fissure opened on the plaza by the passage of the van, and when I could no longer see her a brusque undulation of bodies threw her into my arms and knocked both of us against a tree trunk. As if waking from a bad dream, we found ourselves greedily embracing, her bare legs wrapped around mine and my open hands trembling at her waist and feeling for the first time since I met her the perfumed and delicate attraction, the curved, slender, definite body of Mariana. I brushed her forehead, her chestnut hair with my lips, I raised my eyes to the balcony of the police station and the man in uniform was still there, calm, holding his cigarette at a middle height, looking at the plaza as if there were no one on it, or only us, Mariana and I, embracing under the faded foliage of a tree.

"Let's go, comrades," I heard someone saying to me, one voice very close in the silence in which for ten seconds all the shouts in the plaza had exploded, the butt of a musket and a body that detached me from Mariana as he made his way between the two of us, while we avoided looking at each other and again were lost and inert and trying to pretend that our embarrassment wasn't real, that the embrace like a lightning flash of desire hadn't happened. "Let's go, comrades, let me pass, I want to see the face of that spy when they bring him out," said the voice at my side, a boy summarily dressed as a militiaman who elbowed his way forward raising his musket, probably unloaded and useless, like a banner. "What's going on?" Mariana asked him, "who's been arrested?" and he told us, as if excited by fever, that two days earlier they had arrested a Fascist spy in a Mágina hotel and now they were preparing to take him to the provincial prison in the Assault Guards' van. "But this is where justice should be done. That Fascist is ours. They say he wanted to put a bomb in the House of the People, the murderer." He moved away from us, hitting the bodies in his path with the butt of the musket, and I saw him disappear or sink among the heads, shouting as if he were alone, and then resurface, hanging onto the grating at a window very close to the police station, his musket waving at the end of the overly long strap that held it around his neck. "Now they'll bring him out," he shouted, pointing at the six guards who had climbed out of the van to form a second, tighter line next to the door of the police station, which someone was beginning to open very cautiously. "He's coming out now," announced the boy, and a single great roar extended over the plaza as the crowd pushed with dark violence against the cordon of guards, "they have him at the door, they're going to bring him out right now." The man on the balcony reluctantly threw away his cigarette and disappeared behind the glass, and as if that were a signal, the guards stood more erect until they seemed taller in their blue uniforms, and at the same time they released the bolts on their rifles. When the door to the police station was finally opened, all the voices suddenly became muffled and faded into a sound very similar to silence. Unmoving eyes, raised heads, banners, high and red at midday, quiet among the trees. Without realizing it Mariana painfully squeezed my hand. "There's a guard in the doorway," I said. "He's pointing at someone with a pistol." The guard walked backward, saying something I couldn't hear as he waved the pistol, half-turned toward the encircling crowd. Behind him a man came out with bowed head and cuffed hands, whom the other guards shoved toward the van. Surrounded by them, the man didn't seem to walk but simply to yield as if in a lethargy to the momentum of the rifles hitting him, wounded by the cruelty of the sudden light blinding his eyes after two days of darkness, avoiding it, very pale, already sleepwalking to his death. Before climbing into the back of the van, he stood motionless, as if he didn't understand what they were ordering him to do, and he raised his head for the first time to look at the wall of faces, silent on the other side of the rifles. He had straightened up like someone who hears his name and cannot determine where the call is coming from. Then the boy hanging on the grate shouted "murderer," and abruptly thrust out his hand that no longer held his military cap but something I didn't see, and he whistled and knocked the handcuffed man down among the legs of the guards at the same time that the revived crowd and the long shout and the rage dragged us helplessly toward the door of the police station, knocking down the barrier of rifles and uniforms and lifting into the air the bloodstained body of the prisoner who rebounded against the wall and fell to the paving stones and was again hoisted up and thrown by unanimous open hands that came up to hit him or claw at his face or his torn shirt. I saw his eyes, I saw the gleam of blood streaming from the corners of his mouth and the last shred of a black tie around his neck, I saw him get to his knees, panting, and run like a goaded, wounded animal toward the stone columns of the portico. He threw his arms around one of them, his mouth convulsed against the rough yellow stone, turned toward his persecutors who had stopped, waiting for something or merely witnessing his death agony, forming a circle of silence around the column. Without closing his eyes, without moving his mouth away from the stone edge where he seemed to be searching for air, he began to slip to the ground as slowly as the thread of his blood flowed down the column, his hands together, as if hidden in his groin, his tongue torn in a very dark, not red coagulated mass that didn't completely spill out between his lips when he stopped moving.

Then I remember the plaza gradually emptying and the contracted body beside the column, but that image is lost in the image of other bodies I didn't see, my father's, illuminated by the headlights of a truck at the foot of the cemetery wall, the solitary dead body my father saw on July 19, 1936, at a corner of the Plaza of San Lorenzo. Bodies without faces as if biting the bitter earth or the pavement of a street, abandoned to the sun, in an empty siesta hour, dead and alone, rotting and alone, without name or dignity or glory, exactly like dead animals in the mud of a river. Silently we entered the water before dawn, raising the rifles with both hands above our heads, and we stepped on something soft that sank, something slimy and corrupt, mud and corpses of drowned mules under the weight of a machine gun and human bodies that seemed stripped of bones. I remember the Plaza of General Orduña as if I were seeing it from high above, at an hour made even emptier because the tower clock could not announce it: the empty pedestal, Manuel's car, the body that an Assault Guard poked at with the end of his rifle. Mariana and I walked very slowly, keeping our distance from each other, to the car, sat down in it, not saying anything, not asking each other where Orlando and Santiago were now. Mariana placed her tense hands on the steering wheel and looked at the empty plaza or only at the dirty glass that separated us from it. Her disheveled chestnut hair covered her profile like a veil conceived of only to keep me from seeing her. I said her name in a quiet voice, and she looked at me in the rearview mirror without turning toward me. I placed a hand on her knee without daring to acknowledge or feel the shape of her thigh under the thin skirt, as if desiring her at that moment would have been disloyalty. When we returned to Manuel's house, he hadn't come back yet from the country house, and Orlando and Santiago were waiting for us in the library, a little drunk, very close together on the sofa, laughing at something they were whispering in each other's ear, their glasses raised, as if they couldn't remember the reason for having a toast.

8

THE LIGHT, EVERY NIGHT, round and yellow and high like a minor moon that belonged only to the plaza, the one light burning at midnight in the darkness of Mágina, the one consciousness, Manuel thought, not made sluggish by the still intact stupefaction of the war and the extremely long winter that after eight years seemed to prolong it. He returned to the house at dusk, after seeing Medina in his office on his slow walk that normally took him to the watchtower in the wall, and before pushing open the door, he stopped for a while under the acacias to look at the lighted window in the room where Jacinto Solana was writing at that very moment. He imagined he could hear the sound of the typewriter through the rain, and he continued to hear it, confused with the rain or with the murmur of Jacinto Solana's voice, when he woke in the middle of the night fleeing the vast hand that opened his chest to tear out his heart the way you tear a root out of clod-filled wet ground. The multiplied, metallic blows sounded above his head like rain on the balcony glass and the insomniac footsteps of the man who never seemed to sleep or abandon for a single second his perpetual vigil in front of the typewriter or around it, always uncovered, Teresa told him, beginning at dawn, like a mechanical animal on the desk that Solana circled when he couldn't write, pacing blindly through the smoke of his cigarettes and the importunate labyrinth of his memory, walking in circles of obsessive geometry like an insect flying around a lamp. At eleven the electricity was cut off and all the streets and windows in Mágina were erased by the sudden flood of darkness, but then, after a few minutes during which the circle of the window vanished in the high blackness of the house, a yellower, fainter light appeared and in it was outlined the shadow of the solitary man who had lit the first candle of the night to illuminate his insomnia of written or rejected words, and at times Manuel, hidden under the branches of the acacias, would see Jacinto Solana smoking, motionless, in the circle of light, looking at the swamp of shadows where he tossed the butt like someone who throws a stone down a well and waits to hear it hit the water. Then he would close the window, and Manuel would hear again the distant metallic blows of his writing, as usual among the sounds in the house as the beating of blood in his temples, and like a coward he would approach them, going up in silence to the very door of the room, but when he extended his hand to knock, he would stop and listen to the footsteps on the parquet or the sound of the typewriter, and he never knocked because he was afraid Solana would not want to receive him.

"At first I went up to talk to him almost every afternoon, and I'd bring him tobacco, a thermos of coffee, an occasional bottle of cognac. He'd leave the house at dawn to avoid running into my mother or Utrera, and that was when Teresa cleaned the room and made his bed, but gradually he stopped going out or even opening the door for Teresa, and she would leave a breakfast tray outside the closed door, and when she came back for it, she'd find it untouched. There was one afternoon when he wouldn't open for me either. I wanted to believe, and even told Medina afterward, that he probably had fallen asleep after several nights of insomnia and didn't hear me knock. But a moment earlier I had heard the typewriter, and as I waited at the door I was absolutely certain he was sitting in front of the machine, holding his breath, the index fingers of both hands immobile above the keyboard, waiting for me to go away. I heard the click of the lighter and very strange breathing, like that of an invalid, and then, as I was thinking that Solana couldn't write and was trapped in the agony of a blank page, I heard the harsh scrape of the pen on paper, and I knew that not even silence signaled a truce."

Like the blood in one's temples, like wood borers on the most inaccessible shelves in the library, like a spider invisibly weaving the threads of its trap under a cellar hatchway: he was there, in the house, in the room with circular windows, and sometimes he went out or wandered aimlessly at three in the morning along the gallery hallway, but very soon, when the first days of excitement caused by his arrival had passed, it seemed as if he really had left in an irrevocable way, because they never spoke of him or ran into his taciturn figure, and only Teresa's periodic visits to the top floor with the broom and dustcloth or the tray of food indicated that someone was living in that region of rooms unoccupied for so many years: someone, in any case, who was losing the name and face that all their memories assigned to him and little by little was reduced to an obscure presence, the faded and at times fearsome certainty that the top floor was not empty, and if they thought about him because they heard his footsteps on the parquet or the noise of the typewriter, they barely could connect those signs to the memory of the man they knew before the war or to his inexact shadow that stood in the courtyard ten years later. He was in the house like the wood borer is there, even though one cannot hear its gnawing, and after a month his presence had hidden so definitively behind the brief indications that disclosed it that Manuel, when he finally decided to go into his room even if he didn't want to receive him because he feared he might be sick, waited at the door he had knocked on several times without an answer, feeling the awful uncertainty that the man who unbolted the door for him wasn't Jacinto Solana.

"BECAUSE WHAT I DIDN'T understand then, what I understand only now, as I'm telling it to you, a man who didn't know him and has no idea how much he had changed and imagine him, I suppose, as a literary character, is that when I lost him, I wasn't losing only the one man I could call my friend but also the right to remember or know how my life had been before I renounced it forever. Things exist only if there is someone, an interlocutor or a witness, who allows us to recall that at one time they were true. Which is why he would say that the worst misfortune for a lover is not losing his love but being left alone with his memory, left blind, he would specify, remembering some verses by Don Pedro Salinas that he always recited and that perhaps you've seen underlined in that book of his in the library. <u>For there's another being through whom I look at the world, because she loves me with her eyes.</u> Now I know that in the beginning, when without saying anything to him I cleaned the room with the circular windows and put the typewriter in it, I didn't do it to offer him a refuge or the possibility of writing his book, but to have him here, in this city and in this house, to have someone to whom I could say what I hadn't said in ten years and share the memory of the time when Mariana was alive. It was the same before the war, when she and I fell in love. We were always looking for him, because his presence made us aware of our happiness more intensely than when we were alone. But he never talked to me about Mariana during the months he was here. He said her name only once, on the first day, when he told me he was going to write a book about all of us. I imagine that book was like a vampire that robbed him of the use of language and of memories as he wrote it. He gave it his life just as someone gives blood at a hospital or dedicates himself to opium. That's why I didn't recognize him when he opened the door of his room that night. He hadn't shaved for at least a week or eaten the hot food that Teresa left for him in the hall, and the air in the room and his clothes smelled as if he hadn't opened the window or changed or washed since he arrived here. He opened the door and stood looking at me with his coat over his shoulders, and his shadow hit me at the same time that I detected the rarefied odor of the air, because the lamp in the room swayed behind him as if he had bumped into it when he stood to answer the door. He was swaying too, his arms crossed and both hands holding the wide lapels of his coat, and he smiled without my being able to see his eyes behind his glasses. It took me a little while to realize he was drunk and was moving back and forth in alcohol like a fish behind the glass of an illuminated aquarium, beyond the insolent shame of someone who drinks alone until he falls down and immediately gets up because he hears someone calling him and he has to pretend he's sober. Do you have a light, he said, showing me a cigarette that had gone out, which he placed on the edge of the ashtray and soon forgot about, and he asked me to sit down, repeating my name as if he had just remembered it and wasn't familiar with it yet, and abruptly he forgot about me and turned his back to look at the plaza through one of the circular windows. 'You have to let Medina see you,' I said, but he didn't hear me or didn't pay attention to me, and he began to laugh that cold laugh I hadn't known in him until then and that seemed like the laugh of a dead man. To keep from falling he leaned against the window recess, and he walked toward me following an arduous straight line, holding a new cigarette and a glass of cognac that moved slightly with the trembling of his hand. 'Teresa has told me that you hardly taste your food. Medina's downstairs, in the parlor. If you like, he'll come up to see you right now.' He collapsed into a chair, facing the typewriter, and moved his hands and lips to say something, he said Mariana or Solana and showed me with a weary gesture the written sheets on the floor and desk and the blank sheet in the typewriter. 'Excuse me, Manuel,' he apologized in every gesture or word, 'excuse me for not having cleaned this up to receive you. I never was very orderly, you know. Now I think I'm becoming dirty. But I'm not sick. You remember Orlando: when he looked at you with those cold saurian eyes, it was because he was going to die from drinking so much. This afternoon I began to write and couldn't get past the second line. Alcohol works sometimes, but it isn't a substitute. Orlando knew that too.' I drank with him, I asked about the unfinished and frightening book whose pages thrown down next to the table he was treading on or kicking aside with a careless air in which I saw something of voluntary punishment and perversity, but the man I was talking to was no longer Jacinto Solana."

He didn't go up again, he recounts, as if he were telling about a very long, definitive farewell, he spoke to him again only on the afternoon of April 1, when he went into Solana's room and saw him placing his papers and clothes into the cardboard suitcase. He had just shaved and put on a tie, and his breath didn't smell of cognac. Like a traveler about to leave a hotel, he was arranging his things in the suitcase, and he had made the bed and cleaned the ashtrays and was moving, unfamiliar and resolute, around the room. "I'm going to Madrid, Manuel. Nobody knows me there. I'll be safer." Then, like his own guilt, Manuel recalled inviting Solana to go to the Island of Cuba: the slow brown river moving among the oleanders, the solitary house on the hill, surrounded by almond trees, Jacinto Solana's precise and never-again postponed appointment with his desire to die. Manuel called a taxi, and they waited together at the entrance, accepting forever the unfamiliar courtesy of strangers between them, they got into the car and in silence crossed the lanes of Mágina and the Plaza of General Orduña and then the wide straight streets that extend the city to the north, and when they reached the station, neither one had to begin the gesture of good-bye because the yellow train of the Guadalquivir was already moving slowly on the track. Manuel saw him standing on the running board and moving away, the suitcase in his hand and his hat over his eyes, and he waved a good-bye that Solana never saw because he had already gone inside the car and found a seat next to the window to see how the streets of Mágina disappeared forever in a high city hanging over the ruins of a wall, suspended like a line of blue mist over the undulating remoteness of the olive groves.

"For twenty-two years I've been alone," Manuel said, looking at

Minaya as if he were deciphering on his face that period of time, "from the moment Solana went away until you arrived." In the same taxi that had taken them to the station he returned to the house when night had already fallen, and he was surprised not to see the light burning in the circular windows. He was in Solana's room, which still smelled of tobacco smoke and the presence and usury of a body; he covered the typewriter and then went down to the parlor to look at himself in 1937, to look at his own pride and manhood exalted by the buttons and straps of his uniform. In the oval photograph, Mariana looked at him as if she were foreseeing the future dead man before her now. "But Mariana was looking at him, you ought to know that," Manuel said in the library, in front of the fire. "We were in the photographer's studio, and I had put on my uniform and the two stars I never wore because they promoted me to lieutenant when I was dying in a hospital in Guadalajara. She took my arm and looked at the lens when the photographer told us to smile, but Solana was behind him, with Orlando, and I barely could see them because the lights were blinding me. At the same time that she pressed my arm, Mariana moved her head very slightly and found Solana's eyes. That was exactly when the photographer took the picture. No matter from which angle of the parlor you look, she seems to be smiling and looking at you, but the one she's looking at is Jacinto Solana."

9

ABRUPTLY AND WITHOUT ANY foreshadowing of it, the need to escape had disappeared, the incessant fear of time's flight. Now I perceived everything through the sweet desired fog of wine that ripened its effect precisely at the point where the things and faces flowing on the other side didn't matter or seemed to have happened many years earlier. I drank slowly, beginning at dusk, when Manuel had not yet returned from the country estate and Mariana wandered aimless and alone through the rooms, the courtyard, the hallway in the gallery, avidly attentive to the clock in the library and the door where he would appear. I drank the white wine brought up by Amalia from the wine cellar in dusty bottles whose labels Orlando read with an alcoholic's sacred wonder, relics kept in the darkness of cellars not to celebrate the eve of the wedding but simply to allow me the privilege of the serenity and pale golden light that occupied the place of the air and gave everything an appearance of premature distance very similar to the certain possibility of oblivion. Very slowly, not surrendering, as Orlando did, to the immediate fever of the alcohol spilled on my lips and ablaze in my veins, spinning out my gestures as if I were looking at myself in a mirror pretending I was drinking, like someone who prepares and administers to himself in solitude a medicine or the exact dose of poison to commit suicide. The glass between my fingers, the bottle on the nearby table, the curved edge of glass against my lips, the passage of the wine from palate to consciousness. Now, as I write to recover that night and the day and night that ended in two bodies embracing in the light from a window, suddenly burning above the garden, very close to the palm tree and the metal swing whose creaking, because the wind was moving it slightly, I did not stop listening to as I closed my eyes to kiss Mariana's bare breasts, I find I can barely establish a precise chronology of the things I did and saw while the white wine enveloped everything in its mist as light and clear as the transparency Orlando loved so much in the paintings of Velázquez.

I hear his voice that night, Orlando's savage laugh, I see his eyes saturated with lucidity and cruelty and Santiago's profile like that of a page painted on a quattrocento fresco as he sat next to him, absent and docile, the indifferent tenderness with which he let Orlando caress a knee or a hand auspiciously resting on the edge of the sofa. I hear voices, I see faces, but behind them there is nothing that allows me to establish them in a room or in a landscape, only a dark curtain, perhaps an object that they touch or raise as a signal so that the person who looks at them many years later can recognize them. A night and a day and next to the last night Mariana was alive, broken images and flashes and words that remained in the air after being spoken, like the cigarette smoke, like the indolence that left me lying on the bed in my room or slowly moving back and forth on the swing in the garden, shamelessly intending for Mariana to come and ask me why I was alone, why I seemed so sad and had slipped away from the others, from her. Leaning back in an armchair, next to the fireplace, I became drunk with a serene and filthy delicacy as I listened to Medina, who was explaining something to us about the spy they had lynched a few hours earlier in the Plaza of General Orduña, when Manuel came into the library and Medina fell silent—his last words were a name, Víctor or perhaps Héctor Vera, or Vega—because Mariana had stood up to embrace Manuel and now she was kissing him on the mouth, in front of all of us, as if she were defying us, in front of Utrera, Medina, and Amalia, who had just come in with a tray of appetizers and bottles of wine and remained standing in the middle of the library. In front of me and Santiago and Orlando, who took a drink, raising his glass like a countersign or a malevolent toast conceived exclusively so that I would notice.

Orlando, a mask of laughter, a hard voice of accusation and augury. The next morning, when we all drove down to the country estate in the black car to celebrate the wedding feast, Orlando, possessed by the fervor of the light that had excited him since his arrival in Mágina, took his portfolio and pencils and was constantly drawing things he allowed only Santiago and Mariana to see, but he didn't seem to care about the landscape spread out before him, surrounding the hill where the house stood. He was sitting among the almond trees, his portfolio open on his knees and his red and black handkerchief, wet with perspiration, around his neck, and if he raised his eyes from the paper and looked at the olive groves or the river or the distant, gray line of the roofs in Mágina, it was as if he were seeing not what we saw but the definitive and future form of the picture that at that instant he had decided to paint. At times he put down his pencil to look at us. He smiled, holding the glass of wine that Santiago had brought to his retreat, barely drinking from it, as if all he needed for his happiness was the presence of the boy, the lukewarm odor of the river among the almond trees, the sudden sensation of looking at a scene that secretly obeyed the intention of his imagination as the pencil obeyed his hand. And for that reason I don't know now if when I write I'm recounting what happened then or simply imagining the picture Orlando never painted, the watercolors I saw in January 1939 in a funereal, icy apartment in Madrid. I see the esplanade and the house from the spot where Orlando was sitting among the almond trees. Manuel's black Ford covered with dust to one side of the gate with its baroque metal fittings, in the shade of the grapevine, the obsessive, absurd phonograph playing tangos and extremely long blues erased by the wind, the table with its white tablecloths, Mágina in the distance, the pale green or gray of the olive groves and the river and the hills and lunar ravines that extended the world toward the south, toward the blue sierra where I've never gone.

He knew, he was to one side among the almond trees, his pencil, its point as harsh and precise as his eye, suspended over the paper and his glass recently filled with wine by the solicitous hand of the only creature in the world who mattered to him. Now I know that all of us, Mariana, Manuel, myself, existed that day only so that Orlando could draw his discerning labyrinth of figures entwined in despair and desire. Frasco and his wife had cleared the table at the end of the meal, and they, not Orlando or I, were talking about the bombing of Guernica because a squadron of very high-flying planes was crossing the Mágina sky, and about someone, a spy—"A fifth columnist," Medina specified, as if he were saying the exact name of an illness—arrested three days earlier in Mágina. "There are laws," said Utrera. "There's a penal code. If a man commits a crime, he deserves a trial, and if necessary to be condemned to death, but they have no right to lynch him. It's barbaric, like when they burned the churches." "Those things do more harm to the Republic than a rebel offensive. You should have seen the condition of that man's corpse when it reached the hospital. I'm saying this because I was on duty, and I had to perform the autopsy." Medina, composed, drinking his coffee, citing clinical details and speeches of Don Manuel Azaña, whose hand he once shook before he was president of the Republic and came to give a talk at the Athenaeum of Mágina. Then Orlando's voice resounded like a severe invocation: "The Spanish people have the right to burn churches and lynch Fascists, because what they do will be much worse if we're unlucky enough to lose this war. Think of Guernica, or the bullfight ring in Badajoz. The people are hoping not for the revolution but the Apocalypse."

Straddling a chair, leaning on the back as if it were a windowsill, I looked at the white gleam of the sun on the wings of the silent planes that were disappearing beyond the hills, my back to the others, who were still sitting around the table with a pensive or rigid ceremonial air refuted by the light and the wind that disturbed the tablecloths, raising them at times like the sails of ships. I thought that perhaps my father had looked up from the ground at that same instant to watch the passage of the planes, forgetting them immediately, as if they were birds taking shelter after the first October cold and not emissaries of the war. The wind came up from the ravine of the Guadalquivir, heavy with the odor of mud and wet earth, and it carried away the voices and the music on the phonograph, a fox-trot, a tango, then a trumpet, intermittent and gradually moving away like the rhythm of a train, with the slowness of all the things that one will lose forever. On the ground, within reach of my hand, so that I only had to lean over a little to pick it up, was my glass of white wine, delicate and slow like the music and the faint smell of rotting algae that came from the still waters of the river, illuminating things with a tepidness similar to that of the threads of light that crossed the trellis next to the door of the country house and floated above the dust or pollen, around the crude black stain of the car, above the music recovered and dispersed and the sound of voices behind me becoming confused with the chink of spoons against the porcelain of the cups of coffee and the thin crystal of the glasses that a gust of wind overturned on the tablecloths. Mariana came over, before I saw her I knew she was coming because I recognized her step and the way her presence made the air tremble, to bring me coffee and a lit cigarette, and she remained crouching at my side, facing the city and the wind from the river that lifted the hair on her forehead, as if she had come to an appointment that only for the two of us was not invisible. When she gave me the cup, she placed a hand on my shoulder, and her hair covered one side of her face. Exactly like Orlando's sketch: not a face, but the pure shape of a desire, and that night, back at the house, when he gave me the drawing, he was offering me the sign of a temptation too undeniable for my cowardice.

"Mariana's alone, in the library," he said. "She's sitting and smoking, like you, watching the smoke while she listens to music, waiting for you. Even Manuel knows that if she hasn't gone to bed yet, it's because she wants to see you. Everybody seems to know that here except you. I've been watching the two of you since I got off the train yesterday morning. You wander all over the house, looking for each other, and you pass each other like two sleepwalkers, as if you still had time. For three years you've been looking for each other and hiding from each other like this, don't you remember? You came to my studio and didn't dare to look at her because she was naked. You don't even dare to look at me now. And don't pretend you're drunk or that you're an adolescent scorned by the woman you love. Open your eyes, Solana. It's me, your enemy, it's Orlando."

I close my eyes as I did that night, when I listened to Orlando lying on the yellow-flowered sofa in the parlor, and I hear his voice again, murmuring and serious, as if it were whistling in my ear as he untied the red strings of his portfolio and opened it to show me the portrait of Mariana. It was midnight, and it seemed as if the house and the world were uninhabited. Only Orlando and I, separated by the table in the parlor where the drawing lay under the light of the lamp, only Mariana's profile traced on the paper and perhaps on the dark background of the shelves in the library, Orlando's voice beating like the blood in my temples with the heavy indolence of alcohol. I got up, leaning on the edge of the table, clumsy and cowardly in front of Orlando's not-exactly-human eyes. "Leave me in peace," I said to him, "go away and leave me alone," but he didn't move or take his eyes off mine. He brushed, he tapped very softly the surface of the portfolio with his short, paint-stained fingers, and sweat shone on his neck and beneath the thin hair on his forehead like makeup running beneath the too-close light of the lamp. "It isn't necessary to raise your voice like that, Solana, I'm not your conscience. I don't care what you don't do tonight, or what she doesn't do. When she finishes her cigarette or her drink, she'll go to sleep or try on her wedding dress again, and you'll have the opportunity to give yourself another night of insomnia. I won't be the one to argue with anybody, least of all you, about the right to bring about your own failure. But I suppose you'll understand if I tell you that love has simplified my life. The only thing I care about is painting and having Santiago with me. I know he'll go just like he came, and it's very likely that he'll leave me when we return to Madrid and that I'll die when he goes, but not even that frightens me, Solana, fear is a trap, like shame, and now I'm alive and invulnerable."

Orlando signed the drawing, wrote the date in the margin, and handed it to me with a smile of surrender and tenderness directed at himself, as if when he heard his own words, he had understood all at once the entire feverishness of his love and imminence of the time when he would once again be exiled in solitude. He opened the door of the parlor, and before he went out to the hallway, he turned to look at me. "The music's still playing in the library. She's calling you." When I was alone, the drawing completely took on its imperious quality of invitation and the exact, empty pattern for absence. The wavy, short hair over her cheeks, the grave, pensive smile, not on her lips but in her gaze fixed on a distance of blank paper, of words unspoken, unwritten, of frozen gestures. The wine no longer existed or its excuse or its fog, only the clear line of the drawing against the light of the lamp, and behind it the eyes, the presence of Orlando, who was no longer a witness but the figure and voice in which the only lucid part of my thinking was embodied. And so when Manuel appeared at the door of the library, recently returned from the country estate, and Mariana went to him and kissed him with the greed of someone who has survived too long a wait, I knew that if I lifted my head, I would meet the complicit or accusatory eyes of Orlando, the spy of my rancor, of the plot hidden behind the stillness of things with as much impunity as the geometry that orders the disposition of figures in a painting to make it seem the result of chance.

Motionless figures in the library, as on a stage too brightly lit or in the studio of a photographer where prolonged exposure to the heat of the lights made their faces shine with the brilliance of wax. Medina, still in uniform, because he had come from the military hospital, as he did every night to examine Manuel. Utrera somber and alone among the others, like a guest in a hostile house, censuring in silence all the signs of disorder that the night before the wedding had brought into the house: Mariana's lack of modesty, Santiago's tight-fitting trousers, Orlando's obscene laughter. Amalia, standing next to me with a tray of appetizers and bottles, just down from the upstairs rooms where Doña Elvira murmured things and cursed and looked in the mirrors in her mourning clothes wringing her hands in her lap. Orlando, on the sofa with his knees devotedly joined to Santiago's, allowing himself small indecencies, the light caresses of a sodomite in a furtive park, of a tremulous, besotted, obscene old man who cannot decide to touch a little girl's thighs. Figures turned toward Mágina on the esplanade of the country house, their backs to the proximity of dispersion and death, to the hand and eye for which they posed without knowing it. The painting was going to be called *Une partie de plaisir,* but when I asked about it two years later, Orlando could no longer recall its title or even the intention he once had to paint it.

10

THE BELL AT THE ENTRANCE didn't ring when they arrived, but one of the door knockers sounded on the exterior door, which Manuel or Amalia always locked around midnight, when Medina would leave after having a last drink in the parlor and there was no one left on the ground floor of the house. Manuel hadn't gone to bed yet, he was in the garden, in the dark, waiting for sleep to come on the gentle night in early June, and a wind scented with wisteria had carried from the Plaza of General Orduña the sound of the tower clock striking, but he heard the violent knocking on the door only when Amalia, lighting her way with an oil lamp, opened wide the glass-paned doors that led from the dining room to the garden. She was barefoot and in her nightgown, and the lamp light heightened on her face, still puffy with sleep, the horror of someone who has awakened from a nightmare. "Don Manuel," she called, looking for him in the darkness, "they're knocking at the door. I asked who it is, but they don't answer." For a moment he thought or wanted to think it was Solana who had come back, driven by one of those fits of rapture that long ago had been the ordinary traits of his character and were always preceded by a singularly indolent state. "He's finished the book," he thought before he left the garden, where the clamor of the bronze door knockers sounded muffled and distant, "he's finished the book and has come back to Mágina to show it to me or simply has decided he's sick of the country house and wants to leave tonight for Madrid or someplace where they'll give him a forged passport so he can leave Spain," but when he went out to the courtyard and heard up close the banging that shook the glass in the gallery and the dome, he knew that at no time had he expected it to be Solana knocking and he didn't have to open the door to know the faces and uniforms he would find on the other side. "Don't open it, Don Manuel, they'll take you away like they did when the war was over." Amalia, holding the lamp at the height of Manuel's face, with her back to the door, held his hand to stop him from sliding the bolts, and between their two bodies the light trembled behind the shade of smoked glass as if it too were shaken by the increasingly peremptory sound of the knocking. "Move away, Amalia, go up to your room right now," said Manuel, and he took the lamp from her, noticing that his own hands stopped trembling only when they grasped the cold metal of the bolts, when he took a step into the interior of fear and saw before him the men who had come for him. Later, in the basement of the barracks where they ordered him to look at the body lying on the marble table, he remembered that before leaving the house he had heard behind him some steps on the stairs and a voice or a scream that belonged to his mother. "It's nothing, Señora, nothing to worry about," one of the men had said, the one dressed in civilian clothes, turning from the entrance toward the figure, motionless with stupefaction and rage, that Manuel did not wish to look at, "a minor verification. We'll return your son in a couple of hours." Before closing the door, he saluted Doña Elvira, touching the brim of his hat with his fingers, then looked at the fountain without water and the tops of the acacias, still smiling, as if he personally had approved the quiet of the night, took Manuel's arm firmly and gave an order in a low voice to the Civil Guards, who lowered their weapons and walked behind them like an entourage of silence along the deserted lanes where their boots and the brush of rifles against their belts resonated.

In his treatment of Manuel, the man in civilian clothes, whom the guards called "Captain," adopted from the very beginning an affable air not completely contradicted by his evident desire to look like Glenn Ford. He was bald and wore excessively long sideburns and an unbuttoned and absurd raincoat that he didn't take off when he sat down behind the desk in his office, beneath an equestrian portrait of General Franco. Before speaking he twisted his mouth and tightened his lips as he looked down at the floor or at a typed paper that was on the desk and whose only purpose, Manuel supposed, was to increase the cowardice and waiting time of the person who would be interrogated. "Manuel Alberto Santos Crivelli," the captain read, then raised his eyes from the paper to look at him thoughtfully, as if searching his face for confirmation that the name attributed to him was correct, "owner of the country property called the Island of Cuba, situated at the edge of Mágina, beside the Guadalquivir River. Am I mistaken?" Barely moving his head, Manuel sustained the captain's glance. He was standing, his hands together and his legs slightly separated, and the dark hand of his wound, revivified by fear, climbed steadily toward his heart, cutting like a knife through the wet tissue of his lungs, and each prolonged silence extending between the captain's words was a pit that augmented his vertigo and the throbbing that made a path for the avid edge of the knife drawing closer and closer to his heart. "Is it true that on your invitation, the individual called Jacinto Solana Guzmán moved to the above mentioned property on the first day of April of the current year?" The captain read with difficulty, or perhaps he was pretending to read and didn't remember all the words he needed to say or the exact manner in which he had to repeat them. "He was ill," Manuel said in a voice so low he didn't think the captain had heard him, "the doctor advised him to spend some time in the country." As in some dreams, he didn't have enough breath to raise his voice, and a feeling of asphyxia or of something oozing in his throat erased the words, leaving only the brief, empty movement of his lips. The captain brusquely rose to his feet, folded the paper, and put it in the pocket of his raincoat. "He is ill," he repeated, his face looking down toward the floor, his tightened lips inaccurately feigning the sad smile he had seen in movies. "Come with me, if you don't mind."

The basement smelled of hospital, and damp stone, and something penetrating and rotting that Manuel recognized before the captain turned on the light and remained next to the door while he walked in. The smell of old, wet clothes, saturated with algae or mud or still water. Under a light like the one in a wartime operating room the body was lying on a marble table whose edges were stained with blood, like the counter in a butcher shop. The black socks, still wet, had slipped down toward his ankles, revealing dead flesh, soiled like the light and the grayish white surface of the marble. The metal frames of his eyeglasses, Manuel recalls, twisted and broken, driven into the clot where the blood was a little darker than the mud, the deep hole like a cut windpipe that he looked away from when he discovered it wasn't his mouth, the black thread that had attached the arms of his eyeglasses. Like details of a bad dream, he recognized the trousers he had given Solana when he left for the country house and the checked jacket with a cigarette burn on the lapel. "It wasn't enough for them to kill him. Maybe he was already dead when they pulled him from the river, but they couldn't accept the hunt ending like that. He was dead and they trampled him and somebody continued shooting at very close range until the magazine was empty." He stepped back, not turning yet toward the captain, not looking at the ruined face or the hand that hung half open, casting a shadow resembling a tree branch on the floor, only at the swollen shoes, the too-short socks over the sharp, definitively frozen ankles in the mourning of an operating room. Now the captain was smoking as he leaned against the wall, his hands in the pockets of his raincoat. "Do you recognize this man?" From a distance he already knew was more lasting than sorrow, because he had inhabited it, a stranger to everything, from the day he saw Mariana lying dead on the floorboards of the pigeon loft, Manuel said Jacinto Solana's name like a vindication and an homage, and when he pronounced it for an instant he felt that the man to whom he alluded was safe from the degradation of death, immune to the solitude of his own body lying on a marble table.

"So he was your friend. Your friend Jacinto Solana, you say. He used your country house to hide bandits hunted by the Civil Guard. Didn't you know that? We knew it. Last night, when we went to interrogate him, he fired at us. There's one guard dead and another seriously wounded. You ought to find other kinds of friends, Señor Santos Crivelli. Your name may not always be enough, and we may forget who you are." The captain turned out the light and locked the metal door with a key when they left the basement. Manuel walked beside him to the offices and interrogation rooms, overwhelmed by an intense feeling of disloyalty and guilt, as if when the light was turned off over the table where Jacinto Solana was lying, he had left him alone in the cold and in death. He thought about the broken glasses, about the broken, open hands, about the body abandoned in the dark, and he didn't care about or didn't hear the captain's questions or the noise of the typewriter or even the things he said in response, and when he left the barracks and saw the blue light of dawn it was as if the basement, the interrogation rooms, the smoke, the voice of the captain had disappeared along with the immediate, distant night in which they had occurred: as if his identity and his life had also been canceled at the end of the night, so that now, as he walked toward the Plaza of San Pedro, when he saw the white facade and circular windows beyond the acacias, he perceived with a clear-sightedness uninflected by compassion or tenderness the empty space that surrounded him forever, its boundary as thin and precise as the line on a compass, as irrevocable as the metal door behind which the body of Jacinto Solana had been left.

II

I WAS TREMBLING when I opened the door to the library, but the footsteps I had heard in there from the courtyard didn't belong to Mariana. Kneeling beside the desk where Manuel usually sat to catalogue the books or pretend he was reviewing the administrator's accounts, Utrera was looking for something in the lower drawers, a confusion of papers scattered around him, which he rushed to pick up when he saw me come in. Hurriedly he closed the drawers and got to his feet, smoothing his hair, his jacket, smiling as if he wanted to excuse himself or explain something. "I couldn't sleep," he said, "I came down to look for a book." For a moment I stood silent at the door of the library, and I didn't say anything when Utrera walked past me, explaining again about his insomnia and moving his head as he took his leave with the servile deference of someone who has been caught committing a reprehensible act and who smiles knowing that pretense is useless. He walked in front of me, and his face vanished from my consciousness as if I had seen him from the window of a train. That was how I looked at everything then: it all fled, devoured by the magnet of time while I, motionless, advanced toward the empty future where Mariana didn't exist, where I didn't exist. "Mariana's alone in the library; she's waiting for you," Orlando had said, but there was no one in the library or in the courtyard with its marble flagstones and columns or any place where I could go. The light was on in the dining room, and through the high glass doors painted white the night breeze came in carrying a scent of mock orange and the rhythmic sound of the chain on the swing. There was a box of English cigarettes on the piano, and a bottle of whiskey whose presence I accepted as an invitation.

I drank as I sat facing the door to the garden, facing the yellow path sketched by the light on the gravel, which stopped just at the foot of the swing and the palm tree. Mariana liked to swing there very slowly, brushing the ground with the tips of her white sandals, so deep in thought and rhythmical in her movement that her gestures seemed like a way of measuring time or of yielding life up to its vacant duration. When she and Manuel came into the dining room, I had finished my cigarette and my drink and was getting ready to go up to my room, estimating beforehand the fear with which I'd cross the courtyard again and climb the stairs where perhaps she would appear, the fear of seeing her and not saying anything to her or of not seeing her and confirming the disillusionment of each one of my steps along the empty hallways. I imagined that my return to the bedroom and insomnia would never end because I couldn't accept the possibility of not seeing her again that night. It had been the same on other occasions, in years past, when I would walk with her to the door of her house counting the steps and the minutes left until we reached it and knowing that I would leave her as she looked for her key and then walk back along the same streets hoping with an infinite feeling of desire and failure that the steps I heard behind me were hers, that her voice had come to ask me to go back with her, inventing some excuse, offering me a last drink. Just like then, when I would turn around believing that someone was calling me and that it was her voice saying my name, I heard her now, close, impossible, I heard a burst of her laughter in the dining room, and when I turned toward the door, fearing that the illusion of her voice would be nothing but one of desire's usual deceptions, I discovered them, Mariana and Manuel, with their arms around each other, and they separated when they saw me because they never embraced when they were with me.

WE AVOIDED ONE ANOTHER'S EYES, and nothing was more frightening than silence, or a glance checked in silence. While Manuel filled the glasses and we lit cigarettes, we were still safe; it wasn't absolutely necessary to speak and not leave a single pause or chink between the words, but afterward, when the three of us sat down, the conversation acquired the apprehensiveness of a flight from a horseman who pursued us and was always at our heels, and we listened to our own words, feeling the pressing nearness of their conclusion, behind which was silence and the only words we cared about and weren't going to say. A second of silence was as unbearable as an empty glass or a hand not holding a cigarette, and that game of calm words interlocked by despair became more difficult, because there were very few things we could talk about that didn't contain the possibility of an affront or allude to the trip that would separate us in two days. Just as they had moved away from each other when they saw me in the dining room, they spoke now of their trip to Paris, avoiding any sign of excessive enthusiasm, indicating the probable discomfort of the plane they would take in Valencia, the official red tape awaiting them when they arrived in France, their fear of not knowing how to establish themselves in a foreign country and in another language. "I," Manuel said, "who have almost never left Mágina," and he bowed his head as if suddenly overwhelmed by a melancholy that wasn't part of the game of mitigating their happiness so as not to exclude me from it. "Manuel's afraid," said Mariana, looking at me for the first time with such fixed intensity that I saw a well of loneliness in her gray or blue eyes. Now the words began to name the things obscurely kept in silence, and for a moment I sensed that it wasn't only guilt or shame that we were running from. "He's afraid we'll lose the war and we won't be able to return to Spain." She and Manuel and I knew it wasn't that or not exactly that, but she was defying him and looked at me to know she was on firmer ground, with that portion of coldness in her, that way of hers—and of Beatriz', I thought suddenly, amazed it had taken me so long to discover her similarity to Mariana—of not accepting the cowardice and procrastination of men, capable, like Manuel, like me, of wasting their lives in a perpetual simulation of rebellion or decency that doesn't help them to renounce completely the desires they once deserved and to establish themselves in reality with resignation or serenity or to tear at the limits of shame and a tainted negligence that doesn't permit them to attain those desires. When I understood this I shuddered as if while she looked at me, Mariana was using my presence to inflict the wound of her defiance on Manuel. Now I, who had taken so much pleasure in spying on their mutual tenderness in order to offer it to myself as a counterpoint to my abandonment, my desperation, my rancor, was part of the same scheme that throbbed beneath their embraces, as well as the words unspoken in the silence we no longer knew how to escape. "Manuel's afraid to leave Mágina," said Mariana, wiping her lips after draining her glass too quickly, looking, I knew, for courage in the alcohol, not audacity, only the tempting sensation that words don't obey one's will but a kind of fatality or lethargy that they themselves impel: "He's afraid to leave his house and his library and his pigeon loft. He'd like it if it weren't necessary to pay in order to obtain what one desires. He wants to have it all at the same time, his house, his wife, his city. His friend Jacinto Solana. Tell him now, Manuel, tell him you'd like for everything to go on the way it was on the day he introduced us." When Manuel raised his head, I realized how long it had been that we hadn't looked each other in the eye. He took a breath and partially opened his lips but didn't say anything, he only filled Mariana's glass and mine and put the bottle back on the floor, looking toward the garden, as if he thought he had discovered a furtive presence in the darkness. I took a drink and spoke so that the silence wouldn't completely humiliate us, or to avoid Mariana's calm, cold face and eyes with the same cowardice as on that afternoon in 1933, in Orlando's studio, when I began to look at the recently started canvas and the sketches hanging on the wall in order not to see Mariana naked. "How I wish I could go away. Not to Paris, like you two, but much farther, and never return, or only when I had become a foreigner and could look at everything as a foreigner." "Where?" asked Mariana, leaning toward me. With both hands she held her chestnut hair away from her face and leaned her elbows on her spread knees, as if the alcohol or a devastating sense of banishment would not allow her to hold up her head. She asked where, and the question was a contained, fierce part of her defiance, but I didn't answer, because Manuel began speaking at the same time, and his words didn't erase Mariana's question, they simply left it hanging in the air between us, like the gray or blue eyes that remained firmly fixed on mine: "We always wanted to leave. We'd look at that map in school, you remember, full of cracks, made of oilskin, so old that in the center of Africa there was still a large blank space. You pointed it out to me and said we'd escape Mágina and discover the source of the Nile." "Jacinto escaped," said Mariana, smiling, and for an instant her smile absolved all three of us. "Not enough. If I had, I wouldn't be here now." I stopped speaking with premeditation and Mariana's question, which had remained in the air like the note of a violin extending into another, higher-pitched one when its sound was already fading, returned to her voice at the same time that she stood up for no reason and took a few steps toward the doors to the garden, then turning around to look at us as if we had fallen far behind and she was inviting us to follow her. "Where would you be?" I remembered a map and a book and a hand-colored postcard where you could see ruined stairways and red columns. It had never been an objective, only a name that shone like beaten copper and an impossible place, a junction of longitude and latitude pointed to by an index finger on the inviolate blue of planispheres. "On Crete, for example. Or on the island where Ulysses lived for seven years with the nymph Calypso. I never understood why he left her to return to Ithaca. I liked to imagine that the *Odyssey* is an incomplete poem, and that in the final canto, which must have been lost or perhaps condemned to the flames, Ulysses abandons Ithaca after a few weeks of sleeping with Penelope and goes to sea again to return to Calypso's island. It must be intolerable to live in the place you thought about constantly for twenty years." "Why?" asked Mariana, not looking at me but at Manuel, who still seemed lost in the lethargy of a meditation interrupted by alcohol. "Because there's no one and nothing that deserves so much loyalty." Mariana turned toward us, letting her empty glass drip onto her hip, weaving a little, as if she were high or attempting a dance step she couldn't quite remember. With her the silence came again to take up its place among us, the useless desire to stretch out my hand and open Mariana's blouse a little more and touch her breasts, which I imagined to be as warm and translucent as the skin on her temples, and also the awareness of each of the minutes of the secret truce I had been granting to myself since I saw them come into the dining room and knew I had to leave and that I couldn't leave. Each word, each cigarette and mouthful of smoke, each raw swallow of alcohol burning my lips a truce, a truce and a boundary and a stopped clock when it was no longer possible to attempt any word against the silence. That was why the three of us eagerly felt saved when Orlando's voice and laughter came into the dining room like a gust of wind rattling the panes. He and Santiago had wet hair and shining eyes, and they smelled of clean clothes and a feminine cologne that was like a shameless announcement of their happiness. "Traitors," said Orlando, leaning on Santiago's bare shoulder, pointing at us with his index finger like a drunken marksman who cannot keep his gunsight on the target, "it seemed this whole house was a mausoleum, but you stayed here to drink up the last bottle behind our backs." They looked for glasses in the sideboard, and when they opened the glass door they knocked over a tray, causing a crash of sharp broken glass on the floor that nobody tried to clean up. He and Santiago kicked away the broken pieces and then filled their glasses until the whiskey spilled over the top and onto their hands, which they wiped slowly on the sides of their trousers, laughing and leaning on each other as if fatigue didn't allow them to be completely drunk but only to feign inebriation, an obstinate and vacuous and desperate happiness. "I've been listening to you, Solana," Orlando said, "Santiago and I were behind the door, and we heard you telling those stories of yours about trips you're never going to make. Solana, my brother, you wandering Jew, are you sure your father isn't a new Christian? Because if he isn't, I can't understand this exile of yours, this not belonging anywhere or to anybody, not even to your modesty and your shame, which is Jewish and Catholic. Look at him: you look at him, Mariana. He's still ashamed. All of you are. And I think the Republic is the name you give to your shame, though you know this Republic isn't yours and this war that we're all going to lose would never have been your victory. Whoever wins—and we're not going to win or any of you or whoever that Republic is with its banners and its *Official Gazette*—you'll have lost, Solana, not because your side is weaker or because those son-of-a-bitch French and English have invented that filthy Catholic commandment of nonintervention, but because your Jew-without-a-country blood keeps you from the possibility of belonging to a winning side. Don't look at me like that. I belong to the Iberian Anarchist Federation because I lack the modesty or the shame that obliges my friend Jacinto Solana to be a member of the Communist Party. If at the beginning of this month I had been in Barcelona and not in Madrid, I'd be shot now or locked up in one of those republican jails that defend shame, but God or Prince Piotr Kropotkin wanted me to live in Madrid and for you two to invite me to tomorrow's wedding when you'll marry decency, Mariana and Manuel, just as my friend Solana married modesty when he joined the Communist Party. They say, first the war and then the revolution, exactly like a decent girl puts off her boyfriend at the door, because first come caresses and then happy surrender in marriage.

But that hope is a fraud: this war is the end of the world, and there won't be any future after it."

In Orlando's gestures was the fiction of a fortune-teller who recites poems in old provincial theaters. With what arrogance he moved among us, free, not trapped by our silence, immune to everything, even the sudden old age he already knew would come when love, firm and cruel like a hero recently returned from hell, deserted him. "You've never descended, Solana," he would say to me, "you still haven't written what you ought to write because you haven't gone down to hell, and you don't know what it means to come back and preserve the degree of rationality necessary for remembering." Now Manuel and Mariana and I dissolved at the touch of his words as a dream dissolves when it is shattered by the reality, victorious and obscene, of waking, the cold of dawns beyond the sheets. As if he were posing for a photographer of slightly pornographic postcards, Santiago drank and leaned his elbow on the piano, wearing the red undershirt of a lover for hire, and he shaped his lips into a kiss of dubious tenderness each time Orlando stopped talking to catch his breath and searched Santiago's eyes for a confirmation that he didn't always grant. When I saw him get off the train carrying Orlando's portfolio and mislaid luggage, I thought Santiago was an adolescent, but now, that night, victim of the successive snares of disillusionment and chastisement that knowledge usually set for me, I found him older than Orlando and Orlando's tenderness, older and viler than any of us, antecedent to everything, like a stone statue with painted lips or one of the women with pale thighs who looked at me from doorways on certain streets the first time I came to Madrid. He wore a red undershirt that bared his weak chest darkened by hair that perhaps had grown in recent months not as a declaration of any sort of manliness but to crudely belie the illusion of adolescence that one could find on his face, and white trousers very tight around his hips that moved like mollusks or a woman's hips. Orlando, lost in a drunkenness that he must have imagined as sacred, kissed him on the lips, and with a leap of his ungainly body, he sat on top of the piano, provoking the echo of a single low and very long note. From there, swinging his legs, he looked at us as if from the seat of honor of a pride untouched by shame.

"There's no more need to pretend or renounce," he said, pointing at me, "because what's coming now is the Apocalypse. All of you remember what the papers are saying about Guernica. Phosphorus bombs and scorched earth, fire and brimstone, as in the Cities of the Plain. Your desire makes you afraid because none of you has accepted that it's not possible to choose it without choosing indignity and betrayal at the same time. What all of you have discovered now I found out when I was twelve or thirteen and realized I liked men, not women. That's why you can fall in love and continue to feel the need for decency. You both desire a woman, Mariana, for example, and you feel a little disloyal and a little adulterous, but you don't know anything about fearing a temptation that, if discovered, would make you accept the filthiest word as a sign of shame. I'm going to paint a picture: all of you, this morning, at the country house, in that light Van Gogh couldn't even imagine, united by guilt, and I to one side, like Velázquez in *Las meninas,* looking at you as if you existed only in my imagination and I could erase you just by closing my eyes, like a god."

Then things happened in a way I've given up trying to put into order or explain. I've remembered and I've written, I've torn up sheets of paper where I'd written nothing but Mariana's name, I've stubbornly resorted to the superstitions of literature and memory to pretend that a necessary order existed in that night's acts. During sleepless nights in a cell for those condemned to death, I've caught myself trying to recover, one by one, the most trivial events, gnawed at by the peremptory need not to surrender to oblivion a single one of the casual gestures that later, in memory, shone like signs. I've looked at Mariana's eyes again which, ten years later, when I returned to the house, werc still fixed on me as they were in the photographer's studio, when I still didn't know that what was revealed to me in them was an infinite, motionless farewell. I go outside, to the esplanade of the country house, and the moon that turns the earth white through the branches of the olive trees is the same moon that paused in the May air that night when I turned my back on the others and went out to the garden, still hearing Orlando's voice and the notes of a jazz tune that Manuel had begun on the piano. Mariana was writing something on a paper and covering it with her left hand as if she were afraid that someone might be spying on her, and when she raised her eyes, she looked toward the doors to the garden, but she couldn't see me because for her they were a mirror. Sitting on the swing, I saw them in the squared yellow light of the windows, as if I were watching a film from the unpunished darkness, and like the movie theaters of my adolescence, the piano music infected the figures with its slow, convulsed melody. Mariana stopped writing, looked at the paper, tore it in half and then into very small pieces that she let fall from her closed hand when she stood and crossed the dining room and stopped at the threshold to the garden before moving toward me, walking on the oblique path of the light.

THE MUSIC MANUEL was playing and Mariana's footsteps acquired an undeniable direction. With his head sullenly sunk between his shoulders, Manuel looked at his own hands and at the keyboard as if he were leaning over the edge of a well, weaving with violent delicacy the rhythm of the song, "If We Never Meet Again," which I heard constantly during that time on the phonograph in the library. Behind the white square of the windows, I can remember the red spatter of Santiago's undershirt as he listened in silence, I see or very probably imagine Orlando standing next to him, not listening to the music, looking at Mariana's back when she stopped at the door to the garden and guessing step-by-step what would happen when she began walking again. Sitting on the swing, not moving, I saw her coming toward me, and I looked away from her when she was beside me. Her eyes had the dark brilliance of a lake in the moonlight, a depth untouched and smooth like her temples or her cheeks or the warm skin of her thighs when I moved my hands under her skirt to caress them. "Orlando's right," she said, sitting down beside me, moving the swing a little with the tips of her shoes, "he says you're unsociable. We're all in the dining room listening to Manuel, and suddenly you turn as if you were going away forever and come here, to watch us from a distance." We were together in the space of air marked off by her perfume, and when she pushed the swing she leaned against me a little and brushed my face with her hair, but the proximity of our bodies made the never vulnerable line, the exact distance at which a caress is halted and denied, more intense and physical. "I've had a lot to drink," I said, still not looking at her, "and it's too warm inside." Mariana took my face between her hands and obliged me to look at her, taking from my lips the cigarette I was smoking and tossing it to the ground, as if she were disarming me. Now the brilliance of her eyes dilated in the darkness seemed very close to tears or to a kind of tenderness I had never known how to find in them until that night. "You always talk to me like that, ever since you came to Mágina. You tell me it's hot or that you've had too much to drink or that you're in a hurry to leave for Madrid because you're preparing for that writers' congress, but if I don't look at you, I can't recognize your voice, it's as if someone else were talking to me, and if I look into your eyes to be sure you're still you, it's as if you didn't know me. It's not that you don't look at me or talk to me. It's even worse, because you look through me and talk to me as if I were a statue. I've spent two months in this house thinking about the day you'd arrive, imagining that with you I'd get to see the places where you played as a boy, the plaza with the poplars you told me about so often, and now that you're here, you're farther away than if you had stayed in Madrid. Before you came to Mágina, at least I had the hope of receiving a letter from you. But you didn't write to me in all this time." The music came from a greater and greater distance and was completely erased at times behind Mariana's murmuring voice that was so close, and looking into the dining room while she spoke to me was like spending the night beside the window of a house where the open shutters reveal a remote family supper caught off guard. I meant to tell her that since the day I met her I hadn't stopped writing to her: that all the things I had written and published since then were nothing but the chapters of an infinite letter meant only for her, that even when I went in those unruly trucks of militiamen to recite ballads on the Madrid front and I climbed up on the wooden platform and heard the applause generated by my poetry, I was thinking about her and looking for her face and her impossible smile of complicity or approval among the rows of soldiers standing in their rough military greatcoats. I was going to say something to her, perhaps an ignoble excuse, and I may have been about to suggest that we return to the dining room with the others, choosing the appropriate, neutral tone of voice, but Mariana found my hand in the darkness and pressed it slowly, very gently at first, then grasping it with a serene, sustained violence that did not show on her face when she turned to look at me. Further down, on her skirt, between our two bodies, our hands clutched and intertwined, emissaries of immodesty and unspoken desire. "I'll write to you when I go to Crete," I said, "I'll send you a postcard just for the pleasure of writing your first and last names in a place so far away. I don't think I'll add anything else: just that palace with the stairways and the red columns on one side, and on the other your name, Mariana, Mariana Ríos." "I like to hear you say my name. It's the first time you have since you came here." "Names are sacred. Each thing and each one of us has a true name, and it's very difficult to learn what it is and say it." "Tell me what my name is. Tell me what the name of Crete is." A single word, I thought, I knew lucidly, a single word and the boundary and the fear will be torn apart as if they never had existed, as if that interminable music were not sounding in the dining room and the windows in front of us weren't lit or the doors to the garden not wide open. "Crete is Mariana," I said: in the silence I heard voices conversing and didn't know whose they were. Very slowly, as if in completing that gesture one would hold back all the instants and days that had passed in vain since we met, Mariana brought her lips close to my mouth from the distance of the other corner of the swing, from the afternoon when I had seen her naked in Orlando's studio, from each one of the hours when I had her and lost her without knowing that all the acts of my life, and fear and guilt and postponement, had been meticulously conspiring to clear the way for that island in time when I kissed her and licked her tears and let myself be demolished, trapped in her body, repeating her name just as she was saying mine as if everything we had to say could be summarized in our names. We rolled onto the ground and onto the cold grass like animals greedy for darkness, and I opened or tore open her blouse to look at her white breasts in the light of the moon shining on them while her hands searched and caressed, awkwardly, delicately going down between trousers and shirt, very awkwardly and very delicately going down between skin and the rough fabric of my trousers.

Then I opened my eyes and a violent light that didn't come from the dining room obliged me to close them. We were lying on the ground, and the light from a very high window fell on us covering us with the shadow of a single figure outlined there. Without getting up or entirely breaking the embrace that protected both of us from fatigue and our recovered sense of shame, we fled toward the darkness, and for a moment the light kept shining like a yellow, empty rectangle on the place where it had taken us by surprise, but the shadow spy was no longer at the window. We didn't dare look at each other again until the light went out. Before guilt could rise up around us like a filthy nocturnal tide and drown us, Mariana, kneeling in front of me, touched my lips, my eyelids, the back of my neck, buried her fingers in my hair and drew me once again to her mouth, repeating my name with a dark intonation that made it unfamiliar, as if it no longer alluded to me but to another man whose face she could not see completely in the darkness of the garden, because it was destined to be erased and leave no ashes or attributes of pride in her memory at the precise moment we stood to return to the dining room.

"They've all left," said Mariana, still smiling at me as she fastened the buttons on her blouse. She smoothed my hair with her fingers, and with a handkerchief that smelled exactly like her skin, she wiped my mouth smeared with lipstick, and each gesture was a small sign of complicity and tenderness. As if we were walking through a strange city, she took my arm as we crossed the garden, leaning on my shoulder, and at the door to the dining room she stopped and embraced me for the last time, lifting her hips to press her belly against mine. The piano was open and there were glasses and empty bottles on the table, the floor, next to the broken glass and the stain of spilled alcohol. Mariana lit a cigarette and brushed my face as she placed it between my lips, and then she left, her head bowed, and was about to come back to me when she reached the door, but she didn't, she only stood quietly for a moment and closed the door very carefully when she went out to the courtyard, as if she were trying not to wake someone.

12

AT DUSK THE MIST ROSE over the reddish gullies and the canebrakes and the tall white oleanders on the banks, becoming sluggish in the bends of the river. The mist was dense and blue on moonlit nights and became opaque, solid, white or faintly yellow when the sunlight began to shine on it at dawn, spreading over the course of the river, very close to the ground, like the smoke from the bonfires that on icy December days crept among the packs of olive groves and did not rise above the gray tops of the olive trees. In the mist the whistle of the night trains, emissaries from the sea, the only clocks for measuring how long insomnia lasted, became more intense and more distant, and from the other bank of the river, from the other side of the train tracks, the Island of Cuba emerged at dawn like an island in the mist that still lay in long tatters among the almond trees and detached very slowly from the low roofs of the house, like the last waters of a cautious receding flood whose crest no one had noticed. Before dawn, from the window of his room high above the mist and the slopes of the river like the moat of a castle, Jacinto Solana, just awakened by the passing of an interminable freight train closed like the trains in the war, looked at a darkness turning silver and blue and ashen with the disciplined slowness that time has as it moves on clocks. It was, perhaps, because the entry in his diary was undated, a morning in mid-April, when Solana still saw no proximate end to his book and was desperate with fear of the possibility that he never would finish it, a disorder of truncated pages and sleepless nights and ashtrays filled with stubbed-out cigarettes while the sterile silence was shaken by barking dogs and the noise like a distant storm of a train crossing the metal bridge over the Guadalquivir. It was undoubtedly the time when he still always carried the pistol that Frasco saw on the first day at the bottom of his cardboard suitcase, between the bundles of typed pages that he tied carefully with red ribbon and the dark suit and the shirt that had belonged to Manuel. On the first day, the first afternoon, when Frasco showed him the old barn with the window overlooking the river where twenty-two years later Minaya would find the blue notebook and the cartridge wrapped in a piece of newspaper, Solana untied the ropes around his suitcase and took out the paltry possessions of a fugitive with a kind of methodical absorption that excluded conversation and disorder, like someone who always lives in hotels and knows the desolation of arriving at one on a Sunday afternoon. And as naturally as he arranged his clothing on the bed and his typed and blank pages at the corners of the desk, Frasco saw him take out the pistol, which was very large and looked recently oiled, and place it on the pages like a paperweight, beside the inkwell and the pen, as if it weren't a weapon but a neutral object and somehow necessary for writing, and when he went down to the kitchen to eat that night the pistol bulged in his right jacket pocket. At first he only wrote and waited, Frasco said, and the pistol and the pen always remained within reach of his hand, even when he left the area of his seclusion to take a very short walk among the almond trees or drink a few glasses of wine with him next to the fire where the stew for supper was bubbling. As if he never stopped waiting for someone, he watched the bridge over the river and the path that ended at the house, and sitting next to the fire he remained fixed in the light of the flames, not paying attention to Frasco, searching perhaps behind the crackling of the wood for an indication that at last the footsteps of his pursuers had arrived, calculating the time left in the truce, the blank pages he still needed to fill.

"Lights of Mágina in the dark, above the mist, reflected in it as if in the water of a very distant bay. Uncertain liquid brilliance, candles lit in the last chapels of the churches. Everything seems to sleep, but nothing is sleeping, nobody is sleeping. Lights of Mágina above a great plain of insomnia." Later, when the dogs began to bark and the mules could be heard stirring in the hot breath of the stables, the city was being born at the top of its hill at the same time that the lights went out, emerged from nothing, from the darkness or the mist, materializing as if by chance around a pointed tower higher than the roofs or above the precise line of the wall. Then from the window of his room Jacinto Solana would look in the distance for his father's farm, the small white stain of the house next to the irrigation tank and the poplar tree, but he couldn't make it out in the uniform density that expands and descends between the supports of the wall and the first lines of olive trees like an oasis that surrounds the city, and gradually that failure of vision acquired for him a tonality of relief that also alluded to his memory, as if the distance his eyes could not decipher had also been established between his present consciousness and the fatigued and guilty habit of his memories. Mágina, from the Island of Cuba, was a detail in a landscape or a watercolor by Orlando, not a city but its remote illustration, a docile pretext for contemplation, an empty corner ready to be occupied by literature, and those who had lived in it or still lived in it were losing very slowly and almost sweetly their quality of real creatures in order to conclude completely their transfiguration into characters in a book that at the end of May, as Minaya learned in the blue notebook, was very close to its final pages and no longer loomed as an impossible goal or an intimate form of siege, for it had eventually become for Jacinto Solana an almost peaceful habit of his seclusion in the country house, like the wine and conversation with Frasco and the walks with no destination among the olive trees, which took him very far from the house, toward the sierra, to the slopes of bare slate and harsh valleys of red or sulfur-colored earth as bare of any trace of human presence or eyes as the seas of the moon. After two months of living in the Island of Cuba, the old pain and the old tenderness poisoned by rage and remorse were fading like the shape of a face it is no longer possible to recall, and for that reason the pages in that notebook Minaya found in the lining of a gloomy jacket contained, intermingled with the atrocious story of the last night Mariana lived and the appearance of her corpse in the pigeon loft, short annotations written in the margins or on the back of the squared pages, in which the voice of the narrator until then dedicated to and imprisoned in the plot split in two as if folding over into the attitude of a witness. "28, May, 47. At noon it's very hot and I go down to the river to swim. Icy water. Two pages after lunch, without a single erasure." "May 30, 9 pm, a plane over the vertical of Mágina, at dusk: long trail of smoke tinged with pink paler than in clouds. Maybe include it in chapter on country house, at the end, when they return to city and nobody in the car speaks." In the small hours of May 30, Solana was probably writing a passage that Minaya couldn't find, and to which some annotations in the blue notebook alluded: Manuel enters the marriage bedroom carrying Mariana's dead body in his arms and lays it on the unmade bed. Minaya, who imagined that scene as if it were his own memory, abruptly found it transformed into a question of style: "Correct the fall of nightdress so thighs not exposed. Only her knees, very slim, dirty with droppings. The word 'bloodless' prohibited."

Frasco says that toward the end, Solana hardly was writing, or at least not in the obsessive way he had during the first weeks, and the pistol even disappeared from his desk and his pocket, as if he had forgotten his fear or it no longer mattered to him. Almost at the end, in the blue notebook, in Frasco's words, the man whom Minaya had pursued and constructed until he had given him a destiny as firm as the dates of birth and death that marked the limits of his biography, suddenly got away and left behind nothing more than a few trivial notes and the memory of a peaceful indolence, like a book in whose best chapter the printer inadvertently left a few pages blank: he returned later, but with another voice and a face that in Minaya's imagination was as unfamiliar as the coldness of the final pages of his diary, to recount Beatriz' arrival at the Island of Cuba and her departure for the serene certainty of the death that was waiting for them, her and the two men with her, when they walked out the door of the country house and went into the stand of almond trees, and there was nothing after that, only the squared pages where Solana wrote no more than the exact date of the last day of his life, underlined with a firm stroke of the pen, like a long final flourish: June 6, 1947, dawn, barely twenty-four hours after writing the end of the last chapter in his book. But like those pages where he had summarized and saved himself, though nothing was left of them for the future reestablished by Minaya in the spring of 1969 except some fragments and first drafts as difficult to put in order or explain as the ruins of a buried temple, the final hours of his life were hidden in darkness only partially lifted by the statements of Frasco, who didn't see him die, who only heard the shots and the shouts of the men pursuing him over the roofs of the country house and along the muddy slope of the Guadalquivir and could see, surrounded by the rifles of the guards, how they tossed his corpse onto a truck like a sack of clay.

"I had gone up to Mágina to see my mother and on the way to settle with the administrator the accounts for some day laborers," Frasco said, "and that night when I was back on the estate I saw a light in Don Jacinto's window but didn't want to bother him because I imagined he was writing, and so I put the mule in the stable and went to sleep, and about four or five in the morning I woke up sweating with fear, because I dreamed I was back in the war and was being killed. Then I heard shots very close by and footsteps on the stairs, and three Civil Guards knocked down the door and came into my room and pushed the barrels of their rifles into my chest while one of them held a flashlight so close to my eyes I couldn't see anything. From their shouts and the way they looked at me and hit me, I knew that this time they didn't want to scare Don Jacinto or take him off to jail but kill him on the spot like vermin. But he defended himself, he killed one of them, and even when they had fatally wounded him, he must have hidden in the canebrakes and kept running downriver, because it took them several hours to find his body and the sun was already high when they dragged him back along the bank and threw him in the truck."

FOR FRASCO THIS UNEXPLAINED and sudden eruption of death that came like a gust of winter wind to take his fruit and then left with the sputtering of the truck engine, without leaving any trace of its passing on things, without its infamy lasting in the June morning except for a puddle of mud and algae at the door of the country house, seemed like the confirmation of a destiny of mourning initiated eight years earlier, when a patrol of Falangistas came to the Plaza of San Lorenzo to take Justo Solana away with his hands in cuffs and a bloodstain at the corner of his mouth. They were the same, he always knew, even though they hadn't spoken for so many years, even though his father hadn't known how to read or write and never had left not only Mágina but the Plaza of San Lorenzo and his farm at the foot of the wall and the road that led to it, because those three places constituted the only landscape in the world he cared about. Frasco, who had played with Jacinto Solana as a child and had heard in his youth, in conversations in the barbershop or the tavern, the story of the son who rose up against his father and deserted the land and fled one night to take a train to Madrid, discovered at the Island of Cuba that Jacinto Solana had spent his life inhabited by the shade of his father, and that the never completed flight or desertion he began twenty-two years earlier when he finally boarded one of those trains whose whistles, like those of invisible ships, had stirred him for as long as he could remember was transformed into and ended in his return. His gray hair, his tense unshaven jaws, his hard expression of solitude and disdain took on with every passing day a more interior and darker resemblance to his father's features, and even the way he gave himself over to his insomniac devotion to the written word repeated with mysterious loyalty the obsessive connection that since the beginning of the century Justo Solana had maintained with the land that he himself had broken and cleared and on which he built a house and dug a well of deep, icy water with no help except his own hands and no motive other than his desire not to obey anyone and his pride as the founder and sole owner of his land and life. At night, when Frasco returned to the house and lit the fire and prepared supper in the huge kitchen where on winter dawns the crews of men would gather before going out with their long heather staffs to the olive groves, Solana would come down from his room with a lost or fatigued air and sit next to the fireplace slowly to drink a glass of wine while he looked at or stirred the fire and still didn't say anything, as if he hadn't returned from the place and time where the practice of literature confined him, or reestablished his dealings with reality: he would look at the fire then with the same slow stupor with which he had looked at a blank page, searching its empty presence for the clue to a future word, and only after he'd had several glasses of wine, which Frasco refilled like a silent cupbearer, did he seem to recover the power of speech and the certainty of where he was, the semblance or model of another region and another house situated as firmly on the pages of his manuscript as the Island of Cuba on the bank of the Guadalquivir. He would speak about his father in an indirect way at first, as if hovering over his memory without daring to invoke him, with a sense of shame very similar to fear or the sensation of distance that injured him forever that morning in his childhood when he said good-bye to him in the semidarkness of a corridor in the school, a prefiguration or warning of the definitive leave-taking so many years later, on the dark May night in 1937, when he turned on the path to say good-bye and saw him old and vulnerable and alone in the now-remote light of the fire he had lit to cook the supper he didn't want to share. He spoke at first as if to himself and tended to choose the oldest images he had of his father, but he didn't take long to confirm that Frasco was not only a witness but also an accomplice to his memory, because he told him things about the older Solana that he had forgotten or never had known and that abruptly disproved the fatigued, abstract figure in which forgetting had deposited his memories, so that when he heard Frasco talking to him about his father, it was as if he suddenly had discovered the true face of a stranger, like coming across a fixed, strange gaze that was somehow familiar and finally discovering, after an instant of unrepeatable hallucination or lucidity, that one was seeing oneself in the mirror without realizing it. He learned, for example, that during the last days of his life in Mágina, before the war, Justo Solana had taken to frequenting, always alone and as if secretively, the taverns of melancholy drunks whose lights burned at night in the last houses of the slum district around the wall, he learned that his solitude, his house that was empty and too large, his fierce determination not to accept the excuse of old age when work overwhelmed him, had been wearing him down with slow, pressing constancy, as the passage of time wears down and disfigures a face and levels the places where no one lives. Sometimes Frasco saw him walking toward the Plaza of San Lorenzo feeling his way along the walls, as if he were moving in the dark, and he said that in his jacket pocket he usually carried a well-folded, visible Madrid newspaper with an article signed by Jacinto Solana. He remembered him one afternoon, in a corner of the barbershop, impatient and gruff, passing his hand over his unshaven chin while he waited his turn and paid no attention to the conversation of the others. "Listen, Frasco," he said to him, and took out the paper, unfolding it very carefully, as if he were afraid his large hands would tear that fragile, unknown material, not the paper but the faint weft of the printed words, "you know how to read, find the thing they say my son has in here. But don't read it very loud—I don't want them to hear." Then he put the newspaper back and patted his pocket like someone making certain he hasn't lost a valuable wallet, and he took it out again in the last taverns of the night, already worn out, like his expression, anachronistic, useless, dirty around the edges where he had folded it and at the corners of the pages where he had left the print of his thumb dampened with saliva, and he spread it out and smoothed it on the bar to ask one of the opaque drinkers if he knew how to read and to ask him to look for a first name and a family name on the damaged pages that he was so secretly familiar with.

"They were the same," Frasco said, "and they were killed the same, the way they killed people then, not asking or explaining anything, they would come to somebody's house one day and take him away in a car, and then he'd show up in a ditch or beside the wall of the cemetery with a bullet in the back of his neck and his hands tied with rope or a piece of wire. They said that a lot of people were killed because they'd been marked during the war, but the only thing they could accuse Don Jacinto's father of was that he'd never gone inside a church in his life, and they shot him just the same, as if he had done something, and Don Jacinto thought it had been his fault, 'to take their revenge against me, Frasco, that was the only reason,' he would say to me, and I think that if when he first came here he had that uneasiness that didn't let him rest or sleep at night, it wasn't because of the book he was writing but the guilty conscience he had when he thought about his father's awful death. And in the meantime, the madman Cardeña up there, in the sierra, a step away from the estate, knowing everything he knew and remembering it very well although he seemed to have lost his mind, because he had been in the militia, not one of the men who risked their lives at the front but one of those who always went around with their coveralls clean and their berets at a slant and who were very brave when they marched through the plaza in Mágina or stopped somebody at night to ask for papers. The madman Cardeña was the only one who knew why they killed Don Jacinto's father and who denounced him. One day when he was drunk or really crazy, he told me he was in the patrol that went to look for that Falangista, Domingo González, who spent almost a year hiding in the attic of the house of some relatives, and who finally escaped even though they chased him along the roofs and shot at him. They got to the house before dawn, to surprise them when they were sleeping, but the door was very strong and all the bolts were closed, so they needed an ax to knock it down."

Eyes of a blue as pale as that in the veins visible beneath the skin of his temples, a blue melting and liquid like that in the eyes of the blind, the beard scant on his cheeks, long and hook-shaped on his chin, rigid, as if it were false, crossed by a brilliant thread of saliva that he would lick as he looked at something with his eyes of a hunted animal, standing among the olive trees with his lame, misanthropic dog panting, adhering to his trouser legs, as motionless as a distant tree on the slope he climbed each night followed by the dog and the half-wild she-goats of his flock to return to the shelter of the slabs of slate where he and the goats and the toothless, cowardly dog lived in the obscene confusion of a trash pile or a stable. Before Frasco led him to the hut and raised the filthy curtain to penetrate the darkness where eyes were gleaming neither animal nor human, only circular and staring, stripped of all reference to a body, all connection to the light shining outside in the yellow fennel and the dark splinters of the escarpments, eyes of phosphorus lit by irrationality or horror, Solana had seen the madman Cardeña up close only once, on the riverbank, and it was like meeting straight on an animal that quietly challenges and then flees like a bolt of lightning without any other sign of its appearance remaining except the sudden stabbing of his eyes. As indecipherable as an animal, as the dog whose harsh panting had urged him to turn around impelled by the certainty that he was not alone, the madman Cardeña contemplated Solana with an expression of impassive attention, and before fleeing he was shaken by a convulsion as violent and rapid as a shudder, and he said something or simply opened his mouth and couldn't remember what the language of other men was like, because Frasco said that since the spring of '39, when he came to the sierra fleeing the troops that had occupied Mágina, the madman Cardeña had maintained no other relations in his solitude than with the she-goats and the lame dog who always walked behind him like an extension of his shadow, so that his feigned madness had in the end become true and he no longer knew how to speak except in abrupt monosyllables and brief syncopated phrases like pants or barks that he almost never concluded. The hut where the madman Cardeña lived, attached to a vertical wall of slate, went very deep into a cave in whose final recess he had taken shelter with his dog when Frasco and Solana went in to look for him. He was trembling, holding on knees that were tightly pressed together an old Mauser that he had kept for seven years after running out of ammunition, and caressing the ill-treated back of the dog while he shook his head, not daring to raise his eyes, and cursed and denied as if he were being accused in a dream. "I don't remember anything. It wasn't my fault. It was the other one, he stopped the old man, he says to him, give me the ax. Then he told them it was me." He let go of the rifle, which fell to the ground with the trembling of his knees, and he clawed at his beard or clawed at the air with nails that were long, curved, and hard, like uniform beaks, retreating until he rested the back of his neck against the wall. "Cardeña," said Frasco, taking a step toward him, bent in the semidarkness because the roof of the cave was so low they couldn't stand up straight, and they waited there in an attitude of useless ambush, exhausted by the stink in the air, by the extremely slow waiting, "Cardeña, don't play the idiot with me, you know you can't fool me. Tell us what you told me yesterday, when I gave you the decanter of wine."

He prowled the perimeter of the Island of Cuba and spied on Frasco from a great distance, almost never daring to cross the invisible frontier drawn by the white boundary stones on the ground, but sometimes he and his dog went onto the estate with the wariness of wolves and spied on the house from the grove of almond trees or followed Frasco, hiding behind the olive trees, jumping from one to the other with an unsettling capacity for silence. "Cardeña, come out, I've seen you," Frasco would shout, standing motionless, pretending he still didn't know the place where the madman was stationed, just as when he went hunting and found a very recent trail, and after a while the madman Cardeña and his dog would emerge in the middle of the grove, looking at him with alienated, suspicious eyes and shaken by the panting of hunted animals. The madman prowled around the house and followed Frasco to ask him for a decanter of wine or a packet of tobacco, and when at last he was facing him, he would leave on the ground, not saying a word, a sheepskin or a decapitated kid, like a merchant who doesn't know the language of the distant region to which his journey has brought him, and he would hide again and lie in wait until Frasco returned with the tobacco and the wine. Then he would leave his refuge as if he were catching his prey, and when he fled to the river's embankments, he would shout ancient threats and cowardly curses that in the distance became confused with his dog's barking. He would call Frasco a traitor and a Jew and a lackey of capitalism, and he predicted a rat's death for him if he dared denounce him to the Civil Guard, whose three-cornered hats and dark capes appeared to him each night in the shadows of the trees like an unmoving army against which he waged ghostly battles entrenched inside the fences around the corral where he kept his she-goats, aiming at the valley with his unloaded rifle and shouting blasphemies and challenges that dispersed echoes among the precipices of the sierra.

A few hours after running into Jacinto Solana on the riverbank, the madman Cardeña called Frasco by whistling to him from the almond trees, but this time he wasn't carrying a recently beheaded kid in his bag, and he didn't threaten him with death if he didn't hand over five liters of wine. "I know that man you're hiding," he said, smiling with his empty eyes, his mouth open and as wet as the snout of his dog, panting next to him, hiding between his legs. "The only one hiding here is you, Cardeña. So you can go back the way you came, or I'm calling you know who." Trembling, the madman Cardeña and the dog raised their heads at the same time, as if they had detected the scent or the footsteps of an enemy approaching in silence. "You're hiding him so they don't kill him like they killed his father." Then Frasco turned around: the madman, happy at having trapped him as he was walking toward the house, didn't say anything yet, he remained squatting, looking at him while he caressed the dog, who licked his hand, and acting as if he were following the flight of a bird through the branches of the almond trees. "There was no way to knock down that door," he said, not to Frasco, perhaps to the dog or to himself, to the part of his memory not ravaged by madness, rocking back and forth on bent knees as if he were hearing music, "we were knocking and they didn't open, why would they open if they already knew what we were looking for, and then the old man passed by, riding his mule, and that bastard who denounced us afterward saw the ax sticking out of the saddlebag and says, Comrade, lend us the ax and we'll give it right back, and the old man was scared, he didn't want to, and the other one took out his pistol, if you don't give it to us in a nice way we'll take it in a not nice way, I'm denouncing you, we'll see what you're doing at this hour with an ax, the old man trembling, not getting down from the mule, I remember it as if I could see him now, I went up to Mágina just to get the ax, and now I'm going back to my farm, and the other one put his pistol to his chest and says, well, now you're going to knock down that door, inside there are some fine gentlemen who don't want to let us in, now that's rude, and the old man, who couldn't stand because he was so scared of the pistol, got off the mule and took out the ax and at first he sort of looked sideways and hit the door very slow, like he didn't know how to use the ax, until the other one pointed the pistol at him again and said, we'll see if he's on the side of the

Falangistas inside, and the old man hit the lock three times and knocked down the door, and put the ax back in the saddlebag right away and without getting back on the mule he took the reins and went down the street, but then, when the troops came in, that Judas lost no time going to the Falange and telling them he knew the names of the men who killed the family of Domingo González, and that I was in charge of the patrol, and like everybody knows they asked him for more names, and so to get in good with them, he denounced the old man as an accomplice and was the ruination of us both, since he'll never be at peace as long as I live, because one of these days I'll pick up the rifle and go to Mágina and kill him, and then let them come for me, they won't catch me alive at night or during the day, I'll hang myself before I give myself up to them."

He had spoken as if reciting an interminable litany, in a monotone, indifferent, somnambulistic, his chin rigid against his chest and his hands clasping his knees as if to roll himself into a ball or maintain the monotonal impulse of his rocking, and abruptly, without any variation in his voice announcing that he was about to fall silent, he bit his lips and picked up the rifle again, sitting up slowly against the damp hollow of the cave, fixed now on Solana with an attention sharpened by fear, as if he had recognized in him the other man, the dead man, whom he hadn't seen since that dawn in 1937, returned from the dead to pursue him to the last tunnel of his refuge, to the end of his memory or his madness. They didn't leave yet; they remained still, bending down, facing the man who no longer saw them, waiting for words they could hear, which meant nothing. "Cardeña," said Frasco, putting his hand on his shoulder, as if to wake him, "Cardeña." "Let's go," said Solana behind him, in a very quiet voice. When they left him alone, the madman Cardeña murmured slow tatters of words with his arms around his dog's neck and clawed at his pointed stiff beard with meticulous rage, as if carrying out a methodical flagellation in secret.

13

ALL I HAVE LEFT is the weary privilege of enumerating and writing, of calculating the precise instant when I didn't do what I should have or could have done or the way in which a gesture or word of mine could have modified the passage of time as the erasures or details added to my manuscript modify the story I imagine and recall as stripped of any intention of surviving because of it in anyone's memory as an Egyptian scribe putting the finishing touches on the figures and signs of a funeral papyrus in order to place them in a hermetically sealed chest in the darkness of a tomb. Now I know that if in the small hours of May 22, 1937, when I saw Mariana walking barefoot and as if asleep toward the door that led to the pigeon loft, I had remained a few seconds longer behind the column in the gallery that kept her from seeing me, I would have seen just a few steps away the face of her killer. Now I know that while I looked at myself in my bedroom mirror and wrote in the light of dawn the final verses of my life, someone was grasping a pistol and silently climbing the stairs to the pigeon loft, and my father, who had gone up to Mágina in the dead of night to find an ax and come back to the farm before daybreak, realized too late that he should have obeyed the presentiment of fear he had when he saw the patrol of militiamen and was about to pull on the mule's bridle perhaps and head for another street. He shouldn't have slept that night either while I walked around the bedroom I was going to leave the next morning and sat on the bed without finding the will to take off my glasses or untie my shoelaces and got up again as if I had heard someone calling me, only to sit down not against the pillow but facing the desk where a burning lamp opened a crack of light in the mirror in which my face was a portrait of future dark and an inert prophecy of how I would remember everything and of the past time that concentrated and accumulated there to watch over my insomnia and testify to the last boundary of successive simulations in a biography so tenaciously sustained in them that it suddenly fell apart, like the ash of a paper that did not lose its shape when transformed by fire, when it was no longer possible to use the mask of a new imposture. Not writing yet, not daring to go out to the hallway because I knew that as soon as I stepped on the chess maze of white and black tiles I would walk to the parlor and the door of the marriage bedroom and listen to Mariana's laughter and Manuel's dark breathing and the sound of bodies tirelessly entwined and clinging, I smoked quietly at the desk and looked at myself in the mirror, like an actor so possessed by the character to whom he surrenders his life, that one night, in the empty theater, after the last performance, when he takes off the false eyebrows and the wig and is cleaning off his makeup with routine skill, he discovers that the cotton soaked in alcohol is erasing the features of his true and only face behind which there is simply an oval, livid surface, as smooth and vacant as the glass in two facing mirrors. Like the photographs of Mariana or of our false shared youth that Manuel kept and classified long before the war ended with the melancholy perseverance of a caretaker in a provincial museum, hanging them on walls or placing them randomly on sideboards and on the shelves in the library according to an order as carefully established in the catalogs of his memory as they were invisible to anyone else, my face, that night, was a lucid, brutal prophecy of my past, and everything I never knew or never wanted to know gathered densely around me, at my back, in the shadows and corners of the room, in the hallways of the house, like distant relatives who return in their mourning to hold a vigil for someone who never thought of them when he was alive and about whom they had heard nothing for many years. It was four or five o'clock when I left the bedroom, afraid of running into someone in the hallway. No doubt at that hour he had already got up and harnessed the mule and was going back and forth between the stable and the single room that served as his bedroom and storeroom with the restlessness of excessively early risers: as a boy, before he called me, I would wake, alerted by fear, when I heard his footsteps on the stairs or the violent cough brought on by his first cigarette, and I would hide desperately under the top sheet, as if by remaining still and keeping my eyes closed I could stop or slow down time or dig in the warm hollow of the sheets a burrow where the bitter odor of tobacco couldn't reach or my father's footsteps climbing the stairs again to knock on my bedroom door and throw me with no excuses into the wretchedness of cold and dawn. Recently combed, inflexible, his face red from washing with icy water he had splashed on in the corral, as immune to sleep as he was to fatigue or tenderness, despising me because I walked around groggy and couldn't find the saddle for the white mare. Next to him my clumsy slowness, my physical cowardice in handling animals and tools grew worse, so that his blind resolve when he worked frightened me more than the possibility of punishment. The shape of a hoe was as brutal and intractable as the muzzle of a mule. He noted the ineptitude, the cowardice of my gestures, the absent air with which I carried out his orders, and he shook his head as if accepting an insult he never deserved.

BUT I DIDN'T THINK about him even once that night. Treacherously, while I crushed my cigarette into the marble on the night table and opened the bedroom door, resolved to swallow the indignity or shame, to approach like a wolf the region of the house where it was possible to hear Mariana's laughter and inviting racy words, peremptory commands, brief muffled shouts of exaltation and agony, chance pushed my father like a slow magnet toward his house in Mágina and modulated his step to lead him to the precise place and moment in which a closed door and a pistol and an ax would cause the conspiracy of death against us all to germinate. I want to stop him now, as I write, I want him to choose another street to return to the farm or to take so long to find the ax that when he passes the house where Domingo González was hiding the door is already knocked down and he moves to one side to keep the mule from walking on the splinters. Any small alteration in the architecture of time can or could save him and save Mariana and stop the killer who was already holding the pistol and watching her, quieting his breath against the badly joined boards of the door to the pigeon loft. He saw her from the back, leaning on the windowsill, looking at the line of the roofs and the fig trees in the courtyards above which the distant smoke of chimneys and the icy blue of dawn ascended, as if she were contemplating the sea from the deck of a ship, serene and solitary, like someone who has undertaken a journey announced in a dream, naked beneath the transparent cloth of the nightgown that outlined the shape of her hips and thighs in the faint backlight of air sifted by silence and the sound of sleeping pigeons that woke suddenly and flew into the corners and against the roof of the pigeon loft when the brief shock of gunshots resounded all through the house. I was writing at the time. Before the witness watching me in the mirror with impassive solemnity, incurably sick with literature, I had read aloud the verses I conceived of as a whispered, very long sentence as I prowled the hallway of the gallery and the marriage bedroom like a sleepwalker, and in my voice poisoned with gloom those words that several months later I would find, unfamiliar, printed, indifferent, definitively strange, like the beauty of a woman we once loved who can no longer move us, on the pages of a dirty, tattered copy of *Hora de España* that a soldier left on the train taking us to the front. "Mágina," I wrote, "May 22, 1937," and when I was about to cross out a word to break the excessive rhythm of one of the lines, it was as if all the glass in the gallery and the dome had shattered under the deafening roar of a multitude of pursued men or animals. I had a premonition of sirens and airplane engines rising above the blackness cut by searchlights and the flash of a machine gun, because the instinct of fear returned me to the hideous nights of the bombing of Madrid, but behind the first explosion, in whose immediate recollection I now discerned nearby voices that moved away and a tumult of steps on the roofs and rifle shots, there was only a silence very similar to the one that is prelude to the whistle of a bomb that doesn't explode. I ran to the window and moved aside the curtains, and on the other side of the street I could see, at the edge of the eaves, a very tall shadow that bent forward as it ran and slipped on the roof tiles and finally disappeared as if it had abruptly deserted the body it was pursuing. Then nothing, silence, an empty minute like the foliage in a woods where a hunter's gun has gone off, then footsteps and voices and the weeping of a woman who was Amalia, who came into my room without knocking to tell me that Mariana was dead in the pigeon loft, and the sudden memory of Mariana walking barefoot on the cold tiles a step away from me, my shame hidden behind a corner of the gallery—the curtains were closed across the courtyard windows, and a symmetrical figure invisible to my fascination or my insomnia was stationed behind them, its hand tense on the pistol butt and its ear attentive to the sound like silk swishing of Mariana's footsteps—my stupefaction and desire grown to the now indivisible boundary of my longing to die ever since I learned what the taste of her mouth was like and felt on my fingers the wet warmth that caught at them at the top of her thighs. Some nights, in the house, during this winter, I've left the room with the circular windows, believing I was fleeing the typewriter, and only when I came to the door of the parlor and saw, when I turned on the light, the wedding portrait in which Mariana looks at me with the loyalty of the dead from the distance of that indelible afternoon when she put on her bride's dress and obliged Manuel to put on his now useless lieutenant's uniform to pose for the photographer, I understood and accepted that I was repeating the same steps I took ten years earlier in order to listen to her voice behind the closed door of the bedroom where she was turning over entwined with Manuel and breathing with the same fever that had demolished me beneath her body when she said my name and felt my face like a blind person in the perfumed, avid darkness of the garden. Like that night, with the fervor of someone arriving for an impossible appointment, I entered the parlor and looked beneath the door of the bedroom that no one has occupied since then for a line of light, a sign of the one that shone on the gleam of their bodies and was still lit when dawn came through the window, when Manuel was asleep with fatigue and happiness and Mariana, very carefully moving the arm abandoned to sleep that still held her waist, put on her nightgown and closed the shutters before going out so that the light of day would not wake Manuel. I stood still at the glass door to the parlor and the now-forgotten scent of Mariana's body was not in the air, only the discord between the immobility of places and the headlong flight of time, the persistence of the green-topped table and the bronze clock held up by Diana the Huntress and the sofa with yellow flowers, which had been there long before Mariana came to the house and perhaps will remain in the same indifferent quietude when Manuel and I have died. I stepped forward, after turning on the light, poured less than a glass of anisette from the bottle that Manuel and Medina had left on the table after turning off the radio on which they had listened to the remote music of the "Hymn to Riego" and "The International," lifted a light-tobacco cigarette from Manuel's cigarette case, and when I raised my eyes to the oval photograph, from any angle in the room Mariana was looking at me, fixed on me, as if her eyes were pursuing me in the parlor, just as they had looked for me, without a single gesture or movement of her head betraying her, while the photographer prepared his camera and arranged the lights and Orlando and I talked quietly in the semidarkness that covered the other half of the studio. Like the delicate trace of the touch of a leaf that belonged to a tree that became extinct in another era of the world and survives forever transmuted into a fossil, or a shell's whorls imprinted on a rock very far from the sea with a precision more unalterable than that of the effigies on ancient coins, that was how the moment, when my eyes met Mariana's after an entire day of avoiding each other like two accomplices who do not want to be connected to a crime, endured thanks to chance and the magnesium flash firmer than memory and as undeniable as the bronze profile or light tunic of the Diana the Huntress that was always on the sideboard in the parlor. From there I heard the tenacious, failed panting of Manuel and the laugh and entreaty broken by a long groan in which I didn't recognize the voice of Mariana, and still I didn't move, as attentive as a spy, supported by the darkness, when the silence fell and the respiration of two exhausted bodies reached me like the sound of the sea that one hears and still doesn't see behind a line of tall dunes. I was writing in my imagination, I counted syllables and words as if I were segregating an inevitable material completely foreign to my will, a long thread of drivel and dirty literature as interminable as the flow of thought that followed me everywhere and traced the shape of my destiny and each one of my steps. Followed, pushed by literature, calculating under the remorse and jealousy and fear that someone would surprise me in the parlor, the spurious possibility of recounting that critical moment in the future book I was always on the verge of beginning, I went out to the hallway groping at the walls and furniture, and I was returning to my room when at my back the sound of a loose tile that someone was walking on made me hide behind a corner of the gallery. I saw her pass so close I could have touched her just by stretching out a hand impelled by the instinct to repeat just one caress, but her proximity was as remote and forbidden as that of the blind, like them she was surrounded by an irremediable space of solitude. Disheveled, barefoot, a recently lit cigarette between very pale lips, her face illuminated by the dawn had the mysterious intensity of a gaze that divined everything, a serene light tempered by the devastation of love and the melancholy of fatigue and knowledge, as if at the end of that night her beauty and life had been purged of every banal attribute in order to be summarized in the perfection of a few indelible features, just as a few lines drawn as if at random on the blank space of the paper had been enough for Orlando to sketch a profile of Mariana that could never be captured by photographs.

Afterward, when I saw her stretched out and dead in front of all of us, I realized that perhaps it hadn't been the light of dawn that sharpened her features but a secret divination of the death that was already calling her to the pigeon loft with a voice only she could hear. "Didn't you hear the shooting, Don Jacinto? They killed Señorita Mariana." Amalia was crying and covering her face with both hands, and I didn't understand yet or didn't accept it; I got up from the desk and shook her by the shoulders, I moved her hands away from her face and obliged her to look at me because I didn't comprehend the words blurred by weeping, and she wiped her tears and pointed upward repeating that a stray bullet, that a shot in the forehead, that Mariana was dead in front of the unshuttered window in the pigeon loft, her knees dirty with droppings and her nightgown raised to the middle of her long white thighs, her hands extended and open and her face turned to one side and partially covered by her hair. When I went up to the pigeon loft, Manuel had already closed her eyes. He was kneeling next to her and he wasn't crying; he only extended an almost firm hand in which you could barely notice the violent trembling that shook his shoulders to touch her cheeks very delicately or move away from her mouth a lock of hair that had caught on half-parted lips. He seemed to be shivering with cold next to a fire that had gone out and would never raise his head and stand and come toward us, obscurely gathered in front of the door to the pigeon loft as if an unspoken command or the line of a circle in whose exact center Mariana's head lay prohibited our taking a single step toward her. Standing together, motionless, enclosed in a silence in which Amalia's weeping throbbed against our unified consciousness like the tearing of a wound, we separated momentarily only when Medina and the judge and a captain of the Assault Guard made their way past us to examine Mariana's body, and then immediately, as if the space they passed through had made us vulnerable, we grouped together again to close it, silently driven by the cowardly urgency that brings together a crowd surrounded by fear: Orlando, beside me, squeezing my hand without looking at me, without looking at Santiago, whose eyes were still drowsy with sleep and perhaps last night's alcohol; Utrera, who was blinking and whose respiration was very deep, broken at times as if by a stabbing pain; Doña Elvira, in perpetual mourning, staring not at Manuel or Mariana but at a place in the air that contained nothing, perhaps at the gold and blue strip of May sky that outlined the empty rectangle of the window or the roof where some guards advanced on all fours, looking for something among the broken tiles; Amalia, who cried in screams and wrung large red hands that sometimes tore at her hair or wiped her eyes and mouth in an emphatic gesture. I remember her long weeping like the wailing of a dog and the way Manuel's shoulders and knees trembled when Medina helped him to stand and brought him toward us, moving him as if he were a sleepwalker or a blind man who suddenly had been left alone on the streets of a strange city. I went up to him, said his name in a low voice, "Manuel, it's me, Solana," with desperate tenderness, useless shame, taking him by the arm with a clumsy, blind pity meant for him and myself and the never-denied connection of that mutually sworn loyalty that had begun twenty-five years earlier in the courtyard of a school where we wore blue aprons and had lasted until it was condensed finally in the name of Mariana, but he, lost and alone, didn't recognize me or didn't see me, and he continued trembling as if he were shaken by a fever that blinded him and dilated his pupils, moving his lips as if he were murmuring something, acknowledging the voice of someone calling him whom he didn't see.

As IN DREAMS, in the pigeon loft I am a figure partly removed from myself and more opaque than the others. The pain I remember, the sudden, bitter sensation like the taste of blood in a mouth that has fallen against a damp cement floor, belong to that shadow, and I can't relive them because there are certain kinds of pain that act as anesthesia on memory. At the bottom of a great darkness, the pigeon loft illuminated by the indecent sun of the morning of May 22 that paused at Mariana's waist like the embroidered edge of the nightgown in the middle of her thighs is a cubical space suspended in the air, as far from the house and from Mágina as I am from those days, as Mágina is from me, high above the twilight mist and the gray-bronze of the olive trees, as are the words I write about things I've already given up recovering and naming. I'm alone, the pigeon loft has gradually and silently been emptied, like a church a few minutes after Mass is over, and on the staircase landing, behind me, Medina is talking to the captain of the Assault Guard, who leaned out the window before he left and ordered his men to wait for him in the street. "She died instantly," says Medina, and I hear the click of the metal spring that closes his case with the same unappealable certainty that he and the captain display in establishing how Mariana died. "She heard the shots and went to the window. Or she probably was already looking out and the shot hit her in the forehead before she saw anything. Don't you agree?" The captain doesn't say anything, probably he shakes his head with the sorrow of someone accepting a misfortune that has befallen others. "But let's see, Medina, you're a friend of the family, can you tell me what that woman was doing half-naked in the pigeon loft at that hour? They were married yesterday, weren't they?" I'm alone, and for the first time since I came in, I move toward the empty place where Mariana's body lay, on the thin disturbed layer of droppings and feathers like thistle flowers or tufts of cotton. Leaning on the sill of rotting wood where Mariana may have placed her hands before she died, I look at the impassive scene, the roofs that extend like dunes toward a distance of faded blue where the sierra is outlined, almost wiped away by the glare of a sun that trembles as invisibly as hot air above the chimneys. She had gone up to the highest spot in the house to say good-bye to the city where she always knew she was an outsider and to look for the last time at the things Manuel and I had looked at since we were born, because she would have liked, she told me once, to be part of the oldest paradises in our memories, to remove from hers all the recollections of an earlier life she didn't care about, so that its large, voluntarily emptied area would be ready to receive a new memory never to be divided from ours, a territory as intimately designed for happiness as the memory of certain rooms from childhood. She never spoke to us about hers, and not even Orlando, her oldest friend and the delicate, hermetic confidant of those terrifying chasms in her heart not visible from a distance when she momentarily transformed before me into an unknown woman, knew how she lived or what she did in the years before the spring of 1933, before the precise day he found her sitting in a café at a table on which there was only a glass of water, with her straight hair cut like Louise Brooks' and a resolute determination to model for a painter or photographer who wouldn't rush to touch her breasts as soon as she was naked. "She died in the same way she appeared to us," I thought, looking at the same roofs and blue brightness Mariana saw before she died, as if I could find in them the key her eyes always denied me, "she died and left exactly as she came, as if she had never been here." She didn't feel anything, Medina had said, she didn't even hear the shot or know she was going to die: a sharp blow on the forehead and then darkness and forgetting as she fell on her back and her already inert body rebounded on the dirty planks. But I remembered that her knees were soiled with droppings and that on her forehead, sticking to her hair and the thin border of darker blood surrounding the wound, was a pigeon feather, so small the killer didn't notice it when he wiped her face. He also forgot to pick up the cartridge of his single bullet or perhaps he couldn't find it, driven by the need to get away. It was next to the doorsill, in the crack between two floor planks, hard and vile and hidden, like those insects that fold themselves over when they sense danger until they take on the shape of a little gray ball.

14

BEFORE THEY REACHED THE RIVER, they turned off the engine and
headlights and let the car slide along the thin white dust where the
moonlight revealed bird tracks like the characters in a strange piece
of writing. The car very slowly entered the wet gray fog as it descended to the end of the road, and the low, flexible branches of the
olive trees whipped against the windows and then cracked like slow
whips when they were left behind, perhaps provoking the flight and
shriek of a bat that had watched with no surprise the passage of the
curved black body on which the dust gleamed with a tonality slightly
less livid than on the road. When they reached the railroad tracks,
next to the station's freight shed built at the entrance to the bridge
that extended the road to the country house, they saw above the fog
the grove of almond trees and the esplanade and the irregular building of the Island of Cuba, its baroque pediments covered with whitewash where the moon shone faintly and its roofs laid out at such
unequal heights that they gave the house the air of a rugged, broken
ruin, like those castles whose debris barely stands out on the slope
where they were built and yet they display, especially from below and
at a distance, the traces of an architecture conceived both as a
labyrinth and a watchtower, an arch in the air, a high earthen wall, a
concave roof under which swifts make their nests. On level ground,
very close to the tracks, they used up the car's last impulse forward

to turn it between two olive trees, and they stopped it there, hidden beneath the hard branches at whose ends the olives were already blossoming in fragrant yellow clusters. The leaves on the olive trees scratched at the windows, moved by a breeze they couldn't feel when they got out of the car, and had, at so short a distance, from the darkness of the interior, a metal gleam similar to that of the rails or the river water. On the white, cold earth that shone like sulfur the shadows of the trees had the precision of silhouettes cut out of cardboard, and behind the low volume of fog, beyond the river whose sound was still confused with the wind in the branches, the rise of the Island of Cuba was prelude to a limitless, empty space, mauve, gray and blue, violet at its farthest limits, vast and high like a dome held up only by the light of the moon over the uniform olive trees that sank into precipices of dry torrents marked by yellow broom and then ascended along the side of the hill with the methodical obstinacy of the ocean and stopped their advance at the spurs of the sierra, their roots still adhering to the bare rock, like mollusks clinging to the fissure in a cliff, on slopes of sour thickets where not even the lunatic who planted them there would climb to pick their fruit. Alarmed, exhausted, uselessly on guard, they watched as a night train passed before them, like a long, tremulous ribbon of yellow lights, and its whistle told Solana that it must be between one and two in the morning, because Frasco had taught him to calculate the hour according to the height of the sun or the passage of the trains, and to determine, even if he didn't see them, if they were freight trains or mail trains or express trains, if they were traveling to Madrid or returning to one of those cities on the other side of the sierra that Frasco had never seen and invariably imagined as very large and very close to the sea. Lying on the bed, not yet turning off the light that Beatriz saw before the car stopped knowing it was lit only for him, recognizing him in it just as in another time she would have recognized him in a jacket left on the back of a chair or in the enduring odor of his body between the sheets in the bedroom, Jacinto Solana took pleasure in the certainty of finding himself alone at the Island of Cuba, and the size of the empty house and the olive groves and the landscape surrounding it increased his delight in solitude, no longer driven by literature, because that afternoon, he recorded without emotion in the blue notebook, he had finished the last page of his book, *Beatus Ille,* and now he had before him, on the table that would never again be disordered with rough drafts and the smoke from cigarette butts, a pile of pages as impeccably ordered as those seen on the shelves in stationery stores, but completely covered by a writing that greedily swallowed up the margins and had deserved the absolution of a period. He was mildly calmed and exalted by the mere physical presence of the stacked pages, the solid, certain touch of their corners, the odor of the paper, as if the book were not the score of possible music that other minds and future eyes would bring back to life but an object already definitive and beautiful, closely tied to its weight and the persistence of its volume in space, enclosed in it and its shape like a bronze figure: grown, with the imperious slowness of a tree or a branch of coral, by the addition of the edge of each of the pages that now testified to the duration of its progress, like concentric rings in the recently cut trunk of a tree. He thought about his past life and couldn't understand how he could have survived so many years of empty desperation when the book did not yet exist, and he recalled with distant gratitude the stories he wrote as a boy in his notebooks to show to Manuel later, passing them in secret beneath the desk they always shared, whose somber wood stained with ink blotches was like that of the desk over which he had bent, writing, since he arrived at the country house. He would illustrate those narratives copied from the vicissitudes of silent film with drawings that he colored painstakingly, and at the foot of each he wrote a brief caption between ellipses, as they did in the illustrations for serialized stories, and on the last page he would write *End* in tall block letters, carefully following with a dampened pencil point the line of the squares so that the firm strokes would not swerve. Like successive rehearsals that never could satisfy him completely, he wrote the word *End* many times in the blue notebook, fascinated perhaps by its sound, its shape like the point of a knife, and he probably had written it that same night in the center of the last page of his book, two or three hours before the car with its headlights turned off stopped among the olive trees, on the other side of the river, tracing its letters on the paper with the delicacy and relief of a Chinese calligrapher who concludes, on a silk cloth, the manuscript that has consumed his life.

WHEN HE HEARD THE TRAIN whistle that returned him to time and brought him back from his exhausted lethargy, he got up from the bed and took the candle that was his light to go down to the kitchen, because he had finished a bottle of wine and was not resigned to not prolonging the solitary celebration of the end of his book, as sweet as the last day of school and the lit stove in a corner of the classroom, when he looked at the snow-covered courtyard through the windows of winter and knew that the next morning his father would not shout at him to get up before dawn because all the roads would be blocked by snow. "It's him," said Beatriz, staring at the light that moved away now from the window and swayed back and forth and disappeared and then returned, more opaque and distant, to a front balcony, to the entrance door that poured it over the paving stones when it was half open. "I'm sure it's him," she repeated, as if the others hadn't heard her or didn't believe what she was telling them. "But there must be more people in a house that big. There must be dogs, I suppose," said the man in the light suit sitting next to her, not raising his eyes, not sitting up on the leather seat against which he was resting his unshaven face, as if he had renounced all desire or impulse not to survive but to prolong the flight that had been brought to a temporary halt before the railroad tracks, as if before a definitive, ordinary obstacle. Behind them, in the back seat, the youngest passenger bit his lips and panted quietly as he gripped his wounded thigh with both hands, devastated by fever, by the absurd certainty that the moonlit night and the house where the others spoke vaguely of finding refuge were the final trap that death had set for them. They smoked, not getting out of the car, hiding the lit end of their cigarettes in the hollow of their hands, as if that minor precaution could free them of the Civil Guards who were tracking down the car along nearby highways, or was unavoidable even in the density of the olive trees and the fog. They kept the car windows up, and the smoke, as it thickened, wrenched a gloomy cough from the throat of the wounded man, who leaned against the back of his seat with his mouth open and the right side of his trousers soaked with blood, his eyes brilliant beneath almost closed lids, a cigarette hanging from his lower lip like a thread of saliva. "Let's go," said Beatriz, groping in the dark to pull out the key, "he'll help us. He probably knows some way to cross the sierra without going back to the main highway." She was the one driving the car, Solana noted afterward, the one who had torn one of her silk blouses to make bandages to stop the bleeding from the thigh wound, the one who took the wheel when the other one, the man in the light suit whose profile Solana had seen through the window of that same car six months earlier, began to cry without dignity or tears in the ditch of a forsaken highway and doubled over and vomited when he saw and smelled the blood and remembered the dry, terrifying sound of the shots that tore like horn thrusts into the hip and thigh of the passenger whose name he never knew. "A comrade, she says, perfectly serious," Solana wrote, "a fugitive from the Valley of the Fallen with false documents and a fake mustache and the hair at his temples tinted gray as if for a bad play, a dead man as premature and undeniable as she herself or that guy with white hands and pink brilliant nails who gave them his car and came with them not because he believes in the Republic or in the Party or even in the possibility that they can come out of their trip alive, but for the simple, obscene reason that he's in love with Beatriz and wants to marry her though he knows that's impossible while I'm alive and was even during the years when it seemed I was dead." "I asked him to lend me the car for a few days," says Beatriz, laying out before me like an unformulated reproach the self-sacrifice, the gentlemanliness of the other man, probably her lover, "I told him it was a very long and possibly dangerous trip, and that I didn't want to involve him in something like this, but he insisted on coming with us, he even said he'd denounce me if I didn't let him go. Now he's dying of fear, the smell of blood nauseates him." In love, submissive in advance, prepared to hide bundles of clandestine newspapers in the storeroom of his dress shop or to take her in his own car to a distant city and the door of the prison through which would come the gloomy phantom who once was married to Beatriz and whose face he has seen up close only tonight, in love and avid to carry out all her desires, to guess and anticipate any desire of hers that Beatriz hasn't confessed to him yet, whether it's a handkerchief like the ones she's using now to wipe away blood and perspiration from the wound or a foreign perfume or a reckless, deadly trip to that city on the coast whose name she didn't want to tell me where a smugglers' ship is waiting to take the fugitive to Gibraltar or North Africa, if he lives long enough to get there or they're not killed first in a police ambush. Very pale, his fitted linen jacket stained with blood like a butcher's smock, he looks at me with rancor, with the part of his fear that belongs not to his flight or the memory of the shots and the blood but to the evidence that it is because of me that Beatriz has been denied him and that a single gesture or word from me would be enough for her to leave him with the same serene resolve as on that January morning, in front of the prison, when she got out of the car and walked on high heels across the mud of the highway to go into the tavern where I was drinking beside the fogged window and looking at him, who smoked and counted every minute as he leaned on the steering wheel and couldn't overcome the fear that she was gone forever.

"Let's go," said Beatriz, and she opened the car door, but the wounded man and the other man didn't seem to hear her, as if they didn't believe in the mirage she announced when she showed them the house. She got out with her head bowed to keep the branches of the olive tree from tangling in her hair, and when she looked again for the light she had seen slipping from window to window, like ghosts in the movies, she couldn't find it, but there was a motionless figure in the middle of the esplanade, at the edge of the river embankment, and although from that distance it was impossible for her to see his face, she recognized in a melancholy way, like someone who listens to a piece of music and recovers an intimate feeling that had been forgotten, the shape of his shoulders, the way Jacinto Solana sometimes looked at things with his head tilted to one side and his hands lazily thrust into his pockets. "I'll go alone," she said then, "you two wait here." She crossed the tracks, the bridge, she disappeared in the fog, emerged on the other side of the river, and from there she turned to verify with relief that the car had dissolved in the shadow of the two olive trees hiding it. As indifferent and silent as a tree mineralized by the moon, Solana didn't notice her approach, and saw Beatriz only when she was almost at the end of the road and said his name, first in a quiet voice, as if she were afraid the light that dilated forms and endowed them with the hardness of figures of salt could also enlarge and disfigure the sound of voices, then shouting or perhaps hearing her own voice like the pale shouts in dreams, because the sound of the water erased it, and it vanished in the brilliance of the moon and in the warped space of the olive groves and the liquid blue sierra, as weightless and extended as the fog. "Jacinto," she said again, in a louder voice, but her voice didn't sound to him like a shout, "it's me, Beatriz."

"The three of them are dead," he wrote a few hours later in the blue notebook, after leaving them hidden in the wine cellar and lowering the heavy trap door with the feeling he was adjusting the slab of stone over a tomb, "they're dead and they know it, and maybe I am too, because death is a contagious disease. When they put the car in the shed and I took them to the kitchen, they walked back and forth as if they were in a death cell and ate with the same bitter greed I saw so often in those men who knew they were going to be shot at daybreak. The wounded one shakes and sweats with fever and Beatriz passes him a wet handkerchief for his forehead, and then she returns to scraping the bottom of a can of sardines with her oil-stained fingers, with her long painted nails. They tell me they've gone twenty-four hours without eating, that last night, after the encounter with the Civil Guard, they fled along highways they didn't know and didn't stop until dawn, in an abandoned house, in the middle of a red plain where there was nothing and nobody, not a tree or an animal or a human or a sierra or a city in the distance. At nightfall they left again for the south, and suddenly, Beatriz says, when she had lost consciousness of how many hours she had been driving, she saw in the headlights the sign for a city, Mágina, and then a lit, deserted gas station that might have a public telephone. As on other occasions, in years gone by, when letters hadn't been enough and she would call Manuel to ask if he knew anything about me, she asked the operator for his number and waited a long time until she heard the alarmed voice stupid with sleep that said the Island of Cuba and explained how to get here. The Island of Cuba, she says to me with exhausted irony, 'only you could end up living in a place with a name like that.'"

They were dead, though nobody came to find them in the wine cellar for the whole day they spent there and where they would still be if on the following night, when the wounded one had already lost consciousness and was raving and groaning as he writhed on the pillows and blankets they put down for him in the backseat of the car, they managed to cross the sierra on the road Solana showed them from the Island of Cuba, the old muledrivers' route, abandoned when they paved the main highway, because they carried death with them like fugitives from a city invaded by the plague. They were dead from the precise moment that the passenger, who had not said a single word since they left Madrid, as if silence were a part of his clandestine identity, asked them to stop the car in the middle of a plain through which the highway ran limitlessly in a straight line toward a darkness whose final boundary it didn't seem they would ever reach, got out, tilting his hat over his eyes, then stopping at the ditch, his back to them, as if he were looking for something on the dark horizon, his hand in his jacket pocket where he probably had a pistol. In the rearview mirror Beatriz saw yellow headlights that grew larger until they blinded her and lit the side of the man who was still motionless and taller against the line of darkness. She heard doors open and then a distant voice, a shout, an order, and the passenger turned toward the light and began to run slipping on the gravel in the ditch, and when he was already getting into the car he was paralyzed for a moment against the window, staggering once, and then again, clutching at the edge of the door when the second shot sounded, falling back inside like a soldier wounded as he left the trenches.

Dead, Solana thought as he watched them eat, his elbow on the mantle over the fireplace, witnessing from a solitude untouched by their appearance the devastation caused by flight and fear, the persistence of failure, the clothes abused and covered with dust, the unshaven faces, the border of sweat around the collars of white shirts. Beatriz' high heels twisted when she walked, and her tall hairdo collapsed over her forehead when she bent toward the wounded man. It wasn't the failure and general rout at the end of the war, he recalled, because then the razed fields and the entire universe seemed to share in the defeat of the men who filled the highways like flocks of despair and silence, but a solitary flight, unpremeditated, absurd, the abandonment of a place conquered by fire whose survivors escaped still wearing the clothes of the fiesta they were celebrating, the light jackets and trousers for the June night, the delicate torn stockings, the perfumed handkerchiefs soaked in blood. When she finished eating, Beatriz wiped her oily mouth with the back of her hand, leaving a streak of red on it. She smoked with her eyes closed, exhaling large mouthfuls of smoke, and the other one, her lover, the coward who loved her who hadn't even had the courage to look at Solana when he shook his hand, went up to her and stood behind her, as if he were guarding her sleep, and when he bent down to say something in her ear, he put a hand on her shoulder and extended his fingers very gently until he touched her neck. "I watched them, I knew he wasn't going to say anything to her, that anything he might say would be nothing but a pretext to get closer to her and demonstrate to me, or to his own fear of losing her, that he could talk to her in a tone of voice that only lovers use and put his hand on her shoulder and caress her neck. Then Beatriz opened her eyes and slowly moved his hand away while she looked at me, as if the immobility of her eyes on mine could wipe out the house and the persecution and the night and leave us alone at the beginning of time. Brusquely I pretended I was tending to the wounded man: I looked for water, a glass, I moistened his lips and when I looked at Beatriz again, her eyes no longer searched for mine and the other one's hands lay white and useless on the back of the chair where she was leaning."

He wrote again that night, when he lowered the trapdoor to the wine cellar and recovered as if it were a gift the feeling or appearance of his solitude in the house, he closed all the shutters on the ground floor and checked the chamber and the safety on his pistol and put it on the table while he wrote in the blue notebook as if even after finishing his book he couldn't elude the instinct of literature, Minaya thought, as if things didn't happen completely until he had transmuted them into words that didn't crave the future or the light, only the unmitigated intensity of their own poison, hard words written for oblivion and the fire. He wrote past dawn, and the next night, when the others left, even before the car drove away along the road to the sierra, he closed the outside door of the house and returned to the pen and the blue notebook to recount their departure, but this time he didn't even have time to finish a page, and the last words he managed to write were the prelude to his own death. He heard dogs barking and when he went to the window, he saw the military capes moving, cautiously climbing the embankment, the cold gleam of the moon on the patent leather of the three-cornered hats. That's exactly how Minaya imagined him: unexpectedly liberated from fear and literature, he thought about the others, about Beatriz' gaze, about her pride without supplication and her loyalty firmer than disenchantment and betrayal. Beyond the last line in the blue notebook, in a space free of reality and words, not recalled by any memory, Minaya wanted to contrive the ambiguous figure of a hero: Solana still hears the engine moving away and estimates that Beatriz will press harder on the accelerator when she hears the first shots behind her. While he stays at the window shooting at the pursuers, the car will enter the sierra and gain ten minutes or an hour or an entire day of urgent freedom. Calmly he records the proximity of the shadows that come along the river and fan out on the red clay of the embankment to surround the house, and then, just as he has closed the notebook and replaced the cap on the pen, he puts out the candle, takes the safety off the pistol, leans partially out the window, still protected by the darkness, waiting until the Guards have come so close he can reach them with his bullets.

PART THREE

I am a distant fire and a far-off sword.
—Cervantes, *Don Quixote*, I, XIV

I

ONE BY ONE THE CAPSULES, in the palm of the right hand, between the fingers, rolling between thumb and index finger, small pink bullets that will not wound the temple, that after each sip of water disintegrate in the dark acids of the stomach and the suicidal blood that beats so weakly in eyelids and wrists where hard veins trace a ridge like a scar on yellow flesh, gradual coins for counting and crossing off each minute and hour of the last night, for acquiring not death, which even now is inconceivable and abstract, but an avid pacifying somnolence of thought and of fatigue, a sweetness similar to that of the traveler who arrives very late at the hotel in a distant city where no one is expecting him and, overcome by sleep, slips between cold strange sheets that become hospitable in response to the heat of his body and keep him warm when he falls asleep and loses his hold on time, reason, memory, like the darkness in a childhood bedroom. The capsules on the night table, the glass of water, the cigarettes, the exact curve of the pillow where the back of the neck rests without sinking down completely, which avoids the horizontality of a dead body or a sick person and allows the effortless contemplation of the open window, on the right side of the room, of the door closed so cautiously that nobody will open it now, of one's own body whose shape is erased toward the foot of the bed like a dune eroded by the wind. They are made of a glossy material that fingernails cannot pierce, neutral to the palate, smooth and neutral in the throat, slowly perforated and worn away, like a coin in a cup of acid, when it reaches the stomach and dissolves there, in that lugubrious unknown cavity that forms part of me as surely as my hands or face, their dose of poison and longed-for lethargy, their sweetness of a hand outstretched in the darkness that brushes the eyelids and grants them sleep as if returning sight to the eyes of a blind man. Only the person who chooses the manner and hour of his own death acquires in exchange the magnificent right to stop time. He uproots wrinkles and numbers, leaves the double-inverted receptacle of the hourglass empty, spills on the ground the water of the clepsydra as if he were knocking over a glass of wine. What remains then is the pure, strange shape of the glass, the blank sphere, a wafer or circle of paper, the interminable immobile duration of a stopped watch on the wrist of a dead man or a stopped clock in the living room of a vacant house. There is nothing but sterile time between two heartbeats, between a capsule and a sip of water, between two instants as stripped of their own substance as the extension of a desert, but he, Minaya, doesn't know this, and perhaps never will know it, because he still imagines that time is made to the measure of his desire, or the negation of his desire and he scrutinizes clocks like an astrologer trying to determine the urgent shape of his future in them. In the Mágina station he looks at the large clock hanging from the metal beams of the entrance canopy, walks toward the end of the platform, toward the red lights and the night where the rails disappear, he asks what time the mail train from Madrid will arrive, he confirms on his wristwatch the truth of the voracious advance toward midnight indicated by the hands on the great yellow sphere hanging like a moon above his head. Twelve o'clock, very soon, bells in the Plaza of General Orduña, in the parlor, in the library where the scent of lilies and funeral flowers still lingers, the train that now hugs the bank of the Guadalquivir and blows its whistle when it begins to climb the slope to Mágina, its windows lit and fleeting among the olive trees and its long lead-colored cars, slow and nocturnal like the trains that took men toward a horizon dazzled by the brilliance of a battle that rumbled in the air and over the earth like a distant storm. Passively he waits for the arrival of the train that will carry him away from Mágina and the impossible appearance of Inés, just as he waited for her on other occasions, pretending that he was organizing books in the library or smoking in the dark in his bedroom, without his will ever doing anything to fulfill or hasten his desire, merely paralyzing him in the wait, in the painful consciousness of each minute that passed without her, of each footstep or creak in the silence of the house that announced the arrival of Inés only to unscrupulously prove it false the more certain he was that she was near. And to ease the pain he has imposed on himself a pretense of courage, like a betrayed lover who cultivates humiliation and rancor, wanting to exact from them a spirited will his failed pride denies him, and he looks at the clock and grips his suitcase, telling himself almost aloud that he hopes the train comes soon, because when he gets on and settles into his seat and closes his eyes and the station begins to slip away on the other side of the window through which he swears not to look, the definitive impossibility of searching again for Inés or continuing to wait for her will extinguish in a single blow, he supposes, the slow torture of uncertainty. But the train will probably arrive late, as it does every night, and the fierce, instantaneous, already vanquished intention of leaving disintegrates like a gesture of smoke in the prolonged wait, and Minaya crosses the empty lobby very much to the rear of his desire that precedes him and goes out of the station like a messenger moving too quickly, and he stops at the door, near the line of taxis also waiting for the train's arrival, and leaning against the jamb he puts down his suitcase and smokes melancholically, looking at the double row of linden trees where a shadow approaches to which he assigns the features and walk of Inés until proximity and the harsh white light of the street lamps shatter his illusion. But this is how he always has waited, long before coming to Mágina and meeting Inés, because waiting is perhaps the only way in which he conceives of the substance of time, not as a quality added on to his desires but as an attribute of his soul, like his intelligence or his propensity for solitude and tenderness, and he doesn't know he will go on waiting when he gets onto the train and when he leaves Atocha Station at seven in the morning, numb with cold, somnambulistic, and walks again through the vast city that dawn and absence have made unfamiliar. That was how he waited this afternoon, in the bedroom, as he packed his clothes and books and Jacinto Solana's manuscripts and put on in front of the mirror the black tie someone, Utrera or Medina, had lent him for Manuel's funeral, in this way postponing the moment of going down to the library to confront the faces that undoubtedly were going to accuse him, and the dead transfigured face that by now resembled an inexact mask not of Manuel but of any of the dead men Minaya had seen since his childhood, the double mask of his parents, beneath the glass of their coffins, wrapped in velvet and hospital bandages and absorbent cotton, the dripping, destroyed face on a marble table, the imagined funeral mask of Jacinto Solana. Like inglorious trophies, he kept at the bottom of his suitcase the manuscripts and the blue notebook, the cartridge wrapped in a piece of newspaper, a long pink ribbon with which Inés sometimes tied back her hair and that he untied last night as he kissed her, but before closing the suitcase he moved aside the books and the shirts she had ironed and folded and picked up the cartridge, then kept it, after a moment of indecision, with the relieved gesture of someone who discovers as he's walking out that he's almost forgotten his house key. He thought, he told me, when he had locked the suitcase and examined with cowardly discretion the knot in his tie and the meticulously drawn part in his damp hair, that he had no real right to withdraw into nostalgia, that never, not even in the days when his conversations with Manuel and his usual dealings with books and writing on the file cards gave him the placid sensation of living a life permanently sustained by customs more faithful than exaltation or happiness, so that he could no longer imagine himself living in any city other than Mágina or dedicated to any work other than cataloguing the library, never had he personally ceased being a guest for whom the same standard of hospitality that had welcomed him into the house would end one day by demanding that he leave. The balcony shutters were opened wide, and the sound of the water that fell and rose over the basin of the fountain and the scent of the acacias that recently had bloomed came in like a damp breeze to add to the present and to the proximity of the journey the delicate, dead weight of a sorrow older than his consciousness and more deadly than his memories. The darkly closed suitcase on the bed gave the entire bedroom the gloomy, stripped appearance of a hotel room. As in them, as at that critical moment when the traveler, ready to leave, returns to check he hasn't forgotten anything and once more opens empty drawers and doors to the closet where a solitary hanger moves back and forth, Minaya understood that the city and the house had never accepted him as one of their own, because even before he left, the furniture, the cool odor of the wood and the sheets, the mirror where he once saw Inés coming toward him naked and embracing him from the back, were denying him like suddenly disloyal accomplices and hurrying to erase every proof or trace of the time he had spent among them and to pretend they had recovered the same impassive hostility with which they had received him the first time he entered the bedroom, turning their backs on him as they did that afternoon when he asked them for one final sign not of hospitality but of recognition and farewell. Because downstairs, in the library, the others, the true inhabitants of the house, surrounded Manuel's coffin and murmured prayers or memories or sad judgments on the brevity of life or deadly diseases of the heart, taking refuge in the voluntary semidarkness, waiting for him to arrive in order to receive him with their planned silence of reproval, asking themselves what he was doing, why he hadn't come down yet, why last night, when Medina arrived, he had locked himself in his bedroom and not come out again until very late in the morning, recently showered and silent, as if mourning had nothing to do with him or he didn't know how to respect the details of its ceremony. Utrera knows, he feared, Utrera saw the pink ribbon on the night table and smelled the traces and sweat of bodies, and now he accuses us in a quiet voice with his offended lucidity, with his rancor of an old roué who reproves and condemns what he cannot achieve. Minaya went out to the parlor, because he never left his bedroom through the door that opened to the hallway, and at that moment when the urgency of deciding on an action had removed the image of Inés from his thoughts, he saw her in profile, wearing her mourning blouse, standing in the gallery as if she were lost at a crossroads, and when he tried to reach her, he was alone in the hallway and Inés' face was like those flashes in the dark that one glimpses with closed eyes. He ran toward the corner where she had disappeared and continued to hear her footsteps in the empty rooms and on the staircases where he had walked only once, on the February afternoon when he had gone up to Doña Elvira's rooms. Sweet, impossible Inés, a spy, thorn of persecution, alibi for all desire and all baseness. When he thought he was lost in the successive rooms as alike as a set of mirrors, he found the way he was looking for when he recognized on a chest the Baby Jesus that raised a pale plaster hand beneath a glass bell, pointing an index finger at the hidden turning and staircase that led to the bedroom where Doña Elvira had withdrawn twenty-two years earlier in order not to go on witnessing the decadence of the world and the obstinate failure of her son. But now the disorder from whose menace she had fled in June 1947 like a deposed king who chooses exile without abdicating his crown and his pride, seemed, like an invader, to have broken through the walls and locked doors she had raised against it, which had protected her for twenty-two years, because when Minaya entered the bedroom illuminated by the large windows of the conservatory, he saw before him a place as unfamiliar as those streets that at dawn seemed flattened by a night bombing and one couldn't recognize a single detail of what had been until a few minutes before the long sound of the sirens and the incessant, frightening, earsplitting noise of enemy planes had begun. Just like then, just like those women wrapped in black kerchiefs who searched through the rubble and perhaps recovered an absurdly undamaged family portrait or a crib with twisted bars, Inés, kneeling in the midst of the disaster, deliberately put in order old dresses ripped or trampled in a rage by Doña Elvira after she had overturned chests that may have occupied the same place since the early years of the century, she gathered up letters and postcards, scores of melancholy sonatas and habaneras that Doña Elvira must have danced to in the time of her inconceivable youth, carnival masks, embroidered table linen, long silk gloves that lay on rumpled bedclothes like amputated hands, periodicals about atrocious crimes, old society magazines with lithographs on glossy paper shredded by eager scissors, solemn accounts books on which Doña Elvira had smashed a cosmetics jar and then ground it with her foot. "She began this morning," said Inés, as if stating the effects of a natural catastrophe whose violence cannot be attributed to anyone, "she came here when the undertakers took Don Manuel's body down to the library, and she didn't want any of us to help her. She locked herself in with a key and began to knock everything over and break it and empty all the drawers." Without tears, without a single gesture of despair or evident madness, as methodically determined to create disorder around her as the general of an army who administers and calculates the permanent devastation of a conquered city and sows salt in the pits where its foundations had been. "She called us a little while ago. She kept ringing the bell until Amalia and I got here. She had already combed her hair and dressed for the funeral, and it looked as if she had been crying, but I didn't see any tears, and her whole face was covered with powder." Inés was dressed in mourning too, and the black blouse and tight skirt prematurely added to her body a part of the slim, grave plenitude it would achieve in a few years and that now only some of her gestures were a prelude to, an unknown future body that these hands guessed at in caresses like prophecies and will no longer touch, and that Minaya is ignorant of, because he hasn't learned yet to look at bodies in time, which is the only light that reveals their true nature, the ones an eye and an instant cannot discover. Awkward and cowardly, as he was in the early days, humiliated by the feeling of having lost Inés as inexplicably as she granted him her tenderness, he could only manage to say to her, with a coldness he supposed infected by the coldness he detected in her, a few words that made her feel, him as well, strange and inert, forsaker of the memory of so many nights and days coldly thrown into the acceptance of forgetting, an accomplice not of guilt but of repentance, of simulation, of vile glances fixed on the ground. As it had been the first time he saw her, Inés wore her hair gathered at the back of her neck, smooth and tight at her temples, so that when she completely revealed the shape of her cheeks and forehead, she purified the gracefulness of her profile, but a single chestnut ringlet, translucent, almost blonde, loosened at random when she bent over to pick something up, fell on her face and almost brushed her lips, curled and light like a ribbon of smoke that Minaya would have wanted to touch and undo with his fingers as secretly as at another time he had moved aside the sheets covering Inés' bare breasts and belly and thighs to watch her sleep. Indistinctly he asked her to let him help, and when she moved away as if to avoid a caress she perhaps desired and that Minaya never would have dared to initiate, she dropped the handful of old postcards she had been picking up. White beach resorts with ladies in tall hats seated around tables, casinos beside a sea of pink waves and heraldic views of San Sebastián in hand-tinted twilights, with teams of oxen that removed from the beach the tilting cabanas of the bathers, an illustrated card commemorating the first communion of the boy Manuel Santos Crivelli, celebrated in the parish church of Santa María, in Mágina, May 16, 1912, a letter, suddenly, with a republican stamp, addressed to Don Eugenio Utrera Beltrán on May 12, 1937. "Did you notice this letter?" asked Minaya, standing up, and he removed from the envelope, with extreme care, as if he were raising the wings of a mounted butterfly and attempting to keep it from disintegrating in his fingers, a typewritten sheet, almost torn at the folds. "It's strange that Doña Elvira has it here. It was addressed to Utrera." "That woman has always been crazy," said Inés, barely looking at the letter, "she must have kept it the way she kept everything." The date of the heading, written beneath a letterhead in elaborate calligraphy ("Santisteban and Sons, Antiquarians, Firm Established 1881") was the same as the canceled stamp, and included the letter, even before Minaya began to read it, in the narrow band of time when the wedding and then the death of Mariana occurred, transforming it into a part of that surviving material he could not touch without shuddering, like the cartridge and the piece of newspaper in which he found it wrapped and the white cloth flower that Mariana wore in the wedding photograph and Inés put in her hair one night. "Madrid," he read, "May 12, 1937," thinking that on the same day so impassively indicated by the typewriter, Mariana was still alive, that the time she inhabited was not an exclusive attribute of her person or the history already closing in around her to lead her to her death, but a vast general reality to which that letter and the man who wrote it also belonged. "Sr. D. Eugenio Utrera Beltrán. Dear friend: I am happy to inform you of the arrival on the 17th of the present month of our colleague D. Víctor Vega, whose invaluable skill in the antiquary's difficult art I have no need to describe to you, for you already know the number of years Sr. Vega has been employed in this Firm and the high esteem he enjoys here. As previously agreed, Sr. Vega will inform you with respect to the matters that interest you so deeply concerning our business, in which I hope you decide to take part with the good taste and reliability you have always proudly displayed with regard to the Fine Arts. I inform you as well that on his arrival in Mágina, Sr. Vega will stay at the Hotel Comercio on the Plaza and await your visit there on the 17th. Very truly yours, M. Santisteban."

He looked at the letters of the name, Víctor Vega, he pronounced it aloud, on the edge of a revelation, asking himself where he had heard or read it, then giving thanks to chance for the opportunity of discovering what his intelligence never would have elucidated otherwise. And when he finally went down to the library, when he had before him the semidarkness and in it the hostile, accusatory faces, he carried the letter in his pocket like a certainty that made him invulnerable and wiser, sole master of clarity, like the detectives in books who gather in the drawing room the inhabitants of a closed house where a crime was committed in order to reveal to them the name of the murderer, who waits and is quiet and knows himself condemned, alone, blemished among the others, who are still ignorant of his guilt. It was, this afternoon, like pushing Minaya toward the conclusion of a mystery, like directing his steps and his thoughts from the darkness, from literature, fearing he would not dare to reach the end and yet not wanting him to persist in his search beyond the indicated boundary, it was seeing what his eyes saw and detecting with him the scent of the candles burning at the corners of the coffin and the funeral flowers that surrounded it like the edges of an abyss at whose bottom lay Manuel, like the vegetation of a swamp into which he was sinking very slowly, unrecognizable by now, his hands tied by a rosary that wound around his yellow, rigid fingers and his eyelids squeezed or sewn shut in the obstinacy of dying, without any dignity at all, without that stillness that statues attribute to the dead, humiliated by scapulars that Doña Elvira had ordered hung around his neck and dressed in a suit that seemed to belong to another man, because death, which had exaggerated the bones in his face and the curve of his nose and erased the line of his mouth, also made his body smaller and more fragile, so that when Minaya went up to the coffin, it was as if he were looking at the corpse of a man he had never seen. Except for Medina, who conspicuously did not pray, who remained erect and silent as if affirming against everyone the secular dignity of his grief, a trace of Manuel's transfiguration infected the others, enveloping them in the same gloomy play of light and shifting semidarkness that the candles established and that probably, like the disposition of the catafalque and the black hangings that covered it, had been calculated by Utrera to achieve in the library an effect of liturgical staging. In that light the entire library acquired an oppressive suggestion of chapel and vault, and the old, ordinary smells of varnished wood and leather and the paper in the books had been replaced by a dense breath of church and funeral indistinguishable from the first hints of decomposition already diluting in the air. They were seated in a semicircle around the coffin, shapes without emphasis or the possibility of movement beneath the mourning clothes that tied them to the shadows, barely opening their lips as they prayed, as if the uniform voice marking the rhythm of the litanies did not emerge from their throats but from the darkness or from the scent of the candles, an emanation like a filthy secretion from the rigid weight of sorrow, and when Minaya came in they raised their eyes not to look at him but at a point in space slightly removed from his presence, as if a current of air and not a body had pushed open the door, closing it afterward with a muffled thud. He shook the hand of Frasco, who stood ceremoniously to offer his condolences in too loud a tone of voice, provoking an angry glance from Utrera, an imperious order to be silent. Or perhaps it wasn't the tone of voice, Minaya thought, but the simple fact that Frasco, when he offered his condolences, was recognizing in him a family connection to Manuel that Utrera considered illegitimate. Not daring to say anything to Doña Elvira, whose face was half covered by a translucent veil and who led the rosary as she slipped the beads between fingers as thin and pointed as a bird's claws, Minaya went to sit next to Medina and learned from him the details of the travesty. "They were the ones," the doctor said in his ear, "the old woman and that parasite, that damn hypocrite. Look what they've done to Manuel, that rosary in his hands, those scapulars, the crucifix. He made it very clear in his will that he didn't want a religious funeral, and now see what they've done, they waited until he died to get what they couldn't have when he was alive. And if it weren't for my screaming and yelling, they would have buried him in a Nazarene habit. Where did you get to? I spent all morning looking for you. I have something very important to tell you." Once again Utrera demanded silence, theatrically raising his index finger to his lips, and Medina, with ironic gravity, crossed his hands over his stomach as if parodying the gesture of a canon. "That one already knows. Which is why he's looking at you that way. He's dying of envy." "I don't understand, Medina." Fat and magnanimous, Medina smiled to himself and gave Minaya a kind of pitying look, a look of incredulous astonishment at his youth and ignorance. "Everybody knows by now, even Frasco, who was as happy as I am. A week ago Manuel changed his will. Now you're the sole heir. Of course that won't do you much good for a few years, because Doña Elvira will have all the property at her disposal in usufruct until she dies. And that woman's capable of living to a hundred if she decides to, just as she's lived until now, out of sheer spite." So that now, at the end, when he was concluding the prelude to expulsion, Medina's words abruptly granted him the right not to possession of the house or of the Island of Cuba, because that was a disconnected, abstract condition he could not conceive of, but to ownership of a history in which he had until then been a witness, an impostor, a spy, and that now, in a future he couldn't imagine either, would linger on in him, Minaya, but leaving him, as he would find out very soon afterward when he arrived at the station to buy a single ticket for Madrid, with the same sensation of inconsolable emptiness as the man who wakes and understands that no gift of reality can mitigate the loss of the happiness he just experienced in his last dream. Bewildered, as if he were slowly waking, he abandoned the lethargy into which the waiting, the semidarkness, and the sound of prayers had plunged him and went out to the courtyard searching for the relief of air and the pink and yellow light that turned white only on the marble paving stones, white and cold in the mirror on the first landing, resonant with voices because in that courtyard each sound, a laugh, a voice that says a name, footsteps, the fluttering wings of a pigeon against the glass in the dome, acquires the sharp, dazzling solidity of pebbles in a channel of frozen water, and things that happen there, even the trivial act of lighting a cigarette, magnified by its sonority, seem to be happening forever. Perhaps that was why, when Utrera came out after him and began to accuse him, Minaya was sure of each of the words he was going to say and certain this was the only place where he should say them. Now Utrera wasn't wearing a white carnation in his lapel but a mourning button, and a wide band of black cloth sewn around one sleeve, which gave him the air of a disabled reprobate. He asked for a light, coming very close, like a queer or a policeman, small, exhaling the smoke in rapid mouthfuls, intent on injury, on not holding back a single offense. "I don't know what you're waiting for, I don't know why you haven't left yet, how you dare to remain here, to go into the library, to mock our grief." "Manuel was my uncle. I have the same right to mourn him as any of you." He was astonished by his own audacity, by the firmness of his voice, more certain and clear in the sonority of the courtyard, very close, suddenly, to an appetite for cruelty, involuntarily pleased at acceding to a siege that would turn into an ambush of his accuser precisely when he, Minaya, wanted it to, simply by displaying the letter or the cartridge he had in his jacket or saying one or two necessary words. "Don't look at me like that, as if you didn't understand me. Don't be so sure you've deceived us the way you deceived poor Manuel. You killed him, last night, you and that hypocritical tart you were wallowing with in the most sacred place in this house. I saw you and her when you came out of the bedroom. And before that, I saw you go in, biting each other like animals, and I heard you, but I didn't do what I should have done, I didn't tell Manuel and I didn't go in to throw the two of you out myself, I left so I wouldn't be a witness to that profanation and when I came back it was already too late. That smell in the bedroom, on the sheets, the same one you couldn't get rid of and that I noticed when you came to call on me. Weren't you surprised that I was still dressed at that hour? The ribbon on the night table. Do you think I'm blind, that I can't smell or see? But probably you didn't even try to hide. You're young, you love blasphemy, I suppose, just as you don't know the meaning of gratitude. Do you know what Inés was before she came to this house? She was in the poorhouse without a father or any family name except the one her mother gave her before she abandoned her, a wild creature who would have been expelled from that nuns' orphanage if Manuel hadn't taken her in. But you're different. You come from a good family and you have breeding and an education and carry in your veins the same blood as Manuel. You were a fugitive and a political agitator when you came here, don't think I couldn't find out, even though your uncle, for the sake of courtesy, and hospitality, never told me. He's come to write a book about Solana, poor Manuel told me, as if he didn't realize that the only thing you were doing in this house was eating and sleeping free of charge and hiding from the police and going to bed every night with that maid in order to discredit the hospitality all of us showed you since your arrival. It would be too merciful to call you ungrateful. You are a defiler and a murderer. Last night you killed Manuel." Vain, theatrical, invested with justice and mourning just as he once invested himself with glory and then, as the years passed, with the melancholy and rancor of the overlooked artist, Utrera held his breath as if chewing it with his false teeth and showed Minaya the street door. "Leave right now. Don't continue to profane our sorrow or Manuel's death. And take that slut with you. Neither you nor she have the right to remain in this house." This house is mine, Minaya could have or should have responded, but the crude consciousness of ownership, even one as future and imaginary and founded only on a quiet confidence of Medina's, did not provoke his pride or add anything to his firmness, because the vast white facade with marble balconies and circular windows and a courtyard with columns and the glass in the dome had belonged to his imagination since he was a child with the definitive legitimacy of sensations and desires born and nourished only in oneself and requiring no attachment to reality to sustain themselves, because since less than an hour before, since he found the letter in Doña Elvira's bedroom and confirmed in a passage in Solana's manuscripts who Víctor Vega was, he had taken over possession not of a house but of a history that had been beating in it for thirty years and that he would bring to a close by stripping away its mystery, granting to the scattering and forgetting of its details the dazzling, atrocious shape of truth, its passionate geometry, impassive like the architecture of the courtyard and the beauty of the statues in Mágina, like the style and plot of the book that Jacinto Solana wrote for himself. "You know my uncle began to die a long time ago, on the day they killed Mariana," said Minaya, like a challenge, without any emotion at all, only with a slight tremor in his voice, as if he still weren't sure about daring to say what he had to say, what was demanded of him or dictated to him by loyalty to Manuel, to Jacinto Solana, to the outlined, broken history in the manuscripts, "and I think you also know who killed her." Utrera's dead smile, his old petulance of a hero of brothels and official commemorations twisting the expression of his mouth and remaining there, in his cold look of contempt, in his regained fear, still hidden. "I don't know what you're talking about. Don't you want to leave any of our dead in peace? You know as well as I how Mariana died. There was a judicial investigation and they did an autopsy. Ask Medina, in case you haven't found that out yet. He came here with the judge and examined the body. A stray bullet killed her, a bullet fired from the roofs." He won't deny it at first, Minaya had calculated, he won't tell me I'm lying or that he's innocent, because that would be like accepting my right to accuse him. He'll say he doesn't understand, that I'm crazy, he'll turn his back and then I'll take out the cartridge and the letter and oblige him to turn around so he can see them in my hands just as he may have seen the pistol Doña Elvira handed him that night or afternoon or morning in May when she thought up the way Mariana was going to die. "Let me alone and leave," said Utrera, and when he turned his back as if with that gesture he could erase the presence and the accusation not yet spoken by Minaya, he saw Inés on the first landing, next to the mirror, and for a moment he stayed that way, his head turned, as if repeating the arrogance of any of his statues, and then, Inés said, he was unexpectedly defeated and moved toward the dining room, knowing that Minaya was walking behind him, and even if he could elude or deny his questions, he would not escape the interrogation he had seen in the girl's eyes, transparent and precise like the sonority of the courtyard, earlier than all reasoning or suspicion, all doubt, born of an instinctual knowledge whose sole, frightening method was divination. He lit a cigarette, poured a glass of cognac, put the bottle back on the sideboard, and when he went to sit down, Minaya was in front of him, on the other side of the same long, empty table where they'd had supper together the first night, obstinate, unreal, gathering proofs and words and courage to go on saying them while Inés, in the doorway, without even hiding, witnessed and heard so there would be nothing later on, right now, surrendered to the imperfection of forgetting. "You killed Mariana," said Minaya, he recalled, as if the crime had occurred not thirty-two years ago but last night, this very morning, as if it were Mariana's body and not Manuel's they were mourning in the library, you, it was necessary to say this in another voice that had never been his, picked up the pistol in the small hours of May 21, 1937, and prowled around the gallery, hidden behind the curtains that then, like now, covered the large windows over the courtyard, and Solana almost saw you, but he didn't see you, only a shadow or a trembling of the sheer curtains, and when Mariana began to climb the steps to the pigeon loft on the labyrinthine staircase I've climbed myself at other times, when Jacinto Solana gave up following her and shut himself in his room to write in front of the mirror the verses that twenty years after his death called me to this city and to this house, you walked after her, the pistol in your right hand, which probably was trembling, the pistol hidden in your jacket pocket, driven by a hatred that belonged not to you but to that woman who made you her executioner and her emissary and armed your hand to make certain Mariana would never be able to take Manuel away from this house. "You're crazy," said Utrera, and he got to his feet, draining the glass of cognac, "there was shooting, they were chasing a fugitive, go back up to the pigeon loft and look out the window and you'll see that you can almost touch the next roof. There's no need for you to tell me that Doña Elvira didn't love Mariana. We all knew that. But what had she or Manuel done to me? Why would I kill her?" That's what Solana didn't know, what kept him from finding out the name of her murderer, Minaya thought when he unpacked his suitcase and untied the red ribbons around the manuscripts and searched them for the account of the lynching in the Plaza of General Orduña and the not yet exactly remembered name of Víctor Vega, the antiquarian, the spy. "But Solana found the proof that the pistol had been fired from the door to the pigeon loft." It was the chosen instant, the necessary critical moment of the revelation, just one gesture and he would disarm Utrera with the trivial omnipotence of a man who lifts a foot to step on an insect and then keeps walking without even noticing the dry, light crunch of the animal's shell flattened under the sole of his shoe: it was enough to look at the old man from above, from the certainty of the truth, to examine as proofs of guilt his mouth hanging open because of stupefaction and age and the way the knot of Utrera's black tie pressed like a noose into the flabby skin of his neck, Minaya's slipping his hand inside his jacket like a man looking for a cigarette and taking out a small package and a typed sheet that tore in the middle when he opened it again. Santisteban and Sons, antiquarians, firm founded in 1881, an appointment in Mágina for an accessory in a network of spies and fifth columnists destroyed in Madrid just a few hours before its messenger established contact with you, Utrera, said Minaya, smoothing and joining together the two pieces of paper on the wood of the table and displaying the cartridge that rolled for a moment and then stopped between them, as irrevocable as the deciding card in a game. "Solana found this cartridge. He also noticed that Mariana had traces of droppings on her knees and forehead, which would have been impossible if, as they said then, she had fallen on her back at the window when the shot hit her. She fell face down, because when she died she was looking toward the door of the pigeon loft, and her killer turned her over and wiped the droppings from her nightgown and face so it would seem as if the shot had come from the street, but he forgot to pick up the cartridge, or he looked for it and didn't have time to find it. It was Solana who saw it. Solana wrote down everything. I've read his manuscripts and I've gone where he couldn't go, because he didn't see this letter. Doña Elvira kept it in her bedroom. I think it has the answer." Utrera looked at the cartridge and the two pieces of the letter without yet accepting, without understanding anything that wasn't their double threat, as if he were listening to a judge accuse him in a foreign language whose unknown syllables would condemn him more irrevocably than the meaning of what they said, without yet recognizing in the yellowed, torn paper, the letterhead with the Gothic calligraphy, and the writing in the lost letter he had been looking for throughout the entire house for thirty-two years and that now appeared before him as the face of a forgotten and distant dead man returns in dreams. "Don't make me laugh. Solana's manuscripts, his famous work of genius. After his death a squad of Falangistas came here and burned them all, just as they had done at the country house. They threw his typewriter into the garden from the conservatory window, they burned all his papers and all the books that had his signature, right there, behind you, at the foot of the palm tree. And even if something were left, didn't anyone tell you that Solana was a liar his whole life?" Again he turned to cognac, contempt, useless irony, refusing to look right at Minaya because he wasn't the one he was seeing but the other one, the dead man, the true accuser who had usurped another life to embody in it the obstinacy of his shade, never completely driven away, and it wasn't Minaya's lucidity that made him surrender, or even the way he stood up behind him to hold the letter in front of his eyes like someone bringing a light up to a blind man's face, but the impossible evidence that speaking to him behind that voice was the voice of Jacinto Solana, dead and returned, lodged at the back of Minaya's eyes as if he were behind a mirror that allowed him to see everything and remain hidden. And that voice was also his, the voice of the secret and the guilt, so that when Minaya continued speaking, it was as if Utrera were listening to himself, free at last of the torment of simulating and lying, absolved by the proximity of punishment. "You were going to become a Franco spy," said the voice, Minaya, "you received that letter, and when you were waiting for Víctor Vega to come to Mágina, you learned he had been arrested and then lynched by the mob in the Plaza of General Orduña, and you looked for the letter to destroy it but couldn't find it, and probably Doña Elvira, who stole it from you, who knew as well as you that the letter could lead to your torture and a firing squad, threatened to give it to the police if you didn't kill Mariana." But as Minaya spoke, he began to hear what he himself was saying as if it were a monologue in a book that loses its energy and truth when it is recited by a mediocre actor: he didn't recognize his own brutality and couldn't stop the dirty pleasure he found in it and that incited him to prolong it, just what he had felt, he said afterward, tonight, when he was a cowardly little boy and avenged the fear and humiliations he suffered by hitting those who were weaker and more cowardly than he, and his shame and disgust impelled him to continue hitting until his childhood was over. Utrera looked at the letter and the empty bottom of his glass and moved his bald, humbled head, not affirming or denying, only allowing himself to be struck by each word as if he had lost his will or his consciousness, and it moved back and forth, held up only by his rigid neck and the knot of his black tie, waiting for the blows still to come. It was, suddenly, like hitting a dead man, like closing his fist, expecting muscled resistance and sinking it into decayed or rotted material and pulling back and hitting again with greater fury without anything happening. "Who are you to demand an accounting from me?" said Utrera in a voice Minaya had never heard from him before, because it was the one he used to talk to himself when he was alone, when he returned from the café, at night, and sat down in his studio at the table covered with the dead leaves of newspapers stained with varnish, his useless hands hanging between his knees, "how can it matter to me now that you found that letter? Don't you see? I've spent thirty-two years paying for what I did that day, and I'll go on paying until I die, and afterward too, I suppose. Doña Elvira always says there's no pardon for anyone. Certainly it would have been better if I'd let her turn me in that day, but I was on the Plaza of General Orduña too when they took Víctor Vega out of the police station and I saw what they did to him. I didn't know who he was then. I found out that night, when Medina came back from the hospital and told us his name." Driven by fear, he went up to his room immediately to burn the letter, but there was nothing in the drawer where he was sure he had put it, in the pages of a book he couldn't find either, as if the thief, when taking it, had wanted to emphasize the evidence of the robbery. He looked through his clothes, in the closet, at the bottom of each one of the drawers, under the bed, in the pages of all his books, in the notebooks of sketches he had brought from Italy, he continued searching even though he knew he wasn't going to find anything while he listened in the distance to the sonorous laughter of Mariana or Orlando and the music Manuel was playing on the piano in the dining room, and that night and the following night, when everyone was asleep, he searched with desperate, absurd tenacity on the shelves in the library, in the disorder of Manuel's desk, and when he told Minaya about his search he remembered as if it were an illumination that as he was trying to open the only locked drawer in the desk, Jacinto Solana came into the library and stood looking at him from the doorway as if he had found him out. But Solana left without saying anything to him, or perhaps, he couldn't remember, he was the one who went out with his head bowed, murmuring an excuse, and then he went up to the parlor to continue searching, though he could not possibly have lost the letter there, and then, he said, when after so many hours of constant searching he had lost track of the time, Amalia came looking for him, long after midnight, and with the same indifferent naturalness with which she would have transmitted an invitation to have tea, she said that Doña Elvira wanted to see him, that she was waiting for him in her rooms. "She always looked at the mail, alone, before anyone else saw it. I think she still does. She looked at all the letters that came, one by one, and then she put them back on the same tray on which Amalia had brought them to her and allowed her to distribute them. She never opened any letter, but she studied the return address and the cancellation stamp with that magnifying glass she uses now to go over the administrator's accounts. She herself told me that when she heard the name of the antiquities shop on the radio, she recalled having read it earlier and immediately knew where. That woman is incapable of forgetting anything, not even now." He tapped cautiously on the half-closed door behind which he saw no light, and as he listened in the silence, waiting for a word from Doña Elvira or a sign that she really was there, he heard again from the bottom of the house and the darkness the sound of a tune that grew louder until it seemed very close to him and then began to fade away as if its impulse had been exhausted and abruptly it was extinguished, leaving behind a tense, prolonged emptiness in which the voice of Doña Elvira in front of him, asking him to come in, sounded like an omen. She was standing in the dark, next to the window, lit only by the inconstant illumination of the night, and she raised her index finger to her lips when he tried to ask her why she had called for him, and she ordered him in a quiet voice to come to the window without making noise, pointed out to him something that moved in the shadows of the garden, beneath the fronds of the palm tree, a white blot that seemed trapped in the dark, embracing, lying down, two bodies and then a face still without features, pale, inflamed, locked together like branches in a thicket they were seeking and with which they became confused far away in the garden, behind the glass, in the silence of an aquarium. "Look at whom my son is going to marry. She's been like that for an hour, wallowing like a bitch with the other one, his best friend, he says. And they don't even hide. Why would they?" The strangest thing wasn't that he had been summoned to that place like an ambassador granted a secret audience or that he was there, at one in the morning, beside Doña Elvira, looking at the garden as if from the rear of a box in the theater; it was the silence in which the bodies moved, like avid reptiles, like fish in circular, incessant flight. Since his fear, his certainty that when he entered the dark room he was walking into the prelude to a perdition foretold by the death of Víctor Vega, the two bodies rolling on the grass in the garden as if giving themselves over to being dissolved into a single shadow, and the immutable profile and waved gray hair of the woman leaning her forehead against the glass to continue spying on them, seemed to him as keenly desired and distant as the music that hadn't sounded again. "Turn on the light," Doña Elvira ordered, and she remained motionless in front of the window even after he had obeyed her, and when she finally turned around, with a gesture of tedium, she was holding a paper in her right hand, an extended envelope, exact and brief like a weapon. "As you can understand," she said to him, "I didn't have you come here only to see my shame. That woman has dishonored my son and will take him away the day after tomorrow if I can't stop her. I want you to help me. You aren't like this rabble that has invaded my house. But if you don't do as I say, one telephone call and the Assault Guard will come for you. You should have done a better job of hiding this letter from your friends in Madrid. It took Amalia less than fifteen minutes to find it." Now she had a pistol in her hand, flat, silvery, with an ivory handle, small and cold and gleaming in the light like a razor. She handed it to him as she tucked the letter under the wristband of her black velvet dress, and when he took it and held it as if he didn't know yet how to handle it, she turned her back and looked down again at the darkness in the garden, though no one was there. Later there was only insomnia and the icy touch and memory of the pistol, its shape calculated for secrets and death, its invitation to suicide, the destroyed mouth and coagulated blood on Víctor Vega's lips, his ruined body in the sun beside the arcades on the Plaza of General Orduña, the blindfold over his eyes and his hands tied and the bite of the fire that would throw him against a wall riddled by gunshots or a ditch that was like a pit. "But I knew I was incapable of killing her," he said, "and I was determined to kill myself, but I went out to the hallway thinking that before noon she and Manuel would have left and then I saw her pass by, as close as you are now, and I swear that if I followed her, it wasn't because I intended to kill her, it was as if another man were climbing the stairs to the pigeon loft, because I didn't care anymore about being killed, how could I care if I was already dead?" Without will, without any purpose at all, he kept climbing up to the pigeon loft, conscious of each stair he stepped on, very slowly, without hearing the sound of his own footsteps, as if the design he was obeying had stripped him of physical solidity and was pushing him up the stairs like an ocean swell that picks up a man who before going under when it knocks him down looks at the shore growing more and more distant and knows he is going to drown. Like a magnet the pistol clutched in his hand led him on, the butt wet with perspiration, the short barrel and the trigger that his fingers groped when he reached the top landing afraid Mariana could hear through the closed door the noise of his breathing, but that wasn't what he was hearing, that monotonous sound shaken by the beating of his heart came not from his throat but from the interior of the pigeon loft, it was the murmur of the sleeping pigeons. Perhaps

Mariana believed that Manuel had wakened and had come up to find her, because when she moved away from the window, she had an unsurprised smile on her lips, as if she had been pretending not to hear the footsteps in order to allow Manuel the delicate opportunity of coming up to her silently and covering her eyes as he embraced her. "Utrera," she said, "it's you," in that tone of fatigued indifference she always used to resign herself to the arrival of someone she didn't want to see, and she hadn't seen the pistol yet or understood why he was looking at her that way, so fixedly, as if reproving her presence in the pigeon loft or examining with obscene dissimulation the folds of her nightgown, trying to guess at the lines of her naked body beneath the cloth, the dark shadow of her belly. "Some men with rifles are running along the roofs. It seems they're chasing somebody." Before recognizing what was shining in the hand that rose and rigidly pointed at her and aimed at her eyes wide with fright, Mariana heard shouts and the clatter of feet running on tiles on the other side of the lane, and perhaps a first shot that was still not the one of her death and to which Utrera's pistol responded like an echo, a sudden raging blade above his index finger, then finally still in his hand, pointing now at the smoke and the empty window while his single shot was dispersed in the doubled pandemonium of pigeons and incessant bullets like a hailstorm on the roofs. He turned Mariana over, he said, and wiped her mouth, moving her hair away from her face, her open eyes, in which there remained as if changed into glass the final astonishment of the pistol and her death. Then, when he stood up, wiping the droppings from his knees, he saw the man hiding behind the chimney opposite the window. Barefoot, his feet bleeding, wearing an undershirt, unshaven, as if he had jumped out of bed when they came for him, panting, his mouth wide open, so close Utrera could see the trembling of his chest beneath the dirty undershirt and the hunted, animal sound of his respiration. For a moment, one he would remember forever, they looked at each other, recognizing the other man in the solitude of their fear and their plea for a respite or an impossible refuge, as if they had passed each other in a corridor reserved for those condemned to death. "His name is Domingo González," said Utrera, standing up, finishing in one swallow the glass he hadn't touched while he spoke. "After the war I found out that he saved himself by hiding in a barn, under a pile of straw. From time to time we've passed on the street, but he doesn't remember me, or at least he behaves as if he doesn't know me." He crushed the cigarette he had just lit in the ashtray and left the empty glass on the table, very close to the torn letter and useless cartridge, wiping his lips damp with cognac as carefully as someone cleaning the blood from a small wound. He wouldn't recognize himself either if he could see himself as he was then, Minaya thought, looking without pity or hatred at the mourning button in his lapel and the black band that hung half unstitched from his right sleeve, and I can't even imagine what he's told me or remember what I know in order to call him murderer, because that word, like the crime and the man who committed it, perhaps no longer refer to him, because no one can continue to sustain sorrow or guilt or merely memory after thirty-two years. Minaya suddenly perceived in the dining room this afternoon the immense weight of reality and the ignominy of the guesses that until a few minutes before had exalted him, and he immediately renounced his lucidity like a lover who, when he learns the day will come when his love dies, censures that future treachery with more fury than his present misfortune. He, Minaya, had rescued a book and explained a crime, he maintained intact the power to accuse, to continue asking, to grant not pardon but silence, or to tell what he knew and throw the murderer and his accomplice into a shame more sordid than the old age in which they survived as in an exile with no possible pardon. "Don't look at me like that," said Utrera from the door he had already begun to open, closing it again, "you can't harm me. I have nothing to lose, because I don't have anything. When Doña Elvira dies and you inherit this house, you can throw me out, but by then I'll probably be dead too. I swear that's the only thing I want in this world." Minaya was left alone, Inés said, sitting in the dining room at the long empty table like the client in a hotel who arrives too late for supper and waits in vain for someone to come and serve him, staring with inert fixity, a cigarette between his fingers, at the cartridge and the letter or at the polished wood where the oblique sun of the April afternoon was shining, cross-sectioned by the glass in the white French doors to the garden as if by a lattice window. Inés came to tell him that the undertaker's men had just arrived, with their blue dusters, with their black cars recently parked beneath the acacias on the plaza, with their disrespectful haste that reminded Minaya, when he went out to the courtyard and saw them open the library and house doors wide to carry out the coffin that was closed now, of the afternoon when other men like them emptied his parents' bedroom with pulleys and ropes and loaded their furniture into a truck from which he never saw it emerge again. They put out the candles, passed the candelabras from one to the other and carried them by the armful to the back of a car, took down the wreaths of flowers and the black velvet cloth that had covered the platform where the coffin had been, and then, when they were gone, a great empty space remained in the center of the library, deserted now and still in shadow, like a stage after the last show, and it was in that spot without anything—right there, in another time, barely a week before, where the desk had been, the filing cabinet, the habit of taking notes on the books and waiting for Inés—where Minaya became aware of his own future absence, as irreparable and certain as Manuel's. "Let's go," said Medina beside him, "they're waiting for us." The hearse and the two taxis that would take them to the cemetery were already leaving when he and Medina went outside. He still had to come back after the funeral and burial to pick up his bag, but it seemed to him as he leaned back in the taxi, while the scent of the acacias and the entire plaza was being left behind, that he was saying good-bye forever not only to the house that was closed now and deserted but also to Inés and everyone who had lived there, to a part of his life that very soon would no longer belong to him, inaccessible to returning and to memory, because remembering and going back, he doesn't know yet, are exercises as useless as demanding explanations from a mirror of the face that an hour or a day or thirty years ago had looked into it. He'll come back, no doubt, just as he came back tonight, when it was almost eleven o'clock, hurrying to reach the station on time, crossing the courtyard, I imagine, climbing the illuminated staircase without seeing anyone, like the last passenger on a great ship that is beginning to sink but whose recently abandoned salons have not yet been invaded by the water already flooding the holds, fearing that Doña Elvira or Utrera will appear before him around a corner or in the parlor to subject him to the hateful discipline of saying good-bye, wondering why there is no one anywhere and why all the lights in the house are on. As a last privilege I want to imagine it like this as he leaves it, bright and empty, white in the dark of the plaza as if in the middle of the ocean, because now that Manuel is dead and the book is finished, there is no one left who deserves to live in it. Here, not in the cemetery and even less in the station, is where the end should be, in the illuminated balconies, the circular windows on the top floor, the muffled flash of that light on the rim of the fountain, on the man who from the end of the lane turns to look at it and then grasps the handle of his suitcase and walks toward the Plaza of General Orduña as if assaulting the shadows, with his head bowed, with the posthumous courage of fugitives. I invented the game, I set the rules, I arranged the end, calculating the steps, the successive squares, the equilibrium between intelligence and the blows of chance, and when I did that I shaped for Minaya a face and a probable destiny. Now he is fulfilling it, in the station, now he obeys me and, tall and alone, waits for me as he obeyed and waited in the cemetery while gravediggers moved aside the stone where Manuel's name had not yet been inscribed and Doña Elvira, supported by Utrera and Teresa, bent down to pick up a handful of earth that she would then toss on the coffin with a slow, rigid gesture. He was taller than any of them, and his stature and his youth seemed the visible attributes of his status as stranger, the proof that in spite of the dark suit, the black tie, the summary expression of grief, he did not belong to the group of people in mourning who had gathered around the grave and murmured prayers that in the distance of the afternoon and the empty cemetery sounded like the buzz of insects. Old distant faces, unrecognizable, enervated by heat and oppressive mourning clothes, surrounded by crosses, by the yellow brilliance of the hedge mustard flowers that erased the graves and the paths that separated them and wound around their feet like a swamp of roots. Of all of them, only Medina kept himself partially free of decrepitude, fat and impassive, his arms folded, his hair still black, looking at the men sliding the coffin between rough ropes into the hole of the grave with the composed attention he would bring to looking at a patient who had just died. But Inés didn't look at the grave, Minaya noticed, although she kept her head bowed and her hands folded in her lap and she moved her lips, pretending to repeat the prayers of the others. Only he, who spied on her and her gestures looking for a sign that would allow him to recognize in her the same woman who had embraced him last night, not to get her back but in order not to lose the right to tell himself at least that certain things now impossible had happened to him, realized that Inés had secretively moved her eyes toward a corner of the cemetery, toward a mausoleum shaded by cypresses beside which a man seemed to pray as he leaned on a cripple's crutches. The brim of his hat covered his face, and his head sank between his shoulders, exaggeratedly raised by the crutches. Inés noticed Minaya's questioning and she stared fixedly again at the ground and pretended to pray, but her eyes beneath long lashes slid slowly beyond the still-open grave, over the hedge flowers, as if all of her and not only her gaze were fleeing, just as she did when Minaya was talking to her and she stopped hearing him and smiled at him so he couldn't follow her in her flight or decipher a thought in which she was alone. Taut with the weight of the coffin, the ropes were lowered, rubbing against the sharp marble edges, and one of the men holding them stopped to wipe his brow, interrupting for a single second the voices that were praying. In that fraction of silence, Inés raised her head and looked openly at the man on crutches. He was looking at them too, motionless, leaning on the crutches as if they were a windowsill he had reached using the last of his strength, and although Minaya couldn't see his face, he imagined an indecent curiosity in those eyes covered by shadow and veiled by distance, shining in a sudden reflection of glass when the man began to walk and came out from the cypresses, awkward and very slow, ruined and tenacious between the crutches that preceded him, testing the ground as if looking for hidden graves beneath the hedge flowers. The grave diggers retrieved the ropes, and Doña Elvira took a few steps forward and began to drop earth on the now-invisible coffin without completely opening her hands, as if waiting for someone to capture her gesture in a photograph. The man walked more and more slowly toward the metal grillwork of the cemetery gate, hugging an adobe wall, disappearing at times behind a mausoleum and then reappearing more worn and more awkward, more impossibly determined to reach the exit. He was very close to it when he seemed to give up walking and leaned his back against the whitewashed wall, and now Inés, who could no longer look at him without turning her head, said something to Amalia that Minaya couldn't hear, crossed herself at the grave, and with the same haste moved away from it to go toward the man, who was no longer leaning against the wall. Before he followed her without waiting for the grave diggers to adjust the stone, Minaya remembered that when he came to the cemetery there was a taxi parked next to the gate. He heard the engine starting up and he ran faster, jumping over the graves and the hedge flowers, his heart pounding in his chest as violently as when he had run that winter from the guards along the avenues of Madrid, no longer asking himself what the others would think or who the man on crutches was, but when he reached the cemetery gate, when he stopped on the dusty esplanade where the road to the city began between two rows of cypresses, he saw the taxi driving away leaving behind a translucent cloud of dust and exhaust and the fleeting image as dazzling as a powder flash of two faces that looked at him through the rear window and were immediately erased in the dust, in the distance of rows of cypresses and the first houses in the city. He kept running and waved his hand and probably called to Inés asking her to stop the taxi, but his voice was inaudible and his figure became smaller as the successive shadows of cypresses multiplied in the window, and finally he stood motionless in the distance of the road, still moving his right hand, as if he were saying good-bye, powerless and vanquished, overwhelmed by fatigue, by the incredible certainty that he was partially opening the prelude to the true story when he believed he had left its conclusion behind him. And now it was only a question of waiting for him to come, to cross the fields and the last streets of Mágina, walking very quickly, not seeing or hearing anything of what was happening around him, because the city, the cars, the people he bumped into on the sidewalks were moving out of his way like a sea that parts to show him the only road he should follow, running until he was out of breath and his legs had given out, advancing with no progress, no respite, beyond fatigue, as if only the devastating will to reach the plaza where he had waited so often for Inés kept him on his feet, the plaza where he was tediously condemned to look at Utrera's heroic monument and the hermetic balconies of the house she had never allowed him to enter. "My uncle is sick. He doesn't want to see anybody," she would say. "I'd like to meet him." "He can't, at least not now. I'll let you know when he's better." All that was left was to wait for him with the avid, feigned, wary calm of a hunter who has laid his trap and crouches in the darkness, in the propitious thicket where the muffled movement of a body will sound and then the cold crack of the trap when it closes. "He's here," said Inés from the window when we heard the bell at the entrance. He pulled on the cord several times, but nobody answered, and then he went into the house, into the devastated courtyard above which damp clothes hang on lines, closing off the sky and the railing of rotting wood where the women who live in the rooms along the corridor go to shout at one another or to empty buckets and basins of dirty water, where they lean in the sun, with embroidered housecoats over their shoulders, to dry their hair on Sunday mornings. It always smells of damp, of deep, dark places, of wet lime and stone and cesspool water. From the railing a dry, disheveled woman moved aside the sheets on the lines and pointed to the end of the courtyard when Minaya asked for Inés. "That Inés and her uncle live in the second yard, up top, at the back of the stairs. I saw them come in a little while ago. Now they're riding in a car, like rich people." The sheet fell back like a sopping wet curtain on the woman and her laugh, which was prolonged in other voices along the corridor, in glances of suspicion and mockery that followed Minaya from above until he disappeared into a gloomy passage that took him to another courtyard without a railing or wooden columns, a courtyard like a well, with high unwhitewashed walls, with a single window and a tree whose topmost branches stretched toward it, brushing against open shutters. "Now he's coming up," said Inés, and she moved away from the window, picking up again the needle she had just threaded and the frame where she was embroidering something, a sketch of blue flowers and birds that she looked at meditatively as she sat down in the chair she always used to sew, so absorbed in the needle and the movement of her fingers that touched the taut cloth, searching for the exact spot where she should make the next stitch, that she seemed to have forgotten that Minaya was climbing the stairs, coming closer and closer to me, to us, to the instant when his eyes would meet the eyes of a dead man and when he would hear the impossible and somehow revived voice of a manuscript he hadn't found yet, of so many words deceitfully calculated and written to trap him in a book that had existed only in his imagination, that has ended now, as if he, Minaya, had closed it just as he closed the door when he left here. But perhaps, as he climbed the stairs knowing he was approaching me, he was tempted to turn around, to close his eyes and his intelligence and his sleepless desire to know and leave for the station and Madrid as if he hadn't seen the man on crutches in the cemetery, as if not a single doubt was left that could stain or undo the history he had looked for and now possessed. He climbed up as if going down to a dark basement, he stopped in front of the only door in the corridor, abruptly I was no longer hearing his footsteps, and I guessed he was standing still behind it. "Come in, Minaya, don't stay out there," I said, "we've been expecting you for an hour."

2

Very tall in the doorway, taller and younger than I had imagined, with an air of attentive stupefaction and accepted misfortune that he probably had kept intact since his adolescence and that I suspect he'll never lose, like that way he has of looking at things with his head bowed, of assenting as if he didn't believe completely or never could accept in his innermost thoughts a destiny that he never will stop deferring to, because he was born for a kind of rebellion effected only in silence, in imaginary flight, in tenderness or despair revealed solely when the fulfillment of one's desire has become impossible. Tall and strange, obvious, cowardly, standing in the doorway, at the boundary of deception and astonishment, looking at me as if to confirm that it was I, the vague face wearing glasses in the photographs, the crippled man who walked among the graves with a black hat over his eyes, I, the dead man, the pale worn mask that sat up in bed to receive him, to extend a hand that he hesitated for a moment to shake, as if afraid I might infect him with death, that I would never let him go. He avoided my eyes, without glasses now because I had taken them off to see him better when he came close, he looked at the bed, the night table, the low ceiling in the room, he looked at Inés, sitting next to the window, leaning over the frame and the cloth she was pretending to embroider that spread out in hard white angles over her knees. Fixed on the pattern of the threads, Inés raised her right hand, and it seemed as if she held nothing between her fingers, but then in a slender beam the light caught the tip of the needle or the taut thread that extended it, just as at times, in empty space, very close to one's eyes, the curved, long outline of a spiderweb appears and is immediately invisible again. Before he arrived, while the footsteps that were undoubtedly his were coming down the hall, Inés looked up from her needlework and kept her hand raised and motionless, holding the needle as if the tension of the thread were the only indication of how attentively she waited, and that was exactly how Minaya saw her when he came in, lost in the indifferent tranquility of a figure in a painting in which the artist hadn't wanted to depict her face so much as the artless repose of her hands resting on the frame, sharply delineated on the white cloth and in the oblique light from the window that fell on her bare, bowed neck and was quiet all around her, on the floor tiles, without illuminating the rest of the room, as if in a stillwater where it would endure when its coppery brilliance had been extinguished on the highest bell towers in the city. "Excuse me for not getting up to receive you," I said, "but I came home from the cemetery very tired. Sit down, here, on this chair, I want to see you better. I want to know what you're like, Minaya." He didn't say anything, or he only repeated my name, which when it sounded in his voice had a hard, strange, remote quality, because I didn't name myself, the man I really am, but someone else, perhaps a hero, a shadow hidden in the manuscripts and photographs, the body Manuel saw on a marble table, the man who died at the Island of Cuba, beside the Guadalquivir, in its muddy waters, twenty-two years ago. "Solana," he repeated, incredulous, crushed by questions that devastated him, by evidence that frightened him. I recognized in him, in his large chestnut eyes that looked at me as if they hadn't yet surmounted the temporal distance from the day when I was supposed to have died to that moment when we had met, the signs of a race of reckless seekers, an excessive, never-submissive intelligence insistent on lucidity even at the cost of failure, a fervor and a will predestined to disappear impetuously into the void. I knew he was fated since birth to know much more than was good for him, to deserve exactly what never would be granted him, to not be satisfied if he ever, by chance, achieved it. I saw what Inés hadn't seen—every night when she came home I demanded that she tell me everything—what she wouldn't have been able to tell me: that by virtue of the same aberration of the blood that had made Manuel not resemble his father or his mother or inherit the slightest trace of his paternal grandfather's rough incessant energy but receive instead the delicate features, blonde hair, and blue eyes of his Aunt Cristina, in Minaya an elegance survived that had belonged to Manuel. And that resemblance was even more substantive and undeniable because in no way was it evident at first glance, and it couldn't be isolated in a single individual trait but in a certain internal attitude that could be glimpsed in his eyes, in the way he moved his hands, lit a cigarette, filled a glass, in some unlearned, almost always fleeting gesture that made its way to the intelligence of the person who knew how to see it, like those clues in old novels that allow one to discover the beautiful, high-born lady voluntarily hidden beneath rough peasant clothes. Perhaps that's why I permitted him to know I was alive, out of loyalty or gratitude to that gaze that demanded wonder and knowledge, to Manuel, who had looked at me the same way so often, to Doña Cristina, the white-haired lady with the high, anachronistic hairdo, who gave us tea on the unreal afternoons of 1920 and always asked me to read the poems her nephew had told her about so fervently, with an enthusiasm for them I was very far from feeling, comparing me to Bécquer, to Rubén Darío, to poor José Emilio Minaya, Doña Cristina's deceased husband, whose only book of verses, *Arpeggios,* dedicated to her, Manuel and I knew by heart, because those poems, which would soon feel the fury of our scorn when a magazine in Madrid allied us to Ultraism, had been the first ones we ever read. "You're still not sure," I said to him, "you still can't believe that I'm the person speaking to you, that I'm alive. Neither can I, young man. For twenty-two years I've been dead, I've enjoyed the incredible privilege of not existing for anybody who knew me before those Civil Guards came for me, of calmly losing my memory and my life, as if I had turned into a statue or a tree. Without knowing it, they did me the biggest favor anyone could ever have done for me when they said they had killed me and smashed in the face of another man's corpse and put my glasses on him and dressed him in trousers and a shirt that weren't even mine but Manuel's, and gave him my name, maybe because the lieutenant in charge had strict orders to return to Mágina with my body and didn't have the courage to confess they couldn't find it in the river or because they wanted people in Mágina to take my death as a warning or a public threat. And so when I opened my eyes in the house where I was taken care of and hidden, and it took me so many hours to remember my identity and my name that I wasn't anybody anymore, I was that oblivion and that empty consciousness of the first hour after I woke, and not even the inert body and the hands touching it under the sheets belonged to me, because they were as unfamiliar and external to me as the metal of the bed and the beams in the ceiling and the constant tumult of water sounding beneath the paving stones, at times very close and at other times as remote as a memory allied to the sensation of water, of wetness, of slime, of someone drowning in dreams who opened his eyes and mouth underwater and struggled in an opaque light that gradually darkened, colored in blood, in the taste of blood and algae drenched in mud, someone who closed his eyes and remained motionless, indifferently vanquished, pushed along by the water, by the sweetness of stillness and asphyxiation. But I could not attribute that memory or dream to my life because I no longer had one, I was only that gaze or images of semidarkness and half-closed window and light that succeeded one another without coming together into a permanent shape, I was only the hand testing the body and the sheets as if they were a singular material, I was the room, immobility, the sound of water, the lethargy that had returned, no one, and after several hours the woman came in with a cup of milk and medicines and told me my name, I still couldn't connect it to me but only to that dream of water, to the drowned man without a face, to a bottomless time of mud and reptiles that no memory could ever reach. But it wasn't simply a matter of a hallucination. It was also a premonition. Because a few days later, the man who found me in the backwater of the mill, Inés' grandfather, who had been my father's comrade-in-arms in the war with Cuba, showed me the newspaper with my photograph and name and the article about my death. 'Red bandits brought down in heroic action by the Civil Guard,' I remember it said, and beside my photograph, the one from the file they made when I went to prison, was one of Beatriz dead and one of the man who accepted death because he was in love with her and who may not even have succeeded in becoming her lover. But the photograph of the other man, the younger one, wasn't there, and the paper didn't mention him, so it was undoubtedly his body they gave my name to, bequeathing me the infinite freedom I had conceived of when I awoke and didn't know who I was, saving me from my entire life and from my failure, from the unshaved face, the frightened eyes of the unknown man in the photograph, the shame of looking at Beatriz' dead, swollen face and remembering all the years when I renounced her loyalty and tenderness with the same silent pretense I showed when I renounced my own life, always, long before I met Mariana and up until the last day, until the last night, when I saw her telling me good-bye and I feigned a little sorrow because she was leaving with the others and I didn't dare acknowledge to myself that the only thing I wanted was to be left alone as soon as possible, to close the door to the country house and go back to my bedroom, not to write or to feel safe but only to know that I was alone, with no one blackmailing me with friendship or love or obedience to those slogans in which Beatriz and Manuel and even the cynic Medina continued to believe as if they were the catechism eight years after we had lost a war we never could have won. I was a deserter and an apostate, and it's possible I always had been one, as Beatriz said that night, but in the newspaper that certified my death, they spoke of me as if I had died in combat, I was that photograph of a man who had confronted the Civil Guard with a pistol and preferred death to surrender. You wanted a writer and a hero. There he is. You must have seen that newspaper among Manuel's papers and given it a precise place in the biography of Jacinto Solana that you expect or expected to write. But let me tell you something I left out of the blue notebook. Jacinto Solana leaves his visitors in the wine cellar of the Island of Cuba and goes back, lighting his way with a candle, to the room that faces the river. He puts out the light, smokes in bed, closes his eyes knowing he won't be able to sleep that night either, thinks about the others hiding in the wine cellar, in a damp darkness not mitigated by the moon, in close air where they smell the sweat of fatigue and fear and the odor of blood, hear the labored breathing of the wounded man. He thinks about them and the way they have of accepting persecution and death, and he knows he is thinking about Beatriz and hoping and fearing she will lift the trapdoor to the wine cellar and come up to find him, because if she came here, it wasn't to elude the encircling Civil Guard or to find a road into the sierra that will take them south but for the same reason that led her six months earlier to ask the other man to lend her his car to travel to a distant city where there was a prison and a man about to be released from it. He doesn't write, as I wanted you to suppose, he doesn't go through the pages of a recently finished book with indolent happiness to correct a comma, a word, to cross out an adjective or add one that is more precise, or crueler, he doesn't recall her obstinacy or her pride because those are two virtues he almost always has ignored. He only waits and smokes in the growing clarity of insomnia, he only remembers the way she said, before going down to the cellar, 'So it's true you're writing a book,' and her weary smile, and her twisted heels, and her fingernails scratching at the bottom of an empty can of sardines as if she weren't invulnerable to indignity either. He's waiting for her, but he shivers when he hears the door open because Beatriz came up barefooted to his bedroom, leaving the other man in the cellar, dying of jealousy and fear beside the wounded man who pants and doesn't sleep, powerless and alone, passed over, waiting, as he did when he watched her get out of the car in the field at the prison and didn't dare go after her and was afraid she would never come back. The coward Solana puts out his cigarette and turns to the wall to pretend he's sleeping, but that doesn't erase the presence of Beatriz from his old, intact cowardice. 'You haven't changed,' she says to him, still standing, 'you do the same thing you did when we lived together. You close your eyes and breathe as if you were sleeping so I won't talk to you. Back then I'd be quiet and try to sleep, but I'm not twenty-five anymore. You don't have to keep your eyes closed. I'm not going to ask you for any explanations.' She searches out my face in the darkness, touches my hair, my lips, with those hands of categorical sweetness that recognize my skin as if more than ten years hadn't passed since they touched me the last time, as if it were April 1937 and I had just opened the letter in which Manuel and Mariana invited me or invited us to their wedding in Mágina in twenty days' time. I hear the springs in the bed and feel next to me the weight of her body, her hips, now broad and solemn, the unfamiliar perfume and the slide of the silk blouse against her skin and of the stockings she folds down over her thighs, her knees, as if tearing at the silk, the long white body I haven't looked at yet that trembles when it joins mine, when it rises up over me, the blonde hair spread out over bare shoulders, the bitter, tenacious belly and the open thighs that grasp my waist as I turn over and raise my eyes to look at her and hers close in a gesture of obstinate sorrow. She comes down now, and her hair falls over her forehead and covers her lips, she moves away my hands that enclosed without emotion the restlessness of her breasts and she withdraws and comes down until she bites me on the neck, until she sinks into my groin as she pulls away the rough cloth of my trousers and takes between her fingers and shakes and demands what she was looking for, what grows and affirms itself between her lips as far from me as the coldness of the moon and abruptly spills out in a mediocre death rattle after which there isn't anything, not even the avid desperation with which she licks and swallows and lifts up her hair, wiping her mouth, not looking at me, looking at the open window or the whitewash of the wall behind the bars of the bed. What was I going to say to her, what lie, what caress was I going to attempt when she fell back beside me and lay there quivering, when she drew up a sheet to cover her thighs and buried her face in the pillow as if it were the foul matter of solitude and silence, as if searching there as she bit into it for a weapon against tears. It was the same darkness and the same heavy silence between us, poisoned by guilt and involuntary, thorough cruelty and words unspoken, abdication into wakefulness, the torment of two bodies entwined between the same sheets and two minds as secretly divided as if they belonged to another woman and another man who never had met, who were attempting, impossibly, to sleep at the same time in two hotels at opposite ends of the earth. I watched her dress from my corner of cold shame and semi-darkness just as I had witnessed her caresses, and when she adjusted her stockings and lowered her skirt, she turned her face illuminated by the end of her cigarette toward me, and she no longer seemed the same woman who a few minutes earlier had trembled humiliated and naked against my body, as if when she dressed she had recovered her pride and the serene possibility of contempt. It was then and not the next night that she said good-bye to me. Do you know what she said to me? Do you know what she had been waiting ten years to say to me? 'The only thing I've never accepted is your leaving me for a woman who was worth less than either one of us.' That was exactly what she said to me, and worst of all is that she probably was right, because Beatriz was never wrong. She was lucidity in the same way that Mariana had been the simulacrum of mystery, but in those years when I met her and fell in love with her—I'm speaking of Mariana—I was like you: I preferred mystery even at the cost of deception, and I thought literature wasn't for illuminating the dark part of things but for supplanting them. Perhaps that was why I never could write a single one of the pages I imagined and needed as urgently as one requires air. Haven't you read my real writing from those years in Manuel's library? I was always the exact and somewhat delayed symbol of any manifesto published in Madrid, I even wrote one, in '29 or '30, with Orlando and Buñuel, but it never was published. It was called the *Abyssist Manifesto,* because we wanted to destroy the deception of surrealism, and we proclaimed something and gave it the name of the Abyss. 'The limit,' said Orlando, drunk, as he wrote on a napkin in a café, 'vertigo, blindness, suicide from the thirty-seventh floor of a skyscraper in New York,' but when Buñuel, who was going to place our manifesto in *La Gaceta Literaria,* found out that Orlando preferred men to women, he wrote me a letter warning me about what he called the perfidy of faggots and didn't want anything more to do with the Abyss. I was the most radical of all the surrealists, but hardly anybody knew it; I published a story entitled 'The Outrageous Aviator' in the *Revista de Occidente,* and before that issue appeared, I was sure I'd be famous at last, but when it came out it was as if everybody had stopped reading the *Revista de Occidente* at the same time. I carried it under my arm to all the cafés, and nobody said anything to me, as if my story and I had become invisible. But I wasn't worse than any of the others: I was exactly like them, decipherable in what they wrote or said, more discreet perhaps, or more cowardly, or poorer, or more unfortunate, because I continued to write and was publishing articles in *El Sol* and they asked me for poems for provincial magazines, and when Alberti and María Teresa León founded *Octubre,* they asked me to write about film, but invisibility was like an attribute of my devotion to literature, like a warning to my pride that I was writing in air and wouldn't be anything until I locked myself behind stone walls to start a book, and all I knew about it was that it would be dazzling and unique and as necessary as those books from the past without which one cannot imagine the world. But it was always necessary to write an article in order to go on living or simply to see my name in the pages of a magazine; I always had to attend a meeting or an assembly about something and inevitably postpone until tomorrow or ten days from now the beginning of real literature and real life, and suddenly we were in the war and there was no time or moral justification left for anything that wasn't the methodical manufacture of ballads against Fascism and theater pieces that I sometimes saw produced at the front with a feeling of shame and fraud as intense and unspeakable then as what I felt when I saw myself dressed in a blue coverall among the militias, among those men who would remain there when we had left again for Madrid with our vans and loudspeakers and uniforms for pretending that we too were fighting in the war, that truth and immediate victory were as certain as the spirit of our verses or the anthems we sang at the end when we raised our fists on the wooden platform. But perhaps imposture and error were not in others but in me, in that part of myself that could not completely believe or accept anything too evident, anything that demanded faith and generosity and closed eyes. That night, before she left, Beatriz said I never had believed in the Republic or in Communism, that I hadn't betrayed anything because there never was anything I was loyal to, that if in the summer of '37 I enlisted as a soldier in the army, leaving my position at the Ministry of Propaganda, it wasn't to fight the Fascists with weapons but to find the death I didn't have the courage to give myself. She did believe, like Manuel, who died expecting the proclamation of the Third Republic. She had inflexible discernment and had drawn a line as firm as her moral integrity through everything. On one side, her love for me and her loyalty to the Communist Party. On the other, the rest of the world. Don't think I'm mocking them: I've spent my life admiring their faith and knowing it was their goodness that made me guilty. Even Orlando was capable of certainties that didn't move me, though at times I supported him in them, in the same way I got drunk with him and admired his pronouncements about painting and then returned at dawn to my house thinking, as soon as I was alone, when the cold air gave me back some distance from his words and my own actions, that tonight, as on all other nights, I had wasted an absurd amount of time. Orlando believed as if it were an article of faith that genius was inseparable from the systematic cultivation of any excess. To console himself for not having been Rimbaud at the age of sixteen, when he went to Mass every day and wasn't named Orlando yet, he wanted to be Verlaine, Van Gogh, Gauguin, the savage, the accursed, the he-goat, the seer. But if he painted when he was drunk, he produced nothing but mediocre canvases, and the great love of his life, the fruit of the audacity that according to him I never would have if I didn't go down to hell, was a crude teenager who left him dying of despair when he went off with another man who probably paid him more. I saw him almost at the end of the war, when I went back to Madrid. He was very fat and had decayed teeth and laughed when he told me about the tricks he had used to be declared unfit when his age group was mobilized, mocking me and the uniform I wore, as if the war and the cold that winter and our inevitable defeat were deceptions in which only he had not been caught. 'My dear Solana, you still have that serious gaze, that air of rectitude. The world is collapsing like the walls of Jericho, but you're still thinking about writing a book. Look at me: I'm tired, I'm sick, I'm happy, I've saved myself from mediocrity, I've renounced painting. Death itself is the only work worthy of an artist. Remember what we were saying ten or twelve years ago: to go on writing or painting in the age of the movies is like insisting on perfecting the stagecoach when propeller planes already exist. Propeller, do you remember? We liked that word so much. It was like the name of an Ultraist goddess.' But I could write that book, you're thinking, and it doesn't matter to you if it was scattered and burned and I was the only one who had seen it complete. A book exists even if no one reads it, the perfection of a statue or a painting endures when the lights have been turned off and no one is left in the museum, and a headless marble torso restores to the world the untouched beauty of an Aphrodite buried for two thousand years. But that book you were looking for and thought you had found never was written, or you've written it yourself since you came to Mágina, from the night Inés heard you ask about Jacinto Solana until this afternoon. Right now your disillusionment and your astonishment keep writing what I didn't write, separating unwritten pages. Do you know the impossibility of writing? Not the clumsiness, or the slowness, or the hours wasted searching for a single word that may be hidden under the others, under that white fissure in the paper, under another word that supplants it or denies it and must be erased in order to write in its place the real, the necessary, the only word. Not the effort of searching for the correct adjective, or a rhythm that is at once more fluid and more secret. I'm speaking about an interminable paralysis like that of the wounded man who after a long period of immobility wants to use his hands again or his legs and cannot manage to direct his steps or bring his fingers together with the precision needed to pick up a pencil or lift a spoon up to his mouth. Haven't you dreamed that you want to run and you sink into the ground and open your mouth to speak and can't find the air or curve your lips to form a single word? It never was easy for me to write, or maybe only until I was seventeen or eighteen years old, before I went to Madrid, when I wrote, moved by despair and innocence, in something like a state of automatic grace that came over me as soon as I touched pen and paper, without the intercession of anything or anybody. Friendship, rage against my fate, the tedium and humiliation of work never mattered to me, because I didn't allow them to interfere with my life. It was later that I degraded myself, but that part of the story doesn't matter. It's enough for you to know that until June 6, 1947, at dawn, I was a ruined rough draft of everything I had wanted to be when I was fourteen, of all the personages I invented to elude the only one to which I was condemned, of all the books Manuel lent me and that I read at night without my father knowing. The war and prison helped me learn I couldn't be a hero or even a victim resigned to his misfortune. But in the six months I spent shut up in Manuel's house and the Island of Cuba, I discovered I wasn't a writer either. I would look at the recently oiled typewriter, the shiny Underwood that Manuel bought so I could write, the stacked blank sheets, the pen, the inkwell, the solid, clean desk in front of the circular windows, and all those things he had gathered there as if he had guessed in detail that the oldest desire of my hands was for the instruments of an unknown science. I touched the typewriter, rolled in a sheet of paper, and sat looking at it hypnotized by its empty space. I filled the pen and wrote my name or the title of my book and no more words flowed from it. The act of writing was as necessary and impossible as breathing for a drowning man. I only smoked, looking at the rectangle of paper or the plaza and the roofs of Mágina, I only smoked and drank and remained interminably immobile, with the story I couldn't write oppressing me entire and intact in my imagination like a treasure next to which I was dying of powerlessness and hunger. Sometimes, impelled by alcohol, I wrote all night, thinking that at last the spell had been broken, knowing, as I wrote, that the fervor was false, that when I woke the next morning I would despise what I had written like the memory of a turbid drunkenness. A man isn't always responsible for the first episodes of his failure, but he is for the architecture of the last circle of hell. Instead of giving up and escaping from the book and that house and Mágina, I persisted in the torment until I transformed it into the habit of a degradation that didn't even have the generosity or excuse of madness. Yesterday, when you and Inés went down to the Island of Cuba, Frasco told you that the Civil Guard had burned all my papers. But most of those burned sheets had no writing on them, and it was I who set them on fire a few minutes before they came. As I burned all the rough drafts and all the blank sheets to deny myself the possibility of continuing to pretend to myself that I was writing a book, it was as if Beatriz were still looking at me the way she looked at me when she got up from the bed, as if the car hadn't started yet on the esplanade of the country house and she was still making a brief gesture of farewell behind the window and on the other side of the death they were carrying with them, in the back seat, in the darkness where the wounded man shook with fever, his eyes closed. There was never a mask that could defend me from that look: she was in front of me, unmoving, not vengeful, serene, in front of the vain gesture of renouncing and burning to which I devoted myself as if to a minor suicide, which instead of saving me from indignity tied me to it at the end of my life. I heard the first shots, and before I turned out the light and looked for my pistol under the pillow, I rushed to set fire to the papers that hadn't burned yet, and I ground my foot into the ashes with the same fury I would have used to grind my foot into the pieces of a broken mirror that kept reflecting me. There was, of course, no blue notebook, no manuscripts I had forgotten in Manuel's house before I went to the Island of Cuba. There was nothing but the ashes of blank pages and a besieged and cowardly man who didn't have the time or the courage to get off a single shot. Literature did not absolve me, as you supposed, as I helped you just a little to think. The loss of my life and my name absolved me, because waking in the house where they hid me was like coming back from the dead, and when you come back you acquire the privilege of being another man or of being no one forever, which is what I chose. Don't ask me what the years were like that I spent hidden in that room in the mill, because I don't know how to remember the way one remembers and measures the time you belong to, the time of the living. There's a single static image, of immobility and semidarkness, the man who came in to see me at night and talked to me about my father, and the woman who always brought me cups of very hot broth and came in without making noise so as not to wake me. She left soon after her daughter, Inés, was born, I suppose because she was ashamed to have had the baby with a man we never knew, and at first she wrote and sent money for the girl, but then the letters stopped coming and the grandfather sold the mill and we came to Mágina, to this house, and we took Inés to that nuns' orphanage. But those details shouldn't matter to you, you came here to look for a book and a mystery and the biography of a hero. Don't look at me like that, don't think that for all this time I've been mocking your innocence and your desire to know. I invented the game, but you have been my accessory. It was you who demanded a crime that would resemble the ones in literature and an unknown or unjustly forgotten writer with the prestige of political persecution and the memorable, accursed work, damned, dispersed, exhumed by you after twenty years. I hated you only at first, when Inés came every night and told me you were asking questions about me and writing a book and looking in the library for the magazines in which I published before the war. You came to remind me that I'd had a name and a life that weren't extirpated from the world, to tell me hatefully to arise and walk with the sole, base intention of writing a doctoral dissertation about me. But on one of those sleepless night when I cursed you and asked myself why you had to come here, I conceived of the game, as if the plot of a book had suddenly occurred to me. Let's build him the labyrinth he wants, I thought, let's give him not the truth but what he supposes happened and the steps that will allow him to find the novel and discover the crime. It was enough to send Inés to a printshop to buy a tablet and a pack of paper that were old enough, and write on them in ink diluted with water, and have you find them later in appropriate places, in the marriage bedroom, in the lining of the jacket that Frasco keeps in a trunk at the country house. It was enough to add to the written words a few objects to make them more real, the cartridge, my pen, the letter that you're surely still carrying in your jacket pocket. It's true: I couldn't have invented it all, and other voices that weren't always mine have guided you. I didn't invent Mariana's death in the pigeon loft or Utrera's guilt, and the letter you found this afternoon through the mediation of Inés wasn't falsified by me either, but it's possible that I wasn't the one who found the cartridge in the pigeon loft or that it didn't come from Utrera's pistol, or that the way I discovered the murderer wasn't as exciting and literary as the one I suggested to you. Reality, like the police, tends to clarify crimes with the basest procedures that cannot matter to you or me tonight, because they're almost never useful for literature. And perhaps the history you've found is only one among several possibilities. Perhaps there were other manuscripts in the house or at the Island of Cuba, and chance kept you from finding them. It doesn't matter if a story is true or false, it only matters if you know how to tell it. If you prefer, think that this moment doesn't exist, that you didn't see me this afternoon in the cemetery or that I was nothing more than an old cripple you saw looking at a grave and then forgot like a face that passes you on the street. Now you're the owner of the book and I'm your character, Minaya. I've obeyed you too."

3

I COUNT THE CAPSULES like last coins, resonant in the glass bottle, se-
cretive with silence and death against the palate and in the stomach,
and now the fragrance of the night and Minaya's words and his solitary figure on the platform dissolve in the heavy presentiment of
sleep, like Inés' eyes unclouded by tears when she leaned over me to
kiss me so infinitely on the mouth and pull the blanket up to my
chin, then plumping the pillow under my neck as if tonight were the
same as every other night and tomorrow there would be a waking as-
sisted by her tenderness, by the warmth and softness of her bare
thighs beneath the sheets and the cup of coffee on the night table,
next to the ashtray and the bottles of medicine. How strange now,
when I'm alone, to remember my voice, the irony, Minaya's bewil-
derment, his presence in this very room, on that empty chair, the
passion with which he continued asking questions and wanting to
know beyond knowledge and disillusionment, in spite of them, and
jealousy, and that glance he directed at Inés when she came to pour
me a glass of wine and left her index finger on my lips for a moment,
as if asking me for silence or invoking in front of him a secret complicity that connects her only to me. He asked until the end, obsessive, immune to irony and play, filling my glass when it was empty
as if to bring on a confession and forgetting about his on the night

table, then getting up, when I asked him to leave and to take Inés with him, with the abrupt gesture of someone emerging from water, facing her, waiting for a movement or a sign from her eyes, more fixed than ever on the cloth she was embroidering, silent and very tall, devastated by love, by fear of losing her, urged on by the thought of the train he is supposed to take tonight and by the bell striking the hour in the Plaza of General Orduña, counting the strokes in silence as I now count the last capsules I've poured into the palm of my hand while my sleepiness grows and reaches my limbs like a flood of sand. "You've written the book," I told him, "for a few days you returned me to life and literature, but you may not be able to measure my gratitude and affection, which are greater than my irony. Because you are the main character and the deepest mystery in the novel that did not have to be written in order to exist. You, who didn't know that time, who had the right to be lacking in memory, who first opened your eyes when the war was over and all of us had been condemned for some years to shame and death, exiled, buried, imprisoned in jails or in the habit of fear. You love literature as we are not even permitted to love it in adolescence, you search for me, for Mariana, for the Manuel of those years as if we weren't shadows but creatures truer and more alive than you. But it's in your imagination where we were born again, much better than we actually were, more loyal, better looking, free of cowardice and truth. Leave now, and take Inés with you. She's over eighteen and it's unfair for her intelligence and body to remain buried here, next to a dead man who never finishes dying, in that house where they'll conspire to humiliate her now that Manuel's gone, if they haven't already decided to throw her out. I've taught her everything I remembered or knew. I've tried to educate her as I educated myself, in Manuel's library. She speaks excellent French and has read more books than you can imagine. With your help she can study in Madrid and find a good job. Take her with you. Tonight, right now." He said nothing, standing against the door, vertical and oblique because of a ceiling as low as the shadow of a light resting on the floor, a stranger, very tall, with his melancholy formal suit and mourning tie, just as he is now, I suppose, while he waits on the platform and doesn't know that Inés is going up to the station along the streets of Mágina, past the corners of closed windows with single lightbulbs under the eaves, at the boundary of dark empty fields where the long walls of the cemetery and the station rise up, in another world. He saw her get up and come toward the bed, brushing him with her perfume and her will to defiance, not looking at him, refusing to acknowledge that he was here, that he existed like us and it was possible to choose him. "I don't want to go," she said, sitting on the edge of the bed, smoothing my hair, taking from my hand the glass of wine that was trembling, curled up against my chest as in the distant days when she was afraid of water and darkness and would lie down with me asking me to tell her again the story of the phantom ship as motionless as stone in the middle of the valley of the Guadalquivir whose whistle we could hear from the bedroom in the mill. He, Minaya, continued in front of us, like a guest who has not yet accepted the obligation to leave, but Inés had already excluded him from her tenderness and from the world and embraced me as if we were alone, telling me she would never leave, and kissed me as she curved her lips to say no and she kept saying no with her eyes and her hands and her entire body that affirmed her will to remain here despite my surrender or indolence, fiercely embracing my neck, as if she were defending me, as if when she turned her back on Minaya and the future, she had expelled them from us. She wasn't a shade, she was the only thing that never had contained even the slightest hunger for lies or guilt, the only body undoubtedly and as precisely modeled for happiness as a god's desire and when I embraced it and knew I was tasting its final caresses I wasn't moved by repentance or the sorrow of saying goodbye but by a sweetness very similar to gratitude for the only gift no one had been able to strip from me and that will not be squandered by oblivion. She said no to Minaya, who was no longer in the room, who had gone out in silence and returned to look at us from the hall as if he were about to leave for an exile longer than his own life, she said she would always stay with me and, standing with the reckless determination to choose loyalty of those adolescents who refuse to grow older and be despicable, she closed the door and leaned against it as if to stop anyone or anything from coming in to separate us, and she said no again and knelt beside me, wanting to stop my words when she saw the bottles of capsules for insomnia, and knew why she had to leave tonight. Now I see her walking toward the station with a clarity firmer than any memory and I see her eyes that have recognized Minaya and rest on him from a distance as serenely as they looked at me when she understood that she could not undo my purpose and that when she left she would fulfill the final, delicate, necessary tribute to our mutual loyalty. When I was young I cursed myself for not being able to remember the faces of the women I loved. Now the darkness to which I am descending as if abandoning myself again to the warm water of that river from which I perhaps never returned, or to sleep beneath the sheets of a wintry bed, is the space of clear-sightedness in my memory that I don't want to and can't distinguish from divination. I see Inés walking alone on the avenue of linden trees, and I know there is not an instant in my life when the exact shape of her mouth or the precise tonality of her eyes will stop being as present in me as the scent of her body that is still in the blouse she left on the bed and that I touch and smooth as if I were caressing the profile of her absence. I see Minaya, I immobilize him, I imagine him, I impose on him minute gestures of waiting and solitude, I want him to think that now too, when he is escaping, he obeys me, I want him not to look up yet at the entrance to the station, and to curse me in a low voice and swear that as soon as he arrives in Madrid and breaks the fabric of my curse, he'll burn the manuscripts and the blue notebook and renounce Mágina and Inés, I want him to know that I am imagining him and to hear my voice like the beat of his own blood and consciousness, and when he sees Inés standing under the large yellow clock, it will take him an instant to realize she is not another illusion constructed by his desire and despair, beatus ille.

Granada and Ubeda,
May 1983–May 1985